TWO SUNS AT SUNSET

Tandemstar: The Outcast Cycle, Book One

GENE DOUCETTE

Gene Doucette

Cover art by Jeff Brown at Jeff Brown Graphics

Map design by Cat Scully

CONTENTS

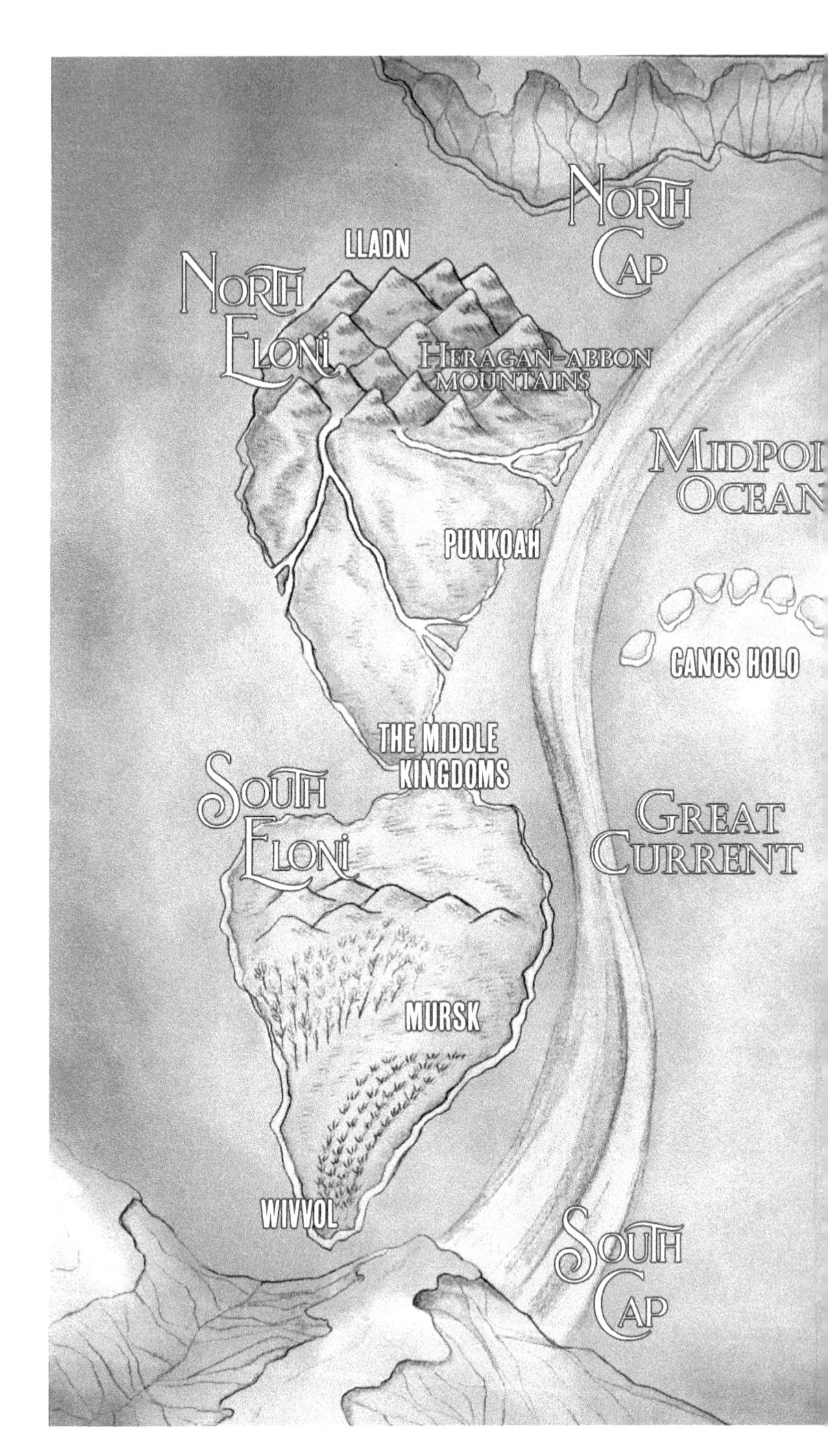
North Cap
Lladn
North Eloni
Heragan-abbon Mountains
Midpoi
Ocean
Punkoah
Canos Holo
The Middle Kingdoms
South Eloni
Great Current
Mursk
Wivvol
South Cap

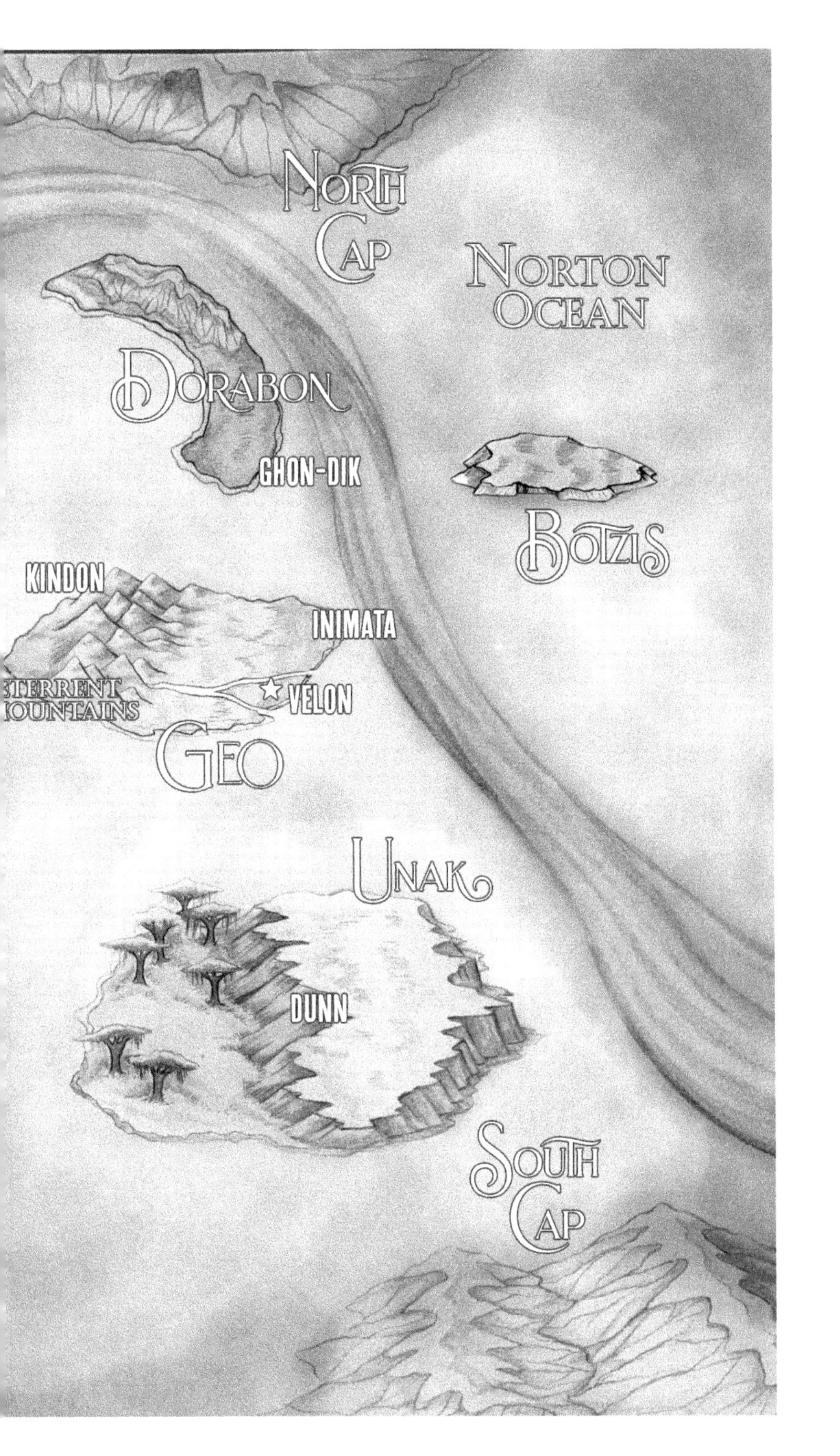
NORTH CAP
NORTON OCEAN
DORABON
GHON-DIK
BOTZIS
KINDON
INIMATA
ETERRENT
OUNTAINS
VÉLON
GEO
UNAK
DUNN
SOUTH CAP

PART I

The Murdered Monk

Chapter One

The clanging on the radiator pipe woke up Makk about ten minutes before his seventeen o'clock alarm was set to go off.

He didn't know what he was hearing at first, nor was it initially clear where he was or what time it was. He'd worked an overnight shift, so bedtime was ten o'clock...or, it should have been. One didn't just go directly from a shift to bed without a drink first. There had to be a little separation between the job and the leisure, and a shot of Dorabonian rye was the quickest way to create that separation.

Also, one didn't have just one drink. One had two, or three, or six, especially when one was an idiot.

Then one went to bed.

CLANG CLANG CLANG

The pipe rang in time with the throbbing behind his eyes, and so he wondered if the problem was that something metallic had come loose inside of his skull. Failing that—and now he was waking up enough to consider things a tiny bit more rationally—it could have been that someone was doing work outside the window.

Makk's apartment was in the Decane Quarter; rather, what it said on the maps. Only tourists (and, presumably, map-makers) called it that, and only if they were confused. It was named after the politician Andon Decane who—some two hundred years prior—had been special envoy to Kindon, among other things. That posting was *nearly* the height of irony, as Andon Decane actively despised the Kindonese, and made no effort to hide this fact. What *was* the height of irony was that the quarter with Decane's name on it was now known as Kindontown by nearly everyone.

Makk wasn't Kindonese, but the rent was cheap, and he spoke fluent Taku, so he got along okay.

CLANG CLANG CLANG

It wasn't work outside; it was Binchagag, whacking the basement radiator pipe with a stick.

"All right, I'm coming," he shouted. Binchagag couldn't hear him, but Makk felt better for having said it anyway. Then he got out of bed, picked up the nearest boot, walked over to the radiator, and hit it a couple of times. Depending on the urgency of the matter, that should buy him at least enough time to clean up and drag himself downstairs. And maybe even get in a shower.

The apartment was indeed cheap, in part because of its location, and in part because it was really small. Makk's bed was his couch, and his bedroom was his living room, and his living room was his kitchen. Thankfully, none of them was also his bathroom, as it was separate.

The walls were thin, the windows let in all kinds of draft, and the radiator his landlord was so very fond of using as a means of communication only occasionally produced heat. But nobody came to Kindontown unless they were Kindonese, or they were lost, which made it was a good place to live if wanting to be largely left alone. Generally speaking, Makk always wanted to be left alone.

CLANG CLANG CLANG

"It's an emergency, then," he muttered. Someone must have been having quite a run of luck in the basement.

He dropped the boot and headed for the bathroom, spotting the empty bottle of rye on the kitchen counter as he went.

"Okay, maybe I had seven or eight drinks," he said. Oddly, this made him feel better about the mass suicide of brain cells that was making it hard to see straight. At least how he felt now had been earned.

He skipped the shower, and the shave. There was a real chance that Binchagag was about to take up the rest of Makk's free time, so a few minutes to make himself presentable was probably warranted, except his shift began at 18:30. Nobody cared how you looked on the overnight shift.

Velon was quite literally the city that didn't sleep. Most of the businesses operated in some form—even if that form was skeletal—all twenty hours of the day, all seven days of the week, all 529 days of the year. Makk assumed this was true for the entirety of Inimata, and possibly true in other countries as well. (It was definitely the case when he was in the military, but the military was run by crazy people who were probably looking for an hour twenty-one and twenty-two to take advantage of.) At some point, everyone just agreed that lowered standards in personal grooming was their reward for what they called *working the over*.

In short, Makk didn't need to shave, and even though the shower would have been nice, it was also unnecessary, so he skipped it too. He did find a clean shirt, and a mostly-clean pair of pants. Then he threw on his jacket, grabbed what he needed for work, and headed out.

Hopefully, somebody downstairs had coffee brewing.

The staircase leading to the apartment was external, and perilously steep, which was a common characteristic in this part of the city. The buildings in Kindontown looked to have been assembled haphazardly by a child god with a poor understanding of the basics of structural integrity. They leaned, and loomed, and most appeared top-heavy. (A lot of them *were*, thanks to probably-illegal apartments built out of plywood on top of roofs. Makk lived in one of them.) From the street level, it felt like the buildings were staring down from directly overhead, as if ripped from the nightmares of a worried agrarian on an unpleasant business trip.

In Makk's version of this nightmare, the buildings were gaming tiles, stacked on their narrows and awaiting that child god to come along and tap the building at the end, sending them crashing down one by one.

He took a minute on the landing outside of his front door, in order to take in the city. Even at night—and the Dancers had set at least a couple of hours earlier—and even in this backchannel part of town, Velon was entirely too busy to cope with, absent a pause to recalibrate. Makk had spent the early part of his life in a uniform, running drop ships and guarding borders, but none of that elevated his pulse rate as much as just walking out his own front door on a busy evening in downtown Velon.

A merchant bazaar was going on across the street, spilling people off the curb and into traffic, which could have been a problem if any of the ground traffic was moving, which it wasn't. Above the ground traffic, every couple of minutes, an aero-car drove by, blasting hot, steamy air from its rear exhaust fans and raising the ambient temperature of all the atmosphere on the block by a couple of degrees. Or so it seemed.

Every crevice of city not taken up by a person or a car was occupied by an advertisement for something, or a streetlight. It was, thankfully, a cloudy night—it had been raining off and on for the past two days—or the sky itself would have been taken up by an advertisement as well, as Lys was scheduled to appear overhead in another hour.

Makk loved everything about the city, when he was on the ground. Up a level, and looking down with the same trepidation as a kid who's about to learn how to swim in a rapidly-flowing river, he couldn't believe anyone allowed themselves to live like this.

He closed his eyes, waited for a little dizziness from what was probably incipient vertigo to pass, and then headed down to the basement, to see what Binchagag wanted.

The ground floor was taken up by a restaurant called Lucky Twins, which specialized in mediocre but exotic variations of Kindonese food. When Makk felt especially adventurous—or if he was just too tired to walk any farther—he'd get food from the place, if only to entertain himself with a game of *guess what part of what animal this thing came from?* This was sometimes pretty easy, because certain body parts came out of the other side of food preparation looking a lot like they did when going into it, and then it became a game of *I dare you to eat this*.

He stopped at a bar halfway between the front door and the back staircase and caught the eye of Lina, the probably-underage girl currently tending bar.

"*Coffee?*" he asked, in Taku.

"*You look like you died six hours ago,*" she said. "*Coffee's old.*"

"*Is it hot and more or less black?*"

"*More or less.*"

She poured a cup, then pushed a bowl of salted chicken skin rinds in front of him, and provided a shot of grain wine as accompaniment.

"*Hangover cure,*" she said. "*Finish it all, vomit. All better.*"

"*No time to vomit,*" he said, downing half of the coffee. It was too hot and too old, scalding the back of his throat and traumatizing his taste buds. He moved on to the chicken rinds, which tasted great by comparison.

"*There's a bottle of pinks under the cash box,*" he said. "*Give me three of those.*"

"*My way works better,*" she said. "*And those are not for customers.*"

"*I'm not a customer.*"

"*No, you're a pain in my ass, Cholem,*" she said. Lina punctuated the name she used for Makk by tapping her chest with two extended fingers. It was meant to ward off evil, but in this case, she was doing it to guard herself against general misfortune. It came from one of Kindon's backwater belief systems, but Makk didn't know which one. Lina probably didn't either.

She pulled the bottle out and extracted three pills for him. Then the pipe behind the bar made the clanging noise.

"*Sounds urgent,*" Lina said. "*Better hurry.*"

Makk took the pills, downed the grain wine, and got to his feet. His stomach commented on his meal choices, but didn't threaten to protest any more stridently, so he figured he was good enough to at least make it downstairs.

Past the bar and at the back of the restaurant, there was a down-staircase with an "employees only" barrier in front of it. Makk pushed the barrier aside, and headed down. Nobody bothered to stop him, which may have been because they all knew him, but he was pretty sure anybody walking to the back and heading down those stairs would have been able to do so unimpeded; knowing it was okay to use the stairs was permission enough to use them.

There was a big guy at the bottom of the staircase, in front of a steel door with a square peekaboo window.

"Evening, Tohai," Makk greeted, in the common tongue—Endish—rather than in Taku.

"Makk," he said. Tohai was not an erudite man in either tongue.

"Bincha hit me up," Makk said. "Someone having a run?"

"I think trouble."

"What kind?"

Tohai shrugged, and pushed open the door.

The basement of the Lucky Twins was a different kind of overwhelming. For starters, there was the smoke from the bacco sticks, which was thick enough to obscure the back half of the room. Makk was never a smoker, but he'd spent enough time around smokers that it hardly mattered. (And he did take a pipe or a stick from time to time, just not habitually.) Everyone in the basement smoked, non-stop, and the ventilation was crap. There were ceiling fans, and half-windows near the top of the outside walls that tilted open, but the air pressure between the inside and the outside was usually equilibrated, so the smoke didn't do much but circle around the room in whorls and waves.

There were fifteen tables in the center of the floor, and a bar along the right side, directly under the restaurant bar and the radiator in Makk's apartment. It was early, so the tables weren't filled, and only a couple of people were standing at the bar. One of those people was Binchagag. Another was a tall, blonde woman who didn't belong there. She and Bincha appeared to be in an argument. Given all of Bincha's gesticulation, it looked like he was losing that argument.

Binchagag pulled Makk into the situation before Makk had even made it all the way to the bar.

"Ah! There, you...you explain it to her," Binchagag said to Makk. "She is accusing us of crimes."

"What kinda crimes?" Makk asked. "I've got my own list, maybe we can compare."

"This is not joking," Bincha said. He was flustered, and when he was flustered, his command of the common tongue tended to break down.

Binchagag switched to Taku.

"*Your kind, your problem*," he said.

Makk took a closer look at the woman, to work out exactly

what Bincha meant by that. She was tall, and well-dressed in a blue pants suit with a white blouse. Her blonde hair was pulled back in a neat braid, revealing a perfectly round face with high cheekbones and blue eyes. Makk, in contrast, was wearing yesterday's clothes (except for the shirt), his hair was standing in three directions, and he needed a shave. He was also shorter and rounder than she was.

They didn't look like they were the same kind of anything. They didn't even look like the same species.

"Hello," the woman said, with a half-smile. She was looking him over, at the same time he was looking her over. Presumably, she was unimpressed.

"Hi," he said, stepping up to the bar. "What can I do for you?"

"Well, that little fellow thinks you can convince me that what I'm looking at right now is something other than an illegal gambling parlor," she said. "Do you think you're up to that?"

Makk shrugged.

"I can give it a shot, sure, but only if you call Bincha here a *little fellow* one more time, because that's damned funny."

Binchagag—who was only short compared to the average Inimatan, but about right for someone from Kindon—swore in Taku and stormed off. She watched him go, and then watched Makk slide onto a bar stool.

"I'm waiting," the woman said.

She was more attractive up close, which was almost never the case with anybody.

"Do you want a drink?" he asked, gesturing to the bar seat beside his, and waving to the tender. The three pinks and belly full of coffee were kicking in; there was a chance he could muster up a small modicum of charm, provided his breath wasn't too bad.

"I'll have a water," she said, accepting the seat. "Is the water here clean?"

"I'd stick with the spirits if I were you. What's your demon?"

"They won't carry it," she said, "but I'll take whatever's amber and comes out of that nozzle over there."

"Deterrent Ridge Draft?" the bartender said. Her name was Phaiet, and Makk knew her entire life's story, including how she ended up with a synthetic leg, tending bar in an illegal gambling establishment in a basement in Kindontown.

It was possible Makk spent too much time beneath the Lucky Twins.

"Make it two," Makk said. He was on shift shortly, but again, people didn't care so much when you were working the over, and besides, beer barely counted as alcohol. His stomach reminded him about the recently-consumed chicken skin rinds and grain wine, and his hangover notified him that any more alcohol at this point would be a poor choice. He ignored both.

"So I'm guessing," Makk said, to the blonde, "based on how much you've rattled my landlord, that you have some kind of authority."

"Is that what you are to him?" she asked. "His tenant?"

"Yeah, I live upstairs."

Strictly speaking, this was an accurate description of his relationship with Binchagag; the bulk of it was transactional in nature. However, Bincha was known to let Makk borrow one of his ground cars in a pinch, and also lent Makk the use of his hunting cabin once or twice a year.

"And he calls you down whenever there's trouble?" she asked.

"Kinda. Are you trouble?"

She reached into her jacket pocket and pulled out a badge. This was a thin piece of metal and synthetic glass that also worked as a camera and a voicer. It was glowing green and yellow, which meant that she was on duty.

"Ohh, you're a *cop*," Makk said. "Maybe the water was a better idea."

"You told me the water was suspect, and I'd barely call D.R. Draft alcoholic," she said. "I'll live."

"Can I see that?"

She handed over the badge. He studied it for about twice as long as he actually needed to, and then handed it back.

"Detective Viselle Daska," he said. "Not just a cop; a detective."

"Yes."

"Daska. What is that? It sounds Unakian."

"My father's from Dunn," she confirmed. "And I think you're stalling. Are you going to explain what's going on in this room better than *he* did, or do you want to go through my whole family tree first?"

"We can do both; I've got time."

Phaiet served up the beer. Detective Daska took a sip, cringed gently, and took another.

"Well, I don't have time," she said. "I'm a few minutes away from ordering backup and arresting everyone."

"Including me?"

"Depends. What else do you do for Mr. Binchagag?"

"It's just Binchagag," he said. "That's his whole name. This is really all I do for him."

"And what is that again? Run down to the basement to charm policemen out of busting an illegal operation?"

He smiled.

"I wasn't even trying to be charming yet," he said. Although he was.

Generally speaking, Makk didn't like other people. But, he liked women just fine. This was not to say that women were not also people, just that he was capable of overriding his instinct to avoid people under certain circumstances. He also knew his relationship with Detective Viselle Daska was shortly going to change into something that prohibited flirting and the general application of charm; he was going to have to get the most out of it while he could.

"I was exaggerating," she said.

"This isn't usually what I do for Bincha, no. I'm more like a professional bad luck charm."

He rolled up his right sleeve and held out the back of his wrist so she could see the mark. It was a small black symbol that looked like a 3 and a 4 having intercourse.

For the first time since they began talking, Viselle Daska looked surprised.

"You're a *Cholem*," she said.

"That's me; professionally unlucky."

"Put that away," hissed Phaiet, from across half the bar, "before you clear out the place."

Makk pulled his sleeve back down to cover up the mark.

"I don't think I've ever seen one of those," Daska admitted.

"The brand? It's more common than you probably think; most times it's just not flashed like that. Still, better than drowning, huh?"

He'd met at least two dozen people with the same mark; most of them only showed him after they'd seen his, and otherwise kept it hidden.

"Oh, I understand now," Detective Daska said. "When your friend Mr. Binchagag is dealing with a hot table, you sit down and show off your little tattoo."

"It's just Binchagag, but yeah. It empties the table, and sometimes the whole place. Not that there's any gambling going on in this establishment."

"Of course not. What's your name, anyway?"

"Makk."

"Do you also not have a last name?"

"Oh, I do."

"Is this your full-time job, Makk? Local *Cholem*?"

She said the last word loud enough to cause a couple of the people in the room to turn around in a mild panic. One of them started closing out his bet.

Even the word was bad luck. There was a whole set of rituals observed by the more superstitious, when the word was said aloud, regardless of whether or not an actual *Cholem* was nearby. Makk had seen people spin around, spit on their hands, and so on. It was the kind of silliness he'd find amusing if he wasn't one.

Detective Daska noticed the same thing he had.

"Maybe I don't need to call in any backup," she said. "I can just say that word loudly."

"I think after you've said it three times you should avoid traffic the rest of the day," he said. "But no, it's not my full-time job. It's just what I do if I happen to be around and Bincha needs a bailout. In exchange, he gives me a discount on the rent; it's nice. Maybe the only benefit I'll ever get out of being a *Cholem*, but I'll take it."

Makk was drastically underselling what it was like to go through life with the *Cholem* brand on his wrist.

It had been put there when he was barely two. Back then, it was an inky black splotch that looked more like a birthmark than a deliberate tattoo. But it grew with him, as the people who put it there knew it would, until it formed the appropriate symbol.

Makk was born on the thirty-fourth day of the month of Sevvitch, in the winter (or 'Do-') season. This was neither his choice nor his fault. Neither—one must assume—was it the fault of his mother and father, or the doctors who delivered him, or the nurses who aided the doctors. It was just a thing that happened, on a day that should have been treated like every other day on the calendar.

The problem was that the month of Sevvitch was only supposed to have thirty-three days. This was the case for all sixteen of the months on the calendar, except for one: the springtime (or 'Ta-') month of Zenita. But Ta-Zenita was a special day, the last day of the year, and a holiday.

It would have been nice if everyone treated the thirty-fourth day of Do-Sevvitch the same way, but they didn't. Do-Sevvitch's 34th day was a leap day that took place only once every four years —all except for one year out of every thirty-three, and then it was skipped—and was considered unlucky by essentially everyone on the planet.

Children born on the Do-Sevvitch leap day were called *Cholem*, which was a derogatory appellation from a pre-Endish tongue. In less civilized times, and places, *Cholem* were routinely drowned, so as to avoid the presumptive string of bad fortune that might befall an entire village. The slightly more civilized expression of this irrationality came in the form of the mark on Makk's wrist.

It was better than drowning, yes, but that wasn't saying much. He still saw the periodic gestures of self-blessing—if not open recoil—in response to his presence, as if bad luck was viral.

The best reaction of all would be if everyone grew up and stopped believing in these things, but that was probably too much to ask for.

"To being professionally unlucky," Daska said, toasting him with her beer stein. She didn't seem at all put off by his mark, outside of a sort of scientific curiosity. "Since I'm about to arrest everyone, it seems especially apt."

"Oh, right," he said. "That. So, this isn't gambling. What you're witnessing is a religious ceremony."

"Ooh, that's almost interesting. Go on."

"That's all I have so far."

She laughed.

"Now I'm disappointed. Look, Makk, I can't be the first cop to walk down those stairs."

"You are definitely not the first cop to walk down those stairs," he agreed.

"Well what did you tell them? *Religious ceremony* and then have a nice day? At least pretend not to insult my intelligence."

"I didn't have to tell them anything."

"Bribes, then?"

"No bribes. They just didn't mind it all that much."

"Give me something better," she said.

Viselle Daska appeared to be genuinely enjoying herself, which could have meant his charm was working, but there were too many other factors in play to be sure what was actually going on. She *had* to know who he was by now.

"How about this," he said. "It's just polite wagering among friends."

"Not nearly as good," she said.

"But it's true. I think most of these folks know each other pretty well."

As if gifted upon her by the gods, a loud argument broke out between two gamblers at a table in the middle of the room. Tohai had to scurry over from the door to break up what was about to become a fistfight.

"I think we can throw away the word *polite*," she said. "And I speak enough Taku to know that those weren't the kinds of words friends usually use with one another."

"Friends fight sometimes! No different from, say...well, we're not friends, you and I. We just met. But a friendly wager between us would still be different from gambling. For instance, let's say you and I bet you're not going to arrest anyone here tonight."

"What are we wagering?"

"The beer. If you arrest someone tonight, in this establishment—which again, is not a gambling establishment—I'll buy you that beer. If not, you'll buy me this beer. How does that sound?"

"Pretty weak odds on your part. All I have to do to win is

arrest someone. I could even leave all of these people alone and just arrest you."

"On what charges?"

"I don't think valid charges are a requirement of the wager," she said.

"You'd have to take me all the way to Twenty-One Central and book me, or else I'm not officially arrested, and you'll lose the bet. I don't know much about you, but you don't look like someone ready to run up a man on bogus charges just to win a beer."

She laughed.

"All right, if this isn't a gambling establishment, as you keep saying, then what is it?"

"A social club."

"A social club. Where people of similar interests..."

"...said interests which happen to include wagering," he said.

"Of course. Where people of similar interests gather for a nice, polite game of five-square."

"Or thirty-three deck. Or tiles. That game over in the corner is called Whin-Whon. I don't understand it at all, but the Kindonese seem to like it."

"But this is just a social event."

"That's what I'm saying."

"In that case," she said, "there's no vigorish. Obviously. And I'm sure they're *only* wagering against one another, and not the dealer. Right? For this to be a set of friendly wagers taking place in a social club."

"Well? I mean, Bincha's gotta keep the lights on. It's a perfectly reasonable expectation."

She shook her head.

"Yes, see, you nearly had it," she said. "Mr. Makk, you are about to lose your bet with me."

"No, hang on, you haven't seen all my tiles yet."

She raised a single eyebrow, which he found weirdly attractive under the circumstances.

"All right," she said, "poorly-chosen analogy aside, go on."

He got off the stool and stretched, as if the next thing he had to say would require some physical activity. He really just needed to straighten his legs for a bit. He had a bad knee, a leftover from his military service. The knee didn't care for barstools.

"Here goes," he said. "You're not going to arrest anybody because you're not a vice cop. You're a detective first grade, and this is only your...second day?"

"It's my sixth," she said. "And now you're getting obnoxious. How'd you know my grade?"

"I know my way around a badge," he said. "Yours isn't the first one I've seen. Homicide, right?"

Detective Daska looked ready to pull her badge back out to see if there was perhaps some information on there that she missed the first hundred times she looked at it.

"Yes..." she said, reluctantly.

"You're the transfer from cyber, huh?"

"How do you know all this?"

"Here, I'll show you," he said. Then he pulled out his own badge. It was glowing blue and white, because unlike Daska, he wasn't currently on duty.

"Detective Makk Stidgeon," she read. "Third class."

She handed it back.

"Also homicide," she added.

"Yep. So like I said, you're not going to arrest anyone tonight, because there aren't any dead bodies in here, and if you were working a case where there was a body somewhere else, I'd already know about it. You can make a *vice* arrest if you want, but I'm going to have to ask really nicely that you don't, and hope I don't have to add that I also outrank you."

"Right."

"And now you owe me a beer."

She laughed.

"Lot of work for a free beer," she said. She slipped a card from her back pocket and swiped it over the bar sensor. "And sorry, but you don't look like a detective."

"Honest mistake."

She made the crinkly face he'd already seen a few times tonight, denoting confusion.

"What time are you on duty?" she asked.

"I don't have to clock in until eighteen-thirty," he said. "Why?"

"Because I think Central has a different schedule."

She pointed to the badge in his hand, which was now red-yellow.

"Aw, come on," he said.

The screen on the badge went from displaying Makk's bona fides to a map image, with a flashing red dot on one part of the map. Then the whole thing began to vibrate.

"Stay right there," he said to Daska, stepping near the door where the sound of the gambling floor was a little less obvious.

He connected the direct, and held the badge up to his ear.

"Hey, captain," he said. "I'm off-duty."

"Not anymore," Captain Llotho said. "You just caught a body."

"That doesn't mean I'm on duty. That means someone who *is* on duty caught a body. That's how work shifts are supposed to go."

"Cut me a break, Makk," Llotho said. "This looks high-profile, and next up is a rook."

Makk looked at Viselle Daska, still at the bar, silently asked him what was going on.

"Anyone I know?" he asked.

"If you met her, you'd know it. I'll have her second-seat on this one, say it's department policy or...the body's in the *House*, Makk. This is some shit. I need someone I trust in front of it."

"You're kidding."

"Not even a tiny bit. Scene officer says it's one of the town-houses. Veesers are already on the grounds; we're putting up a cordon now. It can't wait until eighteen-thirty, you get me?"

"Yeah, all right."

"Thanks, I owe you one."

"You owe me at least five by now," Makk said. "I'm counting. Have the rook meet me at the scene."

Makk disconnected, and walked back to the bar.

"What is it?" Daska asked.

"Dead body in Andel Quarter," he said. "Expect a direct from Llotho."

He finished off his beer, slid the stein across the bar, and headed for the door.

"Hang on," Daska said. "What did he say, exactly?"

"Ask him yourself, detective," Makk said. "I'll catch up with you at the scene."

Whatever response she had in mind was cut off by Llotho's direct on her badge. Makk hit the exit, and headed up to the street.

Chapter Two

Makk made it to the curb, and halfway to the cab stand, before Daska caught up with him.

"Where are you going?" she asked.

"Where do you think?" he said. "I'm hailing a cab. Did you talk to him?"

"Don't you have a car?"

Makk had a few ways to get to Twenty-One Central. The most leisurely was to walk to the edge of Kindontown and grab Hyperline. In that scenario, he also had time to grab food along the way, which clearly wasn't happening now. A *slightly* faster approach would be to hail a cab or order an app-car. Since he was going to Andel Quarter instead of Central (which was in the Geoghis Quarter) a hired vehicle was really the only option.

"Don't usually need one," Makk said, as he kept walking. "Usually, I'm already downtown and can grab a ride from a uniform or requisition an unmarked. And usually, there's no rush because the victim's not going to get any deader in the time it takes for me to get to the scene."

"Hey," she said, grabbing him by the elbow. "Stop walking away from me. What's the problem?"

"The problem is, I don't trust you, Detective Viselle Daska. We're a long way from anyplace someone dressed like you calls home, yeah? You didn't just wander into the Lucky Twins, and we didn't just accidentally meet up, and I don't like being played."

"That's unfair."

"Sure. Let's talk about it later. I've got a body to examine."

It would have been a lot easier to storm off if there had been a cab waiting at the stand, but there wasn't. If anything, traffic on the street had gotten worse in the past hour. If he *had* a street vehicle, it might take an hour to get there, and not even the siren and roof argons was going to change that. Even if he did the same thing half the station did, which was to requisition a car overnight, he had no place to park a ground-based car. Not without paying a ton of credits for the privilege.

He spotted a cab halfway up the street, stuck in the bumper-to-bumper. Its availability flag was off, though.

"Detective," Daska said. "I have a car."

"Good for you."

"I'm saying I can drive us both there."

"I know what you're saying. In this traffic, it won't matter whose car I'm in; we're not getting there any time soon."

"I'll definitely beat you there," she said. "And it won't look good when I do, especially since I already told Llotho I'm also in Kindontown. Don't be an asshole. Accept the ride."

He sighed, and stopped walking to the cab.

"Fine," he said. "Where'd you park?"

They headed down the block and around the corner, to a parking garage that happened to be the tallest structure in the entire quarter.

The Hyperline circuit that replaced private transportation for much of Velon didn't reach Decane. The public reasons for this employed words like *infrastructure* and *cost-benefit*. Privately, Makk was pretty sure the city cognoscenti liked to pretend Kindontown didn't exist, and definitely didn't want tourists to figure out how to get there. It made traffic in the quarter ten times worse, which was probably also not an accident. It all made Kindontown a less-than-ideal place to live if one worked downtown.

But, again, the rent was cheap.

Once at the garage, Daska called the elevator, and then hit the button for the roof.

"You're kidding," Makk said.

"What?"

"I take it this isn't a cruiser?"

"Personal vehicle. What's the big deal?"

He just glared at her and waited for the elevator to reach the top floor. He knew full well there was no way to drive to the roof from the street, and so did she.

There were only five cars on the rooftop, and all of them looked expensive. She headed to what looked like the most expensive of the bunch, and chirped the door unlocked with a fob.

"What?" she asked, again, when it was clear he planned to take a few seconds to review the situation. "Look, it's a ride, and it'll get us there fast."

"It will, yes," he agreed.

"Have you never ridden in one of these?" she asked. "I didn't think to ask. You're not weird about heights, are you?"

"I'm not fond of null-grav tech," he said.

"It's perfectly safe."

"That's what people who've never experienced a null-gravity outage always say. Which is most people. You know why? Because the ones who did experience it aren't around to talk about it after."

She hit another button on the fob, and the doors opened. (They slid up, instead of opening out like a normal damn car.)

"Just get in," she said. "It's too far to walk."

He looked at the interior, which was a combination of burnished leather, brass, and polished hardwood.

"They're paying rookies a lot more than I thought," he said. "I think I need to have a conversation with the captain."

"You know what? Everyone needs to stop calling me a rookie. I'm not a rookie."

She climbed into the driver's seat—on the left—and waited for him to get in. Makk was glad this wasn't one of those cockpit types, with driver in front and passenger in back.

He sat down next to her, pulled his arms in and waited for the door to self-close, while Daska started the electric engine. He caught a whiff of ozone before the door sealed.

Her side of the dashboard lit up, with a variety of gauges unique to aero-cars: altitude, pitch and yaw being the most obvious, but also the gravitation differential factor for the null-grav drive. The power gauge wasn't entirely unique, but most ground-based cars were pure electric, whereas this was a nuclear-electric mix: There was a tiny, deuterium-fueled fusion reactor under the hood of this car. He'd seen a few grounded vehicles with nuclear-electric engines, but only when he was in the army.

The null-gravity drive was, by itself, too expensive for most citizens. Operating one just on an electric battery (while feasible) was suicidal; it ate power too fast. Nuclear-electric was the only solution, but it made the technology twice as expensive.

She checked the gauges, made a couple of adjustments, and then took the car two maders up. He felt his stomach bounce.

"There was an accident, I take it," Daska said. "Null-gravity outage?"

"It's a common concern."

"Not really. Maybe when the tech was new. You're not that old. So what happened?"

"A troop transport dropped out of the sky while heading over the Deterrents. Twenty soldiers died, and I was friends with all of them."

"Ohh, okay. During the Kindon Border Conflict?"

"Yeah."

"I've heard about those old army clunkers. Not near enough power to stay in the air. We're not going to have that kind of problem."

She was looking at his hand, which was clutching the handle that dangled over the door, maybe a little tighter than was really necessary.

"I'm also a good driver," she said.

"I don't doubt it."

"State-of-the-art radar over here."

"I'm sure it is."

She sighed, and gave the rear jet a nudge, took them over the edge of the roof, and into a ten mader dead-drop before settling into a standard travel lane altitude. It was the same sensation as going down a fast elevator. He felt it right in the pit of his stomach, which took that moment to remind him of all the bad dietary choices he'd made in the past ten hours.

"Besides, for someone who's supposed to be all bad luck, you weren't on the transport yourself, right?" she said. "I think you're looking at this all wrong."

He actually *was* on that transport—it was how he wrecked his knee—but this didn't seem like the time to share war stories, not when he was about to die.

"I'd still rather stay on the ground," he said.

"Too late for that."

Once in the lane, Daska got the car up to cruising speed, which—for this altitude—was about half the KPH of the road cars. These things could go a *lot* faster, but then they were hugely dangerous because they were terrible at braking. Another half kalo up and she could have gone faster, but then she'd overshoot their destination. Plus, she probably wasn't licensed for that altitude.

Unless she was. He'd met Viselle Daska only a half an hour ago, and already, she'd surprised him four or five times.

The problem with riding in a car that employed null-grav technology was that it always felt like you were falling. This may have been partly because it wasn't actually null-gravity tech at all: it was artificial gravity that was being applied in the opposite direction as regular gravity. The car went up and down by increasing and decreasing the artificial gravity, which in this case was being applied to the car's floor beneath Makk's feet.

This meant that, when the car was *not* going up or down—when it was hovering—there was a small cavity of space between the car's floor and the buffer plate, in which there was a zero-gravity field. Larger versions of that cavity were used for the zero-g playing fields of Zero-Ball.

When just hovering, it felt a little like standing on top of a hot air balloon. Even with the car's stabilizers to hold the vehicle in place, it still rocked enough for the inner ear to notice. But when the car was *moving*, it felt like one was falling forward, all the time, without ever actually hitting the ground.

Makk's first time in a null-grav vehicle was in an NGT—one of those troop transports—and it was also the first time for the entire squad.

They got sick. Every last one of them. It was a common enough problem that nobody called them NGTs; to the soldiers ordered to ride in them, they were *vomit comets*.

Supposedly, one got accustomed to the sensation over time. But Makk could count on one hand the number of null-grav rides he'd taken since the transport crash. He never had a chance to get used to it, and didn't expect to.

He wasn't *really* expecting Viselle Daska's car to suddenly drop out of the sky and kill them both (along with whoever they landed on.) But his inner ear was telling him he was currently falling, and the amalgam of chicken rinds, grain wine, and beer in his stomach was reminding him of the merits of that old NGT nickname.

He couldn't get sick. Not only would it be criminal to throw up all over this nice interior, in all likelihood he was about to be on vid. Not showing up with sick on your shirt was a minimum requirement.

His discomfort didn't go unnoticed.

"Watch the horizon, detective," Daska said. "I'm told that helps."

"It doesn't help. How long were you at cyber?"

"What?"

"I'm making conversation."

"Seven seasons," she said. "And I had a beat for two seasons before that. Like I said, I'm not a rookie."

"That's not the definition."

"Don't close your eyes," she said.

"Why not?" He had his eyes closed because he was trying to imagine that he was on a boat on a lazy river, instead of suspended at an unreasonable altitude with nothing holding him up.

"It makes it worse," she said.

"I'll try the horizon, then. You ever work a murder case on your own?"

"This would have been my first."

"That means you're a rookie. I don't make the rules, so don't blame me for it. You learn a lot about embezzlement in cyber?"

"I picked up a couple of things," she said. "Why, do you have a case?"

"This is just a really nice car. Must have set you back. Same with that suit."

She sighed.

"Family money," she said.

"You stole it from a family?"

"I come from money, but I'd rather not...look, I know what you're thinking, but I made homicide on merit, okay?"

He actually wasn't thinking otherwise, but he knew enough cops who would jump to that exact conclusion. They'd start with her looks, throw in the money she came from, and go from there.

"How'd you know I came from cyber?" she asked. "It's not on my badge. I checked."

"I'm a master detective."

"C'mon."

"I heard someone was coming over, and guessed it was you."

She laughed.

The car officially left the airspace of the Decane Quarter and banked left onto (or rather, above,) the Wideway. Immediately, the buildings on both sides of the thoroughfare got taller, and the air traffic more common. Daska picked a vertical lane that her instruments indicated was free, and accelerated.

It felt like Makk's head swiveled completely around when the car banked and accelerated. This was *much* worse than he remembered.

"You were trying to find me, weren't you?" he asked. "At Lucky Twins. That wasn't a chance encounter."

She looked at him for just long enough to make him uncomfortable. Mainly because in doing so, she wasn't also looking where they were going.

"I've been in homicide for six days," she said. "But only on desk duty. Captain said the best way to acclimate was to read a lot of case files, but that was a lie. He didn't want me in the field. So I rode the bench, but I also did read those case files. Your name came up a lot."

"You're too impatient," he said. "I rode the bench for two months before I was primary."

"You were second-seat on day *three*, Makk. I told you, I read your cases."

"All of them? I've worked a lot of cases."

"I know," she said, "and you've *closed* a lot of them. More than anyone else in the department."

"Fine, so you swung by for an autograph. Llotho said you were next up. That doesn't sound like desk duty."

"Yeah, I brought that up when I had him direct. Exy and Honuson are working a triple on Suvie. He didn't say so, but I think he tried to pry one of them off to pick up this case, before he asked you."

"A triple in Suvie's kind of a big deal. I can see why that'd be a problem."

"Yeah. It's a banner night for murder," she said.

"Don't do that."

"What?"

She lifted her hands off the steering wheel for a second, as if the offending action he was referring to had to do with the car.

"It's not a murder until we say it is, rookie" he said. "Before that, it's just a body."

"Yes *sir*," she said, with a touch of sarcasm that was almost graceful.

The Wideway cut right through the center of Velon, which was the largest city in Inimata, and the third-largest city on the planet. The road was the longest uninterrupted thoroughfare in the world, passing southwest-to-northeast in a straight line and terminating on both ends at the ocean. It was possible to live an entire life, from birth to death, while never leaving the Wideway, and only traveling in one direction.

"So, you read a bunch of my casefiles," he said. "How does that put you in Binchagag's basement?"

"I was beginning to think he'd never let me off the bench. I got the sense that...I don't know. How well do you know the captain?"

Makk actually knew Yordon Llotho very well. He was a bit of an ass as a captain, but a standup guy otherwise.

"Well enough to buy him a drink," Makk said. "Not well enough to go home with him."

"Right. Okay. I think he looks at me and sees...what I figured you saw when you took a look at this car. I'm saying I don't want special treatment, Detective Stidgeon, but I mean that in either direction."

"That doesn't explain how you ended up in the basement."

"You don't have a partner."

"I'm aware of this."

"That was how."

She wiggled the wheel to adjust to a slight curvature in the road below them, and his stomach lurched again. He felt a little bile in the back of his throat.

Try looking at the horizon, he thought. The problem was, it was night-time, in the city. The farthest thing he could see was a lit billboard on top of a building six blocks away, advertising a brand of disinfectant.

"If I have this straight," he said, "your big plan was to turn up at my *home*, off-hours, and what? Flash your best smile, show off your nicest suit, and charm me?"

"This isn't my nicest suit," she said. "But that's about right. It wasn't the most thought-out plan, but...I guess I figured I'd take your pulse and wing it."

"Right."

He didn't want to look down, but he could tell from the lights that the traffic beneath them wasn't a whole lot better than it had been in Kindontown. It was worse, certainly, in the air; there was another aero-car on their right, and two above. Every now and then, Daska's radar pinged, and the screen readout notified her of a nearby flying object. None of the pings mandated evasive maneuvers—they were proximity alerts, at worst, and picked up the things Makk could already see with his eyes.

One day, driving in the sky was going to be a lot cheaper. He hoped to be retired to the countryside somewhere before that happened.

They were passing the Tether on the right. Makk could see it from just about any part of the city—and really, just about any part of the continent—because the top of the Tether reached lower orbit. He tilted his head to get a look anyway. On clear nights, the beacon at the top was visible, and looked like a pulsing star. This night was cloudy, so he couldn't see nearly that far.

The elevator that took goods and people to the top of the Tether had flashing lights on it as well, but he couldn't see it; either there wasn't one scheduled, or it had made it past the clouds already.

He'd never ridden the Tether, but imagined he'd have an easier time with it, considering it used a pulley system instead of null-grav tech.

"And this was all because I don't have a partner," he said.

"You seemed like a good person to learn from, and yeah: the position's open. And look, you also don't have a car. I'm useful already."

"Skipping the part where I'm about to show you what I ate before that beer you bought me, there's a reason I don't have a partner. I don't work well with others. Nothing you do is gonna change that. And deceiving me is *not* a good start. How'd you find out where I live? Did you break into my personnel file?"

"I...activated the sat beacon in your badge."

"Hah. That's so much worse. How'd you do that?"

"Like I said, I used to work in cyber."

He shook his head.

"You could have just messaged me direct," he said.

"Would it have worked?"

"You think *this* is working? No offense to you personally, Detective Daska, but our partnership isn't going to last beyond the closing of the case. This is not something I do. Ask anyone."

She fell silent for long enough that he got the idea she already *had* asked someone. Either that, or he'd disappointed her somehow. He was fine with either interpretation.

"Anyway," she said, "I wasn't trying to deceive you. If anything, it's the other way around."

"How do you figure?"

"You made me as a cop inside of thirty seconds," she said. "You could have told me who you were."

"We were standing in an illegal gambling parlor. I wasn't showing off my badge until I had no other choice. How'd you even end up down there?"

"Nobody in the restaurant was the right combination of age and gender to be you, so I followed a crowd down the stairs. I didn't know there was an apartment on the roof, or I might've started there."

"Okay. But then you met me, and pretended you didn't know who *I* was, when you were there to introduce yourself."

"Makk, we can play *who deceived who more* all night," she said, resignedly, "but it's going to get tiresome pretty fast. And I didn't peg you until you gave me your name. It probably *should* have been sooner, but it wasn't. I'm sorry I even considered this, but like I said; I don't want the white-glove treatment, and that's what I was getting. I was just trying to nudge this along."

"Well, you did that," he said. "But don't tell me this is about not wanting to be treated special. Every rook rides the bench for a while. You wanted to be the one that didn't."

Past the Tether, the Andel Quarter started to come into view. It was easy enough to see coming because of a different tall monument: The Fingers of the Septal House chapel. It was one of seven such chapels in the city, but was by far the tallest and oldest.

House chapels—the older ones, especially—had a distinctive look to them that was impossible to mistake for something else. Central to the structure was a tall column, flanked on both sides by slightly shorter columns. They were called Fingers, even though there were nine of them.

Nobody was walking around the planet with nine fingers per hand, so the appellation never made a lot of sense. There were some less-than-scholarly theories that people *used* to have that many fingers, back before the Collapse, and the House's columns were honoring that history. There were also a few entirely disreputable quasi-religious arguments that claimed the five gods of the Council all had nine fingers on each hand, but this theory was only respected in certain dark corners of the Stream.

The columns were hollow, like chimneys, although nothing came out of them at any time. Officially. Unofficially, all sorts of claims had been made about what the House was doing with those gigantic chimney-like things. The only thing in common with these claims was that they came from a place of paranoia (mostly expressed in those same dark corners of the Stream) which was the sort of content the House inspired in people who weren't adherents.

These days, that defined more and more people, at least in this city. Makk was a lapsed Septal, and could probably name more locals holding his position than he could name devotees. Not that the Septal House appeared to care. The unspoken message, of this chapter in particular, had always been, "if you don't want to hang out with us, we don't want to hang out with you." It was probably a non-canonical attitude, but it fit Velon nicely.

Immediately surrounding the main chapel was a series of administrative buildings. Beyond that, classrooms and laboratories, of the kind one might expect at a university.

Then came the Brethren neighborhoods. The Septal campus took up roughly three-fifths of the Andel Quarter, and half of the campus was taken up by living quarters for its adherents. The Brethren (they were also called monks, collectively, and Brothers, Sisters or Others individually) were people who'd taken an oath to devote their lives to the Septals, in exchange for which they got a lifetime of room and board, provided they didn't mind living on House land.

It actually wasn't a bad deal. Makk's entire education was through the House, and there was an eight or nine season period in which he was convinced he'd be taking the oath as an adult. The idea didn't last beyond puberty. Not because of some vow of celibacy—monks didn't have to take any such vow, although many did—but because puberty brought with it an anarchic streak that couldn't tolerate the ordered existence of the Brethren.

Housing was a combination of apartment buildings, walk-up townhouses, and standalone one-family homes. (As with the celibacy vow that didn't exist, there were no marital restrictions, as long as it remained within the House. Since there were no gender restrictions on taking the oath, and since the only people monks really hung out with were other monks, finding someone within the House to marry probably wasn't hard.) This meant the neighborhood itself was broken up into smaller neighborhoods. The apartment buildings—three-and-four-story structures—were the farthest from the center, in an area a literal stone's throw from the public streets. The townhouses came next, and then the nice section with houses growing more ostentatious the closer one got to the 'university' portion of the land. Occupancy was doled out according to status and tenure.

Ringing the entire thing was a low rock wall, barely a mader high. It used to be much taller, but one of the High Hats—Dolmet Zi, who held the position until about twenty-two years ago—decided the prior five-mader wall sent the wrong message. She had it cut down to something tall enough to prevent anyone from accidentally walking (or driving) onto the land, but low enough so nobody on the other side felt unwelcome. It did less than High Hat Zi probably hoped it would, for the House's reputation of secrecy—even if the Septals publicized every secret they'd supposedly been keeping in the depths of their vaults, the public would insist they weren't being transparent—the wall at least no longer served as a visual reinforcement of that reputation.

Still in the aero-car travel lane as they approached the neighborhood, Makk could see the dome lights from the police cruisers reflecting off the campus buildings ahead. Captain Llotho said the body was in the townhouses, but until he saw the source of the lights, Makk didn't fully appreciate how far into the campus that really was. This was going to be a big deal. *Lots* of Veesers would be there.

Makk was starting to wish he'd dressed nicer. Or, not answered the captain when he sent the direct. Or, on vacation in Binchagag's hunting cabin, which was half a day's drive away at Zonic National Park.

Professionally unlucky, he thought.

Detective Daska took the aero-car to the ground two blocks before the entrance, on one of the landing strips designed for such a thing. (Every major road in the city featured an extra-lane breakout, about thirty maders long, to allow room for aero-cars.) As soon as the wheels touched down, Makk exhaled for what felt like the first time since they left the garage roof.

"See?" Daska said. "Nice and smooth."

"Right. Pull over, would you?"

"We're just a few blocks..."

"See the shrubs?"

He pointed to a row of decorative bushes that doubled as a property line for a rowhouse back yard.

"Right there," he said.

Daska stopped the car. Makk jumped out before she could ask any more questions, stuck his head behind the bushes, and threw up everything he'd had to eat and drink since Binchagag started whacking the radiator pipe.

Lina was right, he thought, *that* is *a better hangover cure.*

He straightened himself out, and calmly walked back to the

car. Daska pulled a metal tin from her pocket and handed it over, as he closed the door.

"Mint," she said.

"No thanks," he said.

"It's not optional. Trust me."

He took a mint. Daska engaged the electric engine, and merged into traffic.

There were three gated entrances to the Septal campus, spots where the one-mader wall allowed for the existence of a road. Since the lowering of the wall, the gates were largely symbolic, but everyone still used them. Not that ground-cars had any other choice; the wall was an ample deterrent in that regard. It was also considered an insult to take an aero-car over it, whether one's destination was inside or not.

(It was generally frowned upon to take an aero-car over *most* buildings in Velon, but doubly so for Septal buildings.)

"Never been inside this campus before," Daska said, as they came up to the entrance. Traffic in this part of town was considerably lighter than in Kindontown, and on the Wideway, so it didn't take all that long to reach the campus. "Have you?"

"A few times," he said.

The gates were open, as usual. She'd picked what was generally considered the main gate, due to its proximity to the Wideway. There was a much more ornamental gate on the eastern side, which led directly to the front of the chapel without first tripping through the neighborhood, but it was closed except for ceremonial days. The annual march signaling the start of the Tribulations of the Five always ended at that gate.

On the other side of the entrance was a sentry box, with a monk standing next to it. Makk hadn't been inside for a couple of years, but couldn't recall anyone bothering to play security guard there before. Daska slowed next to him, lowered her window, and showed her badge.

"I know where I'm going," she said.

Clothing-wise, it was nearly impossible to tell the difference between most members of the Brethren and an ordinary citizen... from the neck down. The Brothers, Sisters and Others of the order wore a peculiar kind of head-gear: a hood, but with a black veil panel that covered the eyes and (on most) part of the nose. Just the lower half of the face was regularly visible.

Most only wore the hoods in public, and only when there were lay-people around. The rest of their clothing—save for during ceremonies—was normal, everyday city garb. The ceremonial garb was a full monk's robe, and there were some Septals—those who practiced a much stricter brand of faith—who wore robes all the time.

The monk at the gate was not one of the stricter adherents; he was dressed like an ordinary security guard, all except for the hood.

Makk had been around hooded people all his life, and had yet to figure out how to read someone who was wearing one. Not being able to see a person's eyes made their body language largely inscrutable, which was perhaps the point. The hoods also instilled in him a sense of awe, or perhaps fear; an artifact of his child-hood, no doubt, and one he'd been struggling to overcome ever since his *Haremisva*.

One thing that always bugged Makk about the hoods was that the monks who wore them were surrendering most of their peripheral vision in the exchange. When he was a kid, it was sort of funny—if one could figure out where the limit to their vision was, one could make obscene gestures just beyond that point, and so of course that was what he did. As an adult, he didn't think he'd be comfortable with the trade-off.

It was certainly not what he would have chosen to wear if he was on guard duty.

The sentry read Daska's badge for a few seconds, handed back, and nodded.

"Got half the city ahead of you tonight," he said, gesturing up the road.

"You let them all in?" she asked.

"I just got here. Nobody saw fit to man this station until about an hour ago. I guess in case the other half of the city felt like showing. I'm just waiting on orders to close the gates."

"Do they even close?" Makk asked.

"Sure," he said. "We oil the hinges twice a year. Never seen it myself, but everything has a first."

He stepped back and performed a familiar gesture. It involved placing his hand over his heart and pantomiming a grip: his hand went from flat to a fist.

"May the Five be close," he said.

"And with you," Daska said. It was a rote response; she probably didn't even think about it when she said it.

The guard nodded, and they continued on their way.

The streets in the neighborhood were laid out in a well-ordered grid, in contrast to the messy range of odd angles that constituted the rest of the city, which made it perhaps the easiest part of Velon in which to navigate. However, hardly anyone in the Septal neighborhood drove anywhere, unless they were infirm, or they meant to exit the gates. Even on an ordinary night there would be a decent number of hooded monks walking along the streets, regardless of the hour. On this night, that number appeared to have more than doubled, with a bunch of regular non-hooded citizens mixed in.

"Captain didn't give you a name, did he?" he asked Daska.

"For the dead body? No. You?"

"No. Just trying to work out how important you have to be to get half the campus out at this time of night."

"Probably not the High Hat," she said.

"I think Llotho would have let that slip. And Highness lives up there."

He pointed straight up the road to the chapel. The High Hat didn't live *in* the chapel; his residence was in a mansion off to one side.

"Someone on the Council?" she offered.

"Maybe."

The people in the street had a general disinterest in stepping out of the way of Daska's car. They did, eventually, reluctantly, but she had to keep a pace that was going to get them there just as fast as if they parked it and walked the rest of the way.

"I have a portable dome light in the cabinet," Daska said, pointing to the drawer in the dashboard on the passenger's side. "If you want to pull it out, we'll probably make better time."

"Let's not," Makk said. "We're heading into a nest of Verified Streamers. I don't want to get pinned down refusing to answer questions before I even have a chance to figure out if I'm looking at a crime."

"Okay, but our shift might end before we reach the scene," she said. "Unless you want me to start running people over."

"I might be okay with that."

As they continued along the slow creep in the rough direction of the flashing police lights, Makk scanned the crowd.

It was generally the case that members of the Brethren didn't personally broadcast on the Stream. The House had official channels, of course, but those channels were curated, and the content heavily edited. They were nothing like the unfiltered content dumped online, terabyte by terabyte, every day.

Most of those content providers weren't anything he had to worry about. A Verified Streamer—or 'Veeser'—was another story. They had huge built-in audiences, and their broadcasts generally presaged what would later be reported by the curated news organizations. This should have meant that the average Veeser reported information that had a factual basis. In Makk's experience, this ended up being true far less often than the word *verified* implied.

Spotting Streamers was easy enough in a crowd of Brethren; he just had to look for citizens wearing Streamer headgear. Verified Streamer rigs included a tiny blue light (the Unverifieds had a white one) which was supposed to make it easier for them to get into places. Ironically, it usually just made them easier to avoid.

Aside from the periodic sight of Streamers—and so far, none of them had shown any interest in Daska's not-a-police-car—Makk could see little rumor chains traveling along the sidewalk. People who were on their way to the scene interacted with people who had already been there, gossip was exchanged, and expressions of shock ensued.

He had already inferred from the quantity of people milling around that the deceased was someone well-known among this community. What was interesting was the expressions of grief, easily readable as such despite the hoods. The victim was also well-liked.

Assuming there was a victim at all. A happy ending for everyone would be if they were about to witness a suicide or an accidental death. Well, a happy ending for Makk; maybe not anyone else.

The crowd parted about a block out, but only because the uniforms had established a perimeter that began there. Daska got the nose of the car to the edge of one of the police barricades, and parked it.

There were six officers manning sawhorse barriers to keep a sizeable crowd away from the scene. There was a similar cordon on the other side, clearing a space about five townhouse-fronts long. There were two police cruisers in the middle, an ambulance, and a van holding the forensics team. Everybody had their lights going, which was annoying, and probably unnecessary.

Makk took note that nobody involved in the ambulance

looked particularly busy. Whoever's body was inside, they weren't just dead, they were *very* dead.

Makk spotted Swigg, one of the officers holding the do-not-cross line. Swigg had been about to shout at the owner of the fancy aero-car that she couldn't park there, when he saw Makk getting out of the passenger seat.

"Is that you, Makk Stidgeon?" he shouted. "What happened, you marry rich on your off-day?"

"Bod Swigg, this is Detective Viselle Daska. Daska, Swigg. Car's hers."

Swigg was a huge man, both tall and wide. He was always the first cop on call when there was a riot that needed to be settled or a perimeter secured. He was also great to have around when *starting* a riot, emptying a bar, and convincing a drunk cop not to drive anywhere.

All that said, when he got a look at Daska, and her car, he could have been knocked over by a light breeze.

"No kidding," he said. "Well it's a pleasure to meet you miss..."

"Detective," she corrected.

"Detective. Sure."

"Who has the scene, Bod?" Makk asked.

"Tayler," he said. "She's out front."

"Super."

Swigg stepped aside and let the two of them pass through, then closed up the cordon. Already, Makk had spotted two Veesers trying to clear a path through the crowd to get to them. Swigg was a good man to have standing in their way.

"I know you said, you don't want people to think you got any special treatment," Makk said to Daska, as they walked down the street, "but if that's what you really want, you should probably change your ride."

"I tried that already," she said, "when I started in cyber. It was maybe two weeks before word got around that my financial realities weren't the same as everyone else's, and then I had people resenting me for keeping it a secret. *Play-acting at being poor*, they said. I gave up trying to figure out how to make everyone happy."

"Okay then," he said.

"Yeah I know: poor rich girl."

"I didn't say anything."

"Besides, the car got us past the Streamers, right?" she said. "I made five or six on the way."

"Two Veesers at the barricade, probably looping us now," he said. "At least they're getting my good side. Could be a half-dozen drones over us, too."

"You think?"

She looked up.

"Keep your head down, eyes forward," he said. "Yeah, I do think. High profile case like this, you can't control what the Stream gets. If you're lucky, you get to be a willing participant in shaping what's said."

"Good to know, thanks."

From across the street, a couple of the forensic guys waved and applauded when they saw Makk on approach. This was basic sarcasm, and just the surface level of the gallows humor those goons trafficked in regularly.

Velon was the second-largest city on the planet, and one of the most population-dense. This made for enough bodies to clean up that there was a triage approach in place. First cop on the scene generally made a judgment call. If what they were looking at was *probably* a natural death, forensics came in, took pictures and samples and what-not, and then cleared the ambulance to cart the body away. This covered about eighty percent of the daily toll. The other twenty percent of the time, someone asked homicide to double-check. About half of *those* ended up being nothing—just an overly-cautious cop not wanting to make the wrong call.

(Cases where the wrong call was made—where someone on forensics discovered an indication that it was something other than a natural death—happened all the time. They were called cold-scene cases, and everyone hated them.)

The other ten percent were wrongful deaths. Ninety percent of *those* were suicides.

One might think that left a pretty small percentage of the total for actual homicides. It was. But thanks to Velon's size, the raw numbers were larger, per-season, than any other major city in the world. (Probably. Chnta, the world's largest city, reported homicide numbers so low as to be statistically impossible. But that was how things went in Wivvol.)

The reason the forensics team was waving and applauding was that as soon as the scene officer declared this a likely wrongful death, their evening came to a standstill. Having already confirmed that the body inside was deceased, forensics wouldn't be allowed near it until Makk was done, and Makk was a famously slow worker in that regard.

Probably wish they caught the triple on Suvie, he thought.

Notably, the one person from forensics not performing for Makk was the unit boss, Jori Len. She grabbed a device from the back of the truck and headed across the street, to meet up with Makk and Daska at the door.

Meanwhile, the scene officer, Dia Tayler, was on the stoop of one of the townhouses, smoking a stick and looking bored. It was her default expression. Makk didn't much care for her, and the feeling was self-evidently mutual. She called him *Detective Cholem* behind his back, when she was sober, and to his face when she wasn't. She was, however, competent, which was about the best he could ask for from a scene officer.

"I thought I was getting the rook tonight," Tayler said, as they walked up.

"You are," Makk said. "You're just getting me, too. What's the narrative here?"

Tayler came down the steps, eyeballed Daska without a word, and then addressed Makk as if she wasn't there.

"Me and Juo-Ta caught it. Found a body inside, a little ripe, maybe two or three days. Medics stepped in long enough to confirm, and then we sealed it up and called it in. I've got the kid who found the body in the back of the cruiser."

"What kind of kid?" Daska asked.

"The young kind," Tayler said, annoyed. "Student. Says the body inside is their professor."

"How far into the place did the he go to confirm that?" Makk asked.

"He's a *they.* All the way."

"Do they have a key?"

"You'll have to ask them," she said. "But the back door isn't doing a very good job of being a back door right now, so they probably came in that way."

"You ask them what they touched?"

"No, because I'm not a homicide detective, and you guys don't like us talking to witnesses before you do."

"Hey, Makk," Jori said. "The witness was scoped already, if you're worried."

She held up a DNA scope. It was a black box about the size of a pack of bacco sticks.

"Forensics also logged me, Juo-Ta, and the medics," Tayler said. "Not my first corpse, Stidgeon. Not even my first live-Streamer."

She nodded upward; one of the drones had drifted into their eyeline.

Legally speaking, the airspace over a cordoned crime scene was off-limits. Practically speaking, there was almost no way to enforce that regulation without shooting the drone down.

"Super," Makk said. "Where's Officer Juo-Ta now?"

"Around back. We didn't want to risk someone letting themselves in like the kid did, while we stood on the stoop waiting for detectives to free up some time in their busy schedules."

"Okay," Jori said, holding up the scope. "I want to get my team out of here before the suns come up. Which one of you's going in?"

"We both are," Daska said. She stuck her thumb into the scope, waited while it took a microscopic layer of dead skin from it, and then started up the steps.

"Wait for me," Makk said, taking his turn with the scope.

"What, she got a date later?" Tayler asked, under her breath.

"It's her first body," he said. "She doesn't know enough yet to know this isn't supposed to be exciting. Did the kid ID the body for you?"

"Orno Linus. Heard of him?"

"Nope. You?"

"No, but they seemed think we should have. Guess the vic's only a big deal around here."

"Don't call him a *victim*," Makk said, "until we know it's a crime."

Tayler laughed.

"You're not that kind of lucky," she said.

The scope flashed a green all-clear signal. Makk handed it back to Jori, who traded it for a couple of pairs of rubber gloves.

"*Try* not to take too long, Makk," Jori said.

"I can't guarantee that," he said.

He looked over at the cruiser with the kid in the back.

"Get them out of here," he said. "I don't want their face turning up on the Stream."

"You want them in the box?" Tayler asked, referring to the interrogation room at Central.

"No, no. There's a twenty-hour diner just off-campus." He pulled a C-Coin from his pocket and handed it to Tayler. "Have one of the uniforms take them there, get them something to eat. No alcohol."

"Do Seppies even drink?"

"Sure they do. We'll catch up to them after we're done here."

He headed up the steps to the door, where his impatient-looking partner was waiting. He handed her a set of gloves.

"She doesn't like you," Daska said, referring to Tayler.

"Tayler doesn't like anyone," he said.

Viselle looked like she wanted to tell him something, before deciding against it. What she was going to say was that Officer Tayler performed a warding-off gesture behind his back. Daska didn't have to tell him this, and he didn't need to turn around to see it for himself; it happened all the time.

"Let's just go inside," he said.

Chapter Three

Makk had never been into one of the Septal townhouses before. It was about as nice as he expected it to be, but about twice as small. The main entrance led to what in most private quarters would be a living room, at the front of the house, with a kitchen at the back, and a spiral staircase in the middle. And that was it.

Orno Linus didn't appear to have much use for a living room, using the space as an office instead. It had a desk, a bookshelf, a couple of chairs, two markerboards with equations written on them, a small computer, and a little blood.

The blood was obviously a recent addition.

Linus was lying on the floor near the base of the staircase, his feet in the kitchen and his head in the study. His right arm was stretched out toward the desk, his left bent awkwardly, elbow-up. He was in a full monk's cloak, although his head—the back half of which had been caved in by something heavy—was uncovered. He was barefoot.

The body was pretty ripe. Makk had encountered worse (nothing topped the discovery of a woman in a car trunk after three weeks) but knowing there were less tolerable olfactory possibilities didn't lessen the impact of this situation.

Daska coughed, and covered her nose. Makk was suddenly glad he'd already gotten vomiting out of the way for the evening.

"I'm glad that's not your nicest suit," he said. "This kind of smell never goes away."

"Thanks," she said. "This is pretty bad."

"You're welcome. Step out, get some air if you have to."

"I'm fine."

"Just don't get sick on my crime scene."

"I said, I'm fine."

"Okay," he said, walking over to the body. "I'm only saying, there's no shame in it, as long as it's outside. I got sick at my first scene."

"Not my first," she said. "I was scene officer on a couple, when I had a beat."

"Where was that?" he asked.

He knelt down to get a better look at the back of the victim's head. Daska stayed near the door. He couldn't tell if she was doing that because she didn't know how to proceed with the investigation, or because her stomach was recommending she stay near an exit.

"Palavin," she said.

"Nice beat. Not a lot of murders in Palavin Quarter."

"They weren't. Just bodies: a suicide and a heart attack. I made the call on both. Can we call this one a murder now?"

"I think we can, yes."

He pulled out his badge and took a few close-ups of the head wound, and then stepped back for some wide-angle shots. These were mostly for his own use; Jori's team would take the formal scene pics.

"Unless you can figure out how he bashed in the back of his own skull," he added, "and then moved the murder weapon before he died. You sticking around?"

"Yes."

"Then come over here and tell me what you see."

She stepped around the body, slowly.

"Decomp's gonna ruin the wood floor," she said.

"That's all?"

"First thing that came to mind."

She stopped at the victim's feet.

"Based on the blood spatter across the desk and the bookshelf, he got hit around here," she said. "A stick or a pipe, probably."

"What makes you say that?"

"The spray pattern. It arced on the follow-through. And the killer was left-handed."

Makk stood next to her, and considered this point.

If this was a game of bagball, and the back of Orno Linus's head was the ball, the piper at the bag would have to be standing on the right side to swing the pipe freely. A right-handed piper—standing on the left side of the bag—would have to deal with interference from the staircase.

"Good," he said. "But that just means the killer is left-eye dominant."

"Which means they're left-handed."

"Not always."

"Makk..."

"No, it's a good observation. Let's just keep track of what we know for *sure*."

Makk looked up the staircase.

"Only one flight," he said. "Must be bed and bath."

"I can start upstairs, if you want," Daska said. "While you work down here."

"No, stay here. Nothing personal; I'm gonna end up walking the whole place anyway."

Her expression suggested she did intend to take this personally, but she didn't say anything to that effect. She just knelt down next to the body, while Makk turned his attention to the desk. The forensic goons would have more to tell him about the corpse than his eyes could, but the office was another story.

The chair side of the desk was a mess; it looked as if someone had dumped the contents of the drawers on the floor. Makk pulled a couple of the drawers out to confirm that yes, that was exactly what had happened. One had been yanked hard enough to damage the frame.

He thought it was a little interesting that whoever had done this was in a big enough hurry to toss the desk, but not such a big hurry that they couldn't put the drawer back.

"Who was he?" Daska asked. She was taking her own pictures of the body. "Do we know?"

"Tayler said the name's Orno Linus."

"No kidding."

"Do you know him?"

"I know the family. So do you."

"Wait," Makk said. "*That* Linus?"

"Pretty sure. I know Calcut Linus has a brother who took the oath. Maybe this is him. I'd have to see the face to be sure. You think this is related to the family business?"

"I think we're a long way from that kind of assumption," he said. "But if that's a Linus on the floor there, our best move is to sneak out that back door and pretend we were never here. Maybe we can wreck your car in another part of town for an alibi."

"We'd have to bribe all the uniforms first."

"Yeah, but they're cheap."

She didn't answer, because she wasn't taking his suggestion seriously, when he was at least half-serious.

Occupying space between the House and the Linus family was more hazardous than taking a stroll off the moon base without a suit. Even for someone who was professionally unlucky, this was pretty bad luck. The Linuses had a highly cultivated, well-earned unsavory reputation for (for want of a better term) legalized criminal activity. About half of what they were involved in wasn't legal at all, but because it was a Linus endeavor, it may as well have been legal. Publicly, Calcut Linus was a glad-handing influencer with a lot of money and decent political clout. Privately, he was a terrifying man with a violent temper who could make people disappear with a word. Supposedly.

Rumor was, the High Hat of the Velon Septal chapter could also make people disappear. The basis of that rumor was paranoid and conspiratorial in nature—in other words, far less grounded in reality than anything orbiting the Linuses—but that didn't mean it was untrue. The House had a lot of secrets, and it guarded at least some of those secrets in ways that were purported to be quite unsavory.

Basically, short of paradropping into the middle of a dispute between Dorabonian drug lords, Makk couldn't think of a much more perilous circumstance to land in.

Daska didn't seem to understand the nature of the peril inherent in their current circumstance. Or, she didn't care.

She stepped away from the body and into the kitchen to have a look around. Her doing this made Makk uncomfortable immediately, despite her not having left his line-of-sight. He didn't work with partners, yes, but more to the point, he was used to being alone with the dead.

He tried to pretend she wasn't there, and returned his focus to the office.

He'd need a mathematician to translate the equations on the markerboards. The math was next to diagrams that looked like planetary orbit charts, but they could just as easily have been describing the interaction of subatomic particles. He'd need someone to help with those, too.

There was a thin, portable computer on the desktop, open and with a little blood on the keyboard. It was powered down, but the light on the side indicated there was battery life.

They were searching for something, he thought, *but maybe not something you find in an electronic file*.

He wondered if the victim had a voicer. If so, it wasn't near the body, or on the desk. Under the body, maybe. He'd have to ask forensics to check. They'd also bag the computer, after checking it for DNA, but he didn't have to tell them to do that.

"Any proscriptions you know of, on Septals using voicers?" Makk asked.

"Not that I've heard," Daska said. She was near the back of the kitchen, checking out the rear exit.

"How about for the especially devout?"

"You think he was one of those?"

"He's got the clothes for it."

"I don't know the Linuses well," she said, "but I'd be surprised if Calcut's brother was a Fundamentalist. Maybe the robe is just really comfortable. By the way, the back door is definitely busted. I think it was kicked in. Might be how the killer got inside."

"I'll take a look when I'm done here," he said. "My head's in the office right now. How about if you go introduce yourself to Officer Juo-Ta, and tell me what the backyard looks like?"

"Sure."

He didn't look up to see her face, but he could hear her eyes rolling, as she stepped outside.

Rookies are always impatient, he thought.

He turned his attention to the bookcase. It was full of textbooks betraying a range of interests, some not making a lot of sense for a member of the Brethren. The astrology books, for instance.

It had always been the case that the oath-taking members of the Septal House spent their lives devoted to some mix of religious and scientific pursuits. Unlike some of the other religions out there—Unitism, for instance—House adherents were pretty good at partitioning their faith from the things they could prove with some objectivity. It was what made them such good teachers, and scientists: The House was at least partly supported, financially, by income from their patented discoveries.

Makk remembered a conversation he had with Other Yikowshi about it once, back when he was in school. (Yikowshi always struck Makk as the least fanatical—and most approachable—of his teachers, which made them the right person for this kind of question.) On one side, there was the belief that the planet Dib, and all that was on it, had been created by the gods Honus, Javilon, Ho, Nita and Pal. On the other side, it seemed as if each new scientific discovery went a little further toward proving that the gods had nothing to do with anything. It seemed crazy that the Septals could spend so much time believing—and teaching—the first thing, while actively pursuing (and also believing) the second thing.

Yikowshi's answer was that the science illuminated the wonder of the gods' design, and so learning more about how the universe worked was a form of worship.

Their explanation satisfied the young Makk Stidgeon. As an adult, he arrived at a different (and much more popular) conclusion: the Septals were keeping the scientific discoveries that contradicted their belief a secret.

The reason the astrology book in particular stood out was that astrology wasn't a scientific pursuit, and it was a religious pursuit only in the sense that most adherents believed what they believed absent an objective proof of some kind.

It didn't belong on the shelves, essentially.

The other books were a mix of science-based textbooks, and those of a more religious and philosophical bent.

Two books in particular caught his eye. One was a textbook called *Bodies in Motion: Everyday Astrophysics.* The other was called *The Outcast Ascendant: Preparing for the End Times.*

The reason they caught Makk's attention was that both had been written by Orno Linus.

Unless Makk was misinterpreting the titles, these were two

different disciplines. Perhaps it was normal for high-ranking Septal professors to write scholarly works in both the scientific and religious fields, but he didn't recall having seen it before. One *teaching* both, sure. But authorship implied a higher degree of scholarship.

He took a photo of the shelf, then took down the astrophysics book and flipped it open. There was as an entirely unhelpful photographic portrait of the author on the inside jacket: it was Orno Linus, but Orno Linus in a hood.

His eyes fell back on the desk. There weren't any pictures on it, which was only slightly unusual. Makk didn't have any on *his* desk either, but his desk was in a police station, while this was in a man's home.

There also weren't any pictures on the walls.

He'd have to wait until he got upstairs to determine with any certainty that Orno lived alone, but it felt like it. All indications were that the victim had been dead on the floor for at least a few days, so if he was wrong, and Linus shared this space with someone else, that someone else was going to have to be accounted for.

Unless that someone else was lying dead upstairs. Makk wondered if anyone checked.

Tayler's a witch, he thought dismissing the notion, *but she's thorough.*

"Not much of a backyard," Daska said, letting herself back in. Makk jumped, having already forgotten he was working with someone. "I'd have Juo-Ta conduct a search, but there's nothing to search. Scrub grass and dirt."

"Is it fenced in?" Makk asked.

"No, you can just walk through to the other street. The view is the back of the townhouses on the other side."

"Then the search grid is the whole neighborhood. And there's not much point in a search grid. What do you want to look for?"

"I don't know yet," she said. "Murder weapon, maybe. I'm just saying, if we *need* to conduct a search, there isn't much behind the house to look for. I'm assuming the back door was the killer's way in."

Makk sighed.

"Viselle, we're probably gonna be here all night. As soon as that forensic team comes in, we can forget about discovering anything new, so if there's a clue anywhere in this townhouse that will help explain what happened, now is when we're going to find it. I'm not going to release the scene before I'm satisfied that I've seen everything."

"I know all of that," she said.

"I mean, I'm going to look at it all personally."

"You're saying I'm going too fast."

"You're going *way* too fast."

"You could have just said that."

"I was working my way up. Look, this is what you asked for, right? Watch me work, and all that? Well this is how I work."

She nodded, and paced the kitchen a little.

"Alone," she said. "Usually."

"Usually."

"How uncomfortable am I making you, right now?"

He laughed.

"It's obvious?"

"Every time I say something you check the body to see if he was the one who spoke. I get you're used to doing this by yourself, but...look, just give me something to do. And I don't mean some bullshit pretend-something where I walk around introducing myself to all the uniforms in the neighborhood. Do you want me to interview the kid in the cruiser?"

"No, I had Tayler take them down the road for a cup of coffee," he said.

"Right. Okay. Not that, then."

"We'll both interview them later," he said.

"Help me understand your method. Why did it bother you when I said the back door looked like it was kicked in?"

"Because now that's all I'm gonna see when I go look at it. You've biased my first opinion on the subject."

"There's a big boot print on the white paint on the door, and it's splintered under the knob. It's kind of hard to ignore, or confuse as something else."

"All right, fair enough," he said.

"Look at it yourself, if you have to."

"Yes, okay, I'm willing to consider that I may be overreacting."

"I'm just saying, you're going to have to trust me a *little* bit."

"Okay, okay."

He thought of something.

"That boot print," he said, "is it muddy?"

"What? Yeah. I mean, it's dried, but yeah."

"When was the last time it rained? Yesterday?"

"Day before last, I think. I have to check."

"Pull up the weather for the whole week. I've been working the over, so the days are all stacked together in my head, but I'm pretty sure we had a dry week up until a day or two ago."

"I'll put the timeline together," she said. "But I'm not seeing what you're seeing. Why's it matter?"

"Because Orno here's been dead for at least, what? Three days? If the door was kicked in *after*, someone else was here."

"And that someone else didn't direct the cops," she said, finishing the thought.

"That's what I'm saying. Maybe that same someone tossed this desk, and who knows what else."

She nodded.

"All that from a boot print," she said.

"Get a picture of it, before some idiot from forensics cleans the door or something."

"Already done. One more time, Makk: give me something to do."

"How about if you do a pass through the upstairs?" he said. "Don't tell me what you find unless it's breathing. Then we'll swap floors, do the same thing, and compare notes. Does that work for you?"

"Okay."

"But like I said, don't touch anything. If you feel like you have to lift something to look underneath it, don't do that."

She laughed.

"You might have some trust issues," she said.

"Oh, I definitely do. Didn't that turn up in the case files? I barely trust myself."

Makk didn't know enough about the academic aspects of everything going on around Orno Linus's desk to recognize what else might or might not be important, so he took pictures of everything and made a note to have the whole study catalogued and taken downtown as evidence. Whoever searched the office did a pretty good job of tossing it, enough so Makk couldn't say what it used to look like. He also couldn't tell if they found what they were looking for.

It looked like the kitchen had been rummaged through as well. It was a little less obvious, but the stuff in the cupboards had been shoved around and a couple of plates were broken.

Makk made two assumptions. The first was that Orno wouldn't store a broken plate, and the second was that whoever did the search would only move onto the kitchen after they'd searched the study. If they didn't find it in the kitchen either, then if they found it at all, it would have been found upstairs.

He was trying to avoid the conclusion that whatever they were looking for, it was relevant to Orno's death. That seemed like an obvious enough assumption, but he wasn't a fan of obvious assumptions.

Orno's coldbox had a lot of the expected things: some overdue cow's milk, a dozen plover eggs, a drawer of cured meats, a half-empty bottle of white wine, and so on. There was also a glass container holding what looked like bits of dough, another glass container with a thick, white substance, and some bread dough.

Makk unscrewed the second glass container and sniffed. It was a familiar kind of sour: wild yeast. He closed it back up again, took a second look at the bits of dough, and then took another pass around the kitchen, before heading upstairs.

He met Daska halfway up the staircase.

"How long have you been sitting here?" he asked.

"Not long," she said. "Llotho's about to hit you."

Makk's badge flashed and thrummed. He checked the display.

"If you're psychic," he said to Daska, "tell me now."

"He hit me first," she said. "I told him I'm just a doe-eyed rook who knows nothing."

"I know you're joking, but that's probably the smart play."

Makk connected the direct.

"Hi Captain," he said. "Thanks for reaching out, we're both doing great over here."

"I need an update," Llotho said.

"Guy's still dead."

"You know who just directed me? Calcut fucking Linus. *Himself.* Tell me it's not his brother lying dead in that townhouse."

"How'd he hear?"

"What do you mean, how'd he hear?"

"I mean, we haven't formally ID'ed the body yet."

"Every Veeser in the city did it for you, over an hour ago. Are you saying they're wrong?"

"Not wrong, just premature."

"Dammit, I was really hoping they were wrong. It's Orno?"

"We're pretty sure it is. And it's his place; the victim's barefoot and unhooded."

"Barefoot."

"No shoes by the door, so if he doesn't live here, he *stayed* here or walked over without shoes on. I got a photo of him for a comparison, but you know how it is with the Brethren: everything with a hood on."

"Detective, are you ready to positive ID or not?"

Makk looked at the position of the body again. He'd need forensics in here to flip him over and get a decent look at the face, but...

"Yeah," he said. "It's him."

"Damn the Five. All right. Close up the scene *soon*, Makk. I've got Duqo Plaint's office on hold; I need to give them something."

"Tell the High Hat we're done when we're done."

"Just hurry it along, detective."

Llotho disconnected.

"*He* sounded happy," Viselle said.

"Next time, *you* update him."

"Yes sir," she said, getting to her feet. "Any tips for the downstairs?"

"Yeah, don't trip over the dead guy."

As anticipated, the second floor contained the professor's bathroom and bedroom. There was also a second bedroom with no bed in it, being used for storage.

Whoever tossed the first floor did the same thing on the second. There were half-folded clothes sitting in piles and empty drawers tossed aside. The bedroom's closet had been cleaned out, quickly and violently; the clothes-hanger rod had been yanked down, and a hole had been punched in the drywall.

No, not punched.

The shattered remains of an alarm clock were on the floor of the closet after someone threw it at the back wall. It was either a shortcut in determining if the closet had a hidden compartment

—which it clearly did not—or someone was angry at the clock for some reason.

He took a photo, and then flipped over the clock and took another photo. It was an old-fashioned design, with bells-and-hammer on top, an analog face, and a windup key in the back. The impact shattered the glass case, a fragment of which was holding the minute-hand in place.

It was destroyed at fourteen-thirty-two, which was useful, but only a little. Since the clock had no date component to it, he couldn't tell what *day* it had been destroyed. Just that it happened around fourteen-thirty-two.

The second bedroom was mostly empty. It contained a portable cot that was folded and leaning against a wall, an empty closet with a door that needed rehanging—it refused to stay closed—and a half-dozen cardboard storage boxes.

The contents of those boxes had been dumped on the floor. They looked like old academic papers, and were probably only of interest to the man who boxed them. Probably not even then.

Makk made a note to have the papers packed up and sent downtown too; maybe he could find a couple of lay physicists with the time to tell him how much he should care about any of it.

The medicine cabinet in the bathroom was bare, but given the dust on its shelves, it always had been. A free-standing towel cabinet had been overturned, and was now lying halfway in the tub, but there was no other evidence of misbehavior on display.

He returned to the bedroom and let his mind wander.

They didn't find what they were looking for. That much seemed pretty clear. Also clear, there were hardly any hiding places, if one was of a mind to hide something.

The place felt both homey and temporary—a lot like a dorm room. That made some sense, given the way the House promoted adherents. Tenure meant moving closer to the center, which made most residences temporary. At the same time, there were elements to this townhouse that suggested the professor had been there for some time, and planned to stay longer. The centerpiece of that argument was in the kitchen, where it looked like a second oven had been installed.

Regardless, the only things that were supposed to change in a place like this was the occupant, and the occupant's stuff. Therefore, if Orno Linus wanted a hiding place, it wouldn't be in the walls or the floor. It would be in the furniture.

"It's not fair," Daska said, from the top of the stairs. This time, he didn't jump, because he heard her coming.

"Are you done downstairs?" he asked.

"I think I am."

"What's not fair?"

"You get to deduce things by moving stuff around and I don't," she said.

"It isn't a competition."

"No, but it's a test. I see you flipped the clock over."

She took a picture of the clock for herself.

"I did," he said. "Did you check the coldbox?"

"He likes to bake his own bread. You think that got him killed?"

"Depends on the quality of the bread. Does it look to you like the bed's been moved around at all?"

"No," she said. "Why would anyone move it?"

"I can think of at least one reason why they would," he said. "That wasn't the question. The question was, did they?"

She walked around the edge of the bedroom to try out a couple of different angles.

"Doesn't look like it was," she said.

"I agree. Help me out with the mattress."

"In what way?"

"I'm going to move it," he said.

"Okay."

Daska stepped up to the opposite side of the bed.

"I just want to lift it straight up and put it over there," he said, pointing to a relatively unoccupied portion of the floor. "Disturb what's on top as little as possible."

What was on top was the piles of clothing from the drawers.

"Want to tell me why?" she asked.

"Not yet. On three."

He counted to three and then they lifted the mattress together, and moved it to the floor.

Underneath was a flat board.

"Congratulations, you've discovered a bed board," she said.

"They were looking for something," he said.

"Who was?"

"Whoever tore apart this place. But they didn't look here. Get on the floor and have a look under the bed."

She kicked the side of the bed instead.

"It's a box bed," she said. "There is no under"

"That's not true. You just can't access it from the side."

He felt along the center of the bed's platform. It wasn't one board; it was two.

"The thing about box beds," he said, "is that they're mostly hollow in the middle. Someone went through a lot of trouble searching this place, but they were in a hurry. They didn't have time to check the closet for a compartment, so they chucked the first heavy thing they could find at it instead, and upended drawers rather than riffling them. Same with the desk downstairs—although I think they did the desk first. Less evident frustration there. But this bed looks untouched; I'm pretty sure they didn't search it."

"Unless they didn't need to, because they found what they were looking for."

"Doubtful," he said. "But let's find out if they did miss something."

He pulled out a pocket knife and ran it along the seam between the two boards until he could get the blade under one side. Markings along the board indicated this was not the first time someone had done this, which led him to think he was on the right track.

Sliding the blade under one side, he lifted, got his finger under and pulled, until half of the bed's platform came up.

He set it aside, activated the torch on his badge, and shined the focused light into the compartment.

There was only one thing there: a small, leather-bound book, held together by a knotted loop of twine.

"What is it?" Daska asked.

More bad luck, he thought.

He reached in and lifted the book out.

"A book?" she asked.

"Not just any book."

It *smelled* old. He didn't know what that meant, exactly, but that was what he got from it; like an aggregation of dust in book form.

He slipped the twine off and flipped the book open. Daska leaned in to read over his shoulder.

"That's Eglinat," she said softly.

"It sure is. Can you read it?"

"Of course not."

"Neither can I."

The text was written in a neat hand, rather than typed, and in a style of script that made the language somehow more indecipherable.

"We can probably find a dozen people capable of reading this for us," she said, "just by walking outside."

"Maybe," he said. "That depends on how old it is."

"Is that the only thing in there?"

She answered the question by turning on the torch app on her badge and looking for herself, while he thought about what he was going to have to do next. He already knew what that was, but it was going to be a little tricky.

He closed the leather-bound book and slipped the twine back around it.

"Nothing but dust," she said, finishing her search.

"Yeah," he said. "You know those trust issues you said I have?"

"I do."

"I'm gonna work on that problem right now. Can I trust you?"

"Of course you can," she said, a little too fast.

The problem was that nobody, in all of recorded history, ever said, *no, you cannot*, to the question of whether they could be trusted. This was both because everyone thinks they can be entrusted with secrets, and because everyone wants to hear secrets, and so will say whatever they think they need to say in order to hear them.

So he couldn't put a lot of stock in her word. Not that he had a choice.

"This is important," he said.

"You want to work out a secret handshake? Swear a blood oath? Braid each other's hair? What are you looking for?"

I should have worked the scene alone, he thought.

"I'm serious, Viselle."

"Yes, Makk, you can trust me."

"Okay, good," he said. Then slid the book into his jacket's inner pocket.

"We didn't find anything under the bed," he said. "Because we didn't think to check it. Now help me put the mattress back; let's get the forensic goons in here."

Chapter Four

The diner was called Mazel's Brewhouse, and it was indeed a twenty-hour shop, as evidenced by the fact that Makk and Viselle arrived well past the twentieth hour, at around one-thirty.

It took that long to extricate themselves from the crime scene. First, they had to exit the building and notify Tayler that the townhouse was clear, and Officer Len's forensics team could enter. Then they stood around for about an hour, just in case Jori's people discovered something under the body that a homicide detective might think was important, like the murder weapon, the victim's missing voicer, or a note saying "this is who killed me".

They found nothing useful.

Forensics soon had Orno's hands, feet and head bagged. Then the paramedics loaded him onto a stretcher, covered him with a blanket, and ran him out to the ambulance.

By then, there were a half-dozen drones over the street, hoping to catch a shot of Calcut Linus's younger brother on his last trip out of the House. They didn't get that shot, but the odds were decent that one would be turning up on the Stream in short order. All it would take was someone who was suffering from a shortage of funds, with direct access to the body and a flexible moral code.

But Makk wasn't the captain and leaked images weren't his problem.

Llotho scheduled a press conference for eight, which was right around when Makk and Viselle were supposed to be closing out their shift. Despite this, Llotho wanted them available to answer questions.

Makk hadn't shaved, had no clean clothes, and had no answers for the media, all of which made him entirely unqualified to appear on the Stream as the face of the investigation. Viselle Daska, on the other hand, while also having no answers, looked like she was born to appear on the Stream. Therefore, it made perfect sense that *she* be the face of the investigation instead of him.

Captain Llotho didn't agree, but he did credit Makk for such a creative suggestion.

The forensics goons would be at the scene until well past dawn, and Tayler would handle the claiming and carting of all the documents from the office and the upstairs spare room, so once the body left, nobody needed Detectives Stidgeon and Daska around, so after making sure forensics had no surprises, they left.

It took another hour to get to the car and out of the front gates. Along the way, they had to *no-comment* a half-dozen Veesers eager to get the story ahead of the already-announced official morning conference. No doubt one or two of them—or more likely an Unverified Streamer—would take what video they did record and insert some audio to make it sound like Makk or Viselle said something they didn't say, but on that point, there was nothing to be done. The only way to avoid getting manipulated by a talented UnVeeser was to figure out how to turn invisible. Makk had been trying to work out how to do that his entire life, but hadn't managed it yet.

Mazel's Brewhouse was on the other side of the gates, in a

block of stores that both faced the House's neighborhood, and catered to it. The low-rent Brethren apartment houses stood opposite, with nothing but the one-mader wall preventing the hooded masses from walking over. (To that end, someone had put a up a stile on each side of the wall, to allow for easier access.)

The "brewhouse" part of the title was a little misleading. The first time Makk saw the place, he assumed the 'brew' under discussion was beer, when it was actually coffee.

He was disappointed, that first time. Every time after, he was thankful for the availability of coffee at all hours. The Brethren no doubt felt the same.

A uniformed officer Makk barely knew, named Augler, had the kid at a booth in the back. The place was all but empty, with only a couple of hooded customers. If they were curious why one of their fellow Septals was being held by a policeman in the back of a diner, they didn't show it.

"Thank Ho," Augler said, meeting Makk and Daska in the middle of the diner. "I gotta take a leak, but I don't want them to bolt."

"You could have taken them with you," Daska said.

"They don't need to go; I asked. And insisting they go with me seemed..."

"I get it," Makk said. "We'll take it from here."

The kid didn't look up when they reached the booth. With the hood on, it wasn't clear whether they were even awake under there.

Their witness was in full monk's robes, out in public, which indicated either a Fundamentalist upbringing, or a subsequent devotion to the same, if not both. Tayler had said *he is a they*, which meant this Septal was *of Pal*, i.e., a genderfluid monk who aligned with the non-gendered fifth god of the Pentatheon.

"Hi," Makk said, "I'm Detective Stidgeon. This is Detective Daska. Sorry we kept you waiting so long. Mind if we sit?"

"Please," the kid said, sitting up and gesturing to the empty seating.

Makk and Viselle slid into the booth. Makk signaled the waitress, and ordered a couple of coffees and a plate of fried breads. Used to be, the smell of decomp put him off food for the rest of the day. Not anymore.

The waitress—Nacey, according to her nametag—caught a glimpse of the mark on Makk's wrist when he ordered, and automatically performed the sign of the Five. Thankfully, that was *all* she did; he'd been kicked out of plenty of places before because of that little symbol. She was also pretty nice about it, in that she looked a touch embarrassed, after having signed.

"What can we call you?" Makk asked, once the waitress left them alone.

"Other Jimbal, Detective Stidgeon. Or Dorn, if you'd like."

"Dorn, then," Makk said. "I'm Makk, and this is Viselle."

Dorn was already looking Viselle up and down.

"You're very pretty," they said. "I'm sorry, I shouldn't say that, but it's late, and I am tired."

She smiled.

"That's all right," she said. "Dorn, why don't you tell us what you saw, earlier this evening?"

"I assume we're speaking of when I found Professor Linus's body."

"Yes," she said. "Around when was that?"

"I arrived at his door at sixteen-thirty, exactly. I know this, because I had a meeting scheduled with him at sixteen-thirty, and I make a point of punctuality."

"Kind of late for a meeting," Makk said.

Dorn turned, reluctantly. They clearly preferred being questioned by Viselle.

"The professor was supposed to have been unavailable up until then. A trip, or some other thing. I don't know what, but he gave the impression he was going to be away. I have a presentation in the morning, and he promised to review it with me beforehand, and so we came to an accommodation. Sixteen-thirty was the time we agreed upon."

"How long was the trip supposed to be?" Makk asked.

"I don't know for certain that it was even a trip, only that he would be unavailable for a period of time. His schedule was blacked out for a three-day period, and classes hadn't yet resumed, coming out of the holiday."

The holiday in question was the springtide Feast of Nita. It was a traditional harvest celebration that took place over three days in the second week of Ta-Hantober. The city-dwellers of Velon had no harvest to celebrate—at least, none locally—but it was an international holiday nonetheless, and so businesses continued to close for it. The House celebrated with three days of ceremonies in honor of Nita, the god most closely associated with gardening. There would of course be no classes during this period.

Makk did the math. The final day of the Feast of Nita was three days prior. If classes weren't scheduled to resume again until the morning, and Orno Linus's calendar was blacked out for three days *after*...assuming nobody missed him at a feast celebration, he could have been lying dead on the floor of his townhouse for as many as six days. He didn't *smell* six days dead, but that was the window.

"You went to his door at sixteen-thirty," Viselle said. "What happened next?"

"He failed to respond to the bell or the knocker," Dorn said. "And then I became concerned that something was wrong."

"Not that he was simply not home yet?" she asked.

"That would have been out of character."

"Did you try directing him?" Makk asked.

"I did. I was forwarded to his message drop."

"But he did *have* a voicer." Makk said.

"You mean, did he *own* a voicer? Naturally, he did. Professor

Linus was an acknowledged Hohite, but his professional duties mandated the use of one."

The Hohites were a Septal splinter group from a couple of centuries prior who espoused extreme asceticism, taking their name from the god Ho. (Ho was known as *the hunter*, among other things. As would be expected with only five gods, each god became attached to multiple facets of daily existence. Ho was also the god of procreation, war, and medicine, among others.) The original Hohites had long since died off, but one aspect of their teachings—the rejection of modern technology—lived on as a sobriquet for those who either disliked, or were poorly adapted to, technology in some form.

What constituted *modern technology* was subject to interpretation.

The waitress returned, with fried breads and coffee, and Makk took a minute to assuage his growling stomach. He appeared to be the only one at the booth who was hungry, which worked okay for him.

"I considered directing House security then," Dorn said, "but decided against it, absent sufficient facts. I knew the professor had a back door, and the view from the kitchen window was more permissive, so I went around. That was when I found him."

"The back door was open?" Viselle asked.

"It wasn't all the way open, but it wasn't closed. Someone had kicked it. I assume the same person who killed the professor. It had been pulled closed again, but the lock was shattered; a strong wind would have reopened it if I had not."

"Did you direct security then?" she asked.

"No. I bypassed the campus security and directed the police instead."

"Why?" Makk asked.

It was as impossible to discern the full range of facial expressions in Dorn Jimbal as it was for anyone wearing the cowl of the Brethren, but Makk was pretty sure he saw a flicker of fear on the

Septal's face that ran contrary to the explanation that then came out of their mouth.

"Because I wanted to know who killed my friend," Dorn said. "And I couldn't be certain of the rigor applied to an investigation if left in the hands of the House."

"Their role would have been to contact us," Makk said. "Do you have any reason to think that wouldn't have happened?"

"Rumors only. I'm sure you've heard the same ones I have, detective. There's security, and then there are the Sentries. You say their next step would have been to direct the police. I say, it would have been to hand it over to the Sentries."

Makk had heard much the same thing in Stream-based rumors. He never expected to meet an Other who put stock in them.

It had long been a "fact" on the Stream that when a crime was committed on House property, the Sentries made it go away. Statistically speaking, crime rates within the House were *much* lower than the rates just a block on the other side of the property lines, so there was some merit to the claim. But low crime rates could be explained in plenty of other ways, ways that didn't include systemic cover-ups.

Makk wondered how the Sentries might manage to turn Orno Linus's murder into something else without attracting the attention of his older brother. He decided that would have been pretty entertaining, and sort of wished it had played out that way instead.

Dorn took a sip of the coffee, and turned their attention to the fried breads. When they selected one, they looked like a child sneaking a forbidden treat.

"Did you touch the body at all?" Viselle asked. Dorn was biting into dough that was filled with a red jelly, which did not go well at all with discussions of corpses.

"No," they said. "I went no further than the base of the stairs, close enough to affirm that it was Professor Linus, and he was dead. The smell did as much, for the second."

"You knew him pretty well, then," Makk said.

"He has been my guide and advisor for two years, yes. I doubt I would have needed to pass any further than the kitchen to recognize who was on the floor."

"But you did."

"Yes."

"Did he ever cook for you?" Makk asked.

Viselle looked at Makk, surprised by the question, while Dorn tilted his head, like a dog.

"He did," Dorn said. "On a number of occasions."

"Made his own bread," Makk said.

"Among other things."

"How about pasta?"

"Yes," Dorn said.

"I used to work in a kitchen, when I was a boy," Makk said. "Once a week, the matron would prepare fresh pasta for the home. She'd roll out the dough real thin, cut and shape it all by hand. It was really something. But at the end of it, she always had these scraps. They were the bits left over from the edges of the dough. She'd collect the scraps in a jar and once a month, she'd put it in the soup. I saw a jar just like that in professor Linus's coldbox."

"Yes, as I said, he made his own pasta sometimes," Dorn said, sounding impatient. Detective Daska looked like she was ready to ask Makk what his point was, too.

"Did he ever show you how to make it?" Makk asked.

"No."

"It's pretty easy, but you gotta have two things. Other than the raw ingredients, I mean. You need a big counter, and you need a great big rolling pin. Like, a mader long."

He extended his arms to illustrate the size he was talking about.

"Did he have one of those?" Makk asked.

Dorn considered the question.

"He did, yes. Last I saw, it was up against the counter next to the ovens. I don't know if it lived there, but that was where I saw it."

"Was it there the when you found the body?" Viselle asked.

"I couldn't say. I wasn't of a mind to conduct an inventory at that moment. You were in the townhouse; did you see it?"

She looked at Makk.

"We should probably find out where that went," she said.

"Probably."

Provided this was the elusive murder weapon, it was likely long gone. Even if the killer had just dropped it somewhere in the network of yards behind the townhouse, it had rained since; now it was just another random wood dowel without any trace evidence on it.

"Hello, so...am I done?" Dorn asked. "I still have a presentation to ready."

"Nearly," Makk said.

"What's the subject?" Viselle asked. "Of your presentation."

"Orbital mechanics," Dorn said.

"Exciting!" she said, sounding like she meant it, which was a real gift, because surely she did not.

"It is. I've calculated that Dibble's orbit around the Dancers is actually unstable. I'm predicting it will eventually deteriorate, at which time the planet will no longer be habitable."

"Don't mind my saying," Makk said, "but I hope you're wrong about that."

"It won't happen for another seventy-five thousand years," Dorn said. "I would think by then we'd have moved on to the stars. Sooner, if the rumors out of Wivvol hold true, wouldn't you say?"

Makk didn't believe anything that came out of Wivvol's propaganda division, but about everything else the kid was probably right.

"Hey, can you read Eglinat?" Viselle asked. "Out of curiosity."

"Some," they said. "Not on the level of professor Linus, certainly, but I can get along."

"Linus was fluent?"

Dorn looked at both of them blankly.

"He was an intersectional scholar," Dorn said. "One of his circles of expertise was archaic Eglinat. Perhaps five people on Dibble were more accomplished. You should already know this."

"Give us some play," Makk said, standing. "we only just met the man. Come on. I'll have Augler take you back. Don't run home to North Eloni if we have more questions for you."

"I've neither the inclination nor the means," Dorn said. "And this is my home."

Dorn stood, turned to leave, and then came back around to Makk.

"Detective," they said, "how did you know my family hails from North Eloni?"

"Just a guess."

Makk walked Dorn Jimbal out to Augler's cruiser, collected the kid's contact information, and sent them on their way. By the time he got back to the booth, Viselle Daska was on her second bread.

"Should I order more?" he asked, sliding into the booth opposite his suddenly-voracious sort-of partner.

"I don't like to eat in front of people I'm questioning," she said. "And before you ask, no, this isn't the first time I've questioned a suspect in a diner. What do you think?"

"About what?"

"Everything. The case, Other Jimbal, all of it."

Makk held up his empty coffee cup and summoned Nacey and her urn over to resolve the issue of its emptiness, and then selected another piece of fried bread. He would have to add some protein to his evening if he was going to be coherent for the eight o'clock presser, but there was time.

"I think you're supposed to tell me, rook," Makk said. "What did you learn at the scene?"

"Yes, all right," Viselle said, putting down the chocolate glaze. "Linus was killed by someone he knew; he let them inside, and turned his back on them at least once. They weren't there to kill him, though. That was an escalation. The rolling pin was a weapon of opportunity. They swung once, at the back of his head, killing him instantly."

"Possibly," Makk said. "We won't know that until we hear from the autopsy."

"Sure. But the back half of his skull was missing, and from the way he fell it looks like there was spinal damage. Even if he wasn't dead before he hit the floor, he was paralyzed."

"Again, possibly. I agree with you, but..."

"...don't put it into the 'known' category yet."

"Yeah."

"Fair. I was thinking this could have been an accident," she said. "The killer meant to *hit* him, but not necessarily to *kill* him."

"What's the difference?" he asked.

"Intent? Premeditation?"

"That's for the attorneys. Not our problem."

"Right. Assuming the rolling pin is the murder weapon, they took it with them. That was a nice deduction, by the way, I didn't put that together at all."

"Thanks."

"You think it's gone?"

"It's as good as gone," he said. "They're made of wood, and Velon has plenty of fireplaces to go around. Dropping it in a yard somewhere would be stupid, and the only reason to keep it around afterwards would be if it had sentimental value. Plus, it's not like these things have serial numbers on them. Even if we found it, we'd have a time proving it came from Orno's kitchen."

Daska nodded. Makk was starting to learn how to navigate her facial expressions. This one said she was taking notes, albeit just in her head.

"We don't have a time of death yet," she said, "but two or three days ago seems right. We'll have to check his social calendar to see what kind of appearances he was expected to make for the Feast of Nita ceremonies, if any. Maybe nobody *was* expecting to see him for six straight days. He was definitely dead, though, by the time the second person got to the scene, kicked in the back door, and searched the house."

"How do we know the place wasn't tossed before Orno was killed?" Makk asked. "Maybe someone with a key let themselves in, searched the place, and then Orno came home and interrupted them. Later, the second person could have come in, seen the body, and turned right around."

"The blood spatter," she said. "The papers on the desk were moved around after getting sprayed. Besides, a man comes home to find his whole house turned upside-down, with the person who did it still there. Does he turn his back on them?"

"That depends on how well they knew each other. But I'll allow that we don't know which of the two people who spent time with Orno Linus's body also searched the place. It could have been the killer."

"The search *was* conducted in a hurry."

Makk grimaced.

"The list of things we actually know is getting smaller," he said.

"We know he's dead, and we know one of the people who knew this before we did was Other Jimbal. *Everything* else is a guess right now, isn't it?"

"Until the DNA comes back, yes," Makk said. "Then the list of knowns gets a lot bigger. Welcome to homicide."

He held up his coffee to toast, wishing he was back at Bincha-gag's, holding up a beer.

She held up her coffee and completed the toast. Then she put it back down, and stared quietly into the mug, as if there was a fortune to be read at the bottom.

"You knew," she said, quietly.

"I knew what?"

"When we took the mattress off the bed, you wanted to make sure we could put it back again without it looking disturbed."

"I wanted it to look the way it was when we found it, for the forensics team."

She smiled, but not with any real mirth behind it.

"That isn't it. You flipped over the clock, but didn't flip it back again. You moved around some things on the desk and took a book off the shelf. And I know you took photos before you did any of those things. We could have done anything we wanted to do with that mattress."

She leaned in, and got her voice down to a whisper. This probably wasn't necessary, but Makk understood the impulse. There were only two other customers in the diner—Brethren, both of them—sitting at separate tables near the door, while their booth was in the back of the diner, as far from the door as it was possible to be, without sitting in the kitchen. Nacey was at the counter, and theoretically in earshot, but she was having a quiet conversation on her voicer.

"I think you knew you were going to find something in that bed frame, and I think you knew that whatever it was, you didn't want anyone to know you found it. I'd like to know why."

He nodded, and leaned back.

"I didn't know what we'd *find*," he said. "But if there was something to be found, I had a hunch that the bed frame was where it would end up being. Especially after someone else checked the rest of the townhouse. I was also pretty sure whatever was there, it was worth killing a man over."

"Possibly."

"This book came from the vaults, Viselle."

"You don't know that," she said.

"The age of the binding, the pre-type script, the brown pages…it's in archaic Eglinat, which the kid said our victim knew how to read. If he knew how to read it, he had access to examples of it, and the only examples of archaic Eglinat are stored in the House vaults. I think this is a known thing."

"So what if it did?'

"Do you have any idea what the Black Market value is for a book from the House vaults?"

"No," she said. "Do you?"

"Don't be naïve."

"All right, a lot."

"A whole lot. I can think of two equally scary parties who would be extremely interested in getting their hands on it. One is the House. We don't know the steps they'll take to protect their archives, but you've heard the same stories I have. And as soon as this book is entered into evidence, they'll want it back."

"It's an active crime investigation of one of their own," she said. "An *important* one of their own, if Dorn Jimbal is to be believed. They'd be making it harder to catch his killer."

"Which could be exactly what they want."

"For Nita's sake. Makk, the House doesn't *have* a hit squad. You know that, right? That's just Streamer paranoia."

"It's not paranoia."

"Are Walrusman, and the Trench Serpent of Lake Phalailee also suspects?"

"I'll have to check their alibis first," he said. "Look, our man died while keeping this book a secret. It's in our best interests to do the same, for now, and see who comes looking for it."

She sighed, and started on a third piece of fried bread. She was just dissecting it, really; nervous and annoyed and not really hungry.

"Who's the other?" she asked.

"Other what?"

"Two equally scary parties. The imaginary House assassination squad is one. Who's the other?"

"Black Market resellers. Or rather, the organized criminal enterprise that owns and operates the Black Market."

"The Linuses."

"Now you see my concern."

"What I see is paranoia," she said. "But now I understand it."

"Maybe you're right," he said. "Maybe the book's completely unrelated, and Orno Linus was killed in a lover's quarrel. That's what these end up being half the time, so it could be that. I hope so. Because otherwise, we're in the eye of a shitstorm. Since I'm professionally unlucky already, I'm leaning toward the shitstorm right now."

She smiled, genuinely this time.

"I don't think you're *actually* unlucky, even if you do. But if you're that concerned, you can just check the book into evidence."

"And never solve Orno Linus's murder."

"If that's how it plays out."

He considered the suggestion. She was right; he wasn't paid enough to deal with this kind of crap, and at the end of the day, Orno Linus was just another dead body. But somebody out there made him that way, and there wasn't anyone else to speak for Linus. Just unlucky Makk Stidgeon.

"That's not how I operate," he said.

"I know," Viselle said. "That's why I picked you."

Chapter Five

Twenty-One Central was the main headquarters of the Velon Police Force. It sat in the middle of the Geoghis Quarter—at the corner of Twenty-First and Central—which meant it sat in the middle of the quarter most Velonians considered the center of the city. This was because Geoghis contained the two things identified with the middle: Mausoleum Park, and the Tether.

Interestingly, if one took a map and, factoring every quarter, district, borough and exurb, used a ruler to determine the *true* center of the city, one would find that it belonged to a fish market in Hujhon Quarter, right on the border of Geoghis. The owners of the fish market clearly knew this, which was why they called their market Dead Center Fish. Most Velonians, failing to understand the reference—or just not caring—tended to call the place the Dead Fish Center instead.

Geoghis Quarter was also what most people thought of when they thought of Velon. It had the tallest and shiniest buildings, the cleanest and widest streets, the highest commercial real estate property values and the second-highest residential real estate property values. (Palavin Quarter had the highest residential property values.) It was home to the financial district, which also happened to be the financial hub for Inimata as a whole, and since Inimata was the wealthiest country in the world, it was the *de facto* center of commerce for the planet.

Makk could see both the Tether and the trees of Mausoleum Park from his desk, as the homicide corral had a window facing southwest. In the afternoon, he had a great view of the suns setting, through the lattice of the Tether's base. The massive structure was actually quite a distance away, at the very edge of Geoghis, but felt like it was practically overhead from nearly every part of the downtown. He was pretty sure one of the things that appealed to him about his apartment in the Decane Quarter was that he couldn't see the Tether from it: the building across the street blocked the view.

It was seven-thirty. Dyhine and Hadrine had risen forty minutes ago, which he had *not* seen, because the windows weren't facing east. The brightness outside told the story, though, as did his internal clock, which was notifying him that it was time to punch out and go home, and perhaps get some sleep.

He wouldn't be doing that today. He'd already *gone* home once, and didn't know when he was going to make it back again. Such was the nature of a high-profile case like this.

He'd worked a couple before. In 7327, the severed head of Malonist Vindor's grandson showed up in a shipping container on a freighter bound for the southern coast of Botzis. Malonist was, at the time, the undersecretary of Parliament, and his grandson—Roan—was a just pre-pubescent thirty-five seasons, about to celebrate his *Haremisva*. That case was international news for five solid weeks, until the rest of Roan's body showed up in the trunk of a classmate's older brother. The sordid story involved plans to stow away and make for the northern island chain, an authentic Middle Kingdom sword from Extum, and a suicide pact.

It was a racy tale that ended up recreated more than once on the Stream. Nobody bothered to consult Makk on the recreations, or pay him for his story, so of course none of them were remotely accurate. But that was how things went on the Stream.

The other high-profile case was only slightly less newsworthy, but far more significant politically. Someone set off a bomb that killed the Kindonese ambassador to the League of Countries. This happened out in the Pulson Harbor Quarter in 7324, and Makk was only tangentially involved. He'd just made detective, so he wasn't the primary, and thank goodness, because this was a particularly sensitive investigation. The war between Kindon and Inimata had just ended six seasons prior, and Makk was a veteran of that war. Thanks in particular to his war record, he was not the best choice to be the face of that investigation, which was fine. The primary on the case—Yordon Llotho—was a much better option in all respects.

Llotho made captain less than a year after bringing that case in, and when he was shifted to Twenty-One Central two seasons later, he took Makk Stidgeon along with him.

The captain used to joke that Makk was his good luck charm, because Makk recognized the importance of a key piece of evidence in the bombing case, which broke the whole thing open. Llotho was probably the only person to ever refer to Makk as a good luck anything.

All of that was probably why Makk didn't disconnect when Llotho tried to stick him with Detective Daska. Maybe Llotho was minding the politics that would come with putting a rookie face-front on a case like this—Yordon Llotho knew his way around politics better than any non-politician Makk had ever met—or maybe he didn't want to risk wrecking the start of a promising career. Whatever it was, Makk figured he owed Llotho enough to give her the benefit.

Or he saw no promise, knew she'd fuck it on her own, and didn't want to go down with that, he thought.

Captain Llotho showed up at Makk's desk at seven-forty-eight. He had on a crisp, fitted suit, and make-up for the vids.

"You look like shit," Llotho said, no doubt noting that Makk was not also wearing a crisp fitted suit, or make-up for the vids "I take it you didn't have time to change."

"This is me changed," Makk said. "Swung by the apartment before coming here."

"Wow."

"It's a new suit."

"That's not a new suit."

"It's my *newest* suit. I only own two."

"Yeah, stand way behind me," Llotho said. "First impressions."

"All my first impressions involve dead people or suspects," Makk said. "I don't usually have to dress up for either."

"Well, come on and let's get this over with. The media room is jammed. And after this is all over, let's set up time to take you shopping or something."

"You want to wait for Detective Daska? I think she's changing, should be here in a minute."

"No," Llotho said, "just you. Let's keep her out of that room for now."

"Any reason why?"

Llotho looked at his watch, and weighed the value in offering what was probably only going to end up being a partial explanation, before bailing.

"Yes, there are reasons," he said.

"She *is* part of the investigation, Yordon," Makk said.

"I cannot even begin to describe how much it warms my core to hear Makk Stidgeon say that about the partner I forced on him, but we don't have time to hug and celebrate your newfound maturity. I'm sure she'll be upset to be left out of the room, but as I said, there are reasons. Right now, they're waiting on us. You can dry your partner's tears later."

~

In the history of press conferences in which Makk had been directly involved, this one fell somewhere in the middle, which was to say that it could definitely have gone worse. And it would have, if anyone was relying on him to act genial and provide information.

The room had fifteen Veesers in it, four text-based Streamers (or Exters), and five Corpers—reporters for 'print' outlets. 'Print' was a misnomer left over from the days when information in Inimata was disseminated in text on a physical piece of paper; it was now used whenever referencing a privately-owned media conglomerate. For the most part, Corper news was considered less reliable than either Veeser-produced or Exter-produced media, because it tended to be deeply agenda-driven, based specifically on who owned the media outlet.

The nicest form of this kind of bias might express itself in a way similar to how a public relations firm positions its client. Makk remembered a case he had where the victim was stabbed to death with a kitchen knife. Most of the news stories focused on the victim, the killer, and, well, all the other things that tend to be pertinent in this kind of story. But the writer from the Daily Dose began with four paragraphs about the quality and versatility of the knife. Why? Because the Daily Dose was owned by Haevlist Global, a multinational conglomerate that produced many different things...including a brand of kitchen knife that was light enough, well-balanced enough, and sharp enough, to make it the perfect murder weapon. (This was not the explicit angle of their story, but it was definitely implied.)

The worst form of this kind of bias—using the same murder as an example—came from The Clocktower. Most of that story focused on the nationality of the murderer (a second-generation Unakian) and how this was "just like their kind."

Most reliable was probably the Exter-produced media—which of course, hardly anybody read, because that was how the world worked. Good, well-researched longform Exter content was almost never sensational, which meant it didn't get the same kind of headlines. But that was because reality was almost never sensational.

Veeser content fell somewhere in-between. It was substantially better than UnVeeser content, but it remained the case that the motive of any Veeser was self-promotion first, and the story second. This was a feature, and not a flaw; the way to go from being an Unverified Streamer to a Verified Streamer was to achieve some measure of accuracy (adjudicated by the National Communications Division, the government arm dedicated to at least the illusion of accuracy in Streamcasts) coupled with a large following. Good Veesers told the story, but in a way that drew followers. This usually meant making themselves a part of the story. In the case of the murder committed by an Unakian with a kitchen knife, a typical Veeser story began with how this affected *them*, personally.

The presence of so many prominent Veesers in the press room made for a pretty calm, quiet media session, oddly. Each of the fifteen Verified Streamers there had a vested interest in making it look like this was an exclusive, so they took pains to keep things around them quiet. Most of them weren't broadcasting live—the Veesers would edit this later to make it seem like they personally asked each question themselves—but the lack of ambient noise made the edit job easier. The Corpers and Exters didn't have to honor this quiet-in-the-room standard, but they almost always did.

It was surprisingly common for new leads to come out of these sessions, if only by accident. What can happen is that an intrepid Veeser (it's almost always a Veeser) asks a leading question that implies they know more than the cops do. Nobody—other than the Veeser—is happy with this, but it can end up being helpful. It's just that in order to get the information, the police department generally has to wait for the Streamcast to air.

This press conference wasn't one of those instances. It could have been because they were holding it less than twelve hours after the victim had been discovered. It could also have been that this was a bitch of a cold murder before Makk even reached the scene, and there was no other information out there to get. He was pretty sure it was the latter.

It wasn't as bad as Makk had been expecting. Everyone was polite, and nobody had a surprise stumper question that might make Makk and Llotho look like they didn't know what they were doing. Makk even knew one of the Veesers—Elicasta Sangristy, a popular straight-news Streamer—from a prior encounter, although he doubted she remembered him.

All told, the presser lasted about thirty minutes. Makk spoke twice, and both times what he said was, "not at this time." Then it was over, and he was back in Llotho's office.

Detective Daska was waiting there for both of them.

"Good, you're here," Llotho said, as if they had nothing to discuss regarding the media up-front that he'd just stiffed her on. "I got pinged while I was in there; the autopsy's back."

"That was fast," Makk said.

He didn't ask why the results went to Llotho instead of the lead detective. Whoever the captain leaned on for the turnaround probably sent it directly to him for the points; it wouldn't be the first time.

"Everything about this case has got to be fast, detective," he said. "Everything. I'm sending the details to you now, but the tagline is he died on account of having his head bashed in from behind by someone other than himself."

"Was there a tox screen?" Viselle asked.

"Yeah, the guy was clean. Alarmingly clean."

"He had Hohite tendencies," Makk said. "According to the kid who found him."

"That'd explain it."

Llotho stepped behind his desk, but didn't sit, leaving the two detectives in a void in the middle of the room, where neither of them was sure whether this was the kind of meeting where they take a seat or not.

"Look, you're both beat," the captain said. "Stidgeon, you're past your twelfth hour, and this is, what? hour sixteen for you, Daska?"

"Yes, sir," she said.

"Get out of here, get some rest, come back tonight and solve this thing before it goes supernova and takes out the whole city."

Viselle pulled him aside as soon as they were out of the office.

"What the hell, Makk?" she asked.

"What do you mean?"

"You know exactly what I mean."

She was striving to keep her voice down, as they were currently standing in the middle of the homicide desks, and a half-dozen people were in earshot. She wasn't doing a great job of it.

"The press conference," Makk said.

"You know I should have been in there too. I'm a part of the investigation."

"I told him we had to wait. He wasn't interested."

"Sure you did."

He noticed essentially everyone in the room was now following their conversation. He grabbed her by the elbow and led her to his desk, which was in a less occupied part of the room.

"Look," he said, "I don't know why the captain made that call, and to be completely fucking honest, I think you *do* know why he made that call, and it has nothing to do with you being a rook, or rich and pretty. You don't have to tell me, because I don't care. But I stepped up for you, so don't lay this on me."

Viselle Daska looked furious, but temporarily mute. She resolved this by storming off.

Detective Exy poked his head over Makk's cubicle.

"Girl trouble?" he asked.

"Go fuck yourself, Slago," Makk said.

"She's got a temper, huh?"

"Yeah," Makk said. "She also has a car. She was my ride."

A uniform on the other side of the pen walked over. Makk didn't know him; he looked like one of the new recruits, but Makk had reached an age where everyone looked like a new recruit. They also all looked to him like they'd just gotten out of middle school.

"I'm heading out, detective," the kid said. "Where do you need to go?"

"I gotta run an errand," Makk said. "Drop me off in Pant City?"

He looked confused.

"Sure," he said, no doubt resisting the urge to ask Makk what he could possibly be doing in that part of town, that was legal. "Let's go."

The officer's name was Wisgerth, and he'd actually been on the force for more than five years. He talked to Makk like they knew one another, and maybe that was the case; maybe Wisgerth had been involved in a few of the scenes Makk worked over the years, and he just couldn't remember. It happened. Makk was good at remembering dead people and suspects, but didn't always have room for much beyond that.

Wisgerth drove a nice, normal cruiser that stayed on the ground the entire time. Most of the department's cruisers were ground-based, because outfitting the entire force with aero-cars was way too expensive. City-wide, they had only a dozen, and they were used primarily for aerial traffic control...or to create the illusion of aerial traffic control. (The air above the streets was effectively lawless.)

Staying on the ground meant it took a while to reach Pant City, but it was a trip in which Makk didn't feel like vomiting even once, so that was great.

Also great: after basic introductions, Wisgerth didn't talk all that much. Once they got the destination out of the way, Makk was basically given the chance to doze off in the passenger seat.

They were about four blocks out when they hit real congestion.

Much like Kindontown, the Velon city planners didn't really want any tourists visiting the Pantolinar Quarter, so the Hyperline stopped at the edge of the neighborhood. That was because half of it—the part everyone called Pant City—held basically all of the sex-trade business in Velon, with maybe a little drug trafficking thrown in. The only souvenirs they handed out in Pant City were illegal or communicable.

And, without a proper Hyperline hookup, the traffic there was just as bad as in the Decane Quarter.

This was not to say that there was *any* part of the city with decent traffic flow, and it didn't look as if there was anything to be done about it. Some twenty-five years back, the city introduced app-cars, which were self-driving cabs-for-hire. The thinking was that the city would do away with regular cabs *and* private cars eventually, because everyone would prefer the self-driving option.

App-cars were cheaper than cabs, and less expensive than private vehicle ownership (especially when the cost of parking was factored in) so there was reason to think the plan would work, for economic-pressure reasons alone.

But it didn't work; twenty-five years later, the streets were filled with just as many hired- and private-cars as ever, on top of which there were now app-cars adding to the congestion.

A lot of people—Makk included—would rather the city had

taken the money invested in app-car tech and expanded the Hyperline.

"Hey," Makk said, "this is good."

"We're pretty close," Wisgerth said.

"Yeah, but it's another forty minutes for you if you don't turn around right here. I can walk it the rest of the way."

"Cool."

Officer Wisgerth pulled the cruiser over to the curb.

"Thanks for the lift," Makk said.

"No problem," the kid said. "Oh, hey, before you go; I have something for you."

He reached into his breast pocket and pulled out a scrap of paper. He handed it across the seat.

"He said he wants a meeting," Wisgerth said.

Makk unfolded the paper. There was an address in the Palavin Quarter, with a time written beneath.

Makk crumpled up the paper and threw it back into the cruiser.

"I don't come when I'm called," Makk said. "Tell Mr. Linus if he has something to convey, he can give a statement downtown, just like everyone else. If I need to talk to him before then, he'll be the first to know."

"He's not going to like that."

"I don't give a good godsdamn what he likes."

Makk slammed the door and headed down the street.

"That was probably dumb, Detective Stidgeon," he said to himself. "Yep, very dumb."

Chapter Six

Elicasta Sangristy did a quick skim of the feed data, looking for room to mash or trim. It wasn't a full-on edit—there was no time, because she was up against true live. She wanted to hit the Stream on the same beat as the bulk live-dump Veesers, but with better-than-live content. That was the meat. That was how she got the subs.

The feed data was on a direct to her voicer screen, rather than the eyepatch optical. It was slightly less efficient, speed-wise, but it was what she was used to, and besides, it was better to proof the content on the same device her subs were most likely to use themselves. (Elicasta knew the stats; she had higher consumption in the handhelds than the 'tops, at about 65-20, with the other 15 going to miscellaneous wearables.)

"Hold," she said, and the screen froze. "Back two."

There was an extra beat where Captain Llotho took a breath between questions. It was maybe the kind of thing she'd leave in if it was mid-sentence—sometimes there was more information in the silence than in the words—but it wasn't doing any favors here.

"Trim two, forward."

Now, Llotho skipped the breath. His hand also went from

being on the podium to pointing at the optical, without crossing the space between—a blink cut Elicasta never would have tolerated in a proper 'top edit. Here, it was all about pace and turnaround.

Some rand knocked on the door. She was in one of the proof booths the precinct set up for on-scene Veesers, of which there were five. They were supposed to be sound-proofed—hence 'proof booth'—but of course the city cheaped it. Any yack with knuckles could rap on the door and blow an entire live Stream. It was especially rough on the aug-real Veesers. Nothing like putting yourself up with a live cop show in the back, looking like you're in a wide open, and then someone who doesn't look like they're in the shot rattles the door (that the subs can't see in the image) right next to you.

Elicasta didn't do aug-real (sort of) and while she might do a live pickup after a skimmed Stream—if she was really up against it—she knew better than to try it at the precinct, in one of their shitty not-really-proofed proof booths.

"Occupied," she said. "Don't step on my background."

"Sorry," a muted voice said.

She got back to the skim, remembering a point around where Llotho handed off some questions to Detective Stidgeon.

Detective Cholem, she thought.

She could name two or three UnVeesers who would have no problem calling Stidgeon that, not in spite of the fact that it was distasteful—specifically *because* they made their subs by being distasteful.

It wasn't something Elicasta would ever do. She met Makk Stidgeon a couple of years back for a rider. The face-to lasted five minutes, of which she used about thirty seconds. Makk wasn't photogenic, he hated having an optical pointed at him, and as long as the blue light was up he sounded like an idiot.

The thirty seconds was a kindness.

She sorta liked him. He carried himself with a kind of resigned pessimism that roughly translated into a total not-giving-a-shit-ness that was refreshing. Especially compared to the kind of goobs and slags Elicasta usually had to face. *Genuine,* she remembered thinking. Then she shook his hand and saw the mark, and understood where the attitude came from.

He didn't show it off, then or earlier, in the press conference. (He wore his sleeves long and kept it covered the whole time; she was checking.) But, he also never bothered to have it removed, which was probably possible if it was a standard ink job.

That made him interesting, and Elicasta Sangristy's job was to find interesting things in plain sight, or to turn objectively boring things into interesting things, depending. (These were different skillsets.) So she did a little extra research into him, before abandoning the idea of a story. If he couldn't make himself interesting while on vid, it wasn't worth the trouble.

Both his pessimistic attitude and his inability to say notable things popped during the press conference. He did look passably photogenic, though. His hair looked cleaner or something.

She found the spot. It took about ten seconds for Stidgeon to make it to the podium, and he paused for a solid three seconds before each answer. All of that could go.

Once the skim was finished, she'd managed to cut down a twenty-seven-minute presser into a tight twenty-two.

Good enough, she thought.

She uncoupled the eyepatch optical, activated the mini-drone it was attached to, and set it up across the room. She had enough time for a pre-op and a post-op, if she felt like doing both, but she didn't. An intro would be plenty.

Using the app adjustment on her voicer—the optical was slaved to the app—she fiddled with the filters until she got an image of herself that met standards.

Which was to say, it was a good shot. The rig Elicasta used was top-of-the-class, meaning it cost an outrageous sum to obtain. About three quarters of that cost went into getting her to look good in shots like this. Most lenses magnified the center of the image ever-so-slightly, which worked great for distance shots, but less-so for the up-closes, especially when the center was Elicasta's nose. In the old days, before she was a Verified, she combined post-shot digital manipulation (which worked great for the stills, less for the in-motion) with off-angle up-closes. A lot of her early reporting featured her at the edge of the shot, or in profile, instead of face-up.

She was still pretty proud of those early Streamcasts. Every now and then, she'd pull one up, and while there was plenty to critique, there was a lot to be proud of.

Then, as now, she recognized that she wasn't going to get far or do well if she didn't pour resources into making her one irreplaceable asset—her face—look as good as possible, as often as possible.

The tech inside the eyepatch optical drone accounted for the magnification problem by digitally offsetting it in-flight. It meant the face that was being recorded in her up-close was actually a simulation of her—she couldn't think of it as aug-real, even though that's exactly what it was—rather than a true live shot.

It worked great, but only on *her* face. Everyone else got the standard shot, whether the optical was droned or clipped to the main housing over her eye. Which was fine with Elicasta. It was her Streamcast, after all.

Once she was happy with the drone's positioning, she double-checked how she looked using the feed off the voicer.

Good enough, she thought.

"Go to record," she said. The blue light above the optical blinked three times and then settled on a solid blue.

"Hot off the real, babes, this is your girl, Elicasta, downtown and ready to roll with the pollies! We're live-and-go with none other than camera-courting Captain Yordon Llotho and Detective Makk Stidgeon, as we get the absolute latest on the murdered monk in the High Hat's back yard. Who do the pollies want for the death of Orno Linus? 'Casta's here for the answers, babes. Let's get to it!"

Elicasta stopped the recording with the app, waited for the blue light to blink out, and recalled the optical. Once it was in her hand, she popped it into place again—over her left eye—and then reviewed the pre-op. Satisfied, she settled it in front of the already-set-to-go interview footage, merged the two files, and dropped the whole thing into the front of her channel queue. It went live thirty seconds later.

The early reviews were instantaneous, which was something Elicasta always found amusing. How could anyone push a vote on something in less time than it took to consume the thing they were voting on?

Not that she minded much; about 70% of the votes were positive, pushed specifically to offset the anticipated downvotes. It was the nature of the Stream, which was always in the process of devouring itself. Subs from competing niche Veesers would take it upon themselves to bring her agg score down.

Her subs did the same thing to the Veesers they deemed *her* competition, which she didn't appreciate but couldn't do much about. At least three or four times a day, one of these intrepid subs would reach out to her by some direct means, to let her know what they did in her name. She generally ignored them; they were looking for some kind of direct outreach, and sometimes a personalized *thanks* was enough to fill that need. Most of the time, though, it wasn't. That was how she ended up with stalkers.

She started checking on the real reviews—the ones that came in after enough time had passed for the reviewer to have hypothetically watched the thing—after a half an hour. By then, she'd already exited Twenty-One Central and hopped onto the Hyperline, uptown for Palavin.

The Hyperline car was half-full. She boarded with her rig on—it was always on—and her hood up to keep it hidden to anyone not up-facing. She was riding silent: the blue light was out. Technically, the equipment was still recording, but it was on emergency mode.

Used to be, Veesers could only do full-record or off. The problem with that was, the gear wasn't cheap; you could rob a Veeser when they weren't recording. You could also rob them when they *were* recording, but most systems were set up to push all video to the Stream as soon as the equipment was forcibly removed (this was called Panic Streaming) which would include a video of the robber. At the same time, no Veeser moved through the world on full-record 20-7. After a lot of lobbying, the VSU (Verified Streamers Union) and the NCD settled on emergency mode as a compromise. Streamers (Veesers and UnVeesers both) could set their systems to record without a tell-light, but they couldn't *intentionally* Streamcast anything captured that way.

To hold everyone to this mandate, videos were stamped with a status marker. Nothing recorded in emergency mode was supposed to make it past the filter, unless it was a Panic Stream.

She took a seat at the back and kept her face pointed out the window, both so nobody could see the equipment (excluding a fortuitous angle on her reflection) and also so nobody who might recognize her would get an opportunity. This was because the Stream-version of Elicasta Sangristy was one of the most famous people in the world, and getting recognized when she was off-duty was always awkward.

Interestingly—and this became truer as the years went by—Elicasta was only occasionally recognized in the real.

She had a deeply curated version of herself on the Stream. This version was the woman her more fanatical subs wanted to become, be friends with, or stalk. (Or—obviously—have sex with.) She also didn't really exist. Elicasta in the real wasn't as pretty, happy, or clever, and definitely wasn't as interested in being your friend as the Stream-version. And every new wrinkle on her face that she used the eyepatch optical's digital simulacrum to eradicate created distance between Elicasta and Stream-Elicasta.

If she didn't tweak the program, in another twelve seasons or so, people were going to think Elicasta in the real was Stream-Elicasta's mother. But that was something she would worry about later.

As the Hyperline car slid along the dedicated magna-track and past the always-breathtaking Tether, Elicasta took a tally of the consequential votes, and felt satisfied that her latest entry was well-received. Twenty-seven thousand sunlight ratings in a minute-and-a-half, with aud-vid review notices already popping. It'd hit a mil before she reached her condo, and—with a big push from the subject matter—twenty-seven mil at least, by nightfall.

"Thank *you*, Orno Linus," she muttered, before toggling away from the stats tab.

Practical ground-floor access to the hottest story of the season was the kind of lucky she couldn't buy or fabricate. And the brother of one of the richest men in the world being murdered on House grounds was definitely the hottest story of the season; maybe even the year. Between the people who thought the Linuses secretly controlled everything and the people who thought the *House* secretly controlled everything, the Stream was in the early stages of a supernova. Being one of only a handful of Veesers with direct access to the first presser was going to be huge for Elicasta's profile.

Geoghis Quarter fell away behind them. The line of demarcation between Geoghis and Palavin was pretty easy to pick out from elevation, even if the precise distinction—what *made* Palavin look like Palavin—was hard to lay a finger on.

Palavin Quarter was the most expensive place to live in Velon thanks in large part to a six square block section called Norg Hill.

All of the city's ultra-wealthy (hill-toppers, they were called, or just toppers) kept a house there, and about half of them actually lived in that house with some regularity.

Norg Hill was about fifteen blocks from the border with Geoghis, but its very proximity somehow made the rest of Palavin look a little cleaner and shinier. Maybe it was the rarified, top-of-the-tax-bracket air they all got to breathe.

She smirked at the thought. It was obviously not true that the air the toppers breathed was any different than the air any of the rest of them breathed—notwithstanding when they were breathing the air on Lys, which obviously *was* different—but most of them probably imagined it was.

Elicasta was paying entirely too many credits for entirely too little floor space, just to have a condo with a Palavin street address. But it made Stream-Elicasta look ten times sexier, and it got the real-world Elicasta all kinds of face-to's with all kinds of important people. The condo very much paid for itself.

One of her box retrieval algos flashed a message across her eyepatch optical. *HP-IM*, it read. *High probability, important message received.* It flashed alarm truck red, just to emphasize the significance.

She sighed. On average, her public inbox received about seventeen-thousand messages a day—*far* too many for her to scan personally. She employed an intelligent auto-mining program that surfed each message and value-weighted it for her. The program was excellent for daily maintenance. If, for example, she wanted to start some buzz with the subs, she could ask the program to hit her with fan-messages that met specific demo criteria. Just responding to five or ten messages a day kept the subs happy.

It was less than perfect when it came to these alerts, but Elicasta couldn't do much about that. Half the time, the content being sent was just too complex for the algo. Basically, it sucked when it came to verifying video feeds. Roughly two-thirds of the *HP-IM* messages had all the right textual flags, but with video content that consisted of someone showing her their penis. They had yet to turn out to be newsworthy penises, and probably never would be.

Maybe if the High Hat sent me his, she thought. That would definitely be newsworthy, albeit perhaps not for the reason intended by the sender.

She acknowledged the receipt of the notification to get the flashing to stop, and set a reminder to check it after she got home. The Hyperline was no place to see something like that.

"Hey, bitch," Wicha greeted, in a sing-song tone that didn't vibe at all with the words that came out of her mouth. Wicha was on her second-floor balcony, shouting down to the street as Elicasta came up the sidewalk.

"Hey, bitch," Elicasta greeted back. "You on duty, or you just don't feel like putting on clothes today?"

"I got clothes on," Wicha said, pointing to what was either the top half of a sunsuit or a colorful support bra.

"If you say so."

"Don't hate," Wicha said, shaking her assets.

Wicha was an UnVeeser, and probably always would be. She had a sub list that was twice the size of Elicasta's, but there was no way what she put out there was ever getting a V-stamp.

It was interesting, because she and Wicha weren't really *all* that different. Elicasta made her living thanks in part to a pretty face. She bled real-news, which was what kept the subs around—and what got her the Verified honors—but it was the face that brought them to her Streamcast initially.

For Wicha, it was her breasts that did the trick. She didn't have the same kind of hard-news acumen as Elicasta, but she made up for it by doing about half of her face-to's topless.

Every time Elicasta got carried away into thinking what she

did was important and necessary, she reminded herself that Wicha made at least as much as she did without asking anything more probing than, *what do you think of my boobies?*

"Caught your cast," Wicha said. "That story's the cake. I'm jealous, no lie."

"I lucked into the access," Elicasta said, which was only sort of true. She had an in with Twenty-One Central in the form of a person of influence who was sweet on her. She'd also done said person a few favors over the years that made his bosses look pretty good, and he was honorable enough to return those favors when it suited him. Putting her in that room was one such returned favor.

"Yeah, yeah," Wicha said. "Keep to it."

The voicer in Wicha's hand thrummed.

"Oops," she said. "Gotta get this. Hit it hard, girl."

Wicha made a complex hand-gesture that substituted for a wave goodbye. Elicasta made it back, and then laughed because in all the seasons she'd known Wicha, she still didn't understand where this gesture came from or what it meant. For all she knew, it was a Ghon-Dik curse.

Elicasta let herself into the main lobby, called the elevator, and rode up to the top floor.

As one of the most famous people in the world—again, provided 'the world' meant 'the Stream'—she got the choicest condo in the building. This made a little more sense when considering that the owner of the building marketed his properties specifically to Streamers. Those with the most clout got the best view, not to mention direct roof access. Again, it was outrageously expensive—she could buy an entire house with the same credits, in just about any other part of town—but it mostly paid for itself. That was especially the case when she did her up-closes on the roof, with Norg Hill looming directly behind.

She got inside right as the reminder she'd set on the Hyperline went off, and the *HP-IM* signal reasserted itself.

"Hang on, hang on," she muttered.

She dropped her bag in the lived-in part of the place—a living room that never, ever ended up in any of her shots—and stepped into her office. It was, for a normal occupant, an office. For her, it was a tastefully appointed glamour shot room, with each wall designed to give her a different backdrop. Her desk was in the middle of the room, where it would stay out of most shots.

She took a seat and woke up the desktop. It wasn't a top-of-the-line device—she didn't need one for this part of her business—but it *was* quantum-tech, which made it super-fast on the Stream.

After slipping off the headgear and rubbing her forehead for a minute or two, she toggled around on the 'top until she'd located the high priority message her algo thought was so important.

The message text certainly rang all the right bells.

EXCLUSIVE FOOTAGE OF LINUS MURDER, CAPTURED LIVE! it read.

She clicked on the attached vid file, and winced pre-emptively.

"Please don't be another penis," she muttered.

The image filled up the screen. It wasn't a penis; it was a drone shot. It was covering various rooftops, in the first few seconds. All chimneys and shingles. It went in and out of focus, like the driver was still learning how to run the thing.

Reacting, perhaps, to a sound—the vid didn't come with an audio component—the drone panned down from the rooftop level, and held.

It was a steep angle. Elicasta figured the drone was up pretty high and settled at least a half a block away from its subject. The operator probably had a motion detection subroutine built into it. It was, anyway, too far for anyone on vid to know they were on vid.

What happened next was that the back door to the town-house was pulled open from the inside.

Out stepped Orno Linus, in his monk robes, with his hood

down. (This both made him easy to identify and clarified the fact that this was his own home; otherwise, he'd never have the hood down.) He was talking to someone in his yard, but so far, they weren't visible at this angle.

Orno stepped aside, and held open the door, and someone also in full robe—hood up—stepped into the condo. Then the shot cut out. The timestamp jumped ahead twenty-two minutes, to the point when the same be-robed person exited, closed the door carefully, and stared out into the yard. Then they took their hood off, and the vid ended.

A cheap but effective anonymizing filter had been used to make it impossible to identify who this person was. But whoever recorded it had made their point.

The last thing in the vid was this message: IF YOU WANT THE VID WITH ANON OFF, RESPOND WITH A BID. ONLY SERIOUS OFFERS CONSIDERED.

According to the date-stamp on the vid, the drone feed was recorded three days prior to when Professor Linus's body was found. Until she knew if that jibed with the official time-of-death, she had no way of knowing if this was an actual recording of the killer entering and exiting the crime scene, rather than an acquaintance popping by for twenty-odd minutes, and then leaving while Professor Linus was still alive. But if it was real, it was going to be worth a *lot* of credits. How many was hard to say, but the number would be pretty high. Maybe higher than she was comfortable with.

She picked up her voicer and tumbled through her contacts until she reached Ambol's name. He answered on the second buzz.

"What is it?" he asked.

"Hey, it's Elicasta Sangristy, your favorite..."

"I know. What is it?"

Sergeant Ambol Goggam was special assistant to the chief of police. He had a thing for Elicasta that was never actually consummated, in part because he was married, and didn't want his mild obsession with a famous Veeser to cost him that marriage. At the same time, he was deeply paranoid about the possibility that she might ruin his career one day, by playing back something he'd said for her millions of subs. Or something. It probably made sense in his head, even if it didn't in her head; burning sources was a great way to run out of sources.

The fact that Elicasta represented a twin threat to his marriage and his career should have meant he never took her directs. He did anyway. It was one of the only interesting things about him.

"So what is it?" he repeated. "I don't have a lot of time to talk."

"I wanted to thank you for getting me on the list, Amb," she said. Sergeant Goggam was how she'd gained entry to the press conference that was now causing her subs list to explode.

"You already did that."

"You're right, I did. How involved are you with the Linus murder?"

"I get updates. I can't get you any closer than you are now, if that's what this is about."

He meant that the chief got updates, and he was a part of that information chain, which was close enough.

"Following up on something I heard..."

"I can't share details," he said quickly.

"Oh, I know. It was just that another source told me the kid who discovered the body wasn't released at all, that you guys think he did it, and *I* said that doesn't make sense, because the professor had already been dead for three days, and why would the killer even *return* to the crime scene, and..."

"Who told you that?"

His voice had a new urgency to it. She was onto something.

"About the kid? You know I can't..."

"Who told you three days? Coroner hasn't even confirmed that yet."

"Well, not *exactly*," she said. "In the neighborhood."

There was a brief silence. She thought she could hear Ambol's brain churning through possible responses. He was cute, and she enjoyed flirting with him when the situation warranted, but there was a reason he worked in what was effectively a clerical position, and it wasn't because he was a genius.

"The kid's not under arrest," he said. "Don't run with that, because it's not true."

"Okay thanks," she said.

"Now tell me where the three days came from?"

The vid's real, she thought.

"Gotta go, Amb," she said.

"Listen..." he started to say. She hung up before he got any further. She'd probably have to make that up to him later, but there was something more important to do first.

She clicked *respond* to the auction message, and entered an opening bid for the content that was about fifty percent of the amount she was willing to actually pay. It was a large number in its own right; probably more than about three-quarters of the recipients of this message blast could afford.

She sent in the bid. Two seconds later, she had a response.

WE'RE SORRY, it read, BIDDING HAS BEEN CLOSED.

"Dammit," Elicasta muttered. "Too slow."

Someone out there just obtained evidence that could blow open the biggest murder case in years. And she was going to have to wait to see what it was, just like everyone else.

Chapter Seven

There was a lengthy treatise taped to the inside half of the glass window in the door, on paper that had been yellowed by years of exposure to the sunlight that hit it a couple of hours a day. It was nearly impossible to read the words on the pages without a magnifying glass, because in order to get the entire thing printed out in five languages, and still fit it onto the window, the apartment's occupant had to go with a tiny font.

The readability of the pages didn't matter all that much, because the general point was made by the large-type headline—again, in five languages—at the very top of the window, which read: THE OCCUPANT OF THESE PREMISES ASSERTS LEGAL RIGHT TO PRIVACY UNDER ANY AND ALL CONDITIONS. PERMISSION TO ENTER HAS NOT BEEN GRANTED, EXPLICITLY OR IMPLICITLY.

It then cited the legal code that supported this claim, followed by the entire code itself, in the small font.

One of the things that was funny about it—and there was a lot about it that was funny—was that the code Leemie cited pertained very specifically to the defense of a private domicile during a wartime siege. It permitted the owner of that domicile to kill anyone inside, whether or not they presented a visible threat, and regardless of whether he had previously invited them in.

It was a five-hundred-year old scrap of law that the federal parliament simply hadn't gotten around to reversing yet, probably because the conditions under which it might apply were so specific that nobody—aside from Leemie Witts—would ever see a need to lean on it.

Also, in the unlikely event someone entered the apartment during a war and Leemie elected—for whatever reason—to summarily execute them, the law still wouldn't apply, because Leemie didn't own the domicile in question; it was rented. He probably had a second misapplied law that covered that point, and just didn't have space on the door for it.

Makk ignored the yellowed threat in the window and banged on the doorframe.

"Leemie," he shouted. "It's Makk Stidgeon. Open up."

Leemie had a camera above the door. Makk smiled for it.

"Is that Detective Makk Stidgeon of the Velon Paramilitary Force?" Leemie said, through the intercom speaker screwed into the doorjamb next to the camera. "Nobody here named Leemie. Please go away."

"It's just Makk Stidgeon today, Leemie. C'mon, it's been a long twenty. Open up."

"Is that an order?"

Makk sighed. "Only if you need it to be."

Leemie buzzed the door, and Makk pushed his way in.

This only got him as far as the first entryway, where Leemie's locked mailbox sat. Makk was pretty sure his friend went through this nonsense every day with the local mail-carrier: buzzing them in, watching them drop the mail into the steel box, and then walking out again.

There was a thick oak door on the other side of the entryway that—especially in comparison to the wood-framed glass door—looked like it could stall a lengthy frontal assault. Makk listened for the outer door's lock to re-engage and then waited for Leemie to undo approximately seventeen locks in order to open the inner door.

One day, Leemie Witts would die in his apartment and it would be a month before anyone could get to the body.

Finally, the last lock was thrown and the door opened.

"Hurry," said a voice behind the door. Makk stepped into a dark living room, heard the door close again, and waited for his paranoid friend to finish locking them both in.

"Does anyone know you're here?" Leemie asked, as he turned on the light.

"Why would anyone care?"

Leemie's living room was a case study in hoarding, with stacks of print-based news all over the place, along with print books and magazines. In one corner, he had an old-fashioned networked ink printer, which he used to print out things he found on the Stream so as to add them to the room's general disarray. The man was in dire need of bookshelves, a laundry machine, and a visit from pest control. A psychiatrist too, but that was a given.

Leemie pushed past Makk and returned to a creaky chair behind a desk that had seven video monitors.

"Don't think I didn't notice that you failed to answer my question," Leemie whined.

"No, Leemie, nobody knows I'm here."

Leemie Witts was a lot taller than he seemed like he should be, once he crouched down behind the desk. Now gaunt, pale, and in serious need of a dental specialist, he looked like a caricature of the Corporal Lemaighey Witts that Makk served with.

"You shouldn't be here, Makk. You're in the shit right now. I saw you on the news. That case of your smells bad from every angle."

"Yeah, you're not wrong."

Makk moved a pile of folders from one side of a profoundly lived-in couch and sat down. The springs barely held.

"But you maybe aren't the best person to talk about shit that smells," Makk added. "When's the last time you took a bath?"

"You know they killed him, right? Linus must've got too close to the truth."

"What truth is that? And I thought you didn't follow the news."

"Oh, I do. I may be the only one who does."

Leemie was dedicated to a motley assortment of UnVeesers who presented a *truth* that was at odds with reality in ways that was sort of fascinating, from a sociological perspective. These UnVeesers each had a specific agenda, and tended to stick to the elements of actual news which could support that agenda, ignoring the rest. Leemie subscribed to at least a dozen of them and managed to synthesize their reports—which often contradicted one another—into a combined narrative that somehow made sense to him.

If nothing else, it made him interesting to talk to.

"Who is the *they*, Leemie," Makk asked. "And what truth do you think Linus got too close to?"

"Don't know. Something. I've been digging, you know. That's why you're here, isn't it? You came here for the truth."

"Sort of. I need someone who can read Eglinat."

"Every fifth person in Andel can read Eglinat. Why bother me? Unless..."

"There you go," Makk said.

"Unless you don't want the House to know what you have," Leemie finished.

"I don't need a full text translation. Just a rough idea of what I'm looking at."

"Sure. Sure, okay. I can do that."

Leemie scrambled around his desk, until he found a Septal hood in one of the drawers. He pulled it over his head.

Makk laughed.

"Okay," Leemie said. "Show me what you got."

"Is that hood really necessary?"

"Helps me get in character."

"How'd you even get that?" Makk asked.

Leemie Witts was never a Septal. When Makk met him, he was a young soldier, barely of age. They both were. After the war, Makk jumped straight into law enforcement, while Leemie—whose reaction to authority took a far more negative turn in response to his experiences as a soldier—transitioned through a series of technical jobs. That work exposed him to information which, when combined with a deteriorating sanity (there was no other way to put it) eventually made him unemployable. He now did contract work on Black Market jobs that didn't require him to leave home.

Despite all of that (or perhaps because of it) Leemie also happened to be one of the most intelligent men Makk had ever met. In a lot of ways, that just made his paranoia much more fascinating. He saw connections nobody else could, but lacked the balanced wisdom to judge their validity. The upside was, one day he decided he should learn Eglinat—which is never taught outside of the House—and then he did it. His understanding was far short of fluency, but it was better than Makk was going to find anywhere else.

This hardly seemed possible considering these days there were computer programs that could translate every spoken language on the planet into every other spoken language on the planet, with near real-time efficiency. But Eglinat wasn't one of them and it never would be, as long as the only extant samples of the language—and all the fluent speakers—were a part of the House.

Which raised the question, how did Leemie teach himself Eglinat? Makk didn't know the answer, but also didn't want to know.

"You can buy the hoods online," Leemie said. "It's easy, you just gotta know where to look. I bought this from a sexual role-play vendor. People are weird. All right, I'm ready; hit me with what you got."

Makk pulled a memory chip from his pocket and tossed it across the room.

"How clean is this?" Leemie asked, holding it in the light.

"Pretty clean," Makk said. "It's a denatured Credit Coin data shard."

"That's very illegal, Detective Third-Class Stidgeon."

"Central raided a counterfeiting mill a year back; seized about ten thousand of those. I took a handful for personal use, and I know I'm not the only one. It's great for signature-free data storage, if that's the sort of thing you're worried about. This is the first time I've ever been worried enough."

"You put this back in a Coin, it'd be worth something. I know people who can move it for you."

"Yeah, thanks. I'm already up to my neck in shit that's worth a lot of Credits to a lot of the wrong people."

The primary currency for Inimata—and possibly for the entire world—was the C-Coin. It had been developed using blockchain technology, and existed only in electronic form...sort of. It had been developed for the Stream initially, by programmers based in Inimata, where it had existed in a somewhat unstable state (its initial value fluctuated wildly) before settling into nationwide and then worldwide adoption. It was currently considered sufficiently stable that valuation of a single Credit—which was one-sixteenth of a C-Coin—consistently held at between 2.1 and 2.2 times that of the currently recognized global currency, the Fid. (The Fid was the fiat currency of Inimata.)

The Credit was only *sort of* electronic because physical coins did in fact exist. They were called Credit Coins, and consisted of small, round bits of metal and glass, about the same size as a

Dorin. (The Dorin was the first currency in existence, created and backed by the House. It also continued to exist, but was hardly used.) Credit Coins were tiny memory fobs with RFID tags that could hold up to fifteen C-Coins. (*Credit Coins designed to hold C-Coins* is exactly as confusing as it sounds.) Since each C-Coin was worth sixteen Credits—at the current valuation—each Credit Coin could hold up to 240 Credits. As each Credit was worth between 2.1 and 2.2 Fid, a single Credit Coin could hold between 504 and 528 Fid.

Credit Coins were rechargeable; drained Coins were regularly discarded and reused by everyone with a C-Coin account. An example of single-use would be: a consumer wishes to pay a merchant five Credits for some goods, and so the consumer moves five Credits from their C-Coin account to the Credit Coin; the consumer then gives the charged Coin to the merchant; the merchant scans the Coin's RFID tag, clearing out the Credit Coin; the merchant then either returns the Coin to the consumer or (more likely) drops the Coin in a jug with the other depleted Credit Coins.

All Credit Coins came with a display that listed the number of Credits in the Coin's memory. The display, and the Coin charge limit, were both mandated by international banking laws. Naturally, then, there is a thriving black market need for jailbroken, or denatured, Coins, where the display was inaccurate or missing, and the number of Credits allowed on one Coin far exceeded sixteen.

What Makk put the file on wasn't technically a denatured Coin; it was the memory drive for one. However, the fact that it *could* be dropped into the housing of a Credit Coin, where it could store a larger quantity of funds than were allowed by regulation, made the drive itself very valuable to a certain subset of Inimatan citizenry.

~

"So what's on the chip?" Leemie asked.

"Photos."

Leemie put the chip down, gently, as one does a live grenade.

"How'd you take the photos?" he asked. "With the camera on your government-issued badge?"

"A regular old non-networked camera," Makk said. "Are you done worrying?"

"I'm not gonna stick it into anything of mine until I know where it'd been."

"I know, you're like an expensive whore. Take a look at it already."

Leemie popped the chip into a stick, and jammed the stick into a port on one of his computers.

"Ah, it's a book," he said.

"Just the first dozen pages of it."

"And it's in...Oh. No no no."

Leemie physically pushed himself away from the desk. If he could have disappeared through the wall at the back of the living room, he would have.

"That's why he was killed, wasn't it?" he said. "You took that from the scene, and now they're gonna kill *us* for it, thank you very fucking much."

"Why do you say that?" Makk asked.

"That text is from the vault, Makk. Don't even try to lie to me."

"I told you I needed some Eglinat translated. Where do you think it was gonna come from?"

"Not from the godsdamn vault! Is it a whole book? Nita's sake, it is, isn't it? Where is it? Is it here?"

"Calm down."

"I'm not gonna calm down!"

"It's safe," Makk said, lying. "Nobody knows about it except you and me."

"Right. That's what they want you to think."

Leemie was still under his hood, so Makk couldn't see his eyes. Usually, when the crazy started to show up, that was the first place to check.

"You just looked at a picture from a page," Makk said. "What makes you say it came from the vault?"

"What? What?"

"Focus, Corporal Witts."

Makk had seen enough of Leemie's panic attacks to know that the best way to deal with them was to be as calm as Leemie was panicked. Between them, they averaged out somewhere around *moderately concerned.*

"It's archaic," Leemie said. "It's archaic. It's—"

"Tell me what that means."

Makk knew the answer, but having Leemie recite it was a way to get his friend to refocus.

"Okay," Leemie said. He pushed his chair back up to the desk, his head tilting back and forth between the image on his screen and Makk's face. "Okay. People still write in Eglinat, you know? Just the Septals. They say it's a dead language and nobody uses it anymore, but that's not really true because there are classes where they teach it to each other, only they don't use ancient texts to teach it, you get me? They use study guides. That's what I used."

"Black Market?" Makk asked.

"Does it matter?"

"Not really."

"The study guides use ***modern*** letters," Leemie said. "Archaic Eglinat uses a blend. Some of the letters are the same, a few of those are two letters now are only one letter in archaic, and there are over a dozen letters that don't have any modern cognate. There's been a lot of linguistic drift, you get me? Even in a supposedly dead language."

"Is that a long way of saying you can't read it?"

"I'm answering your question, okay? It's in archaic, so it's not something that's *out there*, like the study guides are out there. It came from deep in the House, which means the vault, which means we're fucked."

"And also, you can't read it," Makk said.

"I can't read it *now*. I shouldn't be reading it at all. Any idea how old it is?"

"Not a clue."

"Pre-Collapse?"

"I'm not sure there is such a thing as a pre-Collapse text, Leemie."

Leemie laughed.

"You're so godsdamn naïve," he said.

"I know," Makk said. "It's a failing."

"Of *course* there are pre-Collapse texts. The House pre-dates the Collapse, so why wouldn't the Archives? Look, it's probably not, but if it *is*, it'd be the first time anything that old saw the light of day. That would make it priceless, and we're definitely both dead. They'd probably level this whole city block if they knew about the pages on this drive. But you already know all that, don't you? You factored it in before coming here."

"It's really important that I know what this book is about," Makk said.

"And you think I'm gonna know that from twelve pages?"

"No, I don't."

Makk pulled the book out of his pocket and deposited it on the only clean spot available on the desk.

Leemie looked like he wasn't planning on breathing for a while.

"You're *sure* you weren't followed?" he asked.

"Pretty sure," Makk said. "Let me know when you've figured out something I don't already know. Oh, and it's probably a good idea not to tell anyone you have that."

"You're really...you really plan to leave that with me?" Leemie asked.

"The other options are the precinct evidence locker, and my apartment," Makk said. "I don't like either of 'em. This place looks pretty safe."

"What if I just decide to throw this in the fireplace and forget I ever saw it?"

"You're not gonna do that, Leemie. You're just as curious about what it says as I am. Besides, that fireplace hasn't worked in years."

Leemie's apartment was located at the bottom of a half-flight of steps on the side of a large apartment building that looked like a strong wind would take it down, in the same kind of neighborhood they showed in vid footage about new diseases. By the time Makk got all the way back out again—Leemie had to re-unlock the door, let Makk into the antechamber, and then tell him not to go until the inner door was locked again—and to the street, it was well past midday, and a few hours into the time he was supposed to be using to get some rest. Worse, he was deep in the middle of the wrong part of town.

About the best thing Makk could say about Pant City was that it was pretty easy to navigate as long as the suns were still up. Getting in and out on foot at that time of day didn't require beating back anyone aggressively offering their services. By the time he reached Axton Street—the communally recognized end of Pant City—he'd only had to show his badge once to get someone to leave him alone. That was to a street merchant selling off-brand leather wallets, no doubt with some species of opiate stuffed inside for the right price.

Makk found a manned cab on Axton and rode it to Kindon-town, arriving at the door to his apartment at a little before twelve in the afternoon. There was just enough time to get a couple of hours of sleep before he had to get up and head back downtown again. Technically, he was still working the over, which meant reporting by eighteen o'clock. Realistically, there was no such thing as on-duty and off-duty as long as this case was active.

Maybe, he reflected, he should have asked the guy selling off-brand wallets if he had any greens.

Before even entering the apartment, it was clear that someone else had gotten home before he did; someone who didn't have a key.

The door had been kicked in. Makk's first instinct was to reach for his badge and report an active B&E, but even the local police station was at least thirty minutes out.

His second instinct was to draw his gun, which he did. He shouldered his way inside, ready for whatever.

"Police," he said. "You're conducting an illegal act. Drop whatever weapons you have and surrender yourself."

The whole place had been tossed. In truth, it didn't look *that* much different from how he left it.

"I have legal authority to shoot trespassers on these premises," he said. He stopped short of citing the same legal code Leemie had taped to his door, although it was tempting. As an officer of the law, Makk actually *did* have the authority to shoot an intruder, whether he owned the place or not. "Surrender with hands raised."

He was halfway across the room before he felt comfortable with the idea that there wasn't anybody else there. The apartment just wasn't big enough to hide a person. He put his gun away, closed his front door as well as he could—and then moved a chair in front of it to hold the door closed—and began doing an inventory. Not that he had much of anything of value. Possibly, if a thief was looking for stuff to sell he'd find a couple of things, but Makk was pretty sure this wasn't that kind of break-in.

He spotted a boot-print in the bathroom. Makk had one of those no-skid rugs on the tile floor in front of the shower which was supposed to *not* retain water, something it very obviously did.

Someone stepped on the corner of the rug while searching Makk's largely-empty medicine chest, and the retained-water in the mat captured half of a boot print.

It looked familiar. Makk took a photo of it, and then went through his photograph library until he found the picture Viselle took, of the muddy boot print on Orno's backdoor. It was a match.

The other interesting thing the intruder left behind was in the kitchen, where he or she poured cold coffee on the counter. It was a tad dramatic—Makk definitely had a pen-and-paper somewhere in his apartment—but it worked okay. In the pool of coffee, Makk's unwelcome visitor had written two words.

RETURN IT.

PART II

The Missing Veeser

Chapter Eight

Detective Daska beat Makk to the department by at least a half an hour.

Makk returned to Twenty-One Central, by way of an app-car, at eighteen-fifteen, having gotten just enough sleep to reach that special tired-but-not-sleepy state that was the norm for everyone working the over.

He headed straight to the forensics office, without bothering to stop by his desk first. If there was anything at the desk relating to the Linus case, it would have come from forensics anyway, and if there was something *not* related to the Linus case waiting up there, it could continue to wait.

Forensics was the only part of the building where equipment deserving the moniker *state-of-the-art* existed. Not that this was especially obvious out in the field. Aside from the DNA scanner Len's team used at the scene, anyone watching them work a murder scene would conclude that most of what they did involved taking photos, and bagging and removing stuff. That's because that *was* all they did, at least until they got back to the department.

At Central, Jori Len's team could isolate exposed-surface DNA evidence—something like 90% of what they found was dead skin cells—as much as ten to fourteen days old, catalog and match it to the source with a court-tested degree of accuracy. (They could go more than fourteen days if the evidence was collected from a sealed or otherwise contained place, like a coldbox or a jar. Makk once solved a crime thanks to DNA recovered from the inside of a rubber ball that had been inflated five weeks earlier.) The team's ability to detect everything that *could* be trace evidence was equal parts incredible and underappreciated.

They could also produce scale-model versions of the crime scene, in vid or three-dimensional holograms, should such a need exist. Makk didn't care for the holograms, and so only very rarely asked for them, but if he felt like recreating what he remembered of Orno's townhouse, and didn't feel like driving all the way to Andel Quarter, he could do so easily.

The Linus crime scene was memorialized in a room all its own, and it contained everything they took out of the place except for the body, which was at the morgue.

Most of what was moved—either at Makk's behest or because Len felt like something was important—was professor-related: Orno's books, computer, the markerboards full of equations, and all of the boxes of stuff they found in the spare bedroom. So far, nobody had even tried to do anything with that stuff; it was all sitting on a table in the corner of the room.

There was a larger table in the center of the room, with two tabletop computers attached to six vid screens, only two of which were showing anything at the moment. Officer Jori Len was the one running whatever programs the computers had going on. Viselle Daska was sitting next to her, drinking an expensive coffee in a paper cup.

"There you are," Viselle said. "Got you a coffee." She pointed to the other end of the table, at a second expensive cup of coffee.

"Hey, Makk," Jori said, without turning. "Just bringing your partner up to speed."

Makk liked Jori Len. She was tiny for a police officer, and commanded a team of consistently obnoxious science geeks, who were somehow all afraid of her. She managed to balance being polite and soft-spoken with a sort of weaponized profanity, of which he had thankfully never been the recipient.

More importantly, she was extremely competent, and demanded nothing less than extreme competence from her team, no matter how obnoxious they happened to get.

"Thanks for the coffee," Makk said, to Viselle. "Please tell me you left Central at some point."

"I did," Viselle said. "I don't think Officer Len has."

"I have a very comfortable couch in my office," Jori said. "And a reputation to uphold. Everything ready yesterday and all."

Makk took the coffee, and dragged a chair over to the computer table.

"All right," he said. "Then why don't you start at the top. Tell me about the DNA."

"Counting you two, Officer Tayler, me and my three guys, and the deceased, we have traces of twenty-two people."

"Seven, plus Orno, that's fourteen people. That seems like a lot."

"That's what I said," Viselle said. "That's a lot of guests for a guy who doesn't own a table."

"He was meeting with Other Jimbal in his home," Makk said. "Let's assume for now that the reason for all the foot traffic was that he did this for a lot of the students."

"His schedule should tell us that. I'll see about getting it."

"Good idea. Jori, what do we know about our donors?"

"I started running them against Dee-NAD as soon as we had them isolated," Jori said.

DNAD, or 'Dee-NAD' was the DNA Database. While it was

hardly the case that every citizen of the world was included in Dee-NAD—this couldn't even be said of every citizen of Inimata, or resident of Velon—it was pretty comprehensive. In Inimata, all state and federal government employees and members of the military were required to provide a DNA exemplar. Likewise, everyone on public assistance, or applying for a license to operate a vehicle had to submit a sample. Nearly all the private companies required exemplars as a condition of employment, too.

There was a push to formally mandate everyone be added to Dee-NAD after childbirth, and an equally robust push against such a plan. As a murder cop, Makk loved the idea of a mandatory registration. As a private citizen, he was horrified, and hoped it never passed.

It probably would. The battle against such a thing was lost back when the federal government tied it successfully to public assistance.

None of that would have helped with this case, were it not for the fact that the House also contributed to Dee-NAD. The technology on which the database was founded, and the scanners Jori's team used to collect trace evidence at the scene, originated in the House, so not only were current Inimata-based Brethren included in the database—all of them, supposedly—it was founded using Brethren DNA.

"I've been able to match all but three of the DNA traces to their donors," Jori said.

"Is *all but three* the final word?" Makk asked.

"No, it's still running. So far, every match is to someone in the House. I don't know if that's good news or bad news."

"It's just news. Tell me about where you collected the samples. Did any of the fourteen come from the upstairs?"

She tapped a couple of commands into the computer, to check.

"Yeah, two. Just the stairs and the bathroom, though. Nothing from the bedroom except for Professor Linus."

"Okay," Makk said. "What else?"

"Not too much on the science end of things."

"Murder weapon?" he asked.

Jori shrugged. "You tell me," she said. "I've got a couple of shelves of books. One or two of them are heavy enough to kill a man."

"How about a big stick?" Viselle asked.

"Nothing like that, no."

"We're also missing a voicer," Makk said.

"Didn't find one," Jori said. "I was about to say maybe he ate it, but we've already got the autopsy back."

"This isn't making me happy, Jori."

"It's not my job to make Homicide happy. How about some cement dust and gravel? We have that."

"In the house?"

"Near the front door. I think we all tracked it when we came in that way."

"I was going to check with public works," Viselle said. "See if there was any recent construction in the front of the townhouse. Worth a look, right?"

"Yeah," Makk said. "Maybe the work schedule can put a witness on the street for us." To Jori, he said, "how about on the body? Anything interesting there?"

"Some dough under the fingernails," she said. "Unless he was murdered by a loaf of bread, that's probably not helpful."

"All right. Why don't you take off? The Dee-NAD match doesn't need your help, right?"

"It does not," she said, standing. "And I could use a shower."

She pulled out her badge, tapped a couple of commands, and then Makk's badge thrummed.

"That's the key to the door," Jori said. "I pushed it to both of you, make sure you lock up when you go. And don't direct me unless you want to get yelled at."

"Or unless you missed something," Makk said.

"We didn't miss anything. Usual wager?"

Jori and Makk had a running bet. If, over the course of an investigation, he found something she and her team missed, she owed him a beer. If not, he owed her one. Bets were settled at The Clover, the pub down the road from Central that doubled as every cop's off-duty home away from home. Makk routinely bragged that Jori Len had bought him more beers than the other way around, but in truth they were probably roughly even.

"You're on," Makk said. Then Jori shuffled out, and closed the door behind her.

"So," Viselle said, as soon as they were alone. "Sorry I blew up at you yesterday. I know it wasn't your fault."

"Yordon made the call," Makk said. "I pushed to have you there."

"I believe you."

"You've got a temper."

"I'm apologizing here."

"I'm just pointing out that you have a temper," he said.

"Fine," she said, with a flash of the aforementioned temper. "I don't want to talk about it anymore." She stood up and walked over to the evidence table. "Where do you want to begin?"

"No, no, we're not done yet," Makk said. "I don't know why Captain Llotho excluded you from the presser. But I'm pretty sure you *do* know. Wanna fill me in?"

She sighed.

"I think I do, yes. It would have been bad optics. Not right away, but eventually. My father is Ba-Ugna Kev."

Makk just about fell out of his chair.

"Excuse me?"

"I didn't...I *don't* want people to know that. Captain does, and now you do too. Hopefully not too many more people around here have that information; I'd like to keep it that way."

"You'd have been outed on the Stream inside of an hour," Makk said.

"Right. And then the story wouldn't have been about Orno's murder. It would have been about how Kev's daughter was investigating Calcut Linus's brother's murder. It was a smart play for Captain Llotho."

"I'm surprised he's letting you stay on the case, Viselle."

"I am too, a little," she said. "But it's not *really* a conflict. You know that, right? I meant it before when I said I don't have any direct dealings with my father. I don't. This thing with Linus has just been the past couple of years. I have nothing to do with it."

"But it won't look that way."

"I know."

The *thing with Linus* was a reference to the mostly bloodless technological war currently taking place between two camps: Calcut Linus and the Linus family, and a divisive technologist named Ba-Ugna Kev.

Calcut Linus was one of the first people to recognize the value of Credits, the Stream-based currency. Specifically, he recognized the value of them as a means to exchange funds anonymously, in a manner that was otherwise untraceable.

Credit Coins were, in their way, fungible: they could be handed from person to person, with one Credit *essentially* indistinguishable from another, and with no preserved sender-recipient chain. In this sense, the virtual currency acted exactly like physical cash.

Calcut's insight was recognizing that a large portion of the planet would prefer buying and selling goods and services in an untraceable manner. This was definitely true of those knowingly buying and selling *illegal* products and services, but also for everyone who had no intention of engaging in illegal activity, as well as for people who didn't care whether what they were buying and selling was illegal; they just wanted to buy and/or sell it.

Linus founded an on-Stream marketplace called the Black Market. Every interaction in the Market—from Credit Coin exchanges (Credit Coin being the only allowed currency) to messages, to the code underlying the Market's base functionality—was founded on the same blockchain technology as the Credits.

It was wildly successful, to the extent that most people used the Black Market daily, without necessarily even realizing it. For example, the messaging function—which was meant originally just to negotiate things like prices—was more popular than the marketplace itself, in part because Black Market messages were encrypted more effectively than any non-BM messaging system on the Stream. Nearly everyone in the world had a Black Market message box.

(Notably, the *actual messaging* going through Black Market servers was *not* using blockchain. This would have been a misuse of the technology. The Market used advanced encryption that was a step above Stream standard, but that was all. But it was to the Linuses' benefit that everyone assumed the messaging was as untraceable—and therefore impossible to monitor—as the currency movement.)

The Black Market made Calcut Linus one of the richest people in the world. Non-trivially, Linus was also, without question, a criminal. He made his fortune by standing up the Market, but his dealings within that Market included behavior both legal and otherwise. It wasn't an understatement to say that he *really* created the Market to further his own criminal enterprise, and just accidentally discovered how much non-criminals liked it.

While this was going on, a tech guru by the name of Ba-Ugna Kev was making a name for himself. Kev was something close to a self-made man, a genius rising out of poverty in a technologically backward country (Dunn) on an environmentally challenging continent (Unak) who *also* ended up being one of the richest people in the world.

Ba-Ugna Kev made his fortune by inventing things that made

other things work. His patents touched everything from telecommunications to waste management. It has been said of Kev that while almost nobody could *name* something he'd patented, almost nobody could make it through a day without *using* something he'd patented.

Kev also consulted frequently for governments and private industry. One such recent consultation garnered a great deal of attention, and put him on a direct collision course with Calcut Linus.

A few years earlier, the Inimatan government asked Ba-Ugna Kev to help with the tracking of funds used for illegal purposes, i.e., laundered money. It had become abundantly clear that fighting international financial corruption and illegal commerce was almost completely impossible, thanks to the invention and common use of the Credit Coin. Could he devise a way to help them track financial trades employing virtual currency?

Ba-Ugna Kev rose to the challenge, in part (according to interviews) because he couldn't believe anybody thought Credits were even remotely untraceable. He went on to explain that the very thing that made blockchain technology valuable—that a single Credit couldn't be created out of nothing, copied, or erased—also made it traceable.

"It would be like tracing the serial numbers on physical currency, only far easier," he reportedly said.

Kev began work writing code capable of reading the underlying blockchain technology that supported the (entirely decentralized) functionality of the Credit Coin on the Stream, to enable governments—and whoever else felt like paying him a massive sum for access to the program—to track the movement of funds.

When Ba-Ugna Kev's project became public knowledge, it ran into some significant opposition. Loudest among the opponents was Calcut Linus, who correctly recognized that Kev's work would not just alter the utility of the Credit; it could also unravel the Black Market. A decent number of ordinary, law-abiding private citizens also objected, for equally good reasons: not only would their purchases become traceable, their ostensibly unreadable messages over the BM servers would be available for governments to read, should they desire to do so. (Again, this was incorrect, but it was not in the Market's best interest to make this known.)

Meanwhile, many major corporations saw what Kev was doing as a unique opportunity. Previously, their knowledge of the buying habits of consumers stopped at the border of the Black Market. Considering how many transactions took place there, Kev's program would be of enormous value to them.

All of this created an interesting dynamic, at least in the media: Calcut Linus, whom essentially everyone agreed was a criminal who was simply too wealthy and powerful to actually get arrested for his criminality, was currently looked upon more favorably than Ba-Ugna Kev, a technologist whose inventions had made everyone's lives better.

Kev himself pointed out how curious the public perception of him as a villain was. "All I've done is point out the deficiency in relying upon the Credit Coin as an anonymizing force," he said. "Should I abandon this project immediately, it makes no difference. Knowledge will out; someone else will invent it instead one day."

"He casts a long shadow," Viselle said. "I should have told you before now, but I figured by the time we realized whose murder we were investigating, it was already too late. If you want me off the case, I can't imagine Llotho would have a problem with it."

Makk considered this. If she was too close, or if the Stream outed her down the road, it might make an already hairy investigation that much hairier. Alternatively, she might be uniquely useful.

"You know their world," he said.

"What do you mean?"

"Norg Hill, Lys...the top percent. You have access."

"Well, sure. But you're a homicide cop on an active investigation. You think there are rooms you won't be allowed into?"

"I know for certain that there are rooms I won't be allowed into. But maybe you will be."

She shrugged. "I guess. If that works for you. Where do we start?"

"Let's get to know the professor better," Makk said. He walked over to the markerboards. "What do you think all this means?"

It was Makk's hope that something about Orno Linus's career as a House professor naturally lent itself to murder, but if that were so, it wasn't at all obvious. His books on astrophysics looked like they were new ways to discuss established theory, rather than new theory. And if it *was* new, Makk couldn't envision a circumstance in which such a thing would be worth murdering over.

This was not to say that something connected with the House could *not* be grounds for murder, in the right circumstance.

Education was only one branch of the Septal tree. Religion was a second, and research-and-development was a third. Makk could absolutely see a religious opinion being motive for murder—a fair number of wars started that way—but not in this particular case. Orno did not appear to subscribe to any particular fanaticism, nor did he seem to be some manner of cult leader.

(There *was* the out-of-place astrology book among the scholarly tomes, which was *almost* a cult thing. The book continued to tickle Makk's curiosity, but even after flipping through it for notes

—there were none—he set it aside. There was always a half-dozen unanswered questions by the end of a murder investigation; that looked like this was going to be one of them.)

The R&D wing of the House was the largest division, and also the most secretive. It operated very much like a corporation, in that inventions and discoveries were the property of the House. It was likewise the case that the House chose what to *do* with those inventions and discoveries.

When it came to discoveries, this usually meant going public with what was discovered, thereby advancing the collective knowledge of the planet Dib. With inventions, it usually meant profiting from its use.

Sometimes—and who knew how often this happened—new inventions or discoveries were neither shared with the world nor profited from. Sometimes, they were buried.

Leaked inventions could be very profitable. So could leaked discoveries, possibly, depending on what was discovered and how quickly it could be turned into a profit.

But, it didn't look like Orno was part of the R&D wing of the House. His two areas of expertise were in education and religion, neither of which—again—lent themselves naturally to murder.

Unless the book they found was motive. But even with Makk's own apartment getting tossed in a search for it, that book just didn't seem like enough of an explanation. Why kill the person who could have told you where it was hidden?

There was a lot to this story they were still missing.

"Got another hit," Viselle said. She was at the computer, matching up the names attached to the DNA hits with current whereabout listings. This involved running up the results against the House's public directory.

"How many does that leave us?"

"Two unknowns. Looks like one just might be the result of a sample that was too old. The strand's not complete. The other one *is*, but it belongs to an unregistered."

"Great," he said. "With my luck, that's our killer. Are the rest all Brethren?"

"Looks like. It's a mix of faculty and student."

"That's our suspect list. First thing tomorrow, we start interviews."

"Right," she said. "How are you doing with your formula over there?"

"I scanned it and ran it up against Stream images. Looks like it's a common equation. I can't tell you what he was using it for, but it's not anything reality-altering. I think he put it on the board for easy access."

"He was probably re-proving it," she said.

"What?"

"How far did you go, in your education?"

"I enlisted when I came of age," he said. "So, not far."

"It's a teaching technique. You walk a student through the process by which a formula was reached. You re-prove it."

"How far did *you* go?"

"I did post-grad at Callim."

"No shit."

Callim University, a secular college in northern Inimata, was probably the most prestigious non-Septal educational school in the hemisphere.

"No shit," she said. "Criminology, if you're wondering."

"I sort of was, yes."

"Not my father's choice. He wasn't fond of my holding down a job where I carried a gun."

"Right."

"I know, poor little rich girl."

Makk laughed. "Honestly, Viselle, we just met, so take this however you want, but you should really get past your own money. You've got a nicer car, nicer clothes, probably a nicer place to live, and even the gun daddy didn't want you to have in your holster is nicer than mine. I don't care about any of that if you know how to do your job. I think you'll find most people are the same."

She smirked, and put her gun on the table.

It's not *that* nice," she said.

What she had was a state-of-the-art blaster. They fired a concentrated pulse of energy that could nullify a target from ten maders away. In the military, that was what they called killing people: *nullifying a target*.

They were easier to use under certain circumstances, like having to take out a steel door, or hitting a moving target. (The blast traveled at not-quite lightspeed, but close enough so it didn't matter. With a standard projectile weapon, you had to aim for where the target was *going to be*; with a blaster, you aimed for where they *were*.)

Makk never cared for them. He liked the option of using non-lethal force that a regular old gun provided, and he also liked to be able to fire multiple bullets in rapid succession. Blasters used a rechargeable energy source that needed about five seconds to recover, every time it was fired. Basically, it was hard to miss with one of those, but if you did, you had five seconds to worry about what your target was going to do before you got another chance.

"It's pretty nice," Makk said, putting his standard-issue handgun on the table. "But I'm good with this one. Did you have to submit special paperwork to get that or something?"

"I paid for it myself, if that's what you mean. I did have to jump through a couple of hoops to get it authorized for law enforcement use, but only a couple. So now that we're putting everything out on the table, as it were, what was *your* childhood like? I assume you weren't raised by an egomaniacal, controlling, techno-genius?"

"No such luck. Orphanage. House-run."

"*Really?* The Septals raised you?"

"Yep. It wasn't bad. I don't have other orphan experiences to compare it to, but I wasn't *unhappy*, that I can remember. Near as

I can tell, my parents didn't want to raise a *Cholem*, so after giving me this mark they dropped me off at the nearest chapel. I have to think my childhood would have gone a lot worse otherwise, if that was how they felt."

"Honus's sake. That's terrible."

"Like I said, not really. I made my peace a long time ago."

He was eliding over an enormous amount of his own history. As an eighter, he embarked on a quest to find his birth parents, *did* find them, confronted them about having abandoned him over something that was a lot more in *their* control than it was in *his* control, and nearly ended up with an assault charge on his record. He was saved from a possible stint in juvenile lockdown by Sister Xhvik, the orphanage's matron.

It was probably that experience that led him to joining the military as soon as it was legal for him to do so.

But, he'd made his peace since. That much was true. Also, he kept track of his birth parents and knew that they were both dead now. This was oddly helpful information, as far as his mental well-being went.

"Well," Viselle said, "maybe I do need to get past my own money, but I still feel like an ass for complaining about father to a guy raised without one. Oh, hang on, what's this?"

She was looking at her computer screen.

"What's the matter?" Makk asked.

"Nothing much," she said, performing the blessing of the five, almost absent-mindedly, as if she'd just seen a ghost. "It's just that Duqo Plaint is one of our suspects."

Makk laughed.

"The High Hat himself is in our suspect pool? Perfect."

Viselle continued to look vaguely horrified.

"What do we do?" she asked.

"What do you mean? He's a suspect, so we go talk to him. Just like every other suspect. You act like you've never talked to someone in a position of power, and we both know that can't possibly be true."

"I've never accused one of them of *murder*. Of being a terrible parent? Sure."

"It'll go pretty much the same. You know what? I think we should start with Duqo. I'll direct Captain Llotho and set something up. He'll *love* that."

Chapter Nine

The main business offices for the High Hat of the Velon Septal chapter were located in an administrative building that ran alongside the massive temple anchoring the center of the campus. It was not—to Makk's disappointment—*in* the temple itself.

His disappointment wasn't due to any grand desire to spend some time inside the temple, exactly; it was just that he'd only ever been in the Rotunda, and knew there was a vast warren of rooms on the floors above and below that central hall of worship.

Up, there were probably only two or three floors of space. Down was another story. Nobody outside of the House knew precisely how many sublevels there were. Perhaps only one, but rumors were, it went much deeper than that.

Makk was disappointed because as much as he knew better than to take seriously the idea that there was a secret subterranean city beneath the main temple—or whatever the latest edition of the conspiracy theory that happened to be in favor on the Stream—he had no chance of getting a definitive answer as long as he wasn't even in the right building.

From the window, he could see the side of the temple and the

Fingers jutting out of the top. When he was a kid, he thought they were part of the pipe organ that was installed at the back of the main hall, and used to wonder what songs might use the notes necessary for such a large pipe, and why he hadn't heard one of them yet. It wasn't until he realized not all of the temples had an organ that he decided they must serve some other purpose. He just didn't know what that purpose was. Nobody did.

Viselle, who'd been sitting in one of the uncomfortable wooden waiting room chairs until a minute ago, reentered from the hallway, with her badge in her hand.

"Makk," she said, calling him from the window in a hushed tone.

"What's up?" he asked.

"I just heard back from public works."

His head couldn't make the connection. "Remind me," he said. "Why were we waiting on them?"

"The cement dust at the entrance. You'll like this. They replaced the brick steps in front of Professor Linus's townhouse at the beginning of the week. The front entrance was *unusable* on the night he was murdered."

"Meaning the killer had to have used the back," Makk said. "Were they there around the time he was killed?"

"No. The work was finished the night before his death, but the steps were barricaded until the night before Jimbal found the body."

"The killer had only one means of egress, but it was the one with the lowest chance of a witness," Makk said. "This does not make me happy."

"It's a reduced variable," Viselle said. "That can only help."

"Did they teach you that at Callim?"

"They did, actually. Fine, you're in a mood. I'm going to go sit down again."

It didn't take long to set up the meeting with the High Hat. Makk reached out to Llotho who, after registering the unsavory fact that his lead detective wished to treat the most senior religious figure in the country as a murder suspect, said that not only would it be no trouble to arrange a conversation, he could do it that very morning.

Tragically, the meeting would not involve Plaint being dragged downtown and put into an interrogation room. It turned out the High Hat had been pestering the people Llotho answered to, about having a face-to-face with Detective Makk Stidgeon as soon as possible. Captain Llotho had been declining the request as firmly as he could; discovering Makk wanted to talk to Plaint was a gift.

However, it meant that officially, he and Viselle were there because Plaint wanted to speak to *them*, and not the other way around. It also meant that Makk had to talk to a powerful person at the end of another long overnight, in an environment designed to intimidate *them*, rather than the suspect.

Not that it was that intimidating. They were in a decent-sized waiting area, with a dozen chairs, two entrances, and a half-dozen windows. It was around the size of Makk's apartment, but with nicer curtains and a much higher—and significantly more impressive—ceiling. It came with a chandelier consisting of two different-sized bulbs in the center of a brass loop with a silver ball on it. Makk spent his first ten minutes staring at this odd light fixture before realizing it was modeled on the Dancers, with the planet Dib represented by the silver ball, and its orbit the brass loop. He wondered if they moved the silver ball in correspondence with the 529-day year or if that was too much of a pain.

There was a desk at the far end of the room, behind which was a Sister named Plam, who tersely introduced herself as Duqo Plaint's executive assistant. A large set of double doors at her back led to the office of the High Hat.

Sister Plam looked to be somewhere in her hundred-and-thirtieth season—close to retirement age, if not past it—but carried a *do-not-mess-with* demeanor that Makk didn't even consider questioning. As she looked to be the last defense standing before one of the most important men in the country, it was probably a good thing that she gave off this vibe.

Plam kept looking up at Makk and Viselle. The sister looked vaguely displeased to have them there with her.

After a lengthy enough wait that Makk wondered if he should have taken a nap, right there in the room, the intercom on Plam's desktop buzzed.

"You can go in now," Plam said, nodding with her head toward the double doors.

"Thanks so much," Daska said with a smile.

The doors did *not* lead directly to Plaint's inner sanctum. They led to an antechamber with a guard, with another set of doors on the other side of the guard. It was a setup slightly reminiscent of the two layers of security required to get in to see Leemie Witts.

That's more like it, Makk thought.

The guard was big, squarish, and sturdy-looking, like a support column brought to life. He had a military-grade pulse cannon on a strap over his shoulder, and wore what could best be described as a tactical cowl on his head: a wrap-around visor that preserved his peripheral vision. He was also sporting a projectile-resistant vest.

This, Makk decided, was one of the legendary House Sentries. Makk was raised in a House orphanage on a House campus, and had never seen one before. Nor, he suspected, had most people, in their everyday encounters with the Septal faith. Hence, *legendary*; there was an active debate as to whether or not they really existed.

Yet, when people who claimed to have directly encountered a Sentry described one, this man was essentially whom they described.

"Hold it right there," the Sentry said, when they'd gotten about halfway to the door. "I have to check you for weapons."

"We have weapons," Makk said. "No need to check. We're police officers. Maybe you don't know this, but we're allowed to carry guns."

Makk held up his badge to underline the point. Daska did the same.

"You *are* allowed to carry guns," the Sentry agreed. "Only, not here."

There was a steel cabinet to his right, which he unlocked.

"You're serious," Makk said. "We're officers of the law."

"I *am* serious, detective. Different set of laws here."

"Here where?"

"About where you're standing."

"It's fine," Viselle said. She pulled the expensive blaster out of her shoulder-holster and handed it over.

"All right," Makk said, handing his over butt-first. "Mine's an old-fashioned mechanical handgun, though; try not to confuse it with all the fancy weapons."

"I promise," the Sentry said. He put both into the steel cabinet and re-locked the door. "They'll be here when you come out."

"Super. By the way," Makk said, "I'm pretty sure that pulse cannon isn't street-legal."

The Sentry smiled.

"We aren't in the street," he said. "And as I said, the laws where you're standing right now are a little different than what you're accustomed to."

"You might have to show me what lawbook you guys are looking at, before I go."

"I'll forward the request. You can enter now."

Makk didn't know what to expect on the other side of the doors, but he was leaning toward *throne room*. What he got was... an office. An ordinary-looking, modest office. It had a fireplace, but it wasn't a giant fireplace with an animal-skin rug and ornate leather chairs. Just a small, functional red brick fireplace, with seats in front of it that didn't look like they came from the same set. The desk in the center of the room—rather than being some ornate oak thing—was of the same design and quality as the one in the Linus crime scene. It was less cluttered than that one, though, and was free of blood spatter.

Two walls in the room were taken up by bookshelves whose contents were stacked haphazardly, in an order only the owner could attest to. Light from the rising suns came in through a window on the third wall, which faced east. The fourth wall had —aside from the fireplace—a small cot.

Duqo Plaint, the 237th High Hat of the Velon Septal chapter, was at the desk, in sweatpants and a loose gray shirt with sweat on the collar. He didn't have on his hood.

"Oh, excuse us!" Viselle exclaimed, averting her eyes. Makk did the same, instinctively, and then hated himself a little for doing it.

"No, no, it's fine!" Plaint said. "It's fine! *I* should apologize. Please, no need to look away. Unless you find me particularly hideous."

The High Hat hopped to his feet and crossed the room spryly, sliding into handshakes for both of them.

"I'm afraid I have tended toward far greater informality in my waning years, detectives. Most of my days are spent right here; I feel as though it's an extension of my home."

"But we aren't..." Daska began. She appeared to realize she was about to recite Septal tenets to the highest ranking Septal in the country, and stopped herself.

"Yes, I know. *Fertas nonna fachum*. You are both hereby designated temporary Brethren, and now I don't have to put that uncomfortable thing on. Sorry, I *just* returned from my morning jog; you have no idea how poorly those hoods breathe. Please, sit, relax. Can I get either of you a beverage?"

"We're fine, thank you," Makk said, finding his way to one of the chairs. It was a tattered easy chair near the fire. Daska took a position on a loveseat in the middle of the room that looked as if it ordinarily lived in a different spot.

"But if you don't mind my asking," Makk said, "how do you manage to jog without a hood on? There are bound to be non-Septals around, either in person or by drone."

"That's a secret," Plaint said. Then he laughed. "I'm joking. There are outdoor parts of the campus where non-Septals aren't allowed."

"And the drones?"

"There are ways to block a drone feed. That's not why you're here, though, is it, detective? To ask about my exercise regimen?"

"Actually, you asked *us* here," Makk said. "But since we are, we *do* have some questions for you."

"How felicitous!"

Plaint retrieved some sort of vegetable-based beverage from his desk, rolled the office chair around to the fireplace, and sat, while Makk tried hard not to stare at the man's face. Or rather, at the upper half of it.

High Hats always had strong chins. This was either a job requirement, or there was some kind of unconscious bias that made it more likely for a strong-chinned monk to get the job. Duqo Plaint had been High Hat for most of Makk's adult life, and given the prominence of the role—not just within Velon, but nationally, if not worldwide—it was likely a week didn't go by without Plaint's hooded visage appearing in some piece of media somewhere. All that time, Makk didn't know any more about him than: strong chin, no beard, decent speaking voice. Looking at that entire face now was a little unnerving.

Which may have been the point.

"So," Plaint said, after a long gulp of his green liquid, "I thank the both of you for coming. Whether or not you wanted to.

Detective, you look as if I may have gotten you directly out of bed."

This was to Makk. Viselle looked like she was taking a break between photos for a Smart Business Casual clothing line. Makk was already starting to resent this about her.

"I always look like this, Highness," Makk said, using Plaint's formal title. "But no, we actually worked through the overnight."

Plaint laughed at Makk's choice of self-deprecation.

"No offense intended, Detective Stidgeon," he said jovially.

"None taken. But Detective Daska and I *are* very busy. You put some urgency behind this meeting happening *right now*; is there something we need to know this morning, rather than later?"

"Well," the High Hat said, "to begin, what happened to Orno was terrible. We're all in mourning."

"I can see that."

"What my colleague means..." Daska began.

"No, it's all right," Plaint said, waving his hand. He kept his eyes on Makk. "You're being irascible, to see how I respond. An interesting tactic. More interesting, I think, is the question of why you believe a *tactic* is required at all, Detective Stidgeon. I promise you, the death of Professor Linus was devastating for us all, but if you came here expecting red eyes and rent garments, I am not a man with that kind of free time. Now, since you're not going to begin with why *you* wanted to speak to me, I'll begin with why *I* wanted to speak to *you*. I invited you here to make sure you understood that if there is *anything* you need, I will be sure to avail myself to you."

"We have the full support of the House?" Makk asked.

"Yes, exactly. I'm offering a direct channel to my office. This of course is about anything directly pertaining to the campus, but I have influence that extends further. I'm saying, I can grease gears, if you tell me which ones are sticking."

"That's very helpful," Viselle said.

"In exchange for?" Makk asked.

"I don't understand the question."

"What do you want from us in exchange for the full access you say we'll be getting?"

"I want for you to catch the person responsible for murdering my friend and colleague," Plaint said. "Is that not self-evident?"

"I'm sure you do, but that's not what you want from *us*."

Plaint was beginning to get agitated, which got him out of his chair and back behind his desk. He put down his drink and paced a little.

Daska shot Makk a look.

Make the powerful uncomfortable, he wanted to say. *It's the best way to see what they're hiding.*

"I think it's only fair that the information flow in *both* directions," the High Hat said. "That's all."

"That's all," Makk repeated.

"Yes. I'd like updates on your progress. I'll make sure there are no obstacles to your progress—as much as I can—and you let me know what you find."

"I see." Makk said.

"We can work something out," Viselle said. "Captain Llotho, I'm sure, can provide you with whatever you need."

"Hang on," Makk said. "Look Highness, there's no way to say this nicely, but given where and when the murder took place, the killer was probably one of the Brethren. I'm not in the habit of trading information outside of the force, and I'm *really* not fond of maybe tipping off the killer on what I've found so far."

"I have no plans to disseminate the information widely, Detective Stidgeon," Plaint said. "These updates would only be delivered to me. I assume I'm not a suspect?"

Makk looked at Viselle. "Tell him," he said.

She looked like her head was going to explode.

"Highness," she said, "we found your DNA at the scene."

"Which means yes," Makk said, "technically, you *are* a suspect.

Do you happen to know where you were on the night of the murder?"

Plaint laughed.

"Of *course* you did. You know, that technology was developed right here?"

"I did know that, yes," Makk said.

"I mean to say that it's not only House science, it's *this* chapter's work. We're still very proud."

The High Hat didn't seem at all put off by having been called a suspect. Makk couldn't decide what that meant.

"Now, where I *was* on the night Orno was killed depends on which night that was," Plaint said.

"It was on the last day of the Feast of Nita," Viselle said, "sometime after the final ceremonies."

"Ah. An *exhausting* event. I would have retired to chambers following the Doling of the Bounty."

"Can anyone back that up?" Makk asked.

"Sister Plam keeps my calendar; I can have her check to see if I held counsel with anyone at that time, but it's doubtful. Detective, you aren't *really* being serious right now, are you?"

"Of course not," Viselle said quickly. "Your Highness, we have an obligation to speak to everyone the evidence suggests might have spent time in Professor Linus's townhouse prior to his death. Can you explain why we found your DNA at the scene?"

"Because I was there! About, oh, a week ago. More, perhaps. It should be in my calendar as well; Sister Plam is quite thorough."

"Why were you there?" Makk asked.

"He asked for an audience, and I granted it to him."

"He couldn't go to you?"

"I like to get out from time-to-time, detective. And I've found that a willingness to go to *them* can be greatly appreciated."

"Can you tell us what you talked about?"

"I can't, I'm afraid. House business. But I'm sure you won't have trouble finding Brethren who witnessed my visit. I don't travel unnoticed...well, anywhere, really."

"Unless you're out for a jog," Makk said. "Is an internal investigation being conducted as well?"

"Into the murder? No, we don't do that. I'm sure you've heard stories, but..."

"Into *any* matter involving Orno Linus."

"I'm sorry," Viselle said, jumping to her feet. "I'm sure you're busy. Thank you for the offer to help. Makk?"

"He hasn't said why he wanted us here yet," Makk said, notably *not* jumping to his feet.

"Detective," Plaint said, "I told you..."

"I know. Direct access, blah-blah-blah. This is a murder case, Highness. You're *supposed* to give us full cooperation. It's not something you get to trade. Now I believe you when you say you want to know who killed Professor Linus, and I also believe your explanation for how we picked up dead skin cells belonging to you in his office. But we're not here, in a room where you don't entertain guests, just to look at your hoodless face. What do you *really* want?"

Duqo Plaint turned his back to them, either looking for a book on one of his shelves, or composing himself. If ever there was a time to believe there was no such thing as a secret Septal assassination squad, this was that time.

Viselle Daska looked like she was in the midst of a panic attack. She was staring at Makk and silently mouthing questions like *what are you doing?* It was difficult to tell who would break first: Plaint deciding to speak again, or Detective Daska blurting out another apology.

"What do you know about Professor Linus's scholarship?" the High Hat said, finally breaking the silence. His back was still to them.

"Not much," Makk said. "I saw he wrote a couple of books but I didn't open them."

"Yes. He wrote quite a few. He was an exceptional astrophysicist, but that wasn't where his *passion* took root."

"*The Outcast Ascendant*," Daska said. "I saw that on his shelf. That's not about astrophysics, is it?"

"It isn't," Plaint said, turning. "Very good. Were you raised in the faith?"

"No," she said.

"But *you* were," Plaint said, to Makk. "I could pretend I know from the look in your eye, but that's not so; I looked you up."

"Good for you," Makk growled.

"Who gave you that mark on your wrist, detective?" Plaint asked. "It wasn't us, I'm sure."

"I don't know. I've had it as long as I can remember."

"Barbaric. I'm very sorry; that must have made your childhood much more difficult, and the orphan system is rough enough as it is."

"Thanks."

"And your father," he said, to Daska. "I trust he's well?"

She looked surprised.

"He's...I hear he's doing fine," she said.

"Excellent. Send him my regards, from an old friend."

'Look at all the things I can find out about you', Makk thought.

"You were telling us about the victim's scholarship," Makk said.

"Mm, yes."

Plaint extracted a book from the shelf and walked back to his chair.

"I asked about your faith because my friend Orno was the preeminent expert on the Myth of the Outcast."

With that, he handed Viselle his own copy of *The Outcast Ascendant*.

"Interesting word choice," Makk said, "coming from you."

"Which word do you mean, detective?"

"Myth."

There were a few core tenets in the Septal faith. One was that the world was created by the five gods: Honus, Javilon, Ho, Nita and Pal. The details regarding the nature and application of this creative process differed from House Chapter to House Chapter, thanks to the somewhat odd fact that none of the Septal Houses were working from a single common text. Instead, there were dozens of foundational manuscripts—some estimates put the total in the hundreds—of which each focal Chapter retained a copy. These were called Archival Texts, and they were both sacred and entirely off-limits to all but the most elevated few.

Given each Chapter shared copies of the same essential text, it was reasonable to think that therefore, each Chapter was working from the same basic creation story. There were a number of reasons this was not the case.

First, there were *different* creation stories among the Archival Texts; different Houses preferred different versions for their own reasons.

Second, each archive was copied by hand, at some time in the distant past, from a source text, and then those copies were copied, and so on. This naturally created variation, some of which was quite substantial. The more notable variations were called Divergences, most of which were harmless and somewhat amusing. A few were not. For instance, at least one war was started because of a missing "not" in a passage about the settling of paternity disputes with one's neighbor.

Third, the Septal House structure was deliberately decentralized, which meant there was no single voice of ultimate authority and so, no way to sanctify one set of Archival Texts as *the* texts of record. It was up to the High Hat of each focal Chapter—Duqo Plaint was one such High Hat, speaking for all of Velon and one quarter of the nation of Inimata—to determine which Archival Texts would guide his or her teachings.

Fourth, nobody knew which chapter had the actual source Archival Texts. Nearly every one claimed to, and it was possible every single one of them was wrong and the true source texts were lost to history.

All of this meant that while each House chapter abided by the central idea that the world of Dib (or Dibble, depending on where one was raised) was created out of nothing by the five gods of the Pentatheon, *how* that happened depended on which version of the creation story the local High Hat preferred, and on the version of that story they were using.

The same held for the stories of the Outcast.

Every creation story has to have a destruction story, it seems. For the Septal faith, in every version of the Archival Texts, the Outcast fulfilled that role, both as the destroyer god, and the source of all evil in the world.

There was variance in the finer details. In some of the stories, the Outcast was a sixth founding god who was stripped of his (or her, sometimes) name and banished to another realm, but destined to return one day to undo all of the good done by the Five. In other versions, the Outcast existed before the Pentatheon imposed their will on the world, and before time itself existed. In creating Dib, they beat back his influence and banished him. Thus, his inevitable return would constitute a reclamation of what he considered to be his all along.

The Myth of the Outcast was what adults told children to get them to behave, and the Outcast's mark was the universal symbol for *danger*, *keep out*, and *poison*, among other things.

Makk was intimately familiar with the mark of the Outcast; it was what was on his wrist.

~

Duqo Plaint smiled gently; the patient expression of a lifelong educator.

"Myth," Plaint repeated. "Yes, I understand why you might find that word choice surprising. In my role as High Hat, I have to stand in the middle of two seemingly competitive perspectives. Contradictory, even. I say *myth*, because the foundational stories of our creation are just that: stories. This is the scientific aspect of my Septal faith speaking. Is it literally the case that the Five affixed the firmament, raised the continents, composed the song of the Dancers, spawned all the plants and animals, and created the entirety of Dibble-kind in their images? Not if we're applying the word *literally* accurately, no. But the literal truth would be something impossible for us to comprehend, as we happen to be limited beings. Our stories, our, yes, myths, are shadows of real truths. I don't use the word to diminish the stories, which I gather is how you've taken it. Rather—and this is the *theological* aspect of my Septal faith—I use it to reference a thing which is both *true*, and only *approximate*. I believe in the Five, that they are real, that we all owe our existence to their hand, and that I will meet them in the next life. I can hold that belief without embracing a literal interpretation of the creation stories."

"And the Outcast?" Makk asked.

"I believe there is evil in the world. The mark on your wrist is an example; the action of whoever gave that to you was guided by such evil. Likewise, the actions of Orno's killer. But a literal belief in an *end* day, when the actual, literal Outcast arises and reclaims the universe...no, of course not. It is, as I said, a story told to approximate a thing we all know to be real. We require a manifestation that exists outside of ourselves, even when the *true* Outcast —the true *evil*—is hiding in here."

He tapped his own chest.

"At least," he continued, "this is how I approach my faith, and what I teach. But if you're looking to speak to a literalist High

Hat, I'm sure I can direct you to several Fundamentals. The Middle Kingdoms alone have an overabundance."

"That's all interesting," Viselle said. "Because this book Orno wrote is a doomsday prediction. Isn't it?"

"It is. This is why I asked the question. Brother Linus was a man in great conflict with Professor Linus. I am at peace with the rationalist and theologist aspects of my faith. He was not. Where I saw consilience, he saw only contradiction. His life's work—forever unfinished, now—was to reconcile his far more extreme understandings. You see, Orno believed in a purely atheistic creationism, but he was concurrently one of the most fervent polytheism literalists I've ever met, which meant he held two utterly irreconcilable perspectives at the same time. Detectives, I hate admitting this, but when I heard he'd been found dead, my first thought was that he'd taken his own life. That's how much he was tortured by his own studies."

"Was this an attempt at that reconciliation?" Viselle asked, holding up the book.

"It was a step in that direction. Orno thought that the best way to find his peace was to concentrate on the Outcast myths, narrowly, as a starting point. He arrived at this...quite young, I believe. His talent with Eglinat was renowned before he was even tenured, in large part because in order to pursue the kind of research he wanted to pursue, he first needed to become a foremost scholar in the archaic. And so, he made himself one. He was quite brilliant. That book, Detective Daska, is a cross-examination—a meta-study, if you prefer—of all the variations of the Myth of the Outcast he could get his hands on. The older those editions, the better."

"Did he have to do a lot of travel for that?" Makk asked.

"A tremendous lot, yes. Our Archival Texts are quite old, and our foundational texts comprehensive, but it wouldn't be much of a comparative study had he not looked at other archives. I once told him he was accidentally better-positioned than perhaps anyone in asserting which House archives are originative. But I'm afraid that had he written *that* book instead of the book in Detective Daska's hands, he'd have never been allowed another look into the Archives of the other Houses."

"Can you get us his travel itinerary?"

"Fifteen years' worth?"

"As much as you can."

"If you think it's relevant, detective. I'll have the Sister put something together for you, once she's done establishing my alibi. I would be fascinated to hear, though, why you might think it *is* relevant."

"It's probably not," Makk said. "I won't know until I see it."

"Very well."

He stood, and held out his hand to Daska, who returned the book.

"Now then," he said, walking the book back to the shelf, "you want to know what I *really* want? Very well. What I'm going to tell you next requires absolute secrecy. It cannot leave this room, and it cannot be recorded in your case files. Do you think you can promise me that?"

"Without knowing what you're going to say next?" Makk said. "I don't see how."

"It isn't the name of the killer," he said, "or the murder weapon, or the means of egress, or...I don't know. All of the things relevant to a murder investigation."

"How about motive?" Makk asked.

"It is *perhaps* motive."

"You want to give us something that could be the reason Linus was murdered in his study, and to promise to keep that out of the report."

"Yes," Plaint said. "I don't think it *is* motive. I don't think it's anything but a missing thing, which we require back, which may turn up over the course of your investigation. Perhaps it already has."

"What kind of missing thing?" Daska asked. She was shooting fiery glances at Makk every few seconds, in a way that was so stupidly obvious, Plaint would have to be blind not to notice.

Calm down, Viselle, he thought.

"Why don't you tell us what you have to tell us," Makk said. "And we'll tell you what we can do with it."

The High Hat sighed, and nodded. He moved back to his chair, leaning forward, hands clasped together, knees apart. *Let's work together to solve this*, his stance was saying.

"As I've explained, because of the very nature of Orno's scholarly work, he had access to some of the most sacred archives in existence."

"You mean the Archival Texts?" Makk asked.

"I mean those, but not *just* those."

"Can you be more specific?"

"Not at this time," he said. "We think...this is embarrassing... we think he might have *kept* something from the archives. A... well. An artifact, we'll call it. Something extremely old, and entirely one-of-a-kind."

"But you can't tell us what it is," Makk said.

"That's right."

"You've got a one-of-a-kind artifact, you think it walked off with your personal friend Orno Linus one day, and now you want to know if we found it, and if we *did*, you want us to give it back to you and pretend we never had this conversation."

"Yes, detective. That's precisely it."

"I dunno," Makk said. "We found a broken alarm clock. Was that it?"

"If you had it, you would recognize it as something unique, Makk Stidgeon. There's nothing else quite like it on this planet."

"Huh. I don't remember coming across anything like that. Do you, Detective Daska?"

Viselle shook her head.

"No," she said. "No, nothing."

"We'll check the inventory at the station," Makk said. "I think we have a *nothing quite like this on the planet* section in the evidence room; it probably ended up there."

"Detective, I promise I'm telling you everything I can. Given your education, you understand better than most how critical the sanctity of the archives is."

"Sure, growing up I heard a lot about the House's archives and how the secrets there were *important* secrets. But I never knew why that secrecy was important, and I still don't. And hey, maybe they shouldn't be. Who am I to say? Tell us what we're looking for, and I'll tell you if we came across something like it."

"I'm not going to do that."

"When did it go missing?" Daska asked. "Can you tell us that much?"

"We don't know," Plaint said. "But its absence was discovered before Brother Linus was murdered, as I'm sure you must have realized already. It was over a week ago, the day before the Feast of Nita."

"And you think he's the one who took it," Makk said.

"I don't know *what* to think yet. There are perhaps a dozen people on the campus who are both aware of its existence and have the necessary access. But of that dozen-odd people, he's the only one who has been murdered, and so the question must be floated."

"Your Highness," Daska said, "how many people here know about this artifact and *don't* have the necessary access?"

"A handful," Plaint said. "Thirty, perhaps; I couldn't say precisely. Why?"

"I'm assuming the object in question is valuable?"

"It's priceless," Plaint said. "I mean that exactly; its value is impossible to quantify."

"Yeah," Makk said. "For you maybe. But what about someone on the Black Market?"

"Its value would be in the fact of its existence. It would serve no functional use to anyone outside of the Septal House from which it came. And that use is in itself only theoretical. But knowing only that, the right buyer might be willing to part with a substantial sum. We do have a team looking into that angle."

"What angle?" Makk asked.

"Black Market dealers. If the artifact comes up in an auction, we'll know it. We aren't without our means in this regard." He turned to Viselle. "Your point is well-taken, Detective Daska. Someone else could have perhaps found a way to steal it, provided they knew it existed first. Security-wise, of course, what you're suggesting is utterly impossible."

"Why's that?" she asked.

"I'm not going to elaborate on our internal security measures. Suffice to say, knowing it exists and getting anywhere near it are two profoundly different matters. But all right; perhaps you're correct that this and the murder are unrelated."

"I never said that," Makk said. "Did you say that?"

"I didn't say that either," Daska said.

"You started by saying you thought Orno walked out of the vault with this doodad of yours," Makk said, "and then tried to pass it off by saying it was his murder that put this idea in your head. Is that the only reason you're ready to pin it on him?"

"Detective, there have been two highly improbable crimes in the past two weeks. One was Orno's murder. The other was that someone stole a priceless, irreplaceable artifact. It would be as foolish to *not* think of them as connected as it would be to have you investigating one without being aware of the other. I don't know if they're related, or how, but if the second crime helps us resolve the first crime, all the better. So again, I ask: if you come across the missing item, please return it."

"I get it," Makk said.

"Can you at least tell us *why* it's so important?" Daska asked.

"Have I not been doing that all along, Detective Daska?"

"I guess? I wasn't raised by the House like my partner was. I understand that there are some things the House wants to keep locked up in a vault. Corporations do the same thing, right? Trade secrets and all that. Maybe this is what we're talking about here, too. But it's funny...when I can see your whole face, Highness, it's easier to pick up things. Like, whenever you talk about this missing artifact of yours...you look scared. You can't tell us what it is, but it's not just about wanting to keep a secret. You're worried about what happens if it gets out. Why is that?"

He nodded slowly.

"I'm thinking now that I have forgotten what it's like to be face-naked to the world, and how unguarded that makes a man. The answer, Viselle Daska, is that we don't just keep secrets for our own sakes around here. We're not discussing proprietary chemical formulas or the blueprints for secret inventions, although we have our share of those here as well. No—and this, I hope, answers your questions as well, Detective Stidgeon—there are some things the world should never know about. We guard the secrets that could undo us all."

It took about ten minutes to get from Plaint's office and—after retrieving their guns—to Viselle's car, during which time neither of them spoke. This was mostly because it looked like Detective Daska was about to explode, and Makk didn't want to do anything to help that along.

They both noted—again, without talking—a black panel van sitting at the edge of the parking lot that wasn't there when they parked.

They climbed in, and closed the doors. Viselle started the car.

"You think those are Sentries?" she asked, quietly, as if they could hear her from fifty maders off.

"I dunno. Want me to walk over and ask?"

"No, I want to get out of here."

"Same."

Viselle pulled out, a little faster than she probably intended, and drove past the van.

"Yeah, they're following us," she said.

"Let them follow," Makk said. "We're cops, remember?"

"You'd think the badge would make me feel better, but I'm getting the idea that nobody here cares. I'm pretty sure that van can't fly."

"Don't you dare. Not unless you want me to throw up again."

She grunted. "That guy at Plaint's door. He was a Sentry, right? I didn't think they were a real thing until I saw him."

"Probably. Why are you so spooked?" Makk asked.

"You know exactly why."

Viselle was visibly resisting the urge to break with convention and go airborne from within the House campus. Makk was pretty sure that had the van followed them beyond the wall, she would have done it, never mind her partner's gag reflex. But the van stopped at the gates.

"We're clear," Makk said. "You want to smoke a bacco stick or something?"

"I'll pull over. We need to talk."

"Okay."

She didn't stop until they were around the corner and on a neighborhood side street, therefore theoretically out of view of the Septal campus.

"The *book*," she said, with 'book' coming out like an epithet. "He was talking about the book. We have to give it back to them. We can go back to the townhouse and claim we found it in a crawlspace or something. Do you have it on you? We can do it now."

"No, I don't have it on me, do you think I'm nuts?"

"Let's go get it. Just tell me where to go."

"He really rattled you, didn't he?"

"*Some things the world should never know about?* Tell me he didn't sound dead serious when he said that."

"He did, but...look, all Septals are a little crazy. It's part of their charm. From all I've heard, you have to be as good with Eglinat as Orno Linus was to even *read* the damn thing. Don't think the world is facing an imminent threat just yet."

"Makk..."

"Look, all that's changed between an hour ago and now is the Septals just became suspects, because whatever walked out of that vault is clearly important enough to kill over."

Viselle Daska's nose wrinkled when she was thinking hard about something that she disagreed with. Makk was noticing this for the first time, and found it weirdly cute. Then he was annoyed that he reacted that way.

"I would think the opposite," she said. "I'd think that would take them *out* of the running. If Professor Linus stole something from the vault, I get they may want it back enough to kill over it —they seem that kind of...*charming*, like you said—but killing the guy who can tell them where to find it doesn't make any more sense now than it did before. His murder makes this *harder* for them, not easier. Otherwise, High Hat Plaint wouldn't be talking to us about it at all."

"I agree," Makk said, "if we're still talking about a book."

Viselle sighed, lowered a window, and lit a bacco stick. Makk had been joking about doing that; he didn't know she even smoked. She offered one to Makk, who declined.

"Why wouldn't we be talking about a book?" she asked, after a long drag.

"He kept swapping in the word *artifact* to lead us away from the idea that it was a book under discussion, and I can't think of any reason for him to do that other than it not being a book. So let's say we're not, and Linus took *two* things from the vault. We know the book was in his townhouse. Let's say the second thing wasn't. *Now* are the Septals suspects?"

She thought some more.

"Maybe," she said. "If Orno no longer had it and told the killer all he knew? Like who he gave it to?"

"Or if it was going up for sale in his brother's Black Market," Makk suggested.

"No, it still doesn't make sense. Killing Professor Linus draws all kinds of unwanted attention. Even if it was to send a message, whoever had their missing artifact would just go underground. If they were planning to sell it on the Market, this would *dissuade* them, making it harder for the House to find them."

"You're right," Makk said, smiling. "This was a crime of passion, anyway. Orno wasn't killed with intent by a professional, after having been questioned. The only person more surprised by Orno's death than Orno was the killer, I'm thinking."

"So you were just testing me," she said. "Just now."

"It helps me to know someone else arrived at the same place I had," he said. "Also, you shouldn't be afraid of the Septals. They should be afraid of you. Start thinking of them as just another piece in the puzzle."

"And Plaint's *artifact*?"

"It's probably the book. Seems unlikely that Linus managed to smuggle *two* precious, irreplaceable objects from what's purportedly the most secure place in Inimata. But I don't think he was killed over a missing artifact."

"Then we can return the book," she said.

"I didn't say that."

"At least check it into evidence. Say we found it on a second pass."

"Nope."

"You're exasperating."

"I know."

She tossed the butt of the stick out the window and raised it.

"All right," she said. "Then we're back where we started. What now?"

"Tomorrow go through the other people on the DNA list. One of them killed our guy. As long as we keep that in mind, we'll be fine. The rest of this stuff is a distraction.

"It's a long list."

"Yeah, well these things don't get solved overnight."

Chapter Ten

Elicasta couldn't stop watching the vid. It was looped on the Streamcast of an UnVeeser she never met, whose content she'd never bothered to consume. His name was Zam the Madman, and after a cursory skim of his content, it was apparent that what she was looking at now was the first vid Zam ever streamed in which nobody took off their clothes.

Zam the Madman ran skin content, just about exclusively. She couldn't tell how 'core it was, but the titles didn't sound soft. Elicasta would have to pay a *lot* more to see one of those vids than she did to witness the events recorded in Orno Linus's backyard, and she wasn't sufficiently curious about Zam's content to do that.

"He's flush enough to buy it," she said to herself.

She was watching the vid on her 'top computer, at the end of a frustrating day. She'd been publishing content on the regular, but it was almost all pre-sched content: reviews and recs, mostly. The kind of stuff she can record ahead of time and run whenever. What she *couldn't* do, was post a decent follow to the Linus murder story. She'd done a couple of short bits from outside Twenty-One Central, but all her access points had dried up. Worse, she already knew a bomb was about to drop on the case, and didn't know how deep she wanted to get into it before that happened. Last thing she wanted was to put out something that got contradicted.

Problem being, it took two days for the vid to drop, which was forever in Stream time. It left her paralyzed. She was blue from holding her breath.

It didn't even make sense. Any right-minded Streamer would have flipped the vid as soon as the unedited copy landed in their box, if for no other reason than to beat the rush. No telling how straight-up the seller was. Even if the sold vid was blockstamped, there were ways to source-copy it beforehand.

They could have sold it more than once, essentially. Nobody who knew their business would have risked being *second* to market; not for the amount of money it must have taken to get the deal done.

But Zam didn't do that. Instead, he waited two days. It was maddening. She *had* to know why.

That was just the first of a long list of questions Elicasta had, for Zam the Madman, and for whoever sold the vid to him. (More questions, if the seller also shot the video.) Another good one, was exactly who was in it.

The full vid began the same way as the teaser vid, with the drone orienting on the backyard from a good distance and a great height away. Orno Linus opened his back door, said something—there still wasn't an audio component—and then held open the door. Eventually, and possibly reluctantly, given the delay, a fully robed Septal crossed the threshold. Orno closed the door again, and that was it for act one.

Act two was twenty-two minutes later, according to the timestamp. It was a direct cut, which Elicasta had a problem with. Whoever made it could have opted to skip-speed through in order to make it clear that nothing happened in the middle. They didn't do that. The implication was that it was irrelevant, and maybe it was, but it opened the door to the possibility that something was being hidden in the cut.

If Elicasta had purchased this vid, the first thing she would have asked for was the footage between the takes, so she could determine this for herself.

What happened after the twenty-two minutes was that the lone Septal who entered previously opened the back door and stepped outside, closed the door, and turned around.

Then they lowered their hood, looked up at the sky, and took a deep breath. This act gave the drone an excellent look at the Septal's face.

Then the hood went up, and the Septal disappeared into the night.

Elicasta didn't recognize them, but the Stream came through within seconds of the vid's go-live.

If the consensus idents from the Stream were to be believed, the mystery Septal was Dorn Jimbal, the Other who found the body three days later.

"Why would you come back?" she asked the still image of Dorn on her computer. "I thought Septals were supposed to be smart."

She needed to hit up Zam the Madman, hopefully in a way that didn't make her skin crawl. But regular channels wouldn't do it. Even before he aired the vid, his inbox had to be at least as bad as hers; nothing she could get to him would go through. She was going to have to find someone who could get her a face-to.

According to his stream's launch page, Zam was from Velon. That could be an outright lie—much in the way she benefitted from carrying a residence in Palavin Quarter, tagging yourself as a Velonian was a plus on the Stream—but usually it was easy to spot a counterfeit. Plus, the vid was recorded in Velon and had probably been sold locally.

Elicasta didn't know who else was on the vid pitch blast, but if the seller was smart, it only went to Veesers with the clout to pay, who were already in on the story from the ground. That meant her, and the dozen other Verified Streamers at the presser. And all of them were Velonians.

On the other hand, Zam the Madman was an UnVeeser, and he got in on the bid. Maybe the seller wasn't all that smart.

"Wicha," she said. "She'll know this skeeve."

Wicha wasn't answering.

Elicasta had taken the stairs to her friend's condo and rapped on the door for long enough to figure Wicha had either tuned out or stepped out. It was a little weird, given the time of day. Wicha had a large international follow; she claimed she was the biggest livestream in Lladn from twenty-o'clock to one-o'clock. It was just past ten o'clock local, and while Elicasta wasn't a hundred percent on the time skip, she was pretty sure it was close to a match.

She skimmed her voicer until she landed on Wicha's Stream, and confirmed the girl wasn't live.

Then she started to wonder if something was wrong.

Elicasta exited the voicer's Stream conduit and accessed the key app, then called up Wicha's door lock. This was a mutual thing between them, an emergency-only buddy system set up between two women with a history of dealing with highly motivated stalkers. It had never been necessary before, thankfully.

She swiped the voicer over the sensor, the door went green, and she let herself in.

"Wicha?" she called out. "What's up, bitch? You here?"

No answer.

Wicha's condo was about two-thirds the footprint of Elicasta's, but it was laid out effectively the same way. Only, Wicha didn't have an office with themed walls. She livestreamed in two places: the fake cabana on her porch, and her bedroom.

She wasn't in either place. Nor was she in any other part of the condo.

Which was fine; it just meant Wicha was out running down a story or something. She wasn't much for face-to's to get her stories, but maybe she was trying something new, or working a new location or...well, something. Something not sinister or awful.

Elicasta could only hold onto the non-sinister explanation for a few seconds, which was how long it took for her to find Wicha's headgear.

Wicha's central terminal—where she did all her editing and probably most of her Stream-consuming—was a three 'top setup in a corner of her living/dining room. One of the computers was lit but sleeping. Next to it was Wicha's rig.

It wasn't a state-of-the-art optical rig, like Elicasta's. It was heavier, it had fewer housed edit features, and the aug-real functionality was crude. But if she was anything like Elicasta—and she was—Wicha would have worn her gear in all the same places 'Casta did, which was everywhere except the shower and the bed when she was sleeping. (Wicha probably also took her gear into the shower. The rig was waterproof—so was Elicasta's—and Wicha was the kind of Streamer who might use a shower-shot to boost her sub base.) In other words, short of a sudden retirement. 'Casta couldn't think of one reason for Wicha to leave home without it.

Or rather, no *good* reason.

Elicasta sat down at the desk and woke up the computer.

"Wicha, that you?" asked someone from the hallway.

Bogdis poked his head in, through the open front door. Elicasta hadn't bothered to close it, both because it was a secure building and because she forgot.

"Oh, hey, 'Casta," he said, on seeing her. "Is she around?"

Bogdis was a Veeser from one flight up. He did touristy travel stuff, mostly, with a little shopping porn thrown in. Wicha's place wasn't on the way to his unless he took the stairs and then wandered a little. She'd think this meant he was *checking up* on Wicha for somewhat more salacious reasons, except Elicasta was nearly positive Bogdis was gay.

"She's not here," Elicasta said. "When was the last time you saw her?"

"Strange query. Not positive."

"Today? Yesterday? Answer's not hard."

"Might've been yesterday. I saw her livestream wasn't spinning is all. She must be out."

Elicasta held up her friend's gear.

"Honus's balls," Bogdis said. "She must be in trouble. She *sleeps* with that on. Is the panic flag up?"

"Doesn't look like it. She took it off on her own."

Bogdis fast-walked into the room, an odd little wobble that Veesers without proper headset stabilizers learned to perfect. Bog had long since graduated to the pricier gear, but once you learn that walk it's hard to unlearn it. Elicasta trained herself out of it, but it took time.

He took Wicha's gear from Elicasta and started turning it around, as if he had a higher tech proficiency than she did. Or maybe he was just trying to get a psychic glean off of it or something. 'Casta ignored him and went back to the computer screen she'd just woken up.

The screen was ident-locked. Nothing crazy-sophisticated, but she didn't have one of Wicha's eyeballs, so she wasn't going to be getting any further than the desktop. The security layer was a transparent, so the front screen icons were visible—albeit fuzzy—underneath.

"Wild," he said. "So, you don't know where she is, or when she's due back."

"No. And I'm a little worried. Did she say anything to you, when you talked to her...what was it, yesterday?"

"Um. Kinda. It's why I'm here. She owed me credits."

"Real? How much?"

"I'd rather not say. But it wasn't insubstantial. She said to come back today and she'd have it in-hand. Clean C-Coin."

Wicha, what did you get into? Elicasta wondered.

"Totally face-up, I figured you'd be more in-the-know than I am," he said.

"Well, we're friends, but we're not so tight as that."

"She played you up then," he said. "You sure you weren't working a deal with her? I'm saying, she didn't drop the details on how she was planning to come into all that coin, but she *did* make out like you were complicit."

"That's just the Veeser cred rub-off," she said. "Remember what it was like when you were an Unverified? She must have given you the same kinda respect."

"Not really. My angle's not her thing. But I mean, you had her helping with your messages, right? And you just let yourself into her place. I half-figured you two were coupling on the sly."

"We weren't. What about my messages?"

"She was skimming your hotfile for you," he said. Then he laughed at her puzzled expression, which he evidently interpreted as dishonest. "Come on. She showed me the folder. Don't play."

Elicasta looked at the blurry icons behind the ident overlay.

Maybe...

"Focus," she told her eyepatch optical. Then her high-end gear did its level best to bring what her eye was looking at into focus. She'd never tried doing this on something that was natively blurry before, but the *best-guess* element of the aug-real algo should work effectively the same way.

It didn't help much, but it was enough. Wicha *did* have a folder with Elicasta's name on it.

"You really didn't know this?" Bogdis asked.

"She has a key to my place," Elicasta said. "Just like I have one to hers. She must have let herself in and set up a backdoor dump on my computer. Now I'm thinking she read something she maybe shouldn't have."

"Like what?"

"Like an invite to an auction. Hey, you don't know an Unverified named Zam the Madman, do you?"

Bogdis laughed. "You really did not know her," he said. "This is a trip."

"Why do you say that?"

"Zam's name in the real is Kiz Libbat, and he's Wicha's boyfriend. Why're you asking on him?"

It seemed impossible that Bogdis, the somewhat annoying travel-and-shopping Veeser knew Wicha Reece better than Elicasta, and yet the evidence appeared to be unmistakable. He not only knew Wicha was dating the erstwhile Zam the Madman, who was now perhaps the most famous Streamer alive, but knew his pedestrian real name, and *where he lived.*

Apparently, large portions of the building routinely engaged in social gatherings to which Elicasta was neither privy nor invited. Were it not for the fact that she found most of them annoying, she might have been upset by this news. In this case, it just left her frustrated, because she despised being outside of an information loop.

As much as she wanted to ask Bogdis why none of them saw fit to include her in these events, she decided such questions could wait until after she'd caught up with her friend.

That was provided she still wanted to call the woman a friend after learning that she'd backdoored Elicasta's system, who knows how long ago. The *second* thing she would do, after finding Wicha and interrogating Kiz Libbat, would be to get a cyber espionage expert to take Elicasta through exactly how much of her system had been compromised.

First, she had a story to chase down. As embarrassing as this was, her oft-topless Unverified Streamer erstwhile friend intercepting a private auction message and then, with the financial backing of her core porn UnVeeser boyfriend, outbidding the field for the hottest vid on the Stream, could be a heck of a story... if Elicasta told it right. It was a great way to reinsert herself in the Linus murder, straight-up, and would spin off into a victim card story or three.

Again, if she told it right.

On top of that, there were all the questions she had about the vid, which could spin new angles entirely. She just needed Wicha and Kiz to spill the name of the seller, and maybe finger how much of what Zam the Madman aired was straight from the raw file, and how much he tweaked himself, if anything.

Kiz lived in Geoghis Quarter, a couple of kalomaders from Mausoleum Park, in a decently upscale neighborhood mainly consisting of private brownstones. After shedding Bogdis—who couldn't apparently conceive of a future in which Wicha would *not* return shortly and pay him his credits—Elicasta got there the fastest way she knew how: ordering an aero cab.

It was stupid expensive, but the way she saw it, the only two possibilities here were that Wicha was in serious danger, or Zam the Madman was about to cash out his brand to the highest bidder and skip town with his girlfriend to live in a hut in Canos-Holo. (The last half was pure conjecture, but the *sell out and skip* was a solid assumption.) Either way, urgency was called for.

The aero picked her up from the roof, climbed up to a commercial travel lane—above the Hyperline, and the city traffic and the aero commuters—and then dropped down again to near-street level almost immediately. It gave Elicasta's stomach a tumble, as the car's trajectory stuck to a parabolic arc nearly the whole trip.

"Hoah, check me that address," the driver said. He had a heavy islander accent. Not Canos-Holo, but definitely tropical in flavor. She couldn't quite peg it.

Elicasta rechecked it for him.

"Ya, okay. I don't think I can take you straight," he said. "Maybe a block."

"What's the issue," she asked.

"Check it," he said, pointing down and to their right. Black smoke was pouring out of a building in Geoghis Quarter. Two alarm trucks were at the scene with three police cruisers, and two more of each on the way. A fire helo was inbound too, on the same horizontal as her cab; they'd be shutting down the airspace next.

"Hoping no," she said. "That's not the address."

"You can hope. The on-board say it so. It been wrong, one, two times. This could be another."

"You're saying that's the brownstone I wanted to visit."

"That's what I say."

"Put me down up the block. I'll hoof it."

He set down around the corner from the scene. She hopped out and paid him just as another pollie flew past, with the dome lights spooled and sirens roaring.

She turned her headgear on and ran to the corner, nearly bowling over a couple of UnVeeser alarm truck chasers who always turned up at this kind of sitch. They weren't going to have the whole story.

"Record audio," she said. Then: "This is Elicasta Sangristy, live in the Geoghis Quarter. Something's up, babes. The pollies are heavy, and you'll never guess who lives in that walk-up."

Chapter Eleven

Makk backed up the vid and played it again. It was the twenty or thirtieth time, at least—he'd been at it for close to an hour—but it seemed as if every time he played it he noticed something new, and wrong.

Exactly nothing about it made sense, but that didn't seem to bother anybody but him.

"You're going to wear it out," Viselle said.

They'd set her up at a desk adjoining his, which seemed like a silent affirmation that their partnership would be continuing beyond this case. Makk wasn't sure what to think about that, but was nearly positive he had no say in it either way.

"I don't think you can run down a vid," he said. "It's not like the old magnotapes."

"I know. I was joking. You *are* going to bust that keyboard though, if you keep mashing the back arrow. It's Dorn Jimbal. What else do you need to know?"

"I don't know that at all."

She laughed.

"Come on, Makk. You think it'll turn into someone else on the fifty-first view?"

"Maybe. I'll let you know when I get there."

He didn't make it to view fifty-one, because then Captain Llotho walked in.

~

This was not how Makk's day was supposed to go—although he was thinking this was perhaps something he'd have to get used to until this case got solved. He was *supposed* to be sleeping, though, at this moment and for another three or four hours. Then, after an insufficient amount of sleep (but enough to power through the day) he and Detective Daska were going to be heading directly to the Andel Quarter, to start questioning suspects regarding their whereabouts on the day of the murder.

It would be a nice, normal murder investigation then, and hopefully it would stay that way. DNA tracing wasn't perfect, but it was pretty damn good, and this wasn't an organized, preplanned kill. The murderer was on their list. It might take a while to pin them down, but this was how cases broke.

He was asleep maybe an hour when his badge went active and Llotho hit him up.

"I need you back here as soon as possible," he said, before Makk had a chance to get in so much as a yawn.

"If you want me to solve the Linus murder, I'm going to need to sleep at least another couple," Makk said.

"It looks like the Stream solved it *for* you, detective."

"What's that supposed to mean?" A part of him hoped it meant that he could definitely sleep some more, what with the case solved.

"It means put on some pants and get down here," Llotho said.

Makk watched the vid the first few times on his badge, from the back of an app-car. It was a midday drop—ten o'clock, right when Makk checked in to bed—on a sub-only Streamcast belonging to someone named Zam the Madman. Makk didn't have to pay Zam anything to watch it, because by eleven o'clock it had been picked up by two-dozen Corper feeds.

Central had a loop of the vid waiting for him by the time he reached his desk. Since Captain Llotho wasn't there—although Viselle was, looking as if she'd gotten a full eight of sleep, a shower, and a meal—Makk had time to look at the vid a bunch more.

"You two, with me," Llotho said, on his way by their desks. He didn't sound *angry*, which was potentially good news. He was speed-walking, though, which Makk recognized as a bad sign. His initial absence from the floor was likely due to him being in the middle of one or more meetings with Important People, likely relating to the very same vid that Makk had been obsessing over.

"Close the door," Llotho said, as soon as they were in his office. He had the nicest one on the floor, which wasn't saying all that much given what it was compared to. It was on the corner, with north-facing windows that never quite got the full brunt of the sunlight. He couldn't see the Tether, but he had a nice view of Norg Hill.

"Was Jimbal a suspect?" the captain asked, before he'd even gotten around the desk.

"Everyone's a suspect," Makk said, "until they aren't."

"I'm not interested in a game of semantics, Detective Stidgeon."

"I only mean that we didn't rule them out, because we haven't had time to rule anybody out, all the way up to the High Hat and the people in this room."

"Right, well I have an alibi," Llotho said.

"Me too," Daska said. "We didn't take them *seriously* as a suspect, to answer your question."

"*Thank* you," the captain said. "See, Stidgeon? Nice and direct. Why not?"

"Their only connection to the scene was finding the body," she said. "Linus had been dead for three days."

"You didn't know that at the time."

"He smelled three days' dead," Makk said. "Look, Jimbal's DNA was found at the scene, so they're in the pile of suspects just like all the other matches. But we already talked to them, and we were satisfied with what they had to say. We didn't rule them *out*, but the right course until about two hours ago was to go down the list of other matches. No reason not to circle back on Jimbal if we got something contradictory out of someone else, but we weren't there yet."

"But, as Daska said, you didn't take them seriously," Llotho said.

"Concluding the kid killed Linus, and then when nobody else turned up to find the body decided to go back three days later and call us? Not the most promising theory, no."

"Maybe that was exactly why they went back," Llotho said. "So you'd think that. And then they'd have an explanation for their DNA being at the scene."

"They didn't *need* an explanation; Linus was their professor. Jimbal had been there a bunch of times, just like all the other matches to the professor's students that we got off the scan. Say Jimbal did it. The longer Linus is dead on the floor, the more the physical evidence deteriorates. The kid just wouldn't have benefitted from calling attention to it."

"We're not just *supposing* they maybe did it, detective," Llotho said. "We've got some pretty good visual evidence."

"It's not bad," Makk said. "I'm not convinced."

"You're not convinced," Llotho repeated, flatly.

"I think someone powerful wants this case to be closed sooner rather than later, and served up a doctored vid to the Stream to make that happen."

Captain Llotho stared at him for a few seconds, without commenting. He turned to Daska.

"And you?" he asked.

"The vid's provenance would be nice," she said. "Underlying source data can mark an altered image. Can't do that with a Streamcast; we'd need the raw file."

"Sure, and we'll get that. What do you think about what you *saw*."

She moved around uncomfortably in her seat.

"It didn't look spoofed to me," she admitted. "I spent enough time in cyber to know how to spot a mocked-up vid, and this looked really clean. That could just mean someone who is *very* good at their job mocked it up, but I don't think that's what this was. Sorry, Makk."

"It's fine," Makk said. "Just means we need to find the guy who Streamed the vid and get to who he bought it from."

"That sounds like the least promising of our options," Llotho said. "Go pick up the kid first and see if their story's changed."

"I'm not prepared to do that," Makk said.

"You don't really have a choice here, Makk," Llotho said. He said it in a tone that was friend-to-friend, but what he meant was, he would be ordering Makk to arrest Dorn Jimbal by the end of this meeting, whether or not he wanted to.

"We can only hold him for so long without charges," Makk said, "and I don't see enough to charge him yet. I know getting to whoever recorded that drone shot's a tough ask, but if we don't do it, I guarantee their defense attorney will. We're better off confirming it first."

"And you don't think they did it," Llotho said. "Let's put that on the table."

"I don't." He looked at Daska. "And I don't think you do either."

"I'm still new at this," she said. "I don't know what I think yet."

"When you met them, did they seem like the kind of person who could stove in the back of their professor's head, and then go back three days later to, I dunno, revel in the kill or burnish what was already a perfectly good alibi? And then lie to our faces from a few feet away for a half an hour? Were they that kind of person, detective?"

"No, she said. "They didn't strike me as that sort of person."

"Me neither."

"We have to collect them anyway," Llotho said. "If not to charge them then for their own protection. They just got outed as the prime suspect in the murder of Calcut Linus's brother; they'll *need* protecting. Speaking of, you talk to Calcut yet?"

"Calcut's not in our suspect pool," Makk said. "No DNA at the scene."

"That isn't what I asked."

"Haven't found the time. But he did express an interest in a conversation."

"Find room in your schedule, *after* the two of you have taken Dorn Jimbal into custody. As a favor; it makes my life easier. Now I've got representatives from the House downstairs who are here to assist you in retrieving Other Jimbal."

Makk thought this was interesting.

"Do you now? When did *they* arrive?"

"About a half an hour ago. The vid had been live for 90 minutes, if you're curious about the timing. They offered to hold Jimbal for us, and even bring them to the station. I had to notify them that that's not technically legal. They seemed displeased."

The House sent three Sentries—two men and a woman. They were dressed in matching black uniforms, with those interesting-looking wrap-around visors built into their hoods.

Unlike the Sentry at the entrance to the High Hat's office, none of these three looked like they were armed.

That didn't mean they weren't; Makk couldn't recall if the laws governing concealed weapons applied to the House, but had a feeling even if they did, the Septals would find a way to contravene it.

The head of the team introduced himself as Brother Corland, skipped the part where the other two had names, and then they were all heading for the garage.

"Will there be additional officers joining us?" Corland asked.

"I'm not going to make this a show," Makk said. "We're not hunting down a fugitive and we're not arresting them. We just need some questions answered."

Corland stepped in front of Makk, which was the only way to get Makk's attention, as he was actively interested in pretending the House Sentries weren't even there.

"You mean to do this quietly, you're saying," Corland said.

"That *is* what I mean, yes. I don't want some wandering UnVeeser to hit the Stream with the story of Dorn Jimbal's arrest, and that's what happens if we show up on campus with ten cop cars blazing. Detective Daska and I will go to their residence in her unmarked and politely ask them to accompany us downtown, and that's all that will be happening. Do you think your team can handle that degree of subtlety?"

Corland looked at the other two. It felt like the three of them were conducting a conversation nobody else could hear.

"We're very good at subtle, detective," the unnamed Sister Septal said.

"If you want to draw as little attention as possible, we can help," Corland agreed. "Your arrival on campus will draw attention, no matter how unobtrusive the vehicle. Whereas we will blend in."

"You're going to sneak us onto the grounds, is that what you're offering?"

"I think it addresses your concerns. And we're driving an aero; I'm sure time is a factor?"

Makk so disliked this idea, he was ready to go back to the part about sending in ten police cruisers with the lights up and making a scene. It offended his sense of how this power dynamic was supposed to go—where he was an officer of the law dealing with a security guard with a better-than-average clothing budget—but he also thought if they picked up Jimbal too loudly, Jimbal would clam up and the people above Llotho would press for formal charges.

It was a little easier to take if he thought of Corland as regular police, just from a different section of town, but he was having a lot of trouble making that leap. There was also the little voice in the back of his head (it sounded like Leemie) with warnings about Septal hit squads, and how if he got into the back of a House Sentry car, it would be the last time anyone saw him. This was silly and paranoid, but also very hard to ignore.

"How big is your car?" Makk asked.

"It's a widewagon," Corland said. "Tinted windows. Nobody will know you're there until you want them to."

Makk looked at Viselle. She shrugged.

"Okay, but I need to make a direct first," Makk said.

A few minutes later—after Makk told Llotho to send four cruisers to the campus edge, in case he needed immediate backup—they were sitting in the last row of a decently upscale aero widewagon.

The vehicle could seat twelve. It was the kind of thing temple groups took on outings, or schools used for class trips with a low headcount. Except that this one could fly.

What it was *not*, was the panel van that had followed them off-campus the prior evening.

Makk took the seat in the back, where he had the least chance of throwing up *on* someone. Or he would have, had Viselle not sat in the same row. The three Septals stuck to the front.

"Tell me," Viselle said, as Corland's unnamed male associate drove them to the roof, "what struck you as off about that vid?"

"You want to do this here?" he asked.

She looked at the three Septals, who were far enough away to arguably be sitting in a different car.

"Don't think they can hear us," she said.

"Unless there are listening devices in the wagon. Yes, the House does make me a little paranoid."

"I already knew that. I'm just curious, and we have time to kill. And you're less likely to vomit if you're preoccupied."

He laughed.

"All right. For starters, there's the twenty-two-minute gap. I'd really like to know what happened then. Maybe someone else came out and they don't want us to see that. Even a lousy defense lawyer would start with that."

"Fair," Viselle said. "Could be hiding something."

"Like the *actual* killer exiting. Another thing: the hood. Why'd Jimbal take the hood off? You're running from a crime and you stop and remove the *one* thing that makes you look like everyone else in a ten-block radius, and then what? Smile for the optical? It makes about as much sense as returning to the scene three days later. And are we even a hundred percent sure that's what Jimbal's face looks like?"

"You recognized it as them just as fast as I did," Viselle said.

"Yeah. But you were as close to them as I was the other night, and all I *saw* was their mouth and chin. That could have been someone else on the vid."

"Okay. We can satisfy that much of our curiosity today, right? Compel them to remove the hood?"

"Only if they're formally under arrest," he said. "Before that, all we can do is ask nicely. But even if that *is* Dorn, and they did take the hood off, and it's a match...I'm still not on board with this until I know what I'm missing in that twenty-two-minutes.

Because here's another thing: someone took the murder weapon out of that townhouse."

She gasped.

"And Dorn's hands were empty," she said. "Why didn't you point that out to Llotho?"

"It wouldn't have changed anything. We still gotta pick up Other Jimbal, before the Linus family or one of these helpful Sentries decide we're not moving fast enough in our investigation."

"Detectives?" Corland said, from the front passenger seat. He had a voicer in his hand. "We may have a problem. Nobody can find Other Jimbal."

"Sorry, I must have heard wrong," Makk said. "Did you guys try to detain my suspect after you were told specifically that we did not want you to do that?"

"I arranged to put eyes on them until you got there, that's all. Problem is, we can't put eyes on them. Jimbal's not at home and not at the class that's listed on their itinerary. They haven't logged into any of the libraries, and so far, we haven't been able to locate them on an outdoor path. I had Jimbal's voicer pinged a minute ago, to narrow down the search, but according to the pingback, they're in the apartment. Which we know not to be the case."

"Exactly *when* did you begin this search?"

"I don't think that's relevant right now, Detective Stidgeon. The pertinent issue is that Other Jimbal is hiding, and may have left campus."

Dorn lived in an apartment with three other Septals, one of whom was home, but exactly as helpful as the two who were not.

All he could say for certain was that Dorn Jimbal wasn't there, and he couldn't say when he last saw them. Also, they didn't do it.

"I don't care what vid evidence you have," he said, in the tone of an adult speaking to a mentally impaired dog, "Dorn isn't capable of killing anyone."

"We understand," Viselle said, and it sounded like she *really did* understand, which was a gift. Between Dorn and their roommate —his name was Brother Wollafing—it was clear that questioning young men with Viselle Daska standing next to Makk was significantly easier. "But we can't clear this up without Other Jimbal's help," she continued.

"I mean not only is Dorn constitutionally, physically, and temperamentally incapable of murder; they're *philosophically* incapable of doing so. Dorn is a vegetarian who was raised on a cattle ranch. I don't know that either of you can appreciate how contrary their diet is to that of their family and peers. I once found them carrying a beetle in a scarf. They'd found it in their bedroom, but rather than crush it with a shoe, they took it to a field and set it free. And I doubt I have to tell either of you how unwelcome a disciple of Pal can be in the countryside."

"We get it," Makk said, "they've had a tough life and they wouldn't hurt an actual bug. But that vid's pretty good evidence that they were *there*, and they didn't tell us that the last time we spoke to them. So now we gotta talk to them again, and they're not around."

"I don't know where Dorn could have gone."

"You said that. Can you tell us who *might* know?"

"Not really. Dorn isn't an outgoing sort. They don't make friends easily."

"Are *you* their friend?" Viselle asked.

Brother Wollafing smiled gently.

"No," he said. "I'm their roommate. I've found it's difficult to be both of those things at once."

"Right," Makk said. "Let me ask you this: did you ever see Dorn without the hood?"

Wollafing thought about it. "I don't recall having done so, no. If I had, it would have been an accident."

"Even in front of other Septals?" Makk asked. "I understand that's okay when you're around each other."

"For some. Not for a Fundamentalist like Dorn."

Makk wanted to ask if Dorn Jimbal was really a Fundamentalist or if they just preferred to dress like one. In his experience, Fundies didn't take to science that well, yet Jimbal was working on a thesis relating to orbital mechanics. The only reason he didn't ask was that he didn't think Wollafing knew the answer.

"You're saying they won't even take their hood off in the privacy of this apartment?" Makk asked, instead.

"They never did so in front of me, detective. I'm certain they did when they were alone. Basic hygiene would mandate it."

"And you saw the vid, right?"

"I imagine the entire campus has seen the vid by now."

"You don't think it's a little weird, Dorn taking off their hood?"

He shrugged. "If they thought they were alone, I don't see why they wouldn't. It isn't the most jarring element of the video."

"What *is* the most jarring element?"

"That it exists at all. As I said..."

"I know, I know. Wouldn't hurt a bug."

Makk stepped away from the interview, leaving Daska behind to do the propers.

He caught Corland's attention as the Sentry was getting off a direct. Corland was standing in the dormitory hallway, mainly because the apartment itself was too small for as many people as were currently searching it: four bedrooms orbiting a common room with a tiny kitchen and a tinier bathroom. For most of the city, that many rooms might qualify as a penthouse, except the total amount of space was somehow less than Makk's own living room.

"Still nothing?" Makk asked.

"No," Corland said. "My authority ends at the wall, though. Seems to me you have a potential murderer loose in the city; you should consider alerting the city of that fact."

"This city has plenty of potential murderers walking around. I don't think anyone cares."

"I'm saying—"

"Yes, I understand what you're saying. Before I put out an All-Eyes on some scared kid, I wanna make sure they didn't just decide to go on a long walk. I can't get that worm back in the can once the lid's off."

"We're rapidly exhausting alternatives where the explanation is innocent," Corland said. "We're speaking to their professors now, but they aren't close to any of them. The only one Jimbal *was* close to was killed last week."

Makk appreciated Corland's tact, in not saying Jimbal *killed* that professor.

"Let me ask you something," Makk said. "Does the House keep a, I don't know, a face book of some kind?"

"I'm not understanding you."

"A record of what the Septals here look like without the hoods."

"No, we don't do that. And I'll go you one further. If you think they're going to try and pass as a non-Septal by going face-naked? You won't find a photo of them beyond the age of four. Most of us don't take unhooded photos."

"Is that mandated?"

"Not in this chapter, but we're a bit more liberal. Point being, if you're looking for something to show around town, we can't help you. I'm betting you won't find anything like that in this apartment, and I'm guessing their parents won't have anything either."

"Beyond the age of four."

"That's what I'm saying. If I were you I'd pull a still from the vid and call it a day."

"Thanks for the advice," Makk said. "Hey, I love those boots."

Corland looked deeply confused by the statement, as this seemed to be an inappropriate moment to have a conversation about sartorial choices.

"Thanks?" he said. He lifted his boot and sort-of showed it off. In doing so, he gave Makk a decent look at the treads.

"They look pretty comfortable. Are those standard? I notice you guys all dress the same."

"It's part of the uniform, sure."

"So everyone in the House Sentry Squad or...whatever you call yourselves...has boots like that? I'm just wondering where I can get my hands on a pair. Do you think they're commercially available?"

"Is this a serious question, detective? I think we have more important things to worry about than footwear."

"Yeah, you're probably right."

They couldn't keep the campus manhunt under wraps for long. Eventually, they had to add to the House Sentry team by bringing in patrol officers from Central, and before long the whole city knew Dorn Jimbal was missing.

There was no point, then, in not submitting a formal All-Eyes. Makk's reluctance came from the part where he didn't think the kid did it, but it wasn't going to be long before that didn't matter either.

Night arrived, with no change. He and Daska were set up outside of Dorn's apartment building, in a row of like buildings, about four blocks from the crime scene. Officers and security were conducting door-to-doors, and calling in any tips they got.

The radio had been pretty quiet.

"What do you think?" he asked Daska as the evening wore on.

His stomach was growling, as this stupidly long day didn't have any time built into it for food.

"I don't think we're finding them here. That's what I think."

"There's a lot of House territory to hide in."

"Sure," she said, lighting up a bacco stick. "But if they're here, they'll have to come out eventually, for food or whatever. May not be tonight, but eventually. If Dorn doesn't want to be found, the best place to not be found isn't *here*, it's on the other side of the wall. You know this already."

"Yeah, I do. Problem is, I can't skip ahead, as much as I want to. Did they strike you as the kind of person with the resources to swing a vanish?"

"No, but what do we know about them? They grew up on a farm. Maybe it was a really big and lucrative farm."

"Septals are communal," Makk said. "They don't have private wealth. But you're right; nothing stopping their families from being well-off. I bet Orno Linus could tap his family money any time he needed it. Maybe we start there, with Jimbal's family."

"You called Dorn out as North Elonian," she said. "In the interview. I meant to ask; where did you pick up on that? Their accent?"

"Wild guess. I grew up calling the planet Dib. Dorn called it Dibble. Only a few places where that rolls off the tongue. One of them is Punkoah, and another is the Middle Kingdom."

"Both on North Eloni," she said.

"Yeah."

"It's also the House's stylistic preference."

"In text, sure," he said. "Not in conversation. But that's why it was a guess. We're going to need a full bio on them the longer they're missing, and then we'll know."

"Punkoah has a lot of cattle ranching," she said, referring back to what Brother Wollafing said about Dorn's upbringing.

"Sure does."

There was a Septal Sister standing on the sidewalk across from the cruiser Makk and Viselle were up against. Makk had been watching her for a couple of minutes; she kept acting like she wanted to approach, and then chickening out. But she wouldn't go away.

"Hey," he said. "Give me your pack."

"Sorry, I didn't offer you one. I thought you didn't smoke."

"I gave it up after the army. The stick isn't for me. Lighter, too."

Viselle handed both over. Makk put them into his jacket pocket and crossed the street. The young Sister looked about ready to run, but she didn't.

"Hi there," Makk said. "I saw you eyeing the smoke. Do you want one?"

He extended the pack. She stared at it, but didn't accept the offer.

"We're not supposed to smoke," she said.

"Sure. Septals aren't supposed to kill people either, and we already know it's been a bad week for that."

"No," she said, to the bacco stick. "No thank you."

"Okay. Then why don't you tell me what you want to tell me?"

"I don't know what you mean." She was trying to push herself through the wall at her back.

"Sure you do," he said. "What's your name?"

"Sister Mye," she said. "Fana."

Makk was pretty sure this was one of the names on his suspect list.

"Fana Mye. Nice to meet you. I'm Makk Stidgeon."

He extended his hand for a shake. She got a look at the symbol on his wrist, hesitated, smiled gently, and then shook his hand.

"I'm just trying to find Other Jimbal," Makk said. "I think they might be in trouble. Can you help?"

She nodded.

"Maybe," she said quietly.

"Do you know where they are?"

"I don't. But I think I saw them leave."

"Leave campus?"

"Yes," she said.

"When was this?"

"Last night. Just past sixteen."

"On foot?"

She shook her head. He was trying to work out why she seemed so nervous. It wasn't like *she* was being accused of anything.

"In a car?" Makk asked.

"Yes. It met them around the corner from their building. And I know it was Dorn; we shared a class with Professor Linus."

"Do you know what kind of car it was?"

"I don't know cars. It was expensive-looking."

"Did you see who was driving?" he asked.

"Sort of. Only in profile. It was a Septal, so most of the face was...you know."

"Okay," Makk said. "A Septal driving an expensive car is pretty unusual."

"I thought so too."

"I'm going to want to get a formal..."

She was shaking her head before he could finish the sentence.

"I'm not going on record," she said. "I only...I think Dorn is in trouble, and I want to help. But..."

A Sentry van rounded the corner and started up the street. She saw it and gasped.

"I'm sorry," she said. "I have to go."

Sister Mye spun around and ran down an alley between the buildings before Makk had a chance to get another word in. He nearly ran after her, but decided that would probably be a bad look. Assuming she gave her real name, she wouldn't be that difficult to find again.

He wondered why she was so afraid. The Sentries were intimidating, sure, but they were also Septals, and they were there to protect people like Sister Mye. He would have thought non-Septals had more reason to worry about them.

Once the van had passed, he walked back over to Viselle and returned the pack and lighter.

"Anything?" she asked.

"Yeah. Dorn Jimbal definitely left campus. And they had help."

"What kind of help?"

"Not positive. I've got a loose description of someone wearing a Septal hood and driving an expensive car, who picked up Dorn at around sixteen o'clock last night. I'd tell you more, but my witness is more afraid of Sentries than police officers for some reason."

"Expensive car, sixteen o'clock," Viselle said. "I can work with that."

Makk laughed.

"You want this?" he asked.

"Sure, sounds like fun."

"It's all yours," he said. "Just keep me updated."

Chapter Twelve

The fire burned into the evening. The alarm department managed to keep it from jumping to other properties—a miracle in a city with this kind of architectural congestion—but they couldn't save Kiz Libbat's place. They also couldn't save the two people who were inside of it when it went up.

Elicasta didn't *know* those two people were Kiz and Wicha. Usually, with stories like this, with info she felt pretty solid about but couldn't verify, she held back until that verification. This approach had served her really well; five or six times (out of hundreds) what she *thought* she knew turned out to be straight-up wrong, and her reluctance to let fly saved her from an embarrassing retraction.

This time, she ran with it. Sort of. What she said was: Kiz Libbat owned the place; Kiz Libbat was also known as Zam the Madman; Zam was dating Wicha Reece; neither Zam nor Wicha had streamed fresh since before the fire started; two bodies were found in the fire.

She left her subs to work out the last connection on their own, and skipped saying it out loud. If by some chance it turned out the corpses belonged to some randos—or if Kiz and Wicha staged their own deaths on the way out of town, which would be a twist worthy of the finest fic—Elicasta had cover.

She ended up running four near-live-at-the-scene bits for the Stream. As the only one with the connect between the blaze and Zam the Madman, she was getting tie-in reqs from all kinds of Veesers and Corpers, plus a dozen interview reqs from pretty reputable Exters. Since this story mainlined right to the Linus vid Zam streamed, and since Elicasta was the *only* Veeser with the story, her profile was rocketing.

But, she couldn't get a solid confirm on the identities of the corpses. This could have been because they were straight-up unidentifiable—which would be ideal if Kiz and Wicha were on their way to that theoretical hut in Canos-Holo—but it was hard to tell for certain. None of the pollies or the members of the alert team were particularly impressed with Elicasta's impeccable Veeser rep or her stratospheric profile; nobody was talking.

The murder cops turned up at the scene once the fire was out, as did an alert team arson specialist. Elicasta didn't have a history with any of them. If Makk Stidgeon had been one of the responders, she might have had a shot at wiggling some deets out of him, but no such luck. They also didn't ask for an off-the-optical interview, and didn't seem interested in associating the crime scene with the Linus case. That was assuming this was a crime scene at all, which Elicasta was definitely assuming.

Another thing she didn't say on-Stream, but certainly implied, was that Kiz and Wicha were murdered because of their connection to the drone-witness vid, which meant this was something bigger than some Septal monk killing their mentor in a fit of pique. It meant a conspiracy, and maybe a frame-up. And with both the House and the Linus family involved, there was no shortage of angles where such a thing was legit feasible.

That was the meat.

But maybe Twenty-One Central wasn't interested in such a

messy case. Better if this was unrelated to the other thing, and the Pal kid, Dorn Jimbal, brained their professor. Then all of this would go away.

Elicasta turned in her last Stream of the day at around eighteen, hailed a street cab, and got back to her building by eighteen-forty.

Instead of going straight up, she stopped by Wicha's place on the second floor. She was hoping to find Wicha there—although she didn't really expect to—with an explanation that fit the evidence better than *dying in a massive inferno.* Wicha wasn't, but Bogdis was.

"Did you even leave?" Elicasta asked. He jumped at the sound of her voice.

"By the Five, you startled me," he said. He was at a small table in the middle of the room; the component parts of Wicha's optical headgear were spread out on the table.

"What are you doing?" she asked.

"Trying to help. Hey, I caught your Streams. You must be in bank, huh?"

"For now. It's a hot story. I'm not dwelling."

"Still."

It was somewhat strangely the case that Elicasta didn't care about what her numbers looked like after the day she'd had. True, she knew she was hitting a most-watched status, either direct with her subs or through the ancillary tie-ins she'd approved. (Those tie-ins were bank on their own; she didn't give away anything on her Stream for free.) But she wasn't vibing on any of that. Right now, what she really wanted was to know the *whole* story.

"Real, what are you doing with her gear?" she asked again.

"Like I said, I'm trying to help."

He'd managed to detach the eyeball optical from the main unit, and unhook the skullcap lattice. The pieces for each part were laid out carefully on the table, in roughly the position they would end up being had the headgear been dismantled all at once by some magical force after which all the components settled on the table at equidistant points. It reminded her of the construction guidelines for a *some-assembly-needed* product.

"It's so I can put it together again," he said, on noting where Elicasta's attention had fallen. "You know, in case Wicha turns up and wants it back. Please don't move anything."

"Got it."

His current focus was on the core drive, which was a small rectangular box that rested at the base of the skull for most headsets. 'Casta's high-end gear held a petabyte, about half of which was needed to run the upscale functions. She usually dumped her feed direct to the Stream, so there wasn't much need for the other half of that petabyte's storage, but if it came down to it—if she had to deal with a long-term remote lag or if gods forbid the Stream went down for a time, she could store a ton of liveStreams in the core drive before having to worry about dumping it into her 'top's memory.

Elicasta didn't know Wicha's core drive capacity, but was pretty sure she couldn't afford a peta. It was multi-terabyte at best.

"She dumped her memory on the regular," Bogdis said. "To the tabletop, which we can't get into. But she only sent the true files, and her rig's always been glitchy. She bitched about it up and down."

Elicasta pulled a chair up to the table.

"Why are you thinking we want to get into the 'top?" she asked.

"You were trying to earlier. Wasn't until I caught your liveStream that I got the angle: that vid Zam Streamed was auctioned, only he didn't score the invite. You're thinking Wicha bartered that deal off *your* invite, which means somewhere in that 'top is the back-and-forth with the seller. That's what you're hot for."

"Solid work, for a travel Veeser."

"Thanks, I guess," he said.

"What's all that have to do with her headgear?"

"The glitch."

"You're looking for her glitch files?" she asked.

"She wouldn't have dumped them to the 'top, and who knows how often she cleared the decks of the junk. This old beast doesn't have a *ton* of onboard, so it might not be there, but I only need one file."

"I'm still behind, Bogdis. Walk me up."

"The nature of the glitch is where you're losing the thread. It happened when she was setting the up-closes. She had a balky drone, and a glitchy optical, and sometimes, *sometimes,* those two things would fail together. The drone wouldn't fly, and the optical would *flip,* but it wouldn't wait."

"It wouldn't wait? It would start recording?"

"It would start recording," he confirmed. "While the drone was still linked to the headset. Guess *what* it records when your optical flips while linked?"

"The eyeball," Elicasta said. "You're telling me there's a glitch file in that core drive that caught a super up-close of Wicha's eyeball."

"That's what I'm telling you. If we're lucky. If we're *extra* lucky, it's got the resolution we need to fool the login on her tabletop."

"Bogdis, I...that's super-smart. Thank you."

"I'm doing it for the byline, 'Casta. Don't get all pink."

If someone ever tried to force the core drive from Elicasta's rig, the drive would auto-encrypt. Not to say it would've been an unbreakable encryption, but without the key—which she had—it would take about seventeen thousand years to break it.

Wicha's core was older, and cheaper, and thankfully had no

such protections. It still took them until sometime past one to tap into it. First, Bogdis had to pry the drive from the case, which took an hour. This was mostly because of a need for precision. A hammer would have done it in a few minutes, but it would have destroyed the contents quite nicely.

The naked drive didn't do them much good either. They had to borrow a compatible jack from an UnVeeser named G-Giddy (he streamed club music and soft porn) on the first floor. Getting the drive to talk to one of Bogdis's laptops took them well past twenty-o'clock. Then it was another hour—with a break to consume an order from Kindonoodle at 20:30, because they were crashing—before they found the glitch file they needed.

"There it is!" Bogdis said, on a still of Wicha's eyeball.

"Great," Elicasta said. "Now how are we getting that in front of her computer optical?"

He lifted the 'top, and held it up next to his face.

"Like this?"

"That won't do," she said. "Reso on that 'top's not good enough. Hey, do you have a direct from the laptop to your own optical?"

He smiled. "I get you," he said.

Bogdis jacked the headset into the laptop and did something neither of them did very often: sent a file *from* the computer, *to* the optical.

"Display vid," Bogdis said. "Hold."

Then he took off his headset and flipped around the eyepatch optical.

"What do you think?" he asked.

"Best we can do. Let's give it a try."

She woke up Wicha's tabletop and got back to the ident-lock screen. Bogdis held up the eyeball at a distance from the pinhole camera, and waited.

The lock-screen faded out.

"Score," Bogdis said.

Elicasta went straight to the folder with her name on it and opened it up. As expected, she found her own *HP-IM* file in there.

"Dammit, Wicha," she muttered. "Kinda blew my trust here."

"Is that your dump folder?" Bogdis asked.

"Sure is."

She skimmed through until she found the auction message.

"Here we are."

After the message was the response that Elicasta wrote herself, in which she sent an opening offer, and received the counter that the bidding was closed. But the bid message was also forwarded out of the *HP-IM* file.

"Crap," she said. "It's got a flip tag; Wicha pushed it to another addy. Hope it's hers and not Zam's, or we're done."

"Try her message retrieval cache."

"That's for fan messages. I'm not going in there without a disinfectant."

There were fifty folders on the screen, minimum, organized in a way that only made sense to Wicha.

"One of these folders has gotta be a drop for the anon account," she said, toggling open the search and entering the anon handle. It got no matches.

"Try most-recent," Bogdis suggested.

"Good thought."

She sorted the 'top folders by most-recent-updated and opened the one that came up first. It was titled 'color swatches', which one might expect to contain an array of cleverly named shades of blue or something.

It did not.

"*Here* we are," she said.

It took only a minute to find the forwarded auction message. Beneath it, the response with an opening bid that was *way* beyond Wicha's means. Elicasta would have said it was beyond Zam the Madman's means too, except that he'd come up with it.

The most interesting part, though, was how Wicha signed the message.

"Bitch," Elicasta said, in a non-endearing way.

Bogdis looked over her shoulder. "Seller thought he was dealing with you," he said.

"*I do all my biz from anon accounts. Hope you can deal. Love, Elicasta Sangristy,*" she read.

The next message in the chain was an acceptance of the offer, with details on what account in which to drop the Credits. Wicha responded to that with a dead drop addy for the seller to push the vid.

"Dammit," she said. "It wasn't sent here."

"You're sure?"

"Positive. Look at the server. That's a rented box. No way we're getting into that."

"You're right," he said. "Maybe the source can help. Why don't we go back to them?"

She smiled. "That's a solid idea."

She hit *reply* on the last message in the chain.

Things are messed up, can we meet? she typed. Then she signed and sent it.

The good news was that it didn't ping back immediately, so the box was still active. The bad news, now she had to wait for a reply.

"Maybe I should hijack this addy before her 'top logs us out again," she said. "You want to do me a favor?"

"You mean another one?"

"Hey, you'll get your co-credit after we land this. Promise. You know I'm good."

"Yeah, you're good. What's the favor."

"I want to jack this message box. I can do it with my voicer, but it would be way faster with the 'top in my office."

"Use mine."

"That's not happening. Can you fetch it for me?"

He frowned. "You don't want to leave or the screen will go to sleep, and you don't want to leave me alone with it for long enough to get your laptop on your own. Is that our orbit here?"

"I'm having trust issues today," she said.

"But you trust *me* enough to let me into your condo unescorted."

"I have snacks up there too, if you want to grab something."

He grumbled, and held up his voicer.

"Key," he said.

She flipped to the key app and tapped her voicer against his.

"the key times out in ten minutes," she said.

"Then I guess the engagement's off. Be right back. If this guy replies while I'm gone you better not keep it from me."

"I don't play. Go on, it's the first 'top in the middle of the desk."

Bogdis was gone maybe fifteen seconds before the box flagged with a reply, and for about a half a second, she actually *did* consider reading and deleting before he got back. But he *had* been helpful, and they had non-overlapping sub bases. No harm in giving him the profile bump that came with a co-credit.

That wasn't the vid I sent you, the message said. *Why did you alter it? Who is this really?*

Then the whole building trembled. For a second, Elicasta thought it was an earthquake, but Velon didn't really get earthquakes. Then the sound of the explosion echoed down the hallway, and she realized this was something far worse than an earthquake.

She ran to the door. Smoke was pouring down the stairwell, and the hallway sprinklers had engaged. Someone, somewhere, was screaming.

"They thought it was me," she gasped.

The lights flickered. She ran back to the desktop.

This is the real Elicasta Sangristy, she typed. *I can get the true vid out but not from here. This box isn't safe. I'll give you a face-to, if you tell me where. Don't believe everything you hear about me in the next few hours.*

She tagged it with an anon box addy she owned and told the seller to hit her there. Then she shut down the computer, and exited Wicha's condo by way of the balcony.

This was no great challenge. It was a second-floor perch, but she made it to the first-floor balcony by dangling to the railing, and then dropped to the ground from there.

The entire top floor of the building was on fire, and it looked as if half of it—her entire corner—was gone. She could hear the alarm trucks in the distance, and closer, her neighbors as they poured out to the street. She squatted down behind a row of bushes and pulled her hood over her head.

"Sorry, Bogdis," she said. "I didn't know."

If there was anything left of him, they'd think it was her, and that was fine. This seemed like a good time for everyone to think Elicasta was dead.

Chapter Thirteen

Makk eventually had to send the uniforms home. Most of them were on the afternoon shift, and nobody liked it when 1/3 of the force punched overtime for anything less than an existential threat. He was confident that Corland and his team could continue with the search unsupervised, as they weren't going to find anything anyway.

He had about fifty different threads working through his brain and not nearly enough coffee to cope with all of them. Orno Linus's murder was metastasizing so quickly, Makk couldn't help but think he was missing something obvious, only he hadn't had time to just sit and review the facts, because the facts were updating too rapidly.

All he could address immediately was the insufficient amount of coffee. It was easily rectifiable, as Mazel's Brewhouse continued to be a 20/7 establishment.

"Who benefits," he said to himself, at his table in the corner of the diner, "from framing Jimbal?"

He couldn't bounce this off Viselle Daska, because she was off working the lead Sister Mye gave them. She'd hitched a ride with a cruiser back to Twenty-One Central already. Makk would meet up with her later, assuming she was still at Central when he got there.

"The killer, obviously," he said. "Not that *that's* helpful. I already don't know who that is."

Dorn Jimbal did *not* kill Orno Linus. Makk was sure of that. It didn't matter now, because once they caught up with them, somebody would be leveling charges. That somebody might even be Makk, even if he didn't want to do it. He'd already been forced to issue the All-Eyes.

Plus, there was the part where someone helped the kid flee. It raised the possibility that even if Jimbal wasn't a murderer, they knew more than they were letting on.

"All right, who has the resources to manufacture a bogus vid on short notice? One good enough to fool the forensic techs? The House could do it. So could Calcut Linus. But why would either of them actually *do* it?"

The waitress on the other side of the room looked up. He was the only one in the place, so she didn't have anything to do other than watch the Stream and wonder why her only customer was talking to himself, loudly, in the corner.

"What am I missing?" he asked.

"You need more?" the waitress shouted.

"Sure," he said. He didn't, but saying otherwise was easier than explaining that no, he was just discussing murder with himself.

It was a different waitress than the last time; this one didn't have a problem with the *Cholem* tattoo on his wrist. Or, she didn't see it. Either way. Her name was Bata, and she looked at least thirty.

Bata toddled over with the urn in one hand, and her voicer in the other.

"Anything interesting?" he asked, regarding the voicer and not the coffee.

"Yeah, big fire downtown, earlier today. You follow Elicasta Sangristy?"

"I don't," he said. "But I've met her a couple of times."

Bata laughed; she apparently thought he was kidding.

"Sure. She's reporting on it, you should look her up. Says Zam the Madman died in the fire. Nobody else is, but if 'Casta says it, you know it's true."

"Zam the Madman, right. Should I know that name?"

Bata laughed again, refilled Makk's coffee, and toddled back to the counter.

He streamed the vid, Makk remembered. *That's who Zam the Madman is.*

He pulled out his voicer and jumped on the first news feed that came up. It was a Corper feed belonging to a company that sold chemical products. He found their news to be decently unbiased, if a little overly focused on cleaning supplies. It was also free, which was his favorite feature.

The top result was a tie-in stream file with Elicasta's name on it. He dove in, and found four vid files, all thumbnailed with a still of her somewhat-familiar face. (The Stream version of Elicasta Sangristy was younger and prettier, but also more artificial in a way that was difficult to articulate. He liked the real-life version better.) He watched all four vids in succession, wondering as he did why nobody from Central notified him that a significant witness in his case was dead, and may have been murdered. Then he caught a glimpse of who took the call, behind Elicasta, at the tail end of the fourth vid.

Fent, he thought. *Of course*.

Detective Glayt Fent was not what Makk would call the brightest of the bunch. The most likely reason Central hadn't told Makk about the fire was that Fent didn't know who his victim was. All he needed to do was ask Elicasta Sangristy, or just *watch* her stream, but Glayt was actively hostile to Streamers, Verified or not. Now one of them was making him look like an idiot, just by doing his job better than he was. It wouldn't be the first time.

Unless 'Casta's information was off. Makk didn't know her, or the quality of her facts, all that well, but if he were putting down money he'd trust her over Fent.

Makk nearly directed Central then. But if Zam the Madman was dead in that fire, he wasn't going to be any less dead after Makk made it back downtown.

Which was where Makk should be going. The news of the fire only contributed to the sense that this case was sliding out from under him, and he couldn't do anything about it. Combatting that sensation would mean returning to the office, if only to beat back the tide.

He paid Bata and stepped out into the cool early morning. Lys was overhead now; the space station had an advertisement on its underside for the upcoming Streamcast of the Zero-ball playoffs.

"I'd rather look at the stars," he said. Which was true of everyone in Velon, and probably the rest of the planet when Lys was overhead. The underside of the station usually showed exactly that: the stars. It was a vid feed from the *other* side of Lys, showing the stars everyone was missing because the uber-rich vacation hideaway was in the line-of-sight. But that starlight view was paid for by sponsorships, and so every ten minutes, it was replaced by a fifteen-second advertisement.

It remained an obscenity, but there wasn't much anyone could do about it.

He sighed, and scrolled his voicer over to the app-car order, as it was too far to walk. Then a car up the street flashed its headlights. The driver's side door opened.

"Detective Stidgeon."

Makk squinted.

"Officer Wisgerth?" he said.

"Rilk, when I'm off-duty. Want a ride?"

"Sure, if you're heading to Central."

"I can get you there. We just gotta make a stop first."

"No thanks," Makk said. "I'll get a car."

"Makk, I'm not really asking," Rilk Wisgerth said. "You get that, right?"

"Are you going to shoot me, or run me over? Because it's been a long day, and I don't feel like talking to Calcut Linus right now."

Two unreasonably large men climbed out of the car. They didn't say anything, but they didn't have to.

"Come on," Wisgerth said. "It's a friendly request."

"What's an unfriendly one look like?"

"We can demonstrate that if you really want," the guy at the passenger side door said.

"It's not far," Wisgerth said.

"Fine," Makk said. "But only because you asked so nicely."

It was a big sedan, the kind of luxury vehicle that used to be a lot more common when aero-car tech was too expensive for regular consumers. Makk appreciated it both for being roomy—because he was sharing the back seat with a giant—and for remaining on the ground the entire time.

His hosts were largely silent. The most untoward thing they did was take his gun away before he climbed in. Wisgerth promised he'd get it back after the meeting, while the guy who took it—the one in the passenger seat—implied that him coming back alive after the meeting was at best a fifty-fifty proposition.

They were heading to Norg Hill. Makk didn't even need to look out the window to know that. Locating Calcut Linus was never a problem; he could usually be found either at his estate on the hill or his second estate on Lys. The only way to Lys was by private shuttle, or by riding the Tether. But it was too late to catch the elevator on the Tether—it took six hours to go up and six to come back down, so there was exactly one departure time. A private shuttle would also end up missing the space station, as it was nearly on the horizon already.

So, they weren't going to Lys.

"What's your deal, Wisgerth?" Makk asked.

"My deal?"

"You're supposed to be a cop, but it sure looks like you work for Calcut Linus."

"Can't a guy do both?"

"It's not what I'd call a typical arrangement, no."

"Detective, I think you'll find more than a couple of city officials have been able to negotiate that evident conflict with ease. Besides, everything Mr. Linus does is perfectly legal."

"Sure," Makk said. "Only because he has a hand in passing the laws."

"I don't see that as a contradiction. But to answer your question, he's my uncle."

"By blood?"

"There was some blood involved."

"I mean—"

"I know what you mean. He's always been Uncle Linus, but I'm not a blood relative. He's been there for my family; sometimes we have to be there for him. Like tonight!"

"Sure."

They passed through Geoghis into Palavin. Makk caught a whiff of the fire from a few hours earlier, carried west in the wind from the middle of Geoghis Quarter. Just being reminded of it pissed him off a little. He was off to see Calcut Linus—and probably get kneecapped for some imagined malfeasance—while evidence for his case was sitting in the middle of the wreckage of that fire.

I definitely should have directed Central about it, he thought.

The car went past some mid-to-high-rent housing at the base of Norg Hill before turning onto Norg Drive, a steep climb that corkscrewed up the hill clockwise. The city's very wealthiest lived here. (Or, again, on Lys, if not both.) Makk could identify about half of the estates by the family, and thought most Velonians could do the same. Much harder, explaining how the very wealthy *earned* their riches.

Linus's estate was three quarters of the way up. Whether intentional or not, it looked more than a little like classical House architecture, with lots of marble columns and white stone buttresses and what-not. There was also the 'groups-of-five' patterns: five windows on each side of the main entrance; five balconies; five gables on all five wings. It even had a nine-pipe structure in the middle of the roof, although in this instance smoke was coming out of the central one, indicating that it functioned as a chimney.

It was ostentatious and a little silly-looking, the work of an architect who kept having to change the designs based on the continuously changing whims of his employer.

Wisgerth took the sedan right up to the roundabout at the front entrance. Goon number one got out of the passenger seat, and goon number two from the back. Wisgerth stayed where he was.

"Soon as you're done," he said, "I'll take you wherever you want to go."

"You're a credit to the badge, officer," Makk said.

Wisgerth said something crude under his breath and drove off.

"It's this way, wise-ass," goon number one said.

They took him through a high-ceilinged entryway, past a ridiculously ornate staircase, to a room that was a combination banquet hall and museum, with a series of round tables, and expensive-looking art on the walls. The room was dimly lit by a crystal chandelier dangling from the center of the domed ceiling, and at the far end, on a dais, was a long banquet table.

Calcut Linus was at the table, picking at the meat from a chicken leg.

Calcut looked a lot like his brother—or maybe it was the other way around—except that Calcut had clearly lived a more indulgent life. He was plumper, had a scar on his face under his right eye that Orno didn't have, and wore a hairpiece. He was dressed in baggy brown clothes that might have been pajamas.

"Detective Stidgeon!" he greeted, standing and putting down the chicken. "Come over, sit down! I had the staff lay out some food for us. You're hungry, right?"

Makk left the goons at the door and walked over to the raised dais. His stomach started growling at him before he'd even made it all the way.

"I am, Mr. Linus. Looks like you've planned for ten people here."

He laughed.

"Nah. This is just what we had lying around. I like to feed people. Come, indulge me. I can't eat all of this myself."

"A *battalion* couldn't eat all of this."

"Funny! Come on, sit."

Makk stepped up and slid into a chair opposite Calcut. "Is that Lladnian wine?" Makk asked.

"It is! Good eye."

Calcut grabbed the bottle in his left hand and filled a *goblet* for Makk, which just added to the obscenity of the spread.

It was probably the case that Linus intended—after feeding and watering Makk—to ask for a favor. The play would be *how can you not do me this simple kindness after I've been such a good host, this is an insult,* or something like that. Knowing that, the smart thing to do would be to decline this kindness at the outset. The problem was, Makk really was quite hungry, and he was probably never going to have another chance to drink Lladnian wine. Also, he never intended to do any favors for Calcut Linus one way or another, so he may as well enjoy the food.

He filled a plate with all the meat and vegetables he could reach, and tried the wine. The latter wasn't quite as cosmically wondrous as he'd been told to expect, but it was pretty good.

"So," Makk said, "do you want to tell me why I'm here?"

"I understood that it was customary for a detective in a murder investigation to at least *converse* with the victim's family. My question is, what took so long for you to visit?"

"Didn't need to. As I told your...I told Officer Wisgerth I'd be by when I was ready. I wasn't ready."

"But *I* was ready."

"Good for you. There were a lot of ways you could have done this, Mr. Linus. When the High Hat demanded an audience, he badgered my captain, and boom. My partner and I were in Plaint's office the next morning. I don't want to presume *too* much about you, but I'm nearly positive you have as much pull. Maybe not with my captain, but with somebody. Instead, you send your boys around in the middle of the night to collect me. With that sort of behavior, a man could draw the wrong kind of conclusion."

"Seems to me you got just the right idea, Stidgeon. I wanted to talk to you, and *just* you. Come back tomorrow if you want, with that partner of yours, and we'll have a whole different conversation. This one will be more productive."

"Do you have something against my partner?"

"Sure I do. You *know* who her father is, don't you? If she's anything like that prick, I don't even want her on my lawn."

Makk considered relaying the fact that Viselle Daska would no doubt affirm Calcut's opinion of her father, but he didn't think it would matter.

"Anyway," Linus said, "Now I'm glad. I'm glad we waited until this moment to converse, because now you have a suspect. What can you tell me about this kid? Did he kill my brother, like they're saying?"

"Jimbal's of Pal," Makk said. "They're not a *he*. And whether they killed Orno or not, that isn't a conversation you and I are going to be having."

"Right. That non-binary crap always messes me up. They called him Brother Jimbal on the Stream, but that's wrong, huh? It's *Other* Jimbal. Whatever. Do you think they did it?"

"I'm not answering that, Calcut."

He sighed.

"Well do you have them in custody?"

"If I did, I wouldn't have ordered the All-Eyes. Don't pretend you don't know I did that."

"Yeah, I do. I figured fifty-fifty, you *had* them, and wanted to keep it quiet."

Makk smiled. "You can go ahead and keep thinking that. You're the family of the victim; that doesn't entitle you to anything more than the satisfaction that'll come when we solve the case. I'm not going to tip you off ahead of time, if that's what this is about."

"Ahh. It is and it isn't. But just so I'm straight: what did you offer Duqo Plaint?"

"He wanted updates."

"Updates," Calcut repeated. He said the word like it was a curse. "All right, Stidgeon, I'll be straight. I don't care if you're not sure if this little weasel did my brother. I *am* sure. So is the rest of the world. Least, the ones with eyes."

"And you want...Not sure what you're asking me for," Makk said. "I don't have them."

"Sure, sure, sure, but you *will*."

"I might."

"What I'm getting at is, let's say you when you find them, maybe you don't direct your captain first. Maybe you direct *me* first, and your captain second. Or, don't direct him at all, if that's easier for you."

Makk laughed.

"Let's see if I understand you. I get a line on my *one* lead in the case to solve your brother's murder, and rather than pick him up, find out what he knows and *maybe* figure out who actually killed him, you want me to hand them to you. Then—and I'm just assuming this—Dorn Jimbal 'disappears'."

"Why do you have to make that so crazy? Far as I'm

concerned, Jimbal's disappearance from this world would close the case."

"Your concern isn't the only one in play," Makk said. "I've got a captain who's going to keep on thinking this is an unsolved murder, not to mention the High Hat, and probably the mayor, the governor, and the parliament. Nita's sake, there are probably entire other countries waiting on an answer. On top of which, I'll end up having to solve Other Jimbal's murder too, and you probably won't like how that plays out."

Calcut looked offended. Deeply offended. It was a little alarming, only because Calcut Linus could make Makk disappear just as easily as he was promising to disappear Dorn Jimbal. Easier, since Makk was currently under his roof.

"If you need more evidence that Jimbal did it," Calcut said, "I'm sure I can provide that for you."

"Even if they didn't do it."

"C'mon. I saw the vid. So did you. I get you gotta be gentle here, but the Other did the deed."

"And it's not enough to see them arrested and charged and sent to prison? What's your motivation here?"

He sighed, and wiped his hands on a napkin. He literally had greasy hands that needed attending, but the gesture seemed more symbolic than administrative.

"This is a...reputational problem for me, detective," he said.

Linus effectively owned the Black Market. Officially, it was a decentralized network without a hub, which made it impossible to shut down completely. Not that anyone was really trying to do that. But the designer and operator of this network was Calcut Linus and his organization. (Just as the network couldn't be found and shuttered, the connection to it and Linus couldn't be established in a way that would stand up in court.) This had to mean Linus dealt with a lot of legitimately unsavory individuals, the kind who *could* get arrested for plenty of crimes, if anybody in law enforcement could get their hands on them.

"You're worried one of your business associates will interpret the murder of your brother as a sign of weakness?"

"It's a concern, yeah."

"How would you disappearing the suspect fix that?"

He shrugged.

"Let's say there are plenty of demonstrative ways to make someone go away."

"Oh, I understand. You want to torture and kill Dorn Jimbal and *Stream* it on the Black. Am I getting that right?"

He shrugged again.

"You said it, not me. Great idea, detective. So, what do you say? You help me, I help you? I can do a lot of things for you."

"Really. Like what?"

"For a favor like this? Plenty. Being my friend is lucrative. A guy living above a Kindonese restaurant in the shittiest part of town can use a boost, I'm thinking. Or how about a promotion?"

"I don't want a promotion."

"All right, we'll stick to Credits for now. Name a price."

Makk stood.

"I'm sorry, Mr. Linus. It's a nice offer, but we can't help each other today."

"No, no, no, sit down. Look..." He seemed genuinely exasperated. "I like you, Detective Stidgeon. You're a hard-ass because you gotta be, because of that mark on your arm. I know. It's been a tough life from the jump. Like that thing in the army. Only survivor of a drop-ship crash? That's terrible. I bet everyone blamed you, huh? But look at you now! I admire that."

"You're wrong," Makk said. He stayed on his feet. "I wasn't the only survivor. But you're right about the rest of it."

"Broke both your legs, spent a year in rehab...respect, I'm saying. Do the legs hurt sometimes still? When it's real damp? I broke my knee one time, it still aches when the spring rains come."

"Sometimes," Makk said, without elaborating. He had a bum

knee that he didn't like to talk about, as a general rule. Even with his doctor. In the company of a guy like Calcut Linus, he *definitely* didn't want to talk about it. "Look, I've had a long day, and like I said, I can't help you. But the food was great."

"You might want to give this some more thought," Calcut said, standing as well.

"I can pretend I'm going to, but I wouldn't sit by your voicer waiting on a message. But hey, since I'm here I may as well ask: where were *you* the night Orno was killed?"

This was just dumb, and Makk knew it. Calcut had a well-cultivated reputation as a person with anger issues. About half of the stories supporting this were undoubtedly circulated by Calcut himself, as it served his purposes to be feared. But only half of them.

Makk recalled one story in particular, about Rja Oio, a subordinate of Linus's whose body they found floating in Pulson Harbor one late winter's day. Oio had been beaten badly by someone who used their fists. Ordinarily DNA would have given them something to go with, but the body had been in the water for over two weeks, so Makk had to do things the old-fashioned way.

What he ended up with was a story about Linus beating Oio to death himself, after the man committed the cardinal sin of denting a fender on one of Calcut's town cars. Makk never could prove it, but that didn't make it untrue.

He had to think Rja Oio was surprised to go out that way; he was engaged to Calcut's niece at the time of his demise.

So Calcut had a temper, and now Makk was poking at it to see what happened. It couldn't be because the man was a suspect; his DNA did *not* show up at the scene.

"Why do you ask, detective? You think I'd kill my own brother? Is that the man you think I am?"

He didn't really look angry; just offended. A voice in the back of Makk's head suggested he try harder. He told that voice to shut the fuck up.

"It would be derelict of me *not* to ask, don't you think?" Makk asked levelly. "Given your reputation."

"I let you into my house, I feed you, pour you my expensive wine..."

"And I appreciate all that," Makk said. He wanted to bring up the part about how he didn't *want* to be there, and came only under the threat of violence. This seemed like a bad time, though. "I'm sure the temper thing is overblown. You seem really nice. I still have to ask."

"I don't know, detective. I'll have to check. Can I get back to you?"

"Of course. Now, if our business is concluded?" Makk held out his hand. "It was a pleasure meeting you, and thanks again for the food."

Calcut shook his hand, somewhat reluctantly.

"And I look forward to hearing from you," Calcut said, "after you've changed your mind. The boys will show you out."

He waved to the goons at the door, wiped the hand he used to shake Makk's on his napkin, and walked out of the room through a back door.

Makk crossed the length of the room, to the entrance he came in through. The goons were waiting for him.

"Come along, detective," goon number one said, holding open the door. The other one put his hand on Makk's shoulder, and started leading him to the left.

"Didn't we come in from that way?" Makk asked, pointing to the right.

"Mr. Linus said to give you a tour of the place on the way out," goon number one said.

"I didn't hear him say that."

"I did. Didn't you hear him say that, Doy?"

Doy—the second goon's name, evidently—nodded. "I did indeed hear that."

The tour didn't go on for long. Makk got to see a set of stairs meant for the servants, and a storage room in a basement with no windows. There was a wooden chair in the middle of the room, a dried bloodstain on the floor, and no other furniture.

"Well, this is really nice," Makk said. "Hey, before I forget: can I have my gun back now?"

"Later," the unnamed goon said. "First, I'd like to invite you to reconsider Mr. Linus's extremely generous offer."

"I don't know if it was generous."

"Excuse me?"

"We never got around to talking numbers, so I don't know how high he was willing to go. It might not have been generous at all."

"It was generous."

"If you say so. Anyway, no. If he wants to have a conversation with my suspect, he can talk to them after they've been arrested. Otherwise, I can't help."

"Okay."

He gave Doy a little nod, which meant the time for negotiation was over. Anticipating that he wouldn't appreciate the next part of their conversation very much, Makk opened things by swinging his right fist down in between the larger man's legs, and hitting what he found there as hard as he could.

Doy doubled over. Makk spun around and jabbed him in the throat, then turned back to face the other man.

He wasn't nearly fast enough; the talkative goon had already closed the distance between them. He gut-punched Makk, taking the wind out of him, and then kicked Makk in the left knee.

Makk went down.

"You ungrateful prick," the goon muttered. Then he kicked Makk in the head, and the room went dark.

Chapter Fourteen

Elicasta flipped through the Stream again with the eyeball optical, while keeping watch on the front entrance with the other eye.

The Stream was still assembling the facts that added up to her being dead. So far, nobody had made what she'd call an official pronouncement, meaning something from a respected Veeser, although a statement from the Velon murder police would do it too. She wasn't going blue waiting for the latter given they hadn't even said anything official about Zam the Madman and Wicha yet. But the rumor buzz was kicking up dust. Her subs were noticing she hadn't submitted the morning go-live, only a day after filing reports on the evident assassination of two prominent Streamers. The explosion in Palavin Quarter had also been big news, and since most of her subs knew she lived in Palavin, the two things were being put together in her comments.

Still, nothing official. She needed to keep a careful eye on that, because she didn't want her Streamcast memorialed. That probably wouldn't happen for a little while—a month was her guess, based on what she'd seen before—but it would be one bitch to undo. Memorialing a 'cast meant locking it down from new entries or comments, turning it into a permanent, unchanging artifact of one Veeser's history of Streamcasts. And that wasn't the really bad part. The really bad part was that her sub list would get dissolved and her Stream made public access. About the only thing that would stop *that* was a next-of-kin waive, and she didn't have a designated next-of.

But there was time. Assuming she survived long enough, her next report was going to shatter some records.

A man in a stocking cap and red mirror-shades walked into the restaurant, looked at Elicasta for a few seconds, and then stepped past her table and to the counter. She kept him in the corner of her eye, to see if he approached.

Was that the guy? It could've been. It could also be the woman in the nice suit, noshing on fried octopus tenders and Wivvolian tea while reading her daily Stream summary on a handheld. Or, the older man at the counter audibly chewing a rice bowl. Or any of the six people that had come and gone since Elicasta arrived. Or it could be one of the servers behind the counter. Or, none of them, and they just weren't there yet...if they were turning up at all.

It took most of the early morning to convince the seller, by way of messaging, that she was the real Elicasta Sangristy. It didn't help that they thought they already *were* dealing with Elicasta when they sold the vid a few days earlier, and it *might* not have helped when 'Casta told them that she was about to be declared dead in a fire. (She told them this, knowing it was unlikely for that information to be made public before they met, just in case she was wrong about that. It would be *much* worse to arrange a meet-up and then have the news get out before their face-to.)

The restaurant wasn't her choice. It was a Ghon-Dikian fusion spot just west of the Tether, and Elicasta wasn't a fan of Ghon-Dik cuisine. She was pretty touch-and-go with seafood generally, aside from the occasional Pethisite place.

But she wasn't there to eat. This was a business meeting.

Unless the other party didn't show. Then it was just her sitting out in the open for an hour with her hood down, potentially being discovered by whoever tried to kill her the night before.

Her voicer thrummed. She opened up the message retrieval app. It was the seller, with a new location and time.

Please don't drag this out, she thought. *We're both on a clock.*

The new address was in Axly, an old shipping district in an area that wasn't technically part of Velon city proper. Specifically, the area pinned on the map on Elicasta's voicer was a section known, informally, as Znedo's Gamble.

That section of Axly used to be a full hustle-bustle, with rows upon rows of warehouses along the Moilen River. The warehouses were there for the goods coming off the docks, and the docks were there for the ships and river barges that came downstream from the breadbasket part of central Inimata.

For a number of complicated international economic reasons, the market for domestic goods plummeted at the end of the previous century. The decline was due at least in part to cheaper international goods arriving by ocean (in addition to hosting a river delta, Velon had an ocean port) as well as a change in overall demand. Also, technological advances such as null-grav tech made over-land travel less costly, which made river barges less necessary. And, there were five or six additional proximate explanations that kept economists arguing long after the Axly warehouse district was declared dead.

Znedo's Gamble came later. Dennith Znedo was a real estate developer who became convinced that Velon's future would include legalized gambling. Gambling was already legal in several counties in Inimata; just not Velon County, the part of the country that included Velon city and a dozen other proximate towns.

Znedo became convinced that a legislative bill to legalize gambling in Velon was on the verge of passing. In truth, a *lot* of people thought it was going to pass, but the difference between most of those people and Dennith Znedo was that Dennith had tremendous personal wealth to invest in his belief, and a habit of taking risks.

He bought the entire Axly warehouse district and the land it stood on, right up to the banks of the Moilen, got a commitment from the city to develop the infrastructure necessary to accommodate travel to and from his future resort casino, and broke ground on a shopping mall.

The half-built mall and a nice Riverwalk with a bicycle path and a cleaned-up riverbank was all Znedo got for his enormous investment, as in the end, the legislature didn't pass the bill.

Dennith Znedo spent several years trying to stay afloat while pumping more money into lobbying for legalized gambling, campaigns to attract businesses to his mall, and public awareness ads to try to convince Velonians that Axly was a nice place to visit even without a casino. It didn't work—Znedo went broke, and gambling still wasn't legal in Velon County—but the campaigns did raise public awareness about Znedo's financial problems, which was why Velonians knew all about Znedo's Gamble.

Elicasta had done a couple of stories about the unfinished mall and the still-standing, abandoned warehouses, so she knew her way around in a general sense. Nobody lived there other than the homeless and the rats, but it was a pretty good place to arrange a meet-up if one wanted to keep out of the public eye.

She was given two hours to get there. She took the entire two hours, first by taking the Hyperline in a completely different direction, then hiring a cab to take her to the edge of the Moilen River before renting a bicycle to take the scenic route along the shore.

It had been *forever* since she had an excuse to ride a bike, so it was sort of pleasant. She forgot, for a few minutes, that her whole life had gone up in an explosion less than ten hours earlier.

It would be cliché to say all she walked away with—aside from her life—was the clothes on her back, and the rig on her head. It would also be untrue, because while she did have some C-Coins stored in her condo, most of her money was in a Credit purse. Since Credits were decentralized, nothing in the purse was trackable, and as long as she had the key string, she was the only one who could access it. She still needed to pick a solution for anonymizing the transfer—either by getting her hands on some spent C-Coins and charging them, or using an app to handle the direct transfers—but the funds were there, and they were plentiful. Provided her Streamcast stayed active, the balance would continue to grow, too. It wasn't enough to cover the bid Zam submitted to buy the original vid, but hopefully the seller wouldn't ask for a second payout when both of their lives might depend on her getting the un-doctored version released.

She got to the end of the bike trail, docked the bike, and then walked the rest of the way, arriving at the location ten minutes before the meet.

The location was one of the many abandoned warehouses that Znedo hadn't gotten around to tearing down before he went broke. It was right up on the water. There were a number of broken windows, and the wind off the Moilen could get icy, which was probably why there didn't seem to be any homeless congregating in the area; with all the different abandoned properties to choose from—not to mention the half-finished mall a half kalomader away—might as well go for something cozier.

She lingered at the corner of one of the warehouses opposite the evident front door, stood still, and waited to see if anyone else turned up. Assuming she was going to actually have her face-to at this location, the seller was probably already inside. Elicasta could say with some level of certainty that *she* hadn't been followed on her way here. Could whoever was waiting inside say the same?

After ten minutes in which nothing happened, she took a deep breath and walked over to the door.

It had a padlock on it, but the wood underneath the padlock on the jamb side had rotted away; she had no trouble pulling it open.

The interior was all broken glass and cement dust. Elicasta could just make out footprints in the dust, a trail that probably would have been easier to follow if the lighting was better. There *were* some dangling overheads, but she doubted anyone was paying the electrical bill in this place.

The ground floor was vacant. Large metal doors took up one side of the wall, which must have been how the offloaded freight made it inside when this place still served a function.

She followed the vague trail of footprints until she found a decent-looking one in a spot where the sunlight directly hit, and crouched down to get a better look.

Running shoe, she thought. *Small foot.*

"That's far enough," someone said. The voice came from ahead, in the dark part of the warehouse. It was either a woman or a child. Possibly both.

"Hello," Elicasta said. "I'm here, like you asked."

"Lower the hood."

"Right. Sorry."

The voice was coming from *above* her somewhere. 'Casta didn't have much experience with this kind of space, but had a vague memory of something she saw once—probably in a fic vid, a series or a movie—of a foreman's room perched at a high point over the floor.

"Elicasta Sangristy," the woman/child/and-or-both said.

"That's me. What can I call you?"

"Just X, for now."

"All right, X. What do we do next? Do you want to send me to another restaurant?"

"The thing is, I could have sworn I already did business with

Elicasta Sangristy. And it looks like after I *did* business with her, she died in a suspicious-looking explosion. Unless she actually died in the *other* suspicious-looking explosion."

"I reported on one of them; you know that."

"Fair. Then you didn't die in the first one. You get where I'm going."

"Look, you can actually see me. I am who I say I am. The other times, you were speaking to my friend Wicha. I didn't even know about it. Not until she died."

"Yes, good reporting."

"Thank you."

Elicasta took a few steps closer to the source of the voice, close enough to make out the base of a wooden staircase.

"Hey, hey," X said. "I didn't say you could move."

"We agreed to a face-to," Elicasta said. "And I can't see your face."

"I have a gun pointed at your head, and I'm not satisfied yet."

Elicasta sighed. "No, you don't. Look, we don't have an abundance of time here, X."

"We have plenty of time; nobody knows about this place. Unless you were followed."

"I wasn't. I'm off the Stream, and I think whoever attached a bomb to my front door believes I was killed in the blast. Nobody's looking for me. How about you?"

"I wasn't followed."

"Not what I mean. Whoever killed Wicha and Zam the Madman, and *tried* to kill me, they're just moving down the line on their way to the source of the vid. You understand that, right?"

"That's why the blind auction," X said. "I'm not an idiot."

"How many people did you send that auction clip to? How many of them did you *really* know? Are you completely sure no one got it who shouldn't have?"

"What would that matter?"

"Maybe it doesn't. Maybe all your messages were sparkling.

You filmed the guy who killed the brother of maybe the scariest man alive, and no doubt tripped at least some of that deal on the Black, which *he owns*, but yeah, you're probably *fine*. Oh, and now you're here, talking to me, when you could've taken the Credits, bought yourself an aero car and flown off into the sunset. Why is that?"

X didn't answer. Elicasta took the silence to mean, at minimum, that X wasn't going to blow off 'Casta's head with her imaginary gun, and continued toward the staircase.

"They got it wrong," X said. "That's why. What I sent them... it wasn't that kid. It was someone else."

"Who was it?"

"I don't know. I don't recognize them, any more than I recognize...what's the name? Dorn? They didn't do it, though, and that's not right."

Elicasta reached the base of the stairs and, absent any protest from X, started climbing. The steps creaked as she went, and the wood gave a little; she wondered if the warehouse was actually condemned, and not just closed.

"Too bad you can't prove that," Elicasta said. "Unless Zam was an idiot."

There was a small walkway at the top of the stairs in front of a doorless office enclosed in glass. X was sitting next to the safety railing, with a laptop and a cheap rig. 'Casta pegged her as no more than ten: old enough to buy a rig and start a Stream (there were regulations about doing this before legal adulthood) and young enough to be foolish with it.

"Zam wasn't an idiot," X said. "The vid was blockchained, and he got the only copy. But I'm not an idiot either. I had catch-and-kill insurance. If the vid didn't air as-was, it would snap-back to the source folder. They took it and altered it, so what I sent them never actually aired."

"That's pretty clever," Elicasta said. "On a timer?"

"Yeah. It hit the folder this morning. So now that I know I'm dealing with the *real* Elicasta Sangristy, how much do you want for it?"

'Casta laughed.

"I'm not paying for it. If you want me to air that, it's *my* favor to you. I'm taking a huge risk here."

"I could air it myself. I'm just getting started, but I have some subs."

"Look, X, here's what'll happen if *you* air that. Number one, nobody will believe the first vid's genuine anymore, which is what you want. Number two, nobody will believe the *second* vid either, which you don't want. If you're looking to get the truth out, I'm the only one here who can air it."

"Why you?"

"I have the whole story," Elicasta said. "Or nearly. Tell me how you filmed it."

"It was an accident. I was testing out a refurbed drone."

"Over House grounds?"

"Yeah, I mean...I know the airspace is supposed to be no-fly, but it was my first run, and I needed an area with a *little* activity, but not a ton. The motion detector is glitchy—the whole thing is glitchy, but that was what I was trying to fix—so I figured House airspace was a good control environment."

"That's smart, X."

X got to her feet, stretched, and offered her hand. "It's Mirka," she said. "And I'm sorry about all the, you know, the spy stuff. I didn't know what to believe. It's great to meet you."

Elicasta shook her hand.

"I'm a big fan," Mirka said. "And you're probably right, about who should air it and all. I just want to be done with this."

"Well, we're not there yet," Elicasta said, "but thank you. I need to understand the provenance and then I have to see it, and then we can talk. You say you're just starting out; maybe a co-credit will give you a lift."

Mirka grinned. "That's be great."

"Tell me more. You said it was glitching, is that why there's no audio?"

"It is, yeah. The sensors *react* to sounds just fine, but I can't get it to record anything. Not sure why."

Elicasta could think of three or four explanations for that, but this wasn't the time.

"All right, you put in the air over a House neighborhood. I assume you don't live there."

"I'm not telling you where I live, but no. I was set up a few kalomaders away. The sensors picked up movement in the guy's yard."

"Orno Linus."

"Yeah, him. You saw all that from the teaser vid. Then nothing happened for a while."

"You kept the drone there for another twenty-two minutes, according to the stamp," Elicasta said. "Why did you do that?"

"I didn't mean to, but like I said, the drone was glitchy. It stayed where it was because it thought something else was happening in the yard, but it was just the sensors acting up. Like, the door opens a couple more times. Ten minutes in, you can see Orno holding it, but there's nobody else there, and later it happens again. I'll show you."

"Yes, you will. Showing that missing footage, even if nothing happens, will help prove this is the unadulterated vid. Why didn't you just include a skip-speed of it?"

"I thought it killed the pace."

Elicasta laughed. "Yeah, I guess it would."

"Then there's the end, when the killer ran out. Not this Dorn kid."

"You're sure."

"Very sure."

"Who is it?"

"Like I said, I dunno," Mirka said. "I didn't recognize them."

Whoever actually appeared at the end of the vid could be the key to this whole thing. Someone out there had the means to make sure their identity was masked, and thought it important enough to kill everyone on the evidence chain. The fact that Mirka didn't recognize them was, in that context, a little surprising.

"Okay," Elicasta said, "let's watch it. Maybe I'll know who it is."

"Right. Sure."

Mirka sat back down and woke up her laptop. Elicasta watched as she typed in a series of commands to access the source folder. The vid loaded.

"Want me to skip to the end?" she asked.

"No, I want to see the raw footage straight up."

"Okay."

Mirka handed over the 'top as the footage kicked in, and it was exactly like the teaser vid: Orno opening the door; an unidentified Septal walking in; Orno closing the door. Then came a lot of nothing. The drone's optical drifted up to the roof, where the most interesting thing was chimney smoke, and then it looked back down at the yard again.

"Nothing happens here for like ten minutes," Mirka said. "You sure you want to wait?"

"Let's just double-time it," Elicasta said, toggling the vid. Mirka kept her eye on the timestamp.

"Okay, now slow it down," Mirka said.

The vid returned to normal play. A few seconds later, as promised, Orno opened the back door, stood still for five seconds and then walked away, leaving the door open. It fell closed on its own, and that was it.

"Anticlimactic," Elicasta said.

"I told you. Want to jump to the end now?"

"Maybe we..."

There was something flashing in the corner of the screen, beneath the vid overlay.

"You have an alarm set up?" she asked Mirka.

"Just the drone. It's out front. That's how I knew you were here. Why?"

'Casta handed the laptop back.

"I think it's picked up something."

"Oh. Well it's glitchy, like I said..."

Mirka's expression changed. Elicasta couldn't see the screen but clearly, when the young woman toggled over to the drone feed, she saw something other than a glitch on the optical.

It was then that Elicasta realized they were currently cornered.

"There's no way out from up here, is there?" Elicasta asked.

"It's just the stairs. Shit, it's just the stairs."

"Grab what you need and let's go."

They made it to the bottom of the wooden steps just as the door at the far end of the warehouse opened. 'Casta couldn't make out who walked in because the sunlight on the other side of the door made any clarity in that respect impossible, but it looked like at least two people.

Mirka pulled her behind the stairs and pointed to another door.

"Please tell me that isn't a dead end too," Elicasta whispered.

"There's a back exit."

They got through the door and into a smaller storage room.

"Wake up," Elicasta said to her rig, "give me soft lighting."

A small white light came to life on her forehead, giving them a narrow beam to see with.

"How many were there?" she asked.

"I saw three on the feed," Mirka said.

"I think only two came through the door. The third might be circling around."

"The exit's up ahead. Come on."

She led the way, using Elicasta's headlight to see by.

"I thought you said you were sure you weren't followed," Mirka said. "Looks like you were wrong."

"I wasn't wrong."

"They didn't follow *me*."

"Yes they did," Elicasta said, "after a fashion. They must have seen the snap-back on the file and stuck a tracer on it. They were just waiting for you to open the file."

"That's impossible," Mirka said.

"It's not; it's just difficult and expensive. So is having enough people on string to get a team here in under fifteen minutes. Where's the damn exit?"

"It's coming up. I used to hang out around this place when I was a kid. Never been in this one before this morning, but they all have the same floor plan, and there's a fire exit at the end of this hallway."

"You didn't put a second drone at that door, did you?" Elicasta asked.

"No. But I know it's locked from the outside because I tried that door first. I only have one drone, and it was out there looking for you, not a team of assassins or whatever. That's what this is, right?"

"I think so."

"Why?"

"Whoever's at the end of your recording is pretty important to someone. I think they're taking out anyone who saw it."

"*You* haven't seen it," Mirka said.

"I was about to. And they don't know I haven't seen it. My name was on the transaction, remember? I think it's a good bet that whoever's behind this also funded the purchase. Zam the Madman was probably pretty wealthy, but I saw where he lived; he wasn't *that* wealthy."

"Then they altered the vid and handed it back to him," Mirka said.

"That'd be my guess. Wonder if they executed the tech who did that spoof for them. It's pretty high-quality."

They reached the door. It was indeed a fire exit, with a crash bar and a warning that the door was alarmed. Elicasta wondered if that was really true in a building with no power, and decided probably not. Too bad; the speedy arrival of an alarm truck would be helpful.

"But who *are* they?" Mirka asked, her hand on the door.

"Dunno. If they're waiting on the other side, we can ask."

"Right. Are you ready?"

"Where are we going?" Elicasta asked. "What's on the other side of that door?"

"It's a big open space. The next warehouse is straight. The river is behind us. Where do you want to go?"

"I know I don't want to be in an open area."

"Same. Building-to-building?"

"Why not?"

Elicasta didn't truthfully think she was going to survive long enough to reach the next building, but wasn't going to say that. They couldn't stay where they were, and that was all she was certain of.

"Kill light," she said to her gear. They were plunged into darkness. "Okay, hit it," she told Mirka.

Mirka pushed open the door, and they both went blind for a second, as their eyes adjusted to the light from the suns. Then they were running straight for the next warehouse.

It was just too wide open. Elicasta, weighted down by nothing more than the rig on her head, quickly caught up with, and then passed Mirka—who had to carry a heavy bag with her laptop—in the sprint for the other building. After passing her, 'Casta slowed down a little and tried to grab the young woman's hand, as if this could impel Mirka to run faster. It didn't work, and she never got a hold of that hand, because then a shot from a blaster hit the aspiring Veeser in the back and knocked her to the ground.

Elicasta didn't stop or go back for her, even though the wound didn't appear to be fatal; she kept running. She realized *as* she was doing it that this was a decision that would haunt her for the rest of her life, even if *the rest of her life* was only a minute-and-a-half. She heard Mirka cry out, and saw her fall face-first, and could make out the gunman running for them from the corner of the other warehouse, and then Elicasta was running as hard as she could and that was that.

She cleared the next warehouse—which hypothetically provided cover, given the blaster couldn't shoot around corners—and kept on moving. Then the gun went off a second time. Elicasta arrived at the terrible conclusion that *if* she got out of this alive, it would only be because the assassin had to stop for a kill shot before continuing pursuit.

A lot of blind running came next, with Elicasta weaving between buildings as fast as she could, convinced that at any second another blaster shot would hit *her* in the back. At some point, she managed to get herself turned around, because after the fourth warehouse corner, she reached a dead-end at the riverbank, and the river was supposed to be *behind* her.

She stopped at the edge and spun around to check for pursuit.

Did they give up? she thought. They would have recovered Mirka's bag and the laptop. Was that the end of it?

"Wake up," she said to her eyepatch optical. "Magnify."

She saw two of them between buildings, blasters in hand. They couldn't see her yet, but they would, soon enough.

It wasn't over.

At least this rig's waterproof, she thought. Then she jumped in the Moilen River, and let the current carry her away.

Chapter Fifteen

Makk woke up on his couch to the sound of his badge announcing an incoming direct.

He groaned and rolled over, and then yelped when the giant bruise where his ribcage used to be lodged a protest.

He sat up, and felt around in his pocket for the badge. When he didn't find it there, he looked around the room. It was on an end table, next to his gun, and a note.

Makk only had a vague recollection of being returned to his apartment, of large men carrying him up the stairs and dropping him on the couch, cursing narrowness of the staircase the whole time. He was pretty sure he recalled giving one of them permission to use his bathroom, but this was all he could readily recall.

That he was brought home instead of to the station—where he was expected to be heading after he was done at Mazel's Brewhouse—was probably a good thing. He wasn't sure if that was his idea or theirs. Although given a full array of options, Makk might have picked a hospital over both.

"At least they returned my gun."

He picked up the note. It read: *reach out when you change your mind,* followed by a voicer number.

"Don't hold your breath," he said, slipping the note in his pocket.

He held up the badge, which was still vibrating. There were ten missed directs, all from Viselle Daska. He hit the answer button and pressed the badge up to his face, at which time his face notified him that he'd been kicked in the head.

"Oww," he muttered, right as the connection went live.

"Makk!" Viselle said. "Are you all right? Where are you?"

"Um. Home? What time is it?"

"You sound like you're in pain. I expected you back at Central last night."

"I ended up chasing a lead that didn't pan out. What's the emergency?"

"Okay," she said. The sisters at the orphanage used to have this disappointed tone of voice that they'd managed to weaponize over the years. Viselle had the same gift, even when uttering only one word.

"The emergency," she continued, "is that I've got a lead on Dorn Jimbal, and I'm following it."

"You got a hit on the expensive car?"

"I pulled traffic vids around the campus. There aren't any *on* campus, or if they exist, we don't have access to them."

"No vids on Septal grounds," Makk confirmed. "It's a legal thing, somehow."

"Right. I went through the vids, and found a couple of cars that met the definition of *expensive*."

"By whose standard?"

"Aesthetically. There weren't a lot of cars to look at, around sixteen o'clock in Andel. I clocked one entering the campus before sixteen with only a driver, and leaving after sixteen with both driver and passenger. No good angles on who was driving the car, but I ran the idents against owner records. Got a hit, but not on a person. It's a shell. I'm heading to the address, and I have a bulletin out on the car ID."

Viselle had entirely too much energy to cope with, the first morning after a beating.

"Do you need me to come along?" he asked. *Please no,* he thought.

"No, I'm already halfway. I just wanted you to know."

Thank the gods.

"All right," he said. "Keep me updated."

"I will."

"And be careful."

"You think Dorn is dangerous?" she asked.

"No, but some of the people looking for them sure are."

"Will do."

She disconnected. Makk tossed the badge onto the floor, lay back down on the couch, and wondered if anyone would be upset if he didn't get up again for a couple of days.

But that wouldn't be happening. His brain was awake, and it wasn't going back to sleep again. All the pieces of the case were still drifting around in there, waiting to be assembled in the correct order, but one piece in particular was bothering him a lot.

"Boots," he said.

He sat up again a few minutes later, not thanks to some newly discovered fount of perseverance and fortitude so much as to a full bladder.

The face in the bathroom mirror looked pretty rough. He remembered getting kicked in the head, and not much after that. The blow had left a bruise under his right eye socket, which looked like it wasn't finished swelling yet. It hadn't closed the eye, which was about the most positive thing he could say.

He lifted up his shirt. Bruises on his ribcage and his stomach.

They knew how to make it hurt without killing him, but he definitely had a broken rib or two.

It was neither the worst set of injuries he'd ever endured, nor the worst beating he'd ever absorbed, but it still hurt a bundle.

After a hot shower that didn't do much of anything aside from waking up the rest of his pain receptors, he found a pair of dark sunglasses, quickly concluded that this wouldn't come close to hiding the damage, and decided he wouldn't be heading into Twenty-One Central on this day.

"They'll ask," he told his reflection. "You know they'll ask."

He didn't want to tell anybody what *actually* happened. He wasn't embarrassed about it or anything—those were two pretty large guys taking out their anger on him—but accusing one of the most prominent (and dirty) citizens in the city of assaulting a police officer was just a bad idea, even for an assault by proxy. Makk also didn't care for the options available in plausible lies: *in a barfight* wouldn't make him look good at all, and neither would *falling down a flight of stairs* or *hit by a car*.

He returned to the living room, retrieved his discarded badge, and connected with Jori Len.

"Hey, Jori, it's Makk."

"Makk," she said. "Solve the crime yet?"

"Not yet. Hey, that DNA list you sent us...can you forward a copy to my badge?"

"It's sitting on your desk. What, you can't find it?"

"I'm not at my desk. I'm heading straight to Andel Quarter from here."

"Sure, I'll push it through. Anything else?"

"Not unless you've found the murder weapon," he said.

"I think that's *your* job."

His badge thumped an acknowledgement that he received the file.

"Thanks, Jori."

He disconnected, double-checked to make sure he got the

right list, and then put the badge away and retrieved his gun, and the dark sunglasses.

"Now I just need a car," he said.

"You cannot," Binchagag said.

"Just for a couple of days, Bincha," Makk said. "I'll bring it back. I always bring it back."

Binchagag was at a table in the back of Lucky Twins, eating something that looked like raw egg was one of the ingredients, and raw squid was another part. Makk's stomach was doing flips just spending time in the same proximity as the meal.

"What for? You want to go take care of whoever did that to your face?"

"I know who did this to my face," Makk said. "And no. I *am* going someplace where I'd rather not be obvious."

"Then don't bring that face."

"Funny."

"I know," Binchagag said. "Everyone say so. This is police business, you're saying?"

"It is."

"Then police can give you a car."

"I gotta get all the way downtown to pick up an unmarked and that won't even work. Everybody knows when they're looking at an unmarked. Even the Brethren."

"Oh, you go to the House! It's about that case? You were on the Stream, Wa-Hei told me."

"Yes, big important case and you can help me solve it."

He pondered, and picked at his egg-squid meal.

"If police requisition a vehicle for official business, the owner is compensated, I think."

Binchagag wasn't really like this. Over the past few years, Bincha had shown his appreciation for Makk's particular skill as a bad-luck charm through a variety of means, from cutting him in on the vig to lending out his hunting cabin.

He just felt like being an ass this morning.

"How about if you're just helping out a friend?"

"You're not a friend; you're a tenant."

"Your tenant is about to point a gun at your head and demand the keys to your car. Don't even pretend like you need it; you have three."

"I have *four*," he said, putting the keys on the table. "And you are robbing me. I should direct the police."

"I *am* the police."

"Other police. I'll talk to that yellow-haired woman."

"She won't take your direct. Where's it parked?"

The car was a beat-up sedan made by a company that wasn't known for luxury vehicles. It was sturdy, and it could run forever on an electrical charge, but the solar panels were glitchy and the ignition spark didn't always spark. It was also really heavy compared to most of the sedans on the market—especially the newer ones, which used a metal-glass synthesis—and had a suspension that made it feel like a boat when it turned corners.

Binchagag—or whoever used the car last—had the audio Stream tuned to a news aggregator. Makk was a fan of some of the music Streamers, but didn't feel like fiddling until he found one, so he left it where it was. That was how he found out the city might be dealing with a serial bomber.

"Glad that isn't my case," he said, as the station replayed some of Elicasta's report from the prior day, before revisiting the details on the second bombing. By the time he got the car out of Decane Quarter, he decided he'd better direct Llotho, to see if Fent had worked out who his victim was yet.

"Unless you've solved Linus, I don't have time for you right now, detective," was how Captain Llotho greeted him.

"The first bombing may connect to my case, Yordon," Makk said. "Tell me Fent knows at least that much."

"They both might. We're not sure yet. I know you're not suggesting I combine the two cases. You're not that crazy."

"He can keep it. Why, who was the second bomb for?"

"You know Elicasta Sangristy?"

"Yeah. She filed the reports on Zam the Madman. Why?"

"There you go," Llotho said.

"Wait, the second bomb killed Elicasta?"

"That's what it looks like."

"...Damn," Makk said. "I really liked her."

"Yeah, she was a good one. It's early, but we're looking for a connection between her and this Zam guy and/or the other one who died in the first blast: Wicha Reece. Something more than Elicasta's reportage yesterday. That doesn't seem like enough."

"It isn't. Captain, we needed Zam to get us to the source of the Linus vid. Someone could have figured out that Elicasta can also get us there, before we figured it out for ourselves."

"That's possible," Llotho said. "Or someone just doesn't like Streamers, and picked the most visible one for their next target."

"I think somebody is taking some extreme steps to keep us from the source," Makk said.

"Look, ask Other Jimbal about it once they're in custody. That's still your priority."

"Daska's working a lead on that. I'm on a different trail today."

"Don't bother me with the details, just the results. I'll keep you in the loop on the bombing."

"Thanks, captain."

Makk disconnected, and went back to the news aggregator. It was weird, because he hardly knew Elicasta Sangristy at all—they'd spoken maybe five or six times—but her death put a pall on the whole morning. And this was a day that began with him waking up as a giant bruise.

What were you into, 'Casta? he thought.

Getting onto the House campus presented no problems, as they didn't have the guard station manned. They *never* had it manned, it seemed, except for the night Linus's body was discovered. This was a problem for the investigation, because nobody could provide a list of visitors on the day of the murder. Makk already had the neighborhood canvassed to see if anyone saw a car they didn't expect in the neighborhood of the townhouse on the evening in question—the answer to that was *no*—but a visitor checklist or a surveillance cam or something would have been a much better thing to have.

Now, with Makk stealing onto campus in a civilian vehicle before midday, he was thankful for the lack of a checkpoint. This would work better if he caught people unprepared to speak to the police.

The first person on his list was a third-year brother named Yabb. Jori already ran the DNA matches against the residential directory, so Makk had an address to go with each of the names.

Brother Yabb lived in one of the co-ops: communal groups reserved for married House couples. Makk didn't know much about how these arrangements worked, other than that they all seemed to share a kitchen. It seemed like a weird situation for married-only people—especially the ones who also had children—but none of that was germane to the case.

He parked the car a block from the co-op and walked the rest of the way.

Even if he didn't have a bruised face and dark sunglasses, Makk would have stood out in a neighborhood full of Brethren.

I should have borrowed Leemie's hood, he thought.

There were no legal proscriptions on the books about impersonating a Septal. Not in Inimata, at least. (In other countries? Perhaps.) It was considered disrespectful by most, and sinful by some. Makk didn't care about either respect or sin, but that didn't mean he was ready to impersonate one in order to conduct this questioning unnoticed.

Also, he didn't *really* want to go unnoticed. He just wanted it to look like he was trying to.

He got to the door and rang the bell. A Sister answered after a delay.

"Door's open...oh. Hello," she said. "What can I do for you?"

"Hi, I'm Detective Stidgeon," he said, holding up his badge. "I'm looking for Brother Yabb? I just have a few questions. It's about—"

"Professor Linus, sure. Come on in. Yabb's door's at the top of the stairs on the right. Just look for the name."

"Thanks so much."

"You're welcome. Are you working with the..." she trailed off, deciding mid-sentence that she didn't want to get to the end of the sentence.

"It's just me. Why, has someone been here already?"

"No, never mind," she said, waving her hand in the air. "Sorry."

He waited for a couple of beats to see if she wanted to volunteer more information. It was a pretty basic technique when questioning someone: create deliberate uncomfortable silences and see what they fill it up with. She wasn't biting, though.

"Just at the top of the stairs," he said.

"Yep, and on the right."

He walked up. A couple of Brothers emerged from the downstairs kitchen area to see what was what, while Makk climbed.

He got to the door, and knocked.

"Brother Yabb, hello," he said. "Detective Makk Stidgeon. I'm with homicide. I need to ask you some questions."

The door flew open. A heavy-set Brother was on the other

side in what looked like a hastily pulled-on hood. He looked Makk up and down.

"No," he said. Then he slammed the door closed.

"Just a few questions," Makk said.

"I have nothing to say to you," Yabb said, through the door.

"Can you explain how your DNA ended up at the scene?"

He opened the door again.

"Is this what you asked Dorn?" he asked. "Am I the next one on your list? They didn't do it and neither did I. Now get out of here before..."

He thought better of finishing that sentence, and slammed the door again.

"If you think of anything you'd like to say, message me at the station," Makk said, sliding a business card under the door.

Yabb didn't answer.

Makk went back down the stairs, greeted by seemingly everyone else in the co-op.

"Hey, has anyone else been by to ask about the case?" he asked, directed at anyone who felt like answering.

There was an uncomfortable silence, as seven Septals worked out how best to not answer.

"Not from downtown," one of the Brothers said.

"A Sentry?" Makk asked.

"Please leave," the Sister who let him in said.

It went much like that for the next three interviews, all with students: an ugly combination of hostility, accusations, and dark hints that they'd already been raked over by someone else. Makk thought it was a little odd, only because he was essentially there for answers as to why he shouldn't be considering them a suspect in Linus's murder. He expected them to be interested in establishing their innocence.

He spotted the black panel van after the second interview. It was the same make and model as the one that escorted him and Viselle from campus the day they met with Plaint, and now it was parked up the street from where Makk parked the sedan.

There you are, he thought.

He got in the car and drove to the next interview, ignoring the van. It didn't follow, but by the time Makk was done with Sister Julb, the van was up the street again.

This was the idea that got him off the couch: The boot that made the imprint on Professor Linus's back door belonged to the same person who broke into Makk's apartment; that boot belonged to a Sentry; that Sentry was part of a team that wasn't associated with Corland (who seemed like a straight-up kind of guy); and that team was connected to the van that followed Viselle's car off campus.

Makk figured the van would show up again if he made enough noise. If it didn't? He was probably wrong. If it did...he was probably also wrong, but the van's occupants would be available to question.

He got in the car and drove slowly past the van, not making any particular effort to hide the fact that he was checking it out. The windows were tinted. This should have meant only that he couldn't confirm that it contained Sentries; in his mind, it proved that this was exactly who it contained.

He drove to the next location.

His fifth interview subject was—according to her roommate—in class. Getting this information took almost no time; Makk was pulling out again by the time the van made it to the street. It followed him directly, no longer feigning discretion.

His sixth interview was with another professor. He was home, and—refreshingly—answered the door himself and didn't slam it in Makk's face.

"Yes of course," he said, on seeing Makk's badge. "Please come in."

His name was Professor Gollinshake. He lived in one of the nicer houses right near the center of the campus. It was one step up from Linus's townhouse, geographically and (probably) reputationally. He showed Makk into his dining area and gestured to a seat at the table.

"Can I get you anything? I just put on a pot of coffee."

"Coffee would be great, thank you," Makk said.

"It's no trouble. I was wondering if I'd be speaking to one of you. DNA?"

"Yes, that's right."

He nodded, and walked out of the room.

"I supped with Orno in his home two days prior to the Feast of Nita," the professor said, from the kitchen. "That's why I've come up in your scan."

"Can anyone verify that?"

Gollinshake returned with two coffees, and put one on front of Makk.

"Yes. There were five students. I take it you've not spoken to any of them yet?"

"I'm encountering some reluctance," Makk said. "You're the first of the Brethren willing to talk."

The professor sat down, sipped his coffee, and nodded.

"Yes," he said. "I can understand how we arrived there. Two issues arose at once when poor Orno passed. One was the circumstances regarding his passing. Have you been informed about the other matter?"

"Something missing."

"Indeed. Nobody seems willing to say *what*, precisely. Orno had access to chambers even *I've* never seen, and I'm, well...closer to the throne, if you will."

"What chambers were those?"

He smiled. "You know I can't talk about that. But yes: Something missing that's more important than the identity of Professor Linus's murderer. They've visited here twice already."

"*They*. You mean the Sentries?"

"I do. It seems they think someone was working with Orno to spirit this very important thing off campus."

"And did you?"

"Did I what?"

"Help Professor Linus steal something."

Gollinshake laughed.

"Of course not," he said.

"What do you teach?" Makk asked.

"All sort of things. I'm an ethicist."

"Oh, then no stealing for you," Makk said, with a laugh of his own.

"Not necessarily! Being an ethicist means I'm uniquely qualified to *justify* theft with lofty assertions and large words. If you need conditional justification for something in the future, just drop me a message and I'll see what I can do."

Makk thought of the book now in Leemie's possession. He wondered what Professor Gollinshake would have to say about that.

"I might just do that," Makk said. "Can you remember the names of the students?"

"I'm not sure I can. He conducted these dinners twice-monthly and as far as I know the guest list was never precisely the same. Orno enjoyed seeing what happened when different disciplines collided."

"They were themed, then."

"I wouldn't say *that*, not exactly. I'm sure he didn't know what was going to come out of the dinners any more than the next person. Dorn Jimbal *was* there. That I remember. Fana Mye was there as well. A neurologist, I think...or studying to be one. She made an impression. Dorn the astrophysicist, less so, but enough that I can put him at the event. And me, an ethical scholar."

"My understanding of Professor Linus was that his career was a collision as well," Makk said. "between religious studies and the astronomical stuff."

"I think his mastery of concordant disciplines inspired him. We didn't collide much on this night, however. I'm sure he was disappointed in us. I've been to a few of these gatherings; Orno generally seeded the conversation with initiating questions and then stepped back so the participants could attack the subject. I had a quite edifying evening a few months ago on the nature of the soul."

"But not on this night."

"No, on this night...his question was peculiar. Well, peculiar in context. I don't think we found it odd in the moment. If you know someone...no, that's, I want to get this right. Here it is: assuming such a thing was possible, if you knew without any doubt whatsoever, when and how someone was going to die, would you have a moral and ethical obligation to tell them? Or, and this is interesting, would the obligation instead lie in *not* telling them?"

Makk laughed,

"You're right," he said. "That's a strange question coming from a guy who was murdered a week later."

"As I said, peculiar in context."

"I don't suppose the House has a machine that can predict the future, hidden in its basement."

"Depends on the future," the professor said. "The meteorological department does a decent job of it. As does the astrophysical department. But for a prediction on the scale of one human life, we had to rely upon the neurologist and her cross-studies in general medicine. Even then, the question didn't really stand to muster as something she or a colleague would ever have to legitimately tackle. They can predict the *how*, but certainly not the *when*."

"I was joking."

"I appreciate that. It was still a good question."

"What about astrology?" Makk asked.

Professor Gollinshake frowned.

"Detective, really..."

"No, sorry, I'm not asking because I think the professor's death was predicted in his horoscope. He had a book on his shelf about astrology, and I thought that was odd. I'm wondering if he ever mentioned it."

"Ah. He did not. But I'm not surprised."

"Why not?"

"Astronomy and astrology aren't *that* far apart," Gollinshake said. "Of course they *are* in the sense that one is a science and the other is magical thinking, but they *came* from the same discipline. Orno was interested in the history of many things and old astrological charts have the history of star movement embedded in them. It's hardly shocking to see it included in his personal curriculum."

"Thanks, that's interesting," Makk said. *Not helpful*, he thought, *but interesting*.

"Setting all of that aside, I'm afraid I can't really help you, detective. I don't believe Orno Linus knew he was going to die; the question was an awkward coincidence, and that's all. I don't know who killed him, or why. I have no opinion on whether or not Dorn Jimbal committed the crime, either. I would say they didn't seem the type, but I've also made it my life's work to study ethical decisions, and one of the things I've learned is that we all have our personal compass. If theirs pointed them in the direction of murder, it was no doubt a *flawed* choice, but I won't say they had no capacity to *make* that choice."

"Any thoughts on where they might be hiding now?"

"None. You can check the upstairs if you'd like."

"That's okay," Makk said, standing. "I think I've bothered you for long enough. Send a message if you can think of anything that might be helpful."

Makk put a business card on the table.

"I'm sure I won't, but do direct *me*, if you need an emergency ethical consultation."

"I will."

Gollinshake walked him to the door.

Oh, hey," Makk said. "Where did you sit?"

"Pardon?"

"For Orno's dinner. He didn't have a table. Did you all stand in the kitchen?"

"On the floor," Gollinshake said. "He would put a blanket down. Orno had some odd rules: no table, no chairs, and no hoods. We would sit in a circle, cross-legged, like in the old Septal dialoguing rites. Thank goodness for the blanket; do you know, it's impossible to eat pasta in one's lap without making a mess?"

"No hoods? Including Dorn?"

"*Except* for Dorn. Professor Linus exempted them. I don't know if Dorn is a Fundamentalist by faith, or only by upbringing, but they preferred the full robe and hood in all settings. Orno respected that."

Gollinshake opened the door and looked down the street.

"Ah," he said. "There they are. They'll be coming up the drive as soon as you leave, for a follow-up interview, in which they attempt to learn what we talked about, without coming out and asking. The Sentries are *exhausting*."

"They've put the fear of the gods in all the students," Makk said. "Not you?"

"I have tenure. Good day to you, detective."

They shook hands, and then Makk headed down the street to the sedan.

This time, instead of driving to the next address on his list, he went down the street and turned around, close enough to see Gollinshake's front door and far enough to not be noticed in a collection of parked cars. About five minutes passed before someone got out of the black van with the tinted windows. Definitely a Sentry; hard to say if it was anyone Makk had encountered before.

"All right then," he said, before putting the car into gear.

He stopped the car nose-to-nose with the security vehicle, put it in park, and got out. When nobody climbed out of the van, Makk knocked on the front passenger-side window.

Still nothing. He was pretty positive at least one person was in that car, maybe hoping Makk would just go away, but he couldn't see them through the window without cupping his hand over the glass.

Secret hit squads, he thought. *That's what Leemie would say right now. Secret hit squads and someone blowing up Streamers, and Septals in nice cars sneaking my suspect out of town.*

It seemed like a bad time to poke a bear, but he was running out of ideas. He wanted an answer to at least *one* thing before the end of the day.

Besides, this was why he *really* came to Andel Quarter.

"It's okay," he said, to whoever was in the car. "I can wait."

Then he sat down on the van's hood.

It took ten minutes for the car's only verified occupant to return from the professor's house.

"Can I help you?" he said flatly.

"Yeah, I'm looking for a guy. Maybe you can help. Dresses like you, likes to ransack private apartments and write messages in old coffee. Visited the scene of Orno Linus's murder the day *after* Linus was killed, didn't feel like telling anybody about it. Maybe you know him?"

"I don't think I do. You'll want to get off our car."

"Will I. Let me ask you something else." He pulled out his gun and pointed the barrel at the windshield. "Is this nice, tinted glass bulletproof?"

"It is, yes."

"Good to know. How about the tires? Or you? Are you bulletproof? Thing is, I was having a shitty day *before* learning that the

Sentries have been going around intimidating all the people I need to talk to. I think whoever's yanking your leash doesn't care about the professor's murder, and I'd like to talk to them to find out why. So why don't you direct the person on the other end of your leash, tell them I want a chat, and we'll go from there?"

"And if I say no?"

"I dunno. Say it, and let's find out together."

He put on a sour expression and pulled out a voicer, which was already thrumming with an incoming message. He muttered a response, listened, muttered some more, then shoved the voicer back in his pocket.

"Follow us," he said.

The van led Makk out of the neighborhoods and through the classrooms portion of campus, past the building with the High Hat's office, around behind the chapel, and into a dull-looking cement edifice that he didn't recall ever noticing before. Not that he spent much time on *this* campus. But the Septal-run orphanage that raised him was attached to the Stanto chapter and had a lot of the same *kinds* of buildings—albeit on a smaller campus—as the Velon chapter. In that regard, then, he couldn't recall seeing a building *like* this, growing up.

A steel garage door opened in the side of the building, and in they went. Makk was plunged into darkness that was much worse for the fact that he was wearing sunglasses. He didn't rear-end the other vehicle, but it was close.

The Septal he spoke to, and a driver, got out. Makk put his hand on his gun, and climbed out as well.

"Don't worry," the passenger said, "if we wanted to kill you, we'd bring you to a neutral location. Come on."

They led him to an elevator, which required a security card to use. It quite unexpectedly went *down*.

"Isn't the rest of the building above us?" he asked.

"I wouldn't say the *rest* of it. Part of it is."

The floor they stopped at was another three levels down. The elevator opened to a cold cement hallway with a straightaway that —unless Makk had gotten turned around—extended beyond the footprint of the building above them. It headed right to the chapel.

"Secret tunnel system," he muttered.

"What's that?" the Sentry asked.

"How far's this go?"

He shrugged.

"Dunno. Wrong question though."

"What's the right question?" Makk asked.

"I'm not telling you. But we're not going that way. We're over here."

He led Makk down the left-branching part of the corridor—a much shorter hallway, terminating at a door.

"Go on in," he said.

"You're not coming?"

"No. I would've shot you already, but the boss said not to. Maybe he just wants to do it himself."

"I thought you said you'd only do that at a neutral location."

He shrugged again.

"He's expecting you," he said.

Makk pushed his way into the room.

It looked like a command center that was temporarily between missions: lots of chairs and tables, with unused cork-boards on the walls and a few video monitors not currently in use. Also in the room was a tall, thin Septal, wearing the same commando gear as the rest of the Sentry team.

"Hello, Detective Stidgeon," he said. "You can call me Brother Semit."

"Is that actually your name?"

"Does it matter? Sit. I understand you have questions."

"I had a couple of questions a half an hour ago. I've got about twenty more, now that I've seen this basement here. I asked your man how far it went and he said that was the wrong question. What's the right one?"

"The right one is how deep does it go, but that's not what we're here for. Ask me what you want to ask."

"All right." Makk sat in the nearest metal folding chair. "One of your team kicked down the rear door of the Linus townhouse the day after the murder. Once I realized it was a Sentry, I figured I was dealing with someone acting on their own, but I'm wrong about that, aren't I? This was sanctioned."

"It was, yes. We have a team conducting a separate investigation."

"Do you know which member of the team was in Linus's townhouse?"

Semit looked bemused. "Why does this Sentry in particular interest you?" he asked.

"You must not have heard me. This was the day *after* the murder. The body on the floor would've been hard to miss. That gets them a free interview with the homicide department and a coupon for a cup of coffee."

"You want to ask them why they didn't then report it?"

"It seems like that would be an important thing to do, yeah."

"Let's say...we have a different mandate," Semit said.

"A mandate that's more important than one of your Brethren being murdered, on your grounds?"

"Where we're speaking of this specific division, yes."

"Come on, you guys are basically all campus security, right?" Makk said. This was reductive, because there *was* an actual campus security, with uniforms and all that, and he knew this perfectly well. "I would think Professor Linus's condition at that time would earn a *not secure* label. On top of which, I don't know if you're familiar with the penal code, but *not* reporting it is kind of bad."

"The Sentries are *House* security, which means *our* job—again, I speak of this division specifically—is the continued protection of the *House*. Yes, Professor Linus was a part of the House, but not the part that this group protects and secures. In this specific regard, he was someone our charter mandates we protect the House *against*."

"Because he stole a book."

Semit hesitated. "Brother Plaint told you something was missing from a vault. You've arrived at the *something* being a book. Why?"

"Because that's what you guys keep in the vaults. Old books that only some people are allowed to read and even fewer *can* read."

He nodded. "All right."

"And your mandate is to protect the contents of the vault, above and beyond the lives of the people who go in and out of that vault?"

"Yes."

"A book that nobody can read."

Brother Semit sighed, stood, and paced the room. He seemed to be wrestling with a decision of some kind.

"Orno Linus took...something, from the vault," he said, "meaning to transport it off House grounds and deliver it into the hands of another party. We have an idea of who that other party is, and we have some of their back-and-forths. They used Black Market communiques, thinking it less transparent."

"It's not? Does the House have spy tech you haven't told anyone about?"

He laughed. "Yes, actually, but that isn't what we used. There *is* a project underway to fundamentally decrypt the Black Market. You might have heard of it."

"I've heard rumors," Makk said.

"We're not spearheading it, but some of our proprietary tech is being leveraged, and *that* gives us a window on some exchanges, albeit only on the server level. And what we learned was that before Orno passed—"

"Murdered," Makk said. "Before Orno was murdered."

"Before Professor Linus was murdered, he had multiple exchanges with someone from Twenty-One Central."

"Well. It's a big building." Makk was being flip, because that was his default when taken off-guard. This would have been good information to have at the start of the investigation.

"I'm saying this to explain why your home was searched," Semit said. "We had reason to believe you helped Orno get the stolen vault object off campus, and possibly also had a hand in his murder."

"That's a stretch."

"Yes, the part where it doesn't add up is the gap between the murder and your formal arrival at the scene. Dorn Jimbal makes a much better candidate. That's why you and I are talking right now."

"Because you don't think I did it anymore, and you think I can help you find Other Jimbal."

"What we need is for you to find them, and bring them here, so we can recover what's missing. Then you're welcome to put them away."

Makk laughed. "You're the second person to ask me for that exact favor in the past day, and I don't even have a line on their whereabouts."

He didn't bother to mention that his partner *did* sound like she knew where Jimbal was. That's the sort of thing you share with someone you expect to work with again, and if Makk had his way, this was the last conversation he and Brother Semit would be enjoying.

"Did the other person do that to your face?" Semit asked.

"This? No, I fell down six or seven times. I'm clumsy. Tell me why I should do this thing for you."

"Civic duty?"

"I work for the city, not for the House."

"But the House *raised* you, detective. Actually, that was one reason we considered you a suspect in the first place: a disgruntled orphan, a *Cholem*, someone who would know the value of a vault artifact, looking to bring down an old tormentor."

"Sounds like a good story. What's Dorn's version?"

"We think Professor Linus told Brother Jimbal something they were unprepared to hear."

"Like what?"

Semit shrugged. "I don't have all the answers, but I do believe there are things some of us are not prepared to know, and I believe it when I'm told that Linus knew some of those things."

"So I have this right..." Makk said, "Dorn, in a fit of rage, murders Linus and storms out. Three days later, when Linus's body still hasn't been found, they go back again, finds the book, slips it into a pocket, and *then* directs the police. What'd they do with it after that?"

"We only know they didn't keep it. We searched them and their apartment the following day. Then we interviewed and searched everyone who came into contact with Other Jimbal in the past two weeks, and then everyone who came into contact with Brother Linus in the past two weeks. We've been especially interested in the people on that list you've been going down, as most of them spent time with *both*. Somebody took it from Jimbal, and forwarded it to its eventual destination."

"Which was what?"

"We don't know. It hasn't appeared in any of the auction sites we've been monitoring, but that's all we can be sure of. That's provided the reason for the theft was financial, which we also don't know."

"Right. I have to ask: does your search include blowing up people?"

"You mean the murdered Streamers?" Semit asked.

"I do."

"That wasn't us. The House doesn't *actually* have a secret team of assassins, detective. And if we did, well...there are more subtle ways to kill a person."

"Yeah, that's fair. Well, I'm sorry, but I'm not going to hand over Dorn Jimbal to anyone other than the duty officer at Central. If you want to swing by after they're booked and question them, I'm sure your boss has the pull to arrange it. If Jimbal took your book...you guys probably have plenty of leverage to get that out of them."

Semit hesitated again, debating internally about what he was going to say next.

"It's...not a book, detective." Semit said. "Or, not *just* a book. I'm told we're looking for a *key*. It's a one-of-a-kind."

"Okay, so it's a book that's a key. Is that supposed to convince me to help?"

Semit smiled. "You wanted to be a Septal once, didn't you?" he asked.

"Sure, when I was little."

"I don't know what *you* saw in it, as a child, but what I saw was an opportunity to obtain the hidden knowledge contained in this place. As I said, we don't have secret assassins, Detective Stidgeon, but we do have secrets. The hidden knowledge is real, and what Linus and Jimbal stole is a key to unlocking some. Helping us find it means putting Other Jimbal in my hands for a few hours. Surely you can afford us that."

"If I say yes, will you stop fucking with my investigation?"

"We'll coordinate the efforts of my team with Corland's, going forward. Will that do?"

"Maybe. Let me think about it."

About the only thing Makk was sure of, upon leaving the secret, subterranean lair of the House Sentry team, was that he was running out of explanations for Dorn Jimbal's disappearance.

Sister Mye said she saw Dorn get into a 'nice' car with someone who was at least *dressed* like a Septal. The most plausible explanation—assuming she told him the truth—was that someone from Brother Semit's unit had Jimbal now. That no longer made sense.

If the House didn't have Dorn Jimbal, and Calcut Linus didn't have Dorn Jimbal, who did that leave?

Makk didn't know, but if it was the same party responsible for blowing up Elicasta Sangristy, Other Jimbal was probably dead.

After getting the car out of the garage, Makk parked it on a side street, waited ten minutes to see if any vans were still following him, and then directed Viselle.

"I hope you've had a more productive day than I have," he said.

"Maybe," she said. "I think I know where he *went*, but I don't know how he got there."

"Sounds interesting."

"Mildly interesting. He may be off-planet."

"*Lys*? How would he get up there?"

"The Tether runs daily, you know that."

"Sure. I also know how expensive the sky elevator is, and how unlikely it is that anyone would even allow him to step off the shuttle without an invite from a resident."

"Yeah, Makk, but it adds up, doesn't it?" Viselle said. "It's a big city, but not *that* big. We would have had a lead by now."

When the All-Eyes was put out on Jimbal, the city's ports of exit were put on high alert. Everyone getting on a boat, or going through a toll gate would have been checked. Aero-cars were *not* checked—because it was infeasible—and as far as he knew, neither was the boarding platform for the Tether. If the fugitive was someone with the means to visit the space station Lys, that might not have been the case. But Dorn wasn't that kind of someone.

"This sounds like more than a hunch, Detective Daska," he said. "Who's your source?"

"You don't know her. She said she saw a Septal got off the shuttle this morning, though, and I've spent the whole day trying to confirm that without going up there myself and questioning residents one mansion at a time."

"Your friend lives up there, does she?"

"She does. You know who my family is, Makk. I have a lot of connections in that world. Don't be weird about it."

"No, it's pretty useful. Especially if you're right."

"I think I am. Someone pretty well-connected got them up there, and you know, after that...there are ways off Lys other than the Tether. They could be anywhere in the world by this time tomorrow, and there isn't a thing we can do about it."

"Any idea who helped them?" he asked.

"No, but after the tip I ran the car ident against the vehicles in the garage next to the Tether, and got a hit. I'm thinking whoever drove Jimbal off campus went up too. But the shell ownership of the car is a complete dead-end; unless the driver comes back to retrieve the vehicle, we're not going to be able to make a connection. If you want, we can head up there one overnight and conduct a door-to-door. I don't think we'll find our missing Brethren, but somebody might know something."

Getting to Lys meant riding an elevator to the top of the Tether, at which point one was technically off-planet. To get from there to Lys involved taking a shuttle that intercepted the space station as it passed over Velon. This wasn't really as difficult as it sounded, because the space station didn't move; the planet underneath it did. Shuttles coming off the tether basically had to rise up to an orbit higher than Lys, burn off some of the orbital speed, and fall down to the station. The timing had to be pretty exact—it was nearly impossible to do if the Tether had already *passed* Lys—but the shuttles were built to withstand reentry, so the worst that could happen was that it crash-landed on the surface of Dib somewhere; it had been over a decade since such a thing transpired.

It was supposed to be very safe, in other words. Despite that, Makk couldn't think of anything he'd like to do less. He'd already survived a crash landing in a troop transport where the odds of such a thing happening was about the same. That was only a drop of a hundred maders.

"Let's hope we don't have to do that," Makk said.

"Right. Anyway, I've been reaching out to contacts on the surface to figure out which family stuck their nose in this mess, by other means. No luck so far. What have you been up to?"

He told her about his day, more or less. He went heavy on the details about Brother Semit, threw in a little about Professor Gollinshake, and entirely skipped the part about how it hurt to take deep breaths.

"*Someone at Twenty-One Central*," she repeated. "That's all he said?"

"I think that's all he knew. I'll put in a direct to I.T., see if they have a way to figure out who it was from our end."

"Good idea," she said. "And look, I know you don't want to hear this again, but I think you have to give the book back. Not sure what else we can learn by holding it aside."

"I'm not ready to yet. It's starting to sound like Linus risked his life getting that book out; I want to know why it was so important. But thanks for being predictable."

She laughed.

"Sure," she said. "Is it at least safe? Your apartment can't be that secure."

"I'm not keeping it there."

"Okay. I'm gonna go. I have a couple more old friends I can try. I'll check in later."

"Later."

She disconnected.

Makk checked his mirrors again; still no tail. Maybe they really were going to leave him alone now.

He made a new connection on his badge.

"Leemie, it's Makk," he said. "I'm heading to you. Don't shoot me."

"I don't know what you expect to figure out this time that you didn't get from the last time," Leemie said. Makk was turning the book over in his hands—now gloved in a sterile poly-cloth blend because his friend insisted—as if he was about to witness some sort of revelatory transformation.

"The man said it was a key," Makk said. "Does that make any sense to you?"

"It's gotta have something to do with what it *says*, right? And we don't know what it says."

Makk dropped it on the desk, took the gloves off, and paced around in the extremely limited free floorspace available in Leemie's hole of an apartment.

"Right, we don't know what it says, but you've had it for a few days. Nothing?"

"A couple of words here and there. I'm not even trying a full translation right now. Just looking for letters I recognize."

"Like what words?"

"*Outcast* comes up a lot."

"So it's a religious text."

"Could be," Leemie said with a shrug. "If this is really a pre-Collapse manuscript, it probably is, but what do we know? What else did this Allimitist say?"

Leemie had already concluded that Brother Semit was a member of the Allimites, a secret cult bent on overthrowing world governments. Nobody could prove the Allimites even existed, which was just more evidence that they did, in his mind. Makk didn't even bother to argue.

"He said it's one-of-a-kind," Makk said. "Which doesn't make sense, does it? There'd be a copy of this text in other House vaults."

"No, it doesn't make sense," Leemie said. "Not if we're still talking about the text."

"Which is why I'm thinking there's something else unique about it, aside from the words. Maybe if I tore the binding..."

"Don't you dare," Leemie said, grabbing the book protectively.

"Okay, okay. Look for something, I dunno, key-like in there, would you? My partner is insisting I give that thing back, and I'm starting to think she's right."

"Hold on. You have a partner? And she knows about the book?"

"Yeah, but she doesn't know where it is now."

Makk almost added that his partner was also Ba-Ugna Kev's daughter, just because he thought the total meltdown that would surely follow would be amusing.

"So you lied to me, when you said we were the only ones who knew about it."

Makk sighed. "A tiny lie," he said. "She's the only one."

"Honus's ass," Leemie said, "you're gonna get us both killed. And her too."

"You have to learn to trust people, Leemie."

Makk made it back to Kindontown well after sunset, sore, dog-tired, and in need of a pink for the pain. After putting the car back in the garage, he bypassed the Lucky Twins and went straight to his apartment. Binchagag could have his keys back in the morning.

Or not. About ten minutes after he got in, the pipe started rattling.

"Really?" he said.

Binchagag couldn't hear him, but it sure seemed like he could, as the immediate response to Makk's annoyance was a redoubled CLANG CLANG CLANG.

"Fine, okay."

He shuffled back down, straight through the restaurant. Bincha was at the upstairs bar.

"Saw you go by," Bincha said.

"So you did," Makk said. "Here are the keys. Although I don't know what the rush is."

"This is not about the car. Keep the car if you need it. It's about downstairs."

"Someone running a table?"

"No, *Cholem*, the tables are not a problem. More of your bad luck has showed up in my parlor. I will show."

Binchagag led a confused Makk down the stairs, past the door, and around the basement bar. The tables were hopping, and the room was full of smoke, as per usual for this time of night. It was hard to make out much of anything down there, which was sort of the idea.

There was a figure wrapped in a blanket at the corner of the bar, eating soup.

"Came here asking for you," Bincha said. "Bad shape. Won't talk to anyone but Detective Makk Stidgeon. We took care of her."

"I understand. Thank you for doing that."

"Just get her out of here. She's scaring the regulars."

Makk walked around the bar and took the seat next to his guest. She didn't notice him at first, concentrated as she was on the soup. He put a hand on her wrist; the sleeve was soaking wet.

"Hey," he said.

Elicasta looked up, and smiled.

"Hey," she said. "Sorry, I didn't know where else to go."

"Heard something about you being dead."

"Yeah, it's been a weird twenty. I need protection, Makk. And I have something you're going to want to see. Can you help?"

PART III

The Invisible Man

Chapter Sixteen

Makk led Elicasta up the many stairs to his apartment on the roof, slowly, and with a lot of help. She wasn't weak, just stuck in a perpetual shiver.

"I took a swim in the Moilen," she said, by way of explanation. "It's freezing this time of year; did you know that?"

"I didn't," he said. "Why'd you do that?"

"It was the safest place to be at the time."

Once in the apartment, he found some clothes—his, so they were much too large, but they were also dry—and gave her some time in a hot shower. This necessitated the removal of her rig, which he unwisely attempted to help her with.

"Don't," she said, then: "power down."

She took it off and handed it to him.

"It's waterproof," she said. "Thank goodness; we're going to need it."

After the shower, with her wet clothes drying on the radiator and her self wrapped in Makk's old sweats and a blanket, Elicasta finally stopped shivering.

He set her up with a coffee, and waited for her to start talking.

"Sorry to show up on your doorstep like this," she said.

"I'm glad you did," he said. "I heard you were dead, and you're one of the people in the world that I didn't like hearing that about."

"That's sweet, kind of. What happened to your face?"

"I came across someone who was even more unhappy with the state of the murder investigation than Captain Llotho," he said. "How'd you know where I lived?"

She smiled wanly. "I was doing prework on a story about you, a few years back."

"On *me*?"

"*The Cholem Detective of Twenty-One Central.* You're probably not fond of that angle."

"Not particularly."

"It's moot, but I would have run it by you before I did anything. I never did the piece, but...I'm glad you haven't moved since, or I'd be in a lot more trouble right now."

"Not that I'm disappointed, but why didn't you pursue the piece?"

"Because you're a terrible interview, Detective Stidgeon."

"Only when I want to be."

She laughed.

"If you can turn it off and on, you should turn it on more regular," she said. "Whole world's on vid one time or another."

"Some of us don't want to be," he said. "What kind of trouble are you in?"

She took a deep breath and a couple of sips of coffee, and then walked him through everything she'd endured in the past few days, in great detail, including the shooting death of a young aspiring Streamer named Mirka, ending with a plunge in the river to escape certain death for the second time in fewer than twenty hours.

Makk couldn't quite believe all of this, which undeniably pertained to his case, was going on without him knowing.

"Central only just put the two explosions together with the Linus vid," he said.

"Yeah, well, Fent was working it, and he's an idiot, so..."

Makk laughed. "You sound like you work there."

She shrugged. "He is, though."

"I'm not disagreeing. So, I understand all of this except why you're here instead of downtown. Twenty-One Central can protect you better than I can."

"I'm only riding with people I can trust for now," she said. "If you hand me over to someone downtown that *you* say I can trust...I'll do it. Otherwise, congrats, I'm your new roommate."

Makk thought about what Brother Semit said earlier: Orno Linus was working with someone in Central. If Semit was right, Elicasta's distrust of the downtown office was warranted. That was especially true if whoever was *actually* on the Linus murder vid was important enough to warrant the murder of at least four people, not counting the professor.

"You said you never got a chance to watch the entire vid," Makk said.

"I didn't see the close-out. According to Mirka, that's where the meat is."

"Didn't it die with her? On her laptop?"

"It wasn't local; she was retrieving it from a drop. It's still there, on the other side of a lot of crypto, but I recorded her keystrokes when she entered the string. I can get in from any 'top you want."

"We could watch it right now?"

"Sure, if you don't mind getting interrupted by a death squad. Maybe the stairs will keep them away, but I kinda doubt it."

When it was apparent Makk wasn't making the connection, she elaborated.

"There's a tracer on the file," she said. "It triggered when we looked up the vid in the warehouse, and it'll do the same thing again if we do it now. It's called a poison pill, and before now I thought it only existed in the rant-casts of sketchy UnVeesers. Drop-sites like what Mirka used are supposed to run anti-vi algos on all outgoing file dumps, which is why we weren't on alert. The poison pill skirted the anti-vi, somehow."

"We can't prevent them from finding our location," he said, trying to keep up. Streamers spoke their own language, and he wasn't fully fluent. "Even with programs designed specifically to block our location. Do I have that right?"

"Yes."

"How do we view it, then?"

"The only counter it is to be in a place they can't reach, or that they can't reach quickly. End-to-end, it's a longplay vid, and these guys got all the way out to Znedo's Gamble in under fifteen, so you tell me where we'd be safe. Twenty-One Central maybe, if you think we'd be insulated there. It's your call. I want to see who's on that vid as much as you do, but I also want to live long enough to tell everyone about it."

He doubted she really did want to see the ending as much as he did, but didn't say so. Then he started going through the list of people he could *really* trust downtown. It was a short list.

"Not Central," he agreed. "We need to get out of the city. So *far* out of the city that it would take any team looking *in* Velon too long to reach us."

"Watch it through once and then lightspeed our way to a new location."

"Right."

"You got a place in mind?"

"I think I do," he said. "Ever been hunting?"

The gentlemanly thing to do would have been to give Elicasta his bed for the night while he took the couch. But, his couch *was* his bed—it folded out—so it was either bed-and-floor or bed-and-chair, but once Elicasta saw how difficult it was for Makk to move around, that was out of the question.

"I think if you sleep in a chair with broken ribs you'll die in your sleep," she said.

"Really?"

"Don't know, sounds right. Just lie down next to me on the fold-out, and stop being stupid about it."

So they did that, and of course nothing happened, because she was recovering from a near-death experience and he was a giant bruise. And also, they were adults.

Makk checked in with Binchagag early the next morning.

"You want the cabin now?" Bincha said. "You want privacy with your lady? Apartment is very private."

"It isn't, actually. Someone already broke in once. I meant to tell you; the lock on the door needs replacing."

"How many of my things do you mean to visit with your bad luck, Makk Stidgeon?"

"You don't complain about it when I'm sitting down to gamble. And we're not going to the cabin for *that* reason. We need someplace isolated, for about an hour, to watch something important."

"You can watch fic Streams in apartment too."

Makk sighed. "I don't know how to explain this to you without putting your life at risk, Bincha. Trust me when I say I'm being as honest with you as I can afford to be. We need to get out of the city, and we need a defensible location. I can't promise the car or the cabin will come out of this in one piece...but it's important. It's really important."

Binchagag looked up from his latest stomach-churning meal, which looked like fish, and also looked like it was still alive.

"The face looks better today," he said.

"Thanks."

"You're serious about this."

"As serious as I can be," Makk said.

"If you do whatever this is you have to do, in the apartment?"

"You and I have had our fill of urban warfare already, haven't we?"

Like Makk, Binchagag was a veteran of the Inimata/Kindon border dispute. (It was a war, but "border dispute" was what everyone who wasn't there called it.) Bincha fought on the other side, but that didn't mean his experience differed all that profoundly from Makk's, at least up until Makk's troop transport fell out of the sky. They never talked about their experiences, because they didn't have *that* kind of friendship. But they didn't have to; the wounds were baked in, and easy enough to recognize in others.

"Yes," Bincha said, after a pause. "We have."

He pushed the cabin keys across the counter. "I can repair the cabin and the car, but finding someone to take that apartment, for what I charge you, will be very difficult," he said.

"I'll be careful," Makk said. "Thanks."

He directed Viselle on his way back to the apartment.

"You're going where?" she asked.

"Someplace remote," he repeated. "It's a little much to get into right now, but I have a lead on an unedited copy of the Linus murder vid."

"The missing twenty-two minutes?"

"That too. But the ending *was* spoofed; someone else came out of Linus's townhouse that night. I don't know who, but that's what I'm going to find out."

"By leaving town?"

"Like I said, it's a little much to get into right now. I'll explain later."

She sighed. "You know that vid's been frisked by people a lot more tech-solid than anyone we've got downtown, Makk. It was Jimbal coming out of there at the end. It's the time in-between we should worry about."

"I'll be looking at both soon enough. Unless you found Dorn and can ask them."

"They're definitely in the wind, and halfway to who-knows-where by now."

"That's what I figured," he said. "I'll let you know when I have more. And if Llotho asks, tell him I'm on a hunting trip."

Back upstairs, Elicasta had changed back into her now-dry clothes from the day before, and looked busy skimming the Stream and enjoying a cup of coffee.

"You don't have anything to eat here," she said. "What do you subsist on?"

"Street food. There's a fried kopa vendor up the road that's sending me to an early grave."

"He'll have to get in line," she said. "Are you going to tell me who really beat the crap out of you? Or are you afraid of seeing it reported in my Streamcast?"

"I have concerns in that regard, yes."

"I'll only use it with permission. How's that?"

"If we hit a dull patch on the drive and I can't think of something else to say, I'll tell you. Are you dead yet?"

"I am. My death was picked up by a straight news Veeser about an hour ago, and it's gone global since. I've been reading my Stream messages; most of them are really sweet."

"Only *most?*"

"The Stream is an ugly place. Where are we going?"

"Zonic National Park," he said. "You know it?"

"I know it. Never been. Girl I know used to call it *rapewood.* Doesn't have a stellar rep."

Zonic National Park was a huge place. About one-eighth of it abutted a town called Raighkood, which was a beacon of economic depression. Raighkood used to be a link in a logging industry chain that fell apart some ten years prior. The town was later featured in a true-crime vid series that threw a light on Raighkood's unusually high crime rates in general, and one high profile serial rapist in particular. The title of the series was *Rapewood.*

The fact that Elicasta called it Rapewood signaled that she'd definitely never been to Zonic National Park. If she had, she'd know that the park itself was beautiful, and that the reputation that wafted onto it from the stink of downtown Raighkood was entirely unearned.

"We won't go near the town," he said. "And don't call it that when we're there. You'll piss off the bears."

She laughed. "Maybe they'll rename it after they find our bodies," she said. "Or is that too dark? Sorry, I can't tell; I've been dead all morning."

It was a couple hundred kalos to the cabin. The drive took most of the morning and half of the afternoon, during which time Makk got to listen to Elicasta's freeform critique of other Streamers as their reports came through on the audio news-aggregation Stream in the car.

She reserved most of her scorn for the Veesers eulogizing her.

"Come on, Tabi, you *hated* me, don't even."

"I thought that was nice," he said, regarding what sounded like a tearful tribute.

"Hah. She was reading a script. Don't think she even wrote it. Sounded cribbed. She would've needed at least three brain cells for that and she only has two."

"Remind me never to piss you off," he said.

She laughed.

"Sorry," she said. "Veesers tear each other down all day; it's how we show love. If any of them had the horns for it, they'd say I was a straight bitch with shiny luck that stole every lead. I'd respect that. Are we getting there any time soon?"

"Almost."

"I'm frazzling. You know, this is the longest I've gone without Streaming since I was ten?"

"That's crazy."

"Sure it *sounds* like it, but you live your whole time in the real, and that sounds crazy to *me*."

She hesitated long enough to listen to the next part of the news feed. It was about another presumed-dead Veeser, named Bogdis.

"They're going to memorial me soon, Makk," she said. "It's hard to come back from that."

Elicasta had already explained to Makk what being *memorialed* meant: it essentially turned her entire contribution to the Stream into a gravestone.

"But not impossible," he said. "Besides, even if your Stream is memorialed, *you'll* still be alive."

"You sure about that? Because it seems like the same thing to me."

"Yeah, you definitely need to get away more often. Here we go."

They took the last turn off the public roads and onto the Zonic National Park grounds. It was another half a kalomader from there before they reached the cabin, although it seemed farther than that with all the twists and turns.

Binchagag's cabin felt like it was in an isolated part of the park. In truth, it was one of a string of cabins of the same basic design, separated by tall pines, which made it a difficult place to find and an easy one to misidentify. Makk had been there four times; the first two times he showed up at the wrong cabin, and in one of those two times he didn't realize it until after his fifth attempt to unlock the front door with the wrong key.

"I'll give you this much; it sure is isolated," Elicasta said, as Makk made the final turn leading up to the cabin. "I don't think I've been this far away from civilization in my life."

"I used to go on camping trips as a kid," Makk said.

"As a kid in the orphanage?"

"Yeah. The Septals took us. It was a lot like this. It might have been *exactly* like this; I don't remember where they brought us, but it could have been to this park."

"Real, that's the first happy story I ever heard riding with the word *orphanage*."

"I have a lot of them. It wasn't terrible."

He brought the car to a halt next to an actual log cabin.

"Honus, Javilon and Ho, I didn't think those things were real," Elicasta said, leaning over Makk to get a look at the building. "Is it made of legit logs or is that a decorative façade?"

"Does it matter?"

"Yes!"

"I don't know for sure, but I think they're real."

Makk got out and stretched his legs, while Elicasta climbed out the other side of the car and walked around to the back of the cabin. Her sense of wonder at the natural world was becoming a major source of amusement.

"There's a lake?" she shouted. "What *is* this?"

"It's nature," he said. "You should look into it."

"No thank you." She came back around to the front. "Boy I hope you're as trustworthy as I think you are, Makk Stidgeon. Nobody would ever find me out here."

"They wouldn't find me either."

"They'd know this was a valid place to start looking. Literally nobody would think to sniff me out in the middle of this."

"Then I'd say we made the correct decision."

Makk unlocked the front door with a regular old metal key that Elicasta acted like she'd also never encountered before.

"Real, I didn't think those still existed either," she said.

"You absolutely need to get out more often."

The cabin was extremely standard as cabins went, with a couple of cots, a coldbox, a gas range, a wood table, and some chairs. There was a gunrack on the wall with six rifles. They weren't locked up, but the ammunition was; it lived in a metal safe under the rack.

"Ye olde rifle," she said.

"Those aren't old," Makk said. "Not *very* old. I think that one's ten years; it's the oldest. If you're wondering why no blasters, that's because they're terrible long-range weapons. I wouldn't use it for short-range hunting either; blast radius is too big. End up destroying half the animal if you're not careful."

"Ew."

"They're also expensive."

Makk sat down at the table and set up his laptop. Elicasta no longer had a computer she could work with, not since her condo was blown up. She did have her rig, which was far more important.

"There you go," he said, offering her the computer and the chair.

"Thanks. Blasters are expensive?"

"*I* can't afford one. Don't want one, but also can't afford one."

"The guys who came after me yesterday had them."

"I know," he said. "That means they're well financed. Also might mean they don't really know what they're doing. Jumping in the river probably saved your life, if that was all they had."

"Because they're bad long-range weapons?"

"That, and they're no good with water."

She laughed. "Really."

"A big body of water like that, the energy from the blast will just get absorbed by the liquid. They work *great* through air, but not through a medium as thick as water. They're also not that great in the rain."

"That's hilarious. Is that why they might not know what they're doing?"

"I don't know a lot of trained soldiers who like blasters," he said. "It's what you get if you have more money than training.

Although my partner carries one and she seems pretty competent so far. Could just be my personal bias talking."

The screen flickered to life, revealing a standard entry-image for Stream-skipping.

"Okay," she said, "we're in. I have to talk to my rig for a minute. Not to be rude."

"Sure."

Elicasta issued a series of commands to the computer on her head, none of which made sense to Makk. He got the basic gist of it, though: she asked the device to go back to a specific historical point—she'd already bookmarked it—slow down a sequence, and translate the keystrokes for her. It seemed simple enough, but it took about twenty minutes of trial-and-error, because Mirka's fingers weren't visible the whole time, so probabilistic guesswork was involved.

"Okay, I got it," she said, finally.

"Was that to me?" Makk asked. He was in the kitchen area, reviewing the beverage options. No beer, tragically, but Bincha did have a bottle of Wivvolian vodka. This was probably not the occasion for it.

"It was."

Makk pulled up a chair, as she tapped in the first set of commands, which got them to a gateway on the drop site splash page.

After a second set of commands, the site had to think for a little while.

"If this asks for an ident reconfirm, we're screwed," Elicasta said. "What kind of hunting do you do?"

"What?"

"Sorry, I hate waiting for anything, ever, so I keep busy with dumb questions. What kind of hunting do you do?"

"I don't," he said. "I mean, I could. I mostly fish on the lake. Binchagag hunts deer sometimes, duck sometimes. I don't know what else."

"Sounds exciting. Vacation in the woods and kill things."

"Not a bad slogan."

"Boom, here we go," she said, as the screen advanced. She entered the next set of commands, and then hesitated over the execute key.

"As soon as I do this, the clock starts," she said. "Are you ready?"

"I think we're well past the point where *no* is an acceptable answer. Go ahead."

She hit the button, and nothing terrible happened immediately. In Makk's mind, an exceptionally long fuse was just lit, and he was sitting on the bomb the fuse led to. But that was something to worry about later. They had one chance to watch the vid before it was time to get up and relocate; they had to make it count.

The vid opened up the way he expected: a recognizable Orno Linus opened his door to admit a Septal in full monk's robe and then closed the door. End scene. In the edited version, after few more seconds the vid jumped ahead twenty-two minutes.

That didn't happen this time.

"You're saying this part was edited out by the person who recorded this?" Makk asked.

"Yeah, she said nothing happened and it was boring, so she cut it," Elicasta said. "Professor Linus opens the door again about ten minutes in, then closes it again. I don't know why."

"Keep it here," Makk said.

The optical was acting up, showing the rooftop and some of the trees.

"She was trying to calibrate the drone," Elicasta said. "I think the smoke from the chimney was screwing with the movement sensor. I don't know if you've ever worked with one, but that isn't supposed to happen. It's meant to compensate for wind and smoke and stuff like that. It's also possible there was noise going on in the yard to keep the drone from finding something new to look at."

"There's no audio file here?"

"Right. It's not getting suppressed; the drone was glitchy. It knew when noises were being made and could react to them, but it wasn't tracking them into the vid."

They waited for the optical to calm down, then a little time passed and Orno showed up again. As promised, he opened the door, stood there for a few seconds, and then disappeared inside as the door fell closed on its own.

"Weird," Makk said. "It looks like he's airing the place out or something."

"I know. This is about as far as I got before we had to bolt, but Mirka said nothing else happens until the end. Suspense is killing me; do you wanna skip?"

"It's tempting, but no."

Eight minutes later—or eighteen minutes into the twenty-two-minute gap—the door opened and closed again, seemingly on its own.

"Whoa," Elicasta said. "What was that?"

"Maybe Orno was standing behind the door?" Makk suggested.

"Could be, I guess. Mirka didn't mention that one."

"It's even less memorable than the other one. If it hadn't closed right away I would have thought the wind did that."

"Yeah," Elicasta said.

She was toying with an idea. Makk hadn't known her very long or very well, but he could see what she looked like when her brain kicked in.

"What is it?" he asked.

"Probably nothing."

"Might be something. Let me decide."

"It's something stupid, that's all. Dark Stream rumors. I know an UnVeeser or two who would pop an optical over this. Wait, wait, wait. Here it comes."

They'd reached the end of the twenty-two-minute gap.

About ten seconds passed, and then out came the Septal that was supposed to be Dorn Jimbal.

So far, with the hood on, nothing looked different. They looked around for a few seconds, and then the hood came off...

Makk couldn't breathe. It felt like one of Calcut's thugs had punched him in the gut again.

"Okay," Elicasta said, "All right, well, I don't know who that is. Do you?"

"Yes," he said. "Her name is Viselle Daska, and we're in a lot of trouble."

Chapter Seventeen

"She's your *partner*?" Elicasta asked. "Oh yeah, that's *fantastic*."

He was at the window. Someone was coming up the long road that led only to one place: Binchagag's cabin. They'd already lost their escape route.

"Have you ever fired a gun?" he asked, heading for the ammo cabinet and working the combination lock.

"No, I've never fired a gun, are you joking? Let's just drive out of here before your *partner* gets here."

"Someone's already coming. I don't think it's her; I think it's the team you met at the warehouse."

"No, no, that's not right, that's way too fast," she said. "They had to have been heading here already. Wait, did Viselle Daska know we were coming here? Did you tell her?"

"She was my last direct before we left," he said. "I didn't tell her where, but I didn't have to. She knows how to activate the trace on my badge."

"Seriously."

"She's done it before. Found a way to make it sound charming."

"Nita's sake, Makk. Did she flutter her blue eyes at you too?"

"She did, actually." He was loading the first rifle he could get his hands on. "She also made a bunch of clever observations that don't seem half as clever now that I know she beat me to the crime scene by three days. Here."

He handed her the rifle, and began loading another one.

"I said no, I can't fire a gun."

"You said you *haven't*. Anyone *can*. Point it at something and pull the trigger. Not now; when there's someone to shoot."

"I'm not going to *shoot* someone!"

"That's too bad, because that's what they're going to do to you when they get here. Look, I'm not happy about this either. A minute ago, my partner was still running down promising leads on our suspect, and I was about to blow open the case. Now, I'm pretty sure Dorn Jimbal will go to the grave they're already lying in as the chief suspect, and Viselle is using her daddy's money to make sure that story never changes. That means ensuring you and I don't leave here alive."

"You forgot the part where she killed Linus for some reason," Elicasta said.

"Honus's balls," he said. "The DNA."

"What?"

"We excluded her DNA preemptively. I'm such a godsdamn idiot."

"How about if we made for the woods?"

Makk checked out the window. A team of seven had arrived, in two cars.

"We're in a defensible position here," he said. "We'd never make it in the woods."

"I can run pretty fast," she said.

"I believe you. I can't."

"Bad knee from the army days, right."

He stared at her. "Just how close were you to running that story on me?" he asked.

"Pretty close."

"Glad you didn't. See that corner over there? The one without windows? Crouch down in it, and point the gun at the back door. Someone comes through, pull the trigger. Do I need to show you where the trigger is?"

"No, I can work that out. Can't you order up support or something? I can reach a few million subs that probably also never fired a gun, but you know some armed people, don't you? Other than your partner?"

"Yeah. I can do that."

He pulled his badge out. It was supposed to be lit up, indicating he was on duty. It wasn't. He tapped the face, and got no response.

"Something's wrong with it," he said. "I can't get a signal."

"There's no place in Inimata without a signal, let me see."

She took a look at it.

"Looks dead," she said.

"That's what I said."

"Your last direct was to her? I think she bricked it."

"If we survive this," he said, shoving the badge back into his pocket, "remind me to ask you what you just said. Where's *your* voicer? You can direct an alarm yourself."

"I lost it in the river."

"Perfect. And the rig on your head?"

"It's no more designed to make alarm directs than your laptop," she said. "I can live-Stream my own murder if you think that'll help."

"I'll leave that up to you. Now get in the corner."

She crouched down and pointed the rifle, with the butt in her stomach.

"Not like that," he said. "Watch more fic vids with guns, for Ho's sake. On the shoulder. Otherwise, the recoil will..."

And then the window to his right exploded. Elicasta

screamed. Makk dropped, rolled, and sat up pressed against the wall next to the window.

Blaster shot, he thought. The impact on the wall at the other end of the room gave him a decent idea of where the shooter had been standing, roughly, so after a two-count, he spun around and fired at that spot with one of the rifles.

He had no idea if he hit anybody, because he was already spinning away from the window by then, crawling to one of the undamaged windows to see about getting a better angle.

How well-trained are you guys? he wondered.

He'd been semi-serious when he told Elicasta that the use of blaster might indicate that this team of hitters was inexperienced. At the time, though, his life didn't depend on this assumption being correct.

The way to use blasters effectively, as a team, was to stagger shots to mitigate the five-second lag time. It took about that long for the blaster to recharge, and in the delay—unless they had a second weapon—the shooter was defenseless. If this was a well-trained fire team, Makk could expect to be under fire in a coordinated volley, with blaster fire coming every one or two seconds apart in a cycle.

It required some coordination, and practice as a unit. Since Makk immediately returned fire after the first shot and nobody blew his face off for trying, that could mean they were as inexperienced as he'd been hoping.

It wasn't much to cling to, but it was something.

Makk smashed the undamaged window with the butt of the rifle. This was met with another shot, which took out Binchagag's kitchenette and the rest of the glass in the window, but nothing else. Makk counter-fired, and this time heard a cry. The shooter had been beside one of the cars, standing there like an idiot, and now he was on the ground and pulling himself to shelter around the rear bumper.

"Did you get one?" Elicasta asked.

He put his finger to his mouth, and then pointed to the entrance. Someone was charging the front door.

She nodded. Then he pointed to his eyes and then the back entrance.

Keep your eyes on that door, he was telling her. He hoped she understood, because the front was going to get complicated shortly and he needed her to keep watching his back.

The front door—which Makk didn't barricade, or even lock—flew open with unexpected ease, and the man who kicked it open stumbled into the room. Using the rifle like a club, Makk swept the intruder's legs, took his blaster before he even landed, and fired it once into the man's face. Then he rolled out of the way of another blaster shot that came through the open door.

Predictable, he thought. He kicked the door closed again.

"Gods," muttered Elicasta. She was staring at what was left of the man's head instead of the door.

"Focus!" Makk said. "Back door."

"Sorry!"

Then she screamed and fired a shot, not at the back door but at the window next to it. She didn't hit anyone that he could see, but she did take out the window, which wasn't bad for her first attempt at firing a rifle.

"Did I get him?" she asked.

"I don't know, but you definitely scared him off."

He saw two people running outside now, around opposite ends of the house.

"I'm going to need to go out there," he said.

"What? No. No, you can't."

"They're adjusting tactics. We have to do the same. I count five. You see how they're dressed?"

"Yes."

"Matching outfits?"

"I see, Makk."

"And how I'm not dressed like that? Shoot anyone that looks

like them, and don't shoot anyone that looks like me. I'm going to draw them away. Once I've done that, I'll fire my handgun twice in the air, bang-bang."

He held up the handgun to illustrate this, which wouldn't do a ton of good if she didn't know what a handgun sounded like.

"You hear that, drop the rifle and run straight for the back door, down to the dock, and jump into the lake."

"Then what?"

"Start swimming," he said. "I don't know, I haven't thought that far ahead."

"What about you?"

"I'll be okay."

He opened the front door again. Immediately, two blaster shots filled the space where a human would be standing, if any human were foolish enough to stand there. Makk spun into the opening, fired twice—both times at cars that were probably hiding someone—and then charged across the open space between the front entrance and the parking lot. Even with a bum knee and unable to take a deep breath thanks to the broken ribs, he closed the distance in way less than five seconds.

The first guy he encountered looked ill-prepared for close-up combat. Frankly, he looked surprised that anyone would charge a guy with a hand blaster, which was just poor training. Makk bashed him in the nose with the rifle, hugged him before he fell over, and spun around to put him between Makk and the second active shooter, who wasted his next blaster shot on his partner.

Makk let the dead man fall away, and fired the blaster he lifted off the dead guy in the house, hitting his target in the chest.

The car's windshield to Makk's right shattered. He dropped to the ground.

Lying in the dirt, Makk could see the guy he wounded with the rifle from inside the house, dragging himself away. Then there were the two he'd just taken care of out front, and the one on the floor of the house. Provided his count was right, that left three.

He got up and crouched behind the car's trunk to take a shot at the one who blew up the windshield, which he pegged as being at the corner of the house on the right. Immediately, another shot came from the left corner of the house, narrowly missing his head.

That's two, he thought. He ducked back down and turned. Someone was moving through the woods—a decently-thought-out flanking maneuver.

He fired his handgun in the air, twice.

Go, Elicasta, he thought.

The shooter in the woods—Makk couldn't see him, but could see evidence of him as he moved through the brush—froze at the sound of the gunshots.

The guy probably thought he was out of range where he was. That would have been true for anything except Makk's rifle.

Makk rolled onto his stomach, steadied the rifle, aimed it at the last spot he saw movement, and waited.

The guy in the woods moved. Makk fired. He stopped moving.

Maybe I should *hunt deer sometime,* he thought.

He climbed back up into a crouch to check on the other two. The one on the left was out of breath and kept panting audibly, while the one on the right picked a spot with the sun at his back; they were both still there.

"I've got five to your none, fellas," Makk shouted. "If you run away now I promise not to shoot you in the back. What do you say?"

The door to the cabin creaked open.

"Makk," Elicasta said from the doorway.

Makk was about to yell at her for not running to the pond like he told her to, until he saw what was *actually* going on: Viselle Daska had a blaster pointed at the Veeser's head.

"When did you get here, Viselle?" Makk asked.

"A little late, it looks like," she said. "You and I need to talk. Why don't you put down all those guns and come inside?"

"You've got two shooters ready to drop me if I do that," he said.

"Right, hang on."

Viselle walked Elicasta out past the porch, so she could make eye contact with the men at the corners.

"I can take it from here!" she shouted. "You can go."

Somewhat sheepishly, they emerged from their respective corners, blasters still out but looking unsure about where to point them.

"Put those away," Viselle said. "I told you, I have this. Come on; you know who I am."

They holstered their weapons. Then Viselle took the blaster away from Elicasta's head long enough to shoot the one on the left, spin around—keeping Elicasta between herself and Makk—and kill the one on the right.

She had the blaster pressed up against Elicasta's head again before Makk could do much more than register shock.

"Wow," Makk said. "What kind of blaster *is* that?"

"It's just a newer model. Doesn't have a lot of the power problems as the older ones."

"Nice," he said. "I'm glad *they* didn't have those, or I'd be dead already. How many shots per charge?"

"I'm not telling. Come on, let's talk."

She walked Elicasta back into the house.

Makk walked to the doorway, put the blaster, the rifle, and his service piece down on the stoop, and stepped over the threshold.

"Have a seat," Viselle said, directing him to the chair next to Elicasta.

"Are you okay?" he asked the Veeser.

"I'm unhurt," she said. "But I'm not okay."

Viselle pulled a third chair up to the table, closed the laptop that had somehow managed not to get hit by any stray blaster shots, and then conspicuously checked out the dead body in the middle of the room.

"I'm impressed, Makk," she said. "My father didn't have time to hire the *best,* but the team you took apart was supposed to be pretty good."

"He should probably get his money back."

"I'm sure he'll try."

"Who's your father?" Elicasta asked. "Just so I'm caught up."

"Ba-Ugna Kev," Viselle said.

"You're shitting me."

"Nope. This is all *his* mess. He's a genius, but he can also be an idiot." She pointed at the dead man. "Totally unnecessary. Can't blame him for trying, I guess. Anyway. Makk."

"Yes?"

"I didn't kill Orno Linus."

Makk laughed.

"We saw you," Elicasta said.

"Did you?" Viselle asked. "You saw me enter and leave, but you *didn't* see me kill him. That's because I didn't. Not that I blame you; my father knew I was there the night Orno was murdered, heard about the vid, *bought* the vid, watched it, and arrived at the exact same conclusion you just did. But you're both wrong. I was there but I didn't kill him. Makk, I'm telling you."

"Nobody could use the front door," Makk said. "Just the back. You established that yourself. We only have one person going in or out and I'm looking at her."

"I know what you think you saw, but someone else came in after me, killed Orno, and left before I did."

"Who?" Makk asked.

"This isn't going to sound any better. I don't know."

"You're right; that doesn't sound better. Was he murdered by a ghost?"

"Or someone invisible," Elicasta muttered.

"I was upstairs when it happened," Viselle said. "Hiding in the closet. I wasn't supposed to be there, so...Orno got a message, from someone. He didn't say who, but whoever it was, they were on their way over, so he told me to go hide."

"We didn't find a voicer," Makk said.

"I realize that," she said. "Didn't find a murder weapon either. Whoever it was, they took both with them."

"The phantom killer," Makk said. "Okay."

He sighed, and stood. His ribs were screaming and he was having trouble breathing, because now that his adrenaline had settled down, every part of his body that had been worked over by Calcut's men decided to remind him about it. His balky knee was also not doing all that great. He stood anyway, and tried to pretend he wasn't about to fall over.

Viselle, who had her blaster on the table between them—with her hand on the blaster—didn't seem to mind a little pacing.

"Here's what it *looks* like, Detective Daska," he said. "It *looks* like you dressed as a Septal in order to get into Linus's townhouse without attracting attention, murdered him, and then left. Next day, you started pressing Captain Llotho to get into the rotation—thinking it was only a matter of time before someone found the body—so you could get the case and make *sure* there was a solid explanation for your DNA being at the scene. How am I doing so far?"

"Except for the murder, pretty good."

"How'd you know when Other Jimbal was going to find the body? You were standing next to me when it was reported."

"I didn't. Once it was clear I wouldn't be getting off the bench, I decided to partner with someone. Everything I said about partnering with you was true. I was going to wait until we were both on-duty and make an anonymous tip."

"That put you at the scene with a chance to search the place for any evidence implicating you, and bonus, you got to sit next to me for the whole case, to make *sure* I didn't get close. But then this vid popped up, and you found out about it somehow.

Knowing what it'll show, you directed daddy, who you supposedly haven't spoken to in years, and asked for his help. He bought it through an intermediary, but knew that having done that, he *had* to air something. How'd he get Dorn's face, out of curiosity? Do you know?"

"It's not his face," Viselle said. "It's a reconstruction based on the bone structure of the visible bottom half."

"Great. *Perfect*. So that went out, and we all started looking for Dorn Jimbal. Only, you got to them first. You're the Septal that Sister Mye saw in the car, aren't you? Is Other Jimbal dead?"

"I am," she said. "And no. I wasn't lying about that, either. I arranged to have Dorn moved to Lys. It was the only way to make sure nobody hurt them."

"And also to make sure nobody got a chance to look under that hood to see if Dorn looked the same as in the vid."

"It...served two purposes, yes. But I didn't want them hurt. It wasn't my idea to blame this on them; they didn't deserve this, and I know there are people out there who want to hurt them. Like, whoever did that to your face, for instance."

Makk decided then that Viselle knew *exactly* who was responsible for his beatdown.

"So he's out now; on Lys, or a grave out by Route AB6, it doesn't matter. He's never surfacing, so he'll go down as the killer. Only problem left is everybody who saw the real vid. How did you take care of that?"

"By killing all of us," Elicasta said. "Zam and Wicha, and then Mirka. Then me and Makk. I assume you're still going to do the last thing, before this is over."

"I don't *want* to," Viselle said. "That's why we're talking right now. But yes. You have the basics right. My father bought the vid on the condition that he submit an edited version for the Stream. Then he hired...well, like I said, not the *best* of the best, but these guys. For their efforts, they managed to *not* kill you three times,

Elicasta Sangristy. You're either very hard to kill or they're very bad at their jobs. I'm leaning toward the latter."

"How did Ba-Ugna Kev even find out about the auction?" Elicasta asked. "It wasn't exactly public knowledge."

"I don't know," Viselle admitted. "I never asked."

"All this to keep his daughter from being outed as the killer," Makk said. "And now you want me to believe you aren't even the killer."

"I'm *not*."

"Why were you there?"

"I was picking up something Orno took from the vault," she said. "Something really important."

"The book?" Makk asked.

Viselle hesitated, which Makk found interesting. It was like she didn't want to reveal that she and Makk had managed to successfully hide a pre-Collapse book taken from the Septal vaults, even now, even if only Elicasta was there to hear it. Even when Viselle was probably going to shoot both of them.

She asked me where I hid it, he remembered. *The last time we spoke.*

"Something more important than just a book," she said. "A *lot* more important. Something Orno Linus would be willing to lay down his life for if it came to it."

"This isn't remotely convincing, Viselle," he said.

"I know. I'm sorry. I thought I could explain this without... there are things going on, Makk. This is bigger than both of us. Bigger than Orno, or Calcut, or High Hat Plaint, or my father."

"This is the part where she says she has to kill us for the greater good," Elicasta said. "I think I saw this vid before."

"No, I said I don't want to do that," Viselle said. "I meant it."

She sighed, got up, and did a little pacing of her own.

"Orno was right about the Outcast, okay?" she said. "Some of us are trying to do something about it."

Makk sat back down, to pre-empt falling over from shock.

Only the most hyper-religious Septals believed in a literal Outcast who would arrive one day to bring about the literal end of the world, and Viselle Daska wasn't a hyper-religious Septal. Neither was Orno Linus, from what Makk knew of the man.

"*The Cull*," he said? "You're worried about The Cull?"

"I'm trying to *prevent* it. So are the people I'm working with."

Makk looked at Elicasta, who just shook her head.

"Same," she muttered. "This is off the range."

The last thing he expected was for this conversation to turn in the direction of a horror story parents told their kids to get them to keep them quiet at night.

"Okay," Makk said. "Let's go back. Orno stole something from the vault, and you were there that night to get it from him. And it's supposedly not a book. Did he give it to you?"

"He didn't get a chance. We spoke first; we'd never met face-to-face, and there were matters to settle. Neither of us was aware we were on a clock. Then he got a message on his voicer and told me to get upstairs. I heard arguing, and then nothing. I waited a few more minutes and went back down. I found him, I panicked, and I ran out."

"And the thing you were there to collect?" Makk asked.

"I didn't even stop to look for it."

"Or to direct the pollies," Elicasta said.

"I couldn't message it in, I had no justification for being there," Viselle said. "Makk, to your point earlier, that I only went back to clean up any evidence linking me to the scene: you're only half right. I went back to retrieve what I was there for in the first place."

"Did you?" he asked.

"It wasn't there. I think whoever killed Orno took it."

"Along with his voicer, and the murder weapon," Makk said. "That's quite a haul for your invisible man."

"When you thought it was Dorn Jimbal exiting the back of

Orno's townhouse, you didn't think they were the killer. Why was that?"

"I met them, and they're not a killer," he said. "If you're looking for the same leeway, I just saw you kill two men."

"You killed *five* before I got here," she said.

"Four. The wounded guy is still crawling through the woods, I'm pretty sure. Also, I never said I wasn't a killer, but I wasn't in Orno's condo that night. Besides, this was self-defense. What's your excuse?"

"I was protecting my partner. They would have eventually realized they'll only get paid if you two die. But give me some of the same benefit. If you saw the real ending of the vid, you know I didn't leave Orno's with a murder weapon either."

"That was enough to doubt Dorn's guilt; it's not enough for you. Look, I don't know what you want from us. There's no version of this where we're not surrounded by dead assassins in a cabin, with you holding a blaster to our heads. The snake has already crawled out of Javilon's crate here."

"We could tell a story," Viselle said. "The same one you were already going to tell, except for two things: I came here to back up my partner, and the vid showed Dorn Jimbal coming out of the house."

Elicasta laughed. "Why would we do that?" she asked.

"Because otherwise, you're right," Viselle said. "I'll have to kill you. And I don't want to do that."

"The vid will still get out," Elicasta said.

"You have access to the source file right now, and there are no copies. My father made sure of that. Just delete it," Viselle said. "Makk? You know it's a valid play. And I think you know, deep down, that I didn't kill Orno."

"I don't know anything for sure," he said. "But I *do* know if we delete that vid, there really is nothing stopping you from killing us. If you think you've earned some benefit from me based on our partnership, you've already used all of that up."

"Besides," Elicasta said. "That isn't the only copy." She tapped the side of her head. "I was recording while I watched. Just like I'm recording everything else that's happened in the past hour. Including this conversation."

Viselle was temporarily at a loss for words.

"You're lying," she said, eventually. "Your light isn't on."

"That doesn't mean it's not recording. Sure, I'll get in trouble for Streaming something I caught in lights-out. Might even lose my Verified. But which one of us do you think'll end up in deeper shit? Me or you?"

"She's telling the truth," Makk said. "We wouldn't have seen the unedited Linus vid if Elicasta hadn't recorded the keystrokes."

"Give me your headgear," Viselle said.

"No," Elicasta said. "You know how expensive this rig is? No way. You already blew up everything else I own; I'm keeping this."

Viselle walked up next to Elicasta and held the blaster to her head. "Give it to me, or I'll destroy it with your head still attached."

"Still no," Elicasta said.

Viselle screamed in frustration and then, with her free hand, ripped the optical rig off of Elicasta's head.

"Aaaowww!" Elicasta shouted, as some of her hair went with it.

The optical, now in Viselle's hand, did a curious thing then: The blue light flickered, blinked, went solid for three seconds, and then turned off.

"What was that?" Viselle asked. Then louder, while pointing the blaster at Elicasta's head again: "*What was that?*"

"Sorry," Elicasta said, "I forgot to mention the panic mode. That kicks in whenever someone other than me takes the rig off. It just dumped our whole conversation on the Stream. Congratulations, you're about to be famous."

Viselle screamed, turned around, and threw the rig at the wall. When that didn't satisfy her rage, she spun around and fired the blaster at Elicasta. But by then, Makk had already upended the table. The shot took out a good portion of the wood tabletop, but no parts of Elicasta.

"Viselle!" he shouted. "If you really didn't want to kill us, you don't have to now. There's no point."

He held his breath and listened to his (ex) partner pacing. Elicasta was huddled under his arm, muttering a religious prayer she didn't seem like the type of person to be familiar with.

"Just run," Makk said. "You can probably get out of town before they come looking for you if you leave right now."

Viselle pulled down the table. Elicasta screamed.

"All right, Makk," Viselle said. She'd holstered the blaster. "But don't try to find me." To Elicasta, she said, "one day, I hope you understand the damage you've done."

Then Viselle Daska walked out the back door. A minute later her aero-car was zooming away over the tree line.

"I don't think I like your partner very much," Elicasta said.

Makk laughed.

Chapter Eighteen

Binchagag's cabin was pretty wrecked, but amazingly, his car was fine. It never drew fire because nobody attempted to hide behind it, suffering only slightly from blood Makk was pretty sure came off the first guy he killed.

With a working car, no working voicers, and no idea how long it would be before someone came to help them—or worse, before someone else came to kill them—Makk and Elicasta got back into the car and drove to the nearest town: Raighkood.

Once they reached the main drag, the first thing they did was locate a public alarm voicer to reach Twenty-One Central. It took a few dispatch transfers to make it all the way to Captain Llotho and then a few minutes more to get Llotho to believe what Makk was telling him. It wasn't until the captain Stream-skipped his way to Elicasta's feed—where her emergency flag entry was drawing international attention already—before he really took Makk seriously.

Makk also had to explain that his badge was bricked, (and what that meant, as Llotho didn't know this was a thing either) but that the GPS still worked, so after putting an All-Eyes out on

Detective Viselle Daska and contacting the feds about the mess at the cabin, maybe he could send a local cruiser around.

Then they found a diner.

"I somehow knew I'd end up in Rapewood today," Elicasta said. They were settled in a booth, waiting for food and getting eyed by a curious waiter.

"It's just a small town with a couple of bad neighborhoods," Makk said. "Half the towns outside of Velon look like this. You should get out more."

"Thanks, but I don't run a travel Stream. I knew a guy who did, but..."

"But?"

"But he was killed by the bomb that was supposed to kill me," she said.

The first thing Makk thought was *so there's an opening in the travel Streamer market now*, which he did not say out loud. He drifted toward gallows humor instinctively after combat—and that was certainly what they'd both just survived—because that's how one got through the day in the army. It didn't fly as well outside of the service.

"Sorry," he said instead. "You're talking about that Bogdis guy, right? Were you close?"

"No. Not that it matters. He and Mirka are gonna probably haunt me or something."

"Survivor guilt," he said. "I've been through it."

"I bet."

She disappeared into her optical for a couple of minutes. This behavior came off as rude at first—she did it a lot in the car on the way to the cabin, sometimes in mid-sentence—but now he was mostly used to it. Spend enough time with a Veeser, you have to accustom yourself to the idea that you'll never have their full attention.

"Vid's blown up," Elicasta said. "Hate to say, but looks like I made you into a celeb, Makk Stidgeon."

"Now you can do that story about me," he said.

"Can I?"

"I was kidding."

"Oh. Too bad. You're getting some marriage proposals here."

He laughed. "There's a long application process for the next Mrs. Stidgeon," he said. "And a line."

The waiter brought over their food then—a meat puff for Makk, and a salad for Elicasta—so they disappeared into their food for a few minutes.

"Invisible men," Makk said, eventually, between bites.

"No, no," Elicasta said. She pointed at him with her fork. "Don't tell me you're buying. That whole story was dreamland."

"Hey, you mentioned it first."

"Before I thought it was part of miss crazy's alibi. Is she really Ba-Ugna Kev's daughter?"

"I never tried to confirm it independently, but it adds up."

"Kev's only one of the most powerful people on Dib, and we just implicated him in four murders. Unless she's not his daughter, then I dunno. But that's probably not a good place to be."

"I've been between Duqo Plaint and Calcut Linus all week," Makk said. "You get used to it. Tell me about the invisible men."

"Fine. It's a fake thing, though. UnVeeser playground stuff."

"Pretend I don't care about the provenance."

"It's...ahhh. It's *so* dumb. You know how, like, everything in the real is on vid somewhere? Not really *everything* but a lot. Random shit gets snagged, all the time. What happens is, some of these Unverifieds collect vids of doors opening, and windows closing, and...trees in the wind. Stuff like that, to build their stupid case."

"Which is, invisible people," Makk said.

"Right. With a decent edit and enough examples, you've got something that looks like proof."

"I see. And who do they think these invisible people are, that are opening doors and closing windows, and running through the woods?"

"Depends. Aliens, monsters. Rich people."

Makk laughed.

"Rich people?" he repeated.

"Yeah. I kind of get that one. All these optical drones and what-not, you hardly ever see a real celeb on the Stream who doesn't want to be on the Stream. The patter is that rich people don't show up on optical vids."

"That's interesting," Makk said.

"Nah, it's crazy. Don't bluff."

There are ways to block a drone feed, Makk thought.

"Where'd you go?" Elicasta asked.

"Not far," he said. "Just remembering something someone said to me."

That lunch at the diner was the last peaceful hour either of them would have for the rest of the day. Because after the meal was over, a pair of uniformed federal officers showed up out front to retrieve them, impound Binchagag's car—for trace evidence analysis—and ferry them back to just about the last place either of them wanted to be: the cabin.

Zonic National Park was well outside Twenty-One Central's jurisdiction, as well as Velon city proper. But it wouldn't matter even if it *was* legally in Velon, because national park grounds were under the purview of the federal government. Consequently, Makk had to spend the afternoon dealing with feds, which would be fine except there was some sort of legal mandate that the government only hire assholes. (Or, working for the feds turned you into one. He'd never been sure.)

They made him walk through everything five times, for a variety of audiences. There seemed to be some disagreement as to the likelihood that Makk had dispatched five men armed with blasters by himself, so they kept drilling Elicasta in case she was a secret assassin capable of being fooled by the terribly clever technique of repeatedly asking the same exact question.

The only part where Makk's story changed at all had to do with the number of dead. Last he knew, there was a wounded guy crawling his way out of the park, but he evidently only got as far as the dirt road before bleeding out. Makk was as consistent and thorough as he could be about the rest of it.

It became an even sillier exercise once Elicasta pointed out that parts of the attack had been Streamed; if the feds really doubted Makk's story, they could verify roughly half of it by reviewing the vid.

Captain Llotho arrived around sixteen o'clock to declare that the entire scene was part of the Linus investigation, and therefore did not *actually* belong to the feds at all. That discussion lasted about an hour, and didn't so much conclude as get suspended temporarily, as it was the kind of thing that could continue until the end of the known universe. Especially once the attorneys got involved. Llotho's intercession was enough, anyway, to free Makk and Elicasta from the clutches of the federal question-and-answer circle of death.

Makk filled in Llotho on the entire case on the way back. Yordon didn't seem thrilled to be getting an update on a murder investigation with a Veeser in the back seat, but didn't say so, and Makk didn't care because Elicasta had already heard most of it. Plus, she'd earned an exclusive on the story by now.

"That's a lot," Llotho said, as they reached both the city limits and the end of Makk's story.

"It was quite a morning," Makk said.

"I notice the one thing you're missing is who killed Orno Linus. You don't think Daska actually did it, do you?"

"I have my doubts."

"Without evidence that someone else was there, I'm not sure

we have a choice but to bring her up on charges. I mean, *more* charges. We have her for the murder of two people, on vid, and that's just for starters. I don't think anyone will complain if we throw Linus in with all the rest of it and close the case. Plus, I have to pull you."

"You have to what?"

"Nothing personal. Per the commissioner, the department has to hand over the case. And look, it makes sense; the lead suspect came from our unit."

"When?"

"It's practically done already," Llotho said.

"I need another week," Makk said. "Can you stall it?"

Llotho laughed.

"A week," he said. "He wants a week."

"Come on, you owe me."

"By what figment of your addled mind do you figure that, detective?"

"I didn't want a partner," Makk said. "I *never* wanted a partner. Look at what giving me one led to."

Llotho sighed. "I can get you three days, tops. If you can't make a case in three days, it's going over to Eighty-Five Main."

"Thank you."

"Just tell me you have a suspect in mind," Llotho said, "and you need the extra time to prove it."

"I have a couple of ideas," Makk said.

"He thinks it's the invisible man," Elicasta said, from the back seat.

"You aren't helping," Makk said.

Llotho bought him the three days. Makk spent the first two of them going over the evidence collected at the scene for the hundredth time, re-watching the unedited Linus vid, and talking by voicer to Elicasta Sangristy, who was serving as his temporary sounding-board in the absence of a proper partner.

He did *not* like having partners, but he decided he *did* like having another human being there to discuss sensitive things relating to his case. Especially for a case as annoying as this one.

She'd bounced back from her multiple near-death experiences pretty quickly. It helped that none of what happened affected the credits in her account. Her active Veeser status wasn't going anywhere either, and with the drama of her going from presumed-dead to dramatically-still-alive, all played out on the Stream, things were looking up for her in every way.

"Don't blow a vessel over this," she said at the beginning of one of their directs, "but you may be talking to the most famous person in the world here."

"Remind me to get your autograph," he said, "the next time I see you."

"Make it soon. I'm only going to be the most famous person in the world for another day or two. These things don't last."

She was staying in a downtown hotel until new living arrangements could be sorted, and had invited him to swing by for dinner sometime at said hotel. Makk couldn't tell if it was an invitation for *just* dinner, and was extremely bad at guessing right about these kinds of things, but since the deal was that he had to solve the case first, they were probably never having that dinner-and-whatever anyway.

"You know what I keep wondering," he said to her, on another direct. "Mirka told you the audio was screwy, right? It couldn't record sound, but it could *detect* sound?"

"That's what she said. It was probably a channel problem. Those older models..."

"Yeah, I don't care why. I'm thinking the reason she couldn't get the drone to move on was that it was doing what it was supposed to do. The sensors picked up sound, and it tried to find the source of that sound."

"Your invisible man."

"He'd make noise coming through the yard, and knocking on the door."

"Babe, it was just the chimney smoke and a glitchy old drone model."

She was probably right. Llotho was probably right too when he told Makk—in an effort to get him to drop the case already—that pinning this on Viselle Daska wasn't just in everyone's best interest; she probably actually did it.

Watching the vid over and over again wasn't helping matters. The longer he watched the two empty-doorway scenes, the more convinced he became that someone was there and he just couldn't see them.

If this is Duqo Plaint, I need a lot *more*, he thought. Accusing the High Hat of murder, with evidence of a vid that didn't have the High Hat on it, and an offhand comment about having a way to confound a drone feed, wasn't going to be nearly enough.

On day three, in desperation-mode, he directed Leemie.

"Not over the air," Leemie said, which was just how he answered the voicer, regardless of who was on the other end.

"No choice, I can't make it to you," Makk said. "Look, this case is going to get pulled out from under me by the end of the over, and I'm running out of ideas. Do you have anything?"

"You mean in my research into the thing we're not going to talk about over the air?"

"Yes, that's what I mean."

"Maybe. I was going to wait until I saw you again. Looks like that was a close call a few days back, huh? Boys with toys."

"Boys with toys," Makk agreed.

This was an in-joke from their military days. *Boys with toys* was anyone who thought carrying a big gun was an effective substitute for combat training. At first, they used it to describe their

Kindonese opponents, who were notorious for sending green troops out before they were ready. Later, every new soldier—Inimatan or Kindonese—seemed to fit the description, at least in the eyes of the more experienced troops.

"How about it, Leemie," Makk said. "I could use a break. What do you have?"

"Turns out the word *key* in archaic Eglinat is pretty close to the same as the modern derivation, so I went looking for uses of it. Found one passage. I've only got a few words down."

"Read it to me."

"Ha-ha, sure. Okay, here you go. 'Blah blah blah key, blah the five, keys something something something, something'...and this word, I think it's either 'Cull' or 'Outcast', and then 'blah-blah-something, unity.' Then it goes on for a while."

"Okay, so you really don't have anything yet," Makk said.

"That's what I was saying. But it's a passage that references The Five, the Outcast, and either one key or multiple keys. It's not anything yet, but it's not *nothing*."

"It's also not something."

"Sorry. Look, you'll let me know if I gotta burn this, right? Like, *before* they're at my door?"

"You'll just end up burning the whole building down. That fireplace hasn't..."

Then it all fell into place.

"Gotta go, Leemie, thanks. You've been a big help."

"Have I?" But..."

Makk disconnected, and called up the Linus vid again.

"Chimney smoke, chimney smoke," he muttered.

He got to the spot, and froze the image.

Two chimneys.

He rolled his chair over to the evidence manifest on the table at the other end of the room, flipping through until he found the page he wanted. They'd documented *everything*, including what was in the coldbox.

He grabbed his voicer, and messaged Jori Len.

"Jori," he said, "I need forensics ride-along."

"Hey Makk. For when?"

"Right now. Can you swing it?"

"Depends. Where are we going?"

"Orno Linus's townhouse. You're about to owe me a beer."

Chapter Nineteen

It took absolutely all of Yordon Llotho's clout, favors-owed and bribes-promised to hold onto the case for the additional two days it took to make the necessary arrangements.

One of those days was spent reassembling Orno Linus's townhouse, which was something they usually did only after the case was closed, and only at the request of the family. (Otherwise, they just handed over the stuff in boxes.) By the time it was done, the only thing they didn't have that the original scene *did* have, was the corpse.

Reassembling it was part of a show. It wasn't intrinsic to the solving of the case, but it helped in convincing the two most politically volatile individuals in Velon to come meet them at the crime scene, the following morning.

Makk got to the townhouse early, walked the living room a few thousand times, and considered taking up smoking.

This is going to work, he told himself. *And if it doesn't, well, I'm still famous on the Stream. That must count for something.*

Captain Llotho arrived next, along with Jori.

"I've got unis buttoning up the street," Llotho said.

"Swigg?" Makk asked.

"One-man riot squad," Llotho said. "Tayler's there too, in case we need a brain. Is your girlfriend in position?"

"She's not my—"

"I know, calm down. Ho's sake, you're blushing."

"That's just the bruise. Yes, she's in position."

"Good. Not that we necessarily need her; the line's crawling with Veesers already. Like they were tipped off ahead of time."

"That's shocking," Makk said.

"You're saying they *were* tipped off ahead of time, aren't you?" Llotho said. "You're godsdamn crazy, Detective Stidgeon. And if this doesn't work, I didn't know anything about it."

"It'll work. Do you have everything you need, Jori?"

"I'm good to go," she said. "And for the record: I actually *don't* know what's happening here, so if it goes south, I'm tossing you both in the fire."

"You can't buy that kind of loyalty," Llotho said.

"If it helps," Makk said, "note that the back door still doesn't close on its own."

"That does *not* help, thank you," she said.

The night they returned to the townhouse to check for missing evidence, the first thing Makk did was confirm that if one left open the back door, neither gravity nor some mechanism in the door jamb caused the door to close by itself.

He made quite a big deal out of this discovery, trying it five or six times, and not once did he explain to Jori Len why it was relevant. At first, he wanted to see if she worked it out on her own; now it was just an entertaining way to torture her.

Makk's badge thrummed.

I've got Duqo Plaint coming your way, Elicasta messaged.

Makk went to the front window, and watched as Plaint's private car rolled past the barricade, and then past the front entrance and around the corner.

"Where's he going?" Jori asked.

"To the back," Makk said. "Man like him doesn't want to be

captured on vid walking through the front door to a crime scene where the police are waiting. Not if he can help it."

"And the street's crawling with Veesers," Jori said. "You're a crafty shit, Makk."

"Captain, you want to let the High Hat in?" Makk said.

Llotho stood at the back door, waited a couple of minutes, and then pulled it open to admit Duqo Plaint.

Unlike the last time they shared a room together, Duqo was formally hooded, and in a suit. He shook hands warmly—he had this two-handed double-pump that was weirdly popular with politicians and religious leaders—with Llotho, and then stepped through the kitchen to greet Makk in the same way.

"Stay right there, Highness," Makk said. "Sorry, it's a formality. This is still a crime scene. Jori?"

"Sorry, sir," Jori said, obsequiously. She held out a scanner. "Just put your thumb on the screen."

Plaint looked bemused.

"Really, detective. I thought we were done with this. Your partner...Daska, yes? I understand she's responsible for poor Orno's passing."

"Like I said, this is just a formality. I promised I'd have answers for you, and Professor Linus's murder isn't the only thing you asked me to help solve."

Plaint considered this.

"Yes, all right," he said. He put his thumb on the scanner. "But honestly, I have three law officers here who can attest to how a fresh sample of my DNA might end up at the scene; I see no reason for this."

Makk's badge thumped again. He looked at the screen.

Incoming, Elicasta messaged.

"That's great, Highness," Makk said. "Step on into the living room. We're expecting another, and then we'll get started."

"Who else is coming? Honestly, Captain...?"

"Trust the process, Duqo," Llotho said.

"Trust," Plaint said, mulling over the word.

Makk thought the High Hat was working out when the best time might be to juxtapose *trust* with the actions of Detective Daska.

Calcut Linus showed up a minute later, having similarly opted to drive past the well-videoed front entrance to take the townhouse from the rear. He brushed past Captain Llotho's outstretched hand, heading straight for Makk.

"Stidgeon," he barked, "what's going on out there?"

"Please stop there, Mr. Linus," Makk said. "Officer Len?"

Jori held up the scanner, which Calcut didn't look at with fondness.

"What's this about? I thought I was here to find out about my brother's case."

"You are," Makk said. "But as we've just explained to High Hat Plaint, this is technically still an active crime scene, so we have to follow the protocol."

Calcut still looked unsure. Makk stepped up next to him.

"This can't be the first time you've had to do this, Calcut," Makk said. "Just get it over with so we can start."

Grumbling, he put his thumb on the scanner.

"Didn't expect to see *you* here, Duqo," Linus said.

"Nor I you, Calcut," Plaint said. "Captain Llotho's people have developed an interest in the dramatic arts of late, it appears."

The scanner beeped, and Jori gave a nod.

"Okay, let's begin," Makk said. He led everyone to the bloodstain on the floor.

Stick to the script, he thought. His hand was trembling slightly, an indication that he was more nervous now than he had been when he was facing down armed killers in the cabin. But speaking in front of a crowd was never his thing, and this was quite the crowd.

"I want to walk through the night Orno was murdered," Makk said.

"What for?" Calcut asked.

"Bear with me, Mr. Linus," Makk said.

"I just don't know why I'm here."

"You're here because I promised you answers, personally. I also promised High Hat Plaint answers, personally."

"There were better ways to accomplish this," Plaint said.

"It'll make sense shortly, I promise. Here's what we know. At a little after seventeen-thirty, Professor Linus opened his back door to admit Viselle Daska, disguised as a Septal. According to her, she was there to pick up something Orno stole from the vault." He turned to Plaint. "My understanding is that something is still missing?"

"It is, yes."

"You'll find we've put everything back; once we're done, you're welcome to look for it again, provided the next-of-kin is okay with it."

"Just ship his stuff to my house," Linus said. "Is that all?"

"No," Makk said. "Viselle also said that some ten minutes after she arrived, Orno got a message on his voicer. Based on that message, Orno told her to hide so that he could let someone else in. Then, Orno and that *someone* had an argument, the result of which was that the unknown individual picked up the nearest heavy object and struck Orno in the back of the head. The killer then left, Daska came back down and discovered the body, and fled the scene herself."

"That's...I'm sorry," Plaint said. "That's a *preposterous* story. We all agree on that, yes? Tell me I'm not here because you're taking that seriously."

"You've hit on the problem, Highness," Makk said. "There's no visual evidence of another person entering and leaving."

"That bitch killed my brother," Calcut said. "That's what you're getting at, right? I figured that was why I was here. Where is she?"

Makk smiled.

"Calcut, the last time we were face-to-face, you asked me to hand over Dorn Jimbal, rather than book them downtown."

"I don't know what—"

"It's okay, you don't have to deny it. I won't be handing either Dorn or Viselle Daska over to you today, but you *will* find out who killed your brother. Can I keep going?"

"Let's just get through this, Calcut," Duqo said. He was checking his watch already.

"Thanks," Makk said. "I don't know if either of you have watched the unedited vid, but there *is* evidence that something happened at around those times. The back door opened and closed, twice, but there's no visual proof that anyone went in or out."

"Because there's nobody there, idiot," Calcut said.

"Jori, can you open the back door for me?" Makk said.

Officer Len looked like she'd just figured out where her birthday presents were hidden.

"Sure," she said.

She opened the back door, and let go. The door stayed open.

"As you can both see, once opened, the door stubbornly refuses to close," Makk said. "It has to be shut by someone. Yet on the unedited vid, at the eighteen-minute mark that door opens on its own, and closes on its own, despite nobody appearing to be there. You know what I thought of when I saw this? I thought of something you said, Duqo."

"Something *I* said?"

"In your office. You told me you liked to jog, and you preferred to do it without that hood. When I asked how you could get away with that without being captured by a drone, you said *there are ways to block a drone feed*. Do you remember that?"

Plaint laughed, but it was an uncomfortable sort of laugh.

"Well, of course what I meant was that we have ways to prevent drones from operating *nearby*."

Makk's badge thumped.

Sending both through, Elicasta messaged. *It's what we expected.*

"I thought that was what you meant too," Makk said. "Up until I compared the unedited vid to Daska's claim, and played with Orno's back door. Then I started to wonder if there was tech out there that could digitally exclude a person from a *live* feed."

"Really, detective," Plaint said. "There's no such tech on the market, and we all know it."

"Not on the *market*, no," Makk agreed. "We also all know the House keeps some of its tech to itself, and is also known to share that tech with...friends, from time to time."

He said this to Calcut.

"What is this shit," Calcut said.

"Yordon, really," Plaint said, to Llotho. "I didn't come here to entertain Streamer conspiracy theories."

"Gentlemen, we recorded both of you entering the rear of this townhouse," Makk said. "Duqo, here's you coming in."

Makk held up his badge, screen-forward, so they could all watch as Captain Llotho opened the back door to...nobody.

"And, here's Calcut."

A similarly mystifying event transpired, with Llotho admitting no one.

"These were captured by an overhead drone," Makk said. "The date-and-time stamps on the vids match up, and there are three officers of the law in here ready to testify under oath that Duqo Plaint and Calcut Linus entered this building at those times. So cut the shit."

Plaint and Linus shared a few annoyed looks with one another, before Plaint sighed and shrugged.

"All right," he said. "You've made your point. The technology *does* exist. But we're hardly the only two people employing it."

"You're the only two on my suspect list," Makk said.

"Detective Stidgeon, literally *hundreds* of Velonians have that technology at their disposal. If anything, you've widened your suspect pool substantially."

"That's not why *you're* here," Makk said. "You're here because DNA can put you here, Highness, *and* you've got the tech to make yourself invisible to a drone. Those two things are *also* true of whoever killed Professor Linus."

"Captain, please tell me you're not sanctioning this line of reasoning," Plaint said.

"Duqo, until ten seconds ago, I thought Detective Stidgeon's theory about vid-masking technology was completely insane," Llotho said. "I'm now inclined to give him all the time he needs to make the rest of his case."

"Well, I'm not," Calcut said. "I'm leaving."

"Your brother liked to bake bread, didn't he?" Makk asked. The question stopped Calcut in his tracks.

"Sure, I guess," he said. "He was nuts about that shit."

"Bread, and pasta," Makk said. "Used to have a big rolling pin for the pasta. Kept it in the kitchen, leaning up against the wall, right about where you're standing. We think that was the murder weapon."

"Good for you."

"He was going to be baking bread the night he was killed. The dough is still in the coldbox. Highness, Orno lived here for a few years, didn't he? Long enough to make some changes?"

"It was why he never moved closer," Plaint said.

"Right, he had a second oven put in. Something else I noticed in the unedited vid: this townhouse is the only one with two chimneys. The one in the den is closed off, but the one for the brick oven in the kitchen isn't. He had the oven going that night, and I know because smoke was coming out of it."

"I'm done with this," Calcut said. "You've got nothing."

"It bothered me, this whole time, where that rolling pin ended up," Makk said. "The smart thing, if you're a person who already doesn't appear on video, is to take it with you and dispose of it later. But that isn't what happened. What happened was, the killer threw the pin into the wood-burning brick oven, hoping to destroy the evidence."

"Right. Goodbye," Calcut said. "Captain Llotho, your boss is gonna hear about this shitshow."

He opened the back door to discover the way blocked by Officer Bod Swigg.

"We're not finished yet, Calcut," Makk said. "Let me explain the killer's mistake. His mistake was in not knowing how the oven worked. He threw the pin into the fire, and did something he *thought* would open the flue and stoke the flame. But what he did instead was *close* the flue and choke out the fire. I know this because the smoke wasn't coming out of the chimney at the *end* of the vid. Which *also* meant the rolling pin didn't burn out. Two days ago, Officer Len and I returned with a forensic team and found the remnants. It wasn't much, but it was enough. Jori, what did you find?"

"A thumbprint," she said. "On a partly burned rolling pin."

"Which is why we needed your thumbprints," Makk said. "Thanks again, both of you."

"That nonsense about protocol," Plaint grumbled. "This is all a charade, Captain Llotho, and I can prove it. I saw the trace DNA list myself, and while *I* was on it, we both know Calcut was not."

"That's true," Makk said. "But only because the test doesn't work as well for blood relatives. But now that we have a sample of Calcut's DNA, it should be easy enough to parse. Not that it matters. Fingerprints will do fine. Jori?"

"We have a positive match," she said. She handed Makk her scanner so he could see the results for himself.

He nodded, and handed it back.

"Why did you do it, Calcut?" Makk asked.

"I didn't," he said. "This is a puppet show. You don't have enough."

"The DNA recheck will put you here the week Orno was

murdered," Makk said. "Your thumbprint on the probable murder weapon will put you here the *night* he was murdered. And you're left-handed, aren't you? I saw you pour a wine bottle with your left, the night you had your boys kick the shit out of me for not playing along."

Calcut flew into a rage then, screaming. "*I'll kill you, you goddamn Cholem*!"

He didn't even reach Makk: Officer Swigg corralled him before he made it out of the kitchen.

"I should have let my guys finish you off like they wanted!" Calcut yelled. He looked like a kid, with Swigg's arm wrapped around him.

"*There's* that temper," Makk said. "You found out Orno was doing business with Ba-Ugna Kev's daughter, didn't you, Calcut? They communicated over *your* servers, right? You came here to confront him about it, and he wouldn't listen, and you *lost it*."

"*You can't prove that!*"

"Then when you heard there was a witness hiding upstairs, you asked *me* to turn the witness over to you. Not because you wanted revenge for killing Orno; you thought they could finger you."

"Llotho, I will not *rest* until you and this *asshole* are *fired* and, LET GO OF ME!"

Bod Swigg lifted Calcut off the floor. It was sort of funny.

"Officer Swigg," Llotho said, "take Mr. Linus downtown. He's under arrest."

Linus struggled against Swigg for a few seconds, before giving up.

"You know this won't stick, Stidgeon," he growled.

"Probably not," Makk said. "But that's not my problem."

Captain Llotho and Officer Len followed them out, with the captain hesitating at the door for long enough to nod to Makk. That left Duqo Plaint.

"You're free to go, Highness," Makk said. "Thanks for coming."

"Yes. That was quite a performance."

"Thanks, I like to entertain when I can."

"Is there any reason *I* had to be here for it?" Plaint asked.

"Yes," Makk said. "Until we checked both of your thumbprints, I wasn't positive which one of you did it."

"I am, for the record, also left-handed."

"I figured. In your office, you were holding your drink in your left hand."

Plaint nodded slowly.

"And you...you really thought I was capable of such a thing?"

Makk shrugged.

"I don't know *what* you're capable of. I know you've got a secret police force running around, scaring the shit out of your own Septals on the trail of some magical super-something, and I know *that's* more important, somehow, than reporting the murder of one of your own. They were here, did they tell you? One of the Sentries found Orno's body two days before Dorn, searched the place, and then left without so much of a hello to Twenty-One Central or anyone else."

"I *didn't* know that," Plaint said. "But I'm not surprised."

He paused to study Makk, which made Makk feel unaccountably self-conscious.

"You're...*disappointed*, aren't you?" Plaint said. "We've let you down somehow."

"I guess. I was raised by Septals, and I always thought you guys were *trying* at least. To be something good. Maybe not always succeeding, but trying. Now I'm not so sure."

"I understand. It's hard, without knowing the entire story. But what Orno took really *was* more important than his life. I heard Ms. Daska say this in that video, and she was correct. I don't know how she knows what she knows...but she isn't wrong."

"Then I'm the idiot who thinks nothing's worth that. Maybe that's why it's guys like you that send guys like me to war."

Plaint smiled grimly.

"There are things more valuable than a life. *Many* lives, for instance."

"Yeah, I've heard that before too."

"Well," he said, "I'm sorry to disappoint. I take it your promise was false?"

"My promise?"

"You intimated that you'd recovered the artifact. I take it you have not."

"No, but it seems to me your best shot at getting it back just left. We think Calcut took Orno's voicer with him; he might have your doo-dad too. If not? Like I said, we put everything back. Go ahead and search it all you want."

"I doubt Calcut would know what he had, if he had it. There is scarcely a dozen who do. Possibly including your former partner and whomever she's aligned with, although I doubt that as well."

Makk shrugged.

"It's a key, right? Not exactly a planet-shattering discovery."

Plaint smiled.

"You're correct; it isn't significant on its own. A key's value lies in what it unlocks. But. Enough of that."

Plaint shook Makk's hand.

"It looks as though I'm going to have to prepare an official statement regarding Professor Linus's killer shortly," he said. "Good day, detective."

"And to you, Highness."

Plaint headed for the back door, hesitating in the threshold.

"Calcut was right, you know," he said. "The charges aren't going to hold. I say that not because you didn't prove your case well—I thought you did an excellent job—but because one aspect of that proof is *never* going to see the courtroom."

"The vid filter," Makk said.

"Not only will Linus fight to keep that out of court, so will the House, and very nearly every other powerful figure in Inimata."

"Even if it means Professor Linus's killer goes free?"

"I'm afraid so. Goodbye."

Makk closed the door behind him, walked back to the bloodstain, and took a deep breath.

His hand was still trembling. Everything happened the way it was supposed to, but for some reason he remained largely unsatisfied. Because Plaint was right. All Makk had done was create an enormous headache for the federal attorney whose job would be to attempt to prosecute the case against Calcut Linus. Worse, that same attorney just filed formal charges against Ba-Ugna Kev, to go with the ones submitted against Viselle Daska a few days earlier.

What was probably true was that *none* of them would see the inside of a prison cell.

But as he said, that wasn't his problem. He solved the murder, and now he was done. So why wasn't he ready to leave?

Viselle, he thought. *How much damage did you do to my scene without me knowing?*

He did a lap around the first floor, trying to remember what his first impressions were. Was there anything he could have caught earlier that would have made a difference? Anything he missed because Daska was there too?

And what *did* happen to Duqo Plaint's key? That was the real trigger for this whole mess, and the last mystery to remain unsolved.

Maybe that was why he didn't want to go; he hated leaving unknowns behind.

"Hey babe," Elicasta said, from the back door. "Are we done? Everyone went home."

"Nearly," he said. "You file your story?"

"Soon as I saw Calcut Linus leave in cuffs. *Super* disappointing."

"Why? We got our man."

"I *know*, but Plaint was *so* much meatier. Can you imagine? Whatever. I'll still beat everyone else to the goods by a solid twenty, minimum."

"That's only because you recorded the story beforehand."

She actually recorded *two* stories: one for Calcut Linus and one for Duqo Plaint. He very much hoped she pushed the right one. She was right, though; Plaint being the killer would have been a lot more explosive—or meatier, or whatever she called it.

Elicasta took a couple of steps into the kitchen. Makk was probably supposed to be telling her not to, as this was still a crime scene and she was a civilian, but that seemed like a silly thing to worry about at this point.

"So, I'm done and you're done," she said. "What are we still doing here? I was promised a dinner."

"Yeah...I need a minute."

"Okay."

She tilted her head at him, and smiled.

"What is it?" she asked.

"Nothing. I want to look around one more time, and then I'll meet you out back."

"All right. You know, if there's something you want to talk about, I can keep secrets."

"I know. Five minutes."

"Okay."

She stepped out.

Makk walked around Orno's desk and sat down.

"Mysteries," he muttered. "Too many mysteries."

Between what Viselle said that day in the cabin, what Brother Semit told him about this key, and what Leemie said about the pre-Collapse book that nobody seemed to care was missing, it felt like there was still a lot left to solve.

"That's what it is," he decided. "I've only solved the easy one."

He sighed, got out of the chair, and headed up the staircase.

The bedroom was as he remembered it. Jori and her team had taken a few things downtown, but had put them all back in their original positions.

They'd done a good job; even the broken alarm clock was back in the closet under the dent it had left in the wall. Makk kicked it aside, stepped into the closet and closed the door.

Can you really not hear the downstairs from here? he wondered. Viselle said she couldn't hear the specifics of the argument that took place between the Linus brothers from inside the closet, and —not that it mattered any longer—now that he was *in* said closet, that seemed like a stretch. The closet was too close to the staircase.

He probably could have tested this earlier, when he had people downstairs who could pretend to have an argument.

"There's no point," he muttered. "You solved this damn case, just go home."

He didn't go home. Instead, he went into the spare room, because it also had a closet, and Viselle didn't specify which one she'd been hiding in.

The spare room had been used to store large boxes, which had *not* been returned. Makk didn't know why, and made a note to ask Jori about them later.

Nobody at Central ever really worked out what the boxes' contents actually were. *Research* was the shorthand answer, but they didn't have anyone with enough of an advanced understanding of astrophysics to figure out *what* was being researched. Important stuff, perhaps, but only to Professor Linus. Makk been through all of them himself, and had the paper cuts to show for it.

He stepped into the second closet and tried to close the door. But—and he remembered this from the first time he examined this room—this was the door that was hung wrong. The only way to get it to stay closed was to hold it shut.

She could have done *that*, and maybe then not heard what was going on downstairs. It seemed like a stretch, but maybe.

He let the door go. It flew open again.

He wondered why Linus never bothered to have something like that fixed. Or fixed it himself, even; he was smart enough to figure out something like this.

Makk felt along the jamb, for the hinges, to see if any of them were loose. Around near the bottom of the door, his finger passed a lump.

"Hello."

He opened the door all the way, to get a better angle. Something was *taped* to the inside. He ripped off the tape...and a key fell into his hands.

It was, as promised, not like anything he'd ever seen before: nearly as long as his forearm, flat, and made of a material he couldn't readily identify. It was as firm as metal, lighter than wood, and less delicate than glass. Clearly it was a composite of some kind, but he couldn't begin to guess what the component parts were. The first word that sprang to mind was, interestingly, *alien*. But that was the wrong word. The right word was: pre-Collapse.

He stepped into the bedroom, where the light was better. Elicasta was standing at the top of the steps.

"What is *that*?" she asked.

"Something more important than a man's life," he said. "And what are you doing here?"

"Your five minutes were up, and I'm impatient. Is that a key?"

He shoved it in his pocket.

"Tell you what," he said. "Let's have that dinner, and I'll walk you through everything I know. When I'm done, maybe you can help me figure out what I'm going to do with this."

Epilogue

The clothes itched.

That was Dorn's second thought, on putting on non-Septal clothing for the first time since childhood. The first was, how much *harder* it was to put on the clothes. The robes Dorn was accustomed to slipped over the head and that was that. No pant legs or belt to manipulate. No shirt to button and tuck.

The pants were too large for them. The only reason the pants didn't end up around Dorn's ankles every time they stood was the belt. But when the belt was tight, the material at the waist ended up bunched in a couple of places, and chafed.

Dorn had plenty of time to think about the pants, and the tight-fitting shirt, and the hooded sweatshirt over the shirt, and the loose-fitting hood on their head that didn't come as close to approximating a Septal hood as they'd hoped, because it was a long ride up the Tether.

That Dorn was even riding up the Tether—something they never expected to be doing in their lifetime—was due to a miraculously weird series of events that, twenty-five hours later, still hadn't come together in their head in a way that made any sense.

First, there was the voicer direct from the detective. (The pretty one.) She spoke of a matter of grave urgency requiring that they drop what they were doing and meet her at the curb. In hindsight, Dorn probably should have demanded more specifics prior to committing to a face-to-face engagement, but at the time, they didn't think this would be the last time they would be in their apartment.

It was *supposed* to be a quick interview. Or, that was the impression Detective Viselle Daska gave. Also in hindsight, it was clear that Daska would say anything to get Dorn out of the building and into the car.

"They're going to blame you for the professor's murder," she'd said that night, as soon as they got into the car. Then she put the car in gear and drove away from the campus.

She refused to elaborate on who *they* were, leaving Dorn to speculate. The police? The House? All she *could* say was that she had arrived to rescue them, by getting them out of the city.

The next day, Dorn saw the doctored vid, and understood. Daska had them hidden in an apartment in the Geoghis Quarter by then, a high-end neighborhood in which she said nobody would think to look for a wayward Septal. She provided them clothes to change into, and told them to prepare to move again.

I was so frightened, they thought. *I should have been thinking more clearly*.

When Dorn saw the vid, the first thing they thought of was to do exactly what Daska kept insisting was about to happen: get out of Velon before they're arrested and locked up for something they did *not* do. Every word out of Viselle Daska's mouth that sounded like progress in that direction went unchallenged.

It was foolish. Dorn prided themself on level-headedness in the face of deleterious circumstance. It was how they'd made it off the farm and into a House chapter like Velon, rather than languishing in the backward campuses of Punkoah.

If they were thinking straight, they would have gone directly to the nearest Veeser, face-naked. That would have been enough.

When Dorn was three, their father disciplined them—for some terrible slight that Dorn couldn't even recall—by taking a hot poker to their left cheek. Dorn's mother treated the wound with a palliative that, while soothing, did nothing to address the possibility of infection. By the time they were seen by a proper physician, Dorn had lost sight in their left eye.

The milky, sightless eye and horrible scarring on the left side of Dorn's face defined the next five years of their life. Either because it was assumed that Dorn had committed a crime worthy of such a drastic punishment, or because children were just instinctively cruel, Dorn grew up being called *novine*. (In Broughu, Dorn's native tongue, it meant *outcast*.) Their taking of the House vows were very much inevitable, after that. What better future for someone with such a face, than a career under a hood? Dorn even adopted a Fundamentalist stance, sartorially, to excuse themself from having to explain why they wouldn't remove the hood in front of Brethren.

So, when a vid aired showing an unscarred version of Dorn Jimbal, obviously, the best way to prove their innocence was to simply uncover their face. That they didn't even consider this, in the moment, indicated perhaps the scars from that childhood nickname ran deeper than the ones left by their father's hot poker.

The elevator attached to the Tether was a lot larger than it looked from afar. Since the Tether itself—a bundle of columns composed of nanotube carbon fiber—extended all the way into outer space, it seemed likely anything riding it would look small in scale. Still, Dorn was unprepared.

The only thing that rode the elevator was the shuttle, which didn't seem like much. But the shuttle was large enough to carry as many as fifty people (not including the crew) and four shipping crates' worth of goods.

It was not, on this day, carrying nearly as much into orbit. Amazingly, all it had—again, aside from the crew—was Dorn, and a stack of boxes recovered from Professor Linus's townhouse.

The boxes arrived with Viselle Daska, along with the news that Dorn's escape would be aboard the most conspicuous means of egress from Velon—and from the planet—available. She explained that she'd spirited the boxes from the evidence locker ("Nobody will miss them," she'd said, "because nobody there understands what's in them,") and that they deserved to go with Dorn—who *would* understand them—to Lys.

Then they were heading for the Tether, with Viselle Daska again failing to elaborate adequately and Dorn too terrified of getting captured to press her further.

Dorn didn't fully appreciate that Detective Daska was a person of far greater means than her status as an employee of the police department would imply, until it became clear that she'd secured the *entire* Tether for Dorn. There were no witnesses to later testify that they shared an elevator with a notorious fugitive, and whatever crew there was remained in the pilot's nest and never came into direct contact with their passenger. Even Viselle Daska stayed behind—although she didn't inform them that this would be happening until it was too late to reverse course.

"You'll be greeted by a friend on the other side," she'd told them. "Don't worry; we'll keep you safe."

Thus, over the course of the six hours it took for the elevator to reach the top of the Tether, Dorn had nobody with which to share in the wonder as Velon, then Inimata, then the continent of Geo all grew smaller beneath them.

It was breathtaking. As a Septal, Dorn had never even considered space travel to be something they might one day partake in, because the House—for whatever reason—didn't sponsor a space program of any kind. It was only an avenue for laic scientists. But as the curvature of Dibble became a part of Dorn's horizon—with its alarmingly (from this perspective) thin layer of atmosphere—and they felt, for the first time, like they were actually in space, they wondered if this was perhaps the best possible outcome. Dorn's immediate future was uncertain, and their long-term future as a Septal had been blown up, perhaps irrevocably, but in the moment, it didn't matter.

Dorn Jimbal was in outer space.

Professor Linus would have loved this, they thought.

An alarm sounded once the elevator reached the top of the Tether. It was followed by an announcement notifying all passengers that they had to return to their seats and strap themselves down, as the shuttle was entering a zero-gravity sequence.

According to the *History of Tether Travel* information tableau painted on one of the shuttle's inner walls, up until three years ago, the occupants of the Tether's elevator experienced gradual weightlessness all the way up, reaching near-zero-G's at the acme. Since then, artificial gravity had been installed in the elevator, offsetting the natural decrease. (This wasn't a part of the original design because the Tether predated null-grav tech by a number of years.)

However, the shuttle itself did not have any artificial gravity, so once it detached from the elevator, and until it docked with Lys, there would be no gravity.

Dorn thought it was unfortunate that they wouldn't be able to enjoy weightlessness properly, even for a few minutes.

Connecting from the Tether to Lys was actually one of the most perilous maneuvers to be conducted daily anywhere on or above the planet. As soon as the shuttle detached from the Tether's platform, it launched up at a sixty-two degree angle, rendering the question of weightlessness moot. (Dorn's moment of zero-G was just that: a moment.) This trip took the shuttle *above* Lys. It then reversed engines to burn off the momentum it carried from the planet's rotation, and dropped into a dock on Lys.

At the same time this was happening, a second shuttle left the dock and sped up, to connect with the Tether before it disappeared over the horizon, to begin its six-hour journey back down. On the next rotation, Dorn's shuttle would be the one reconnecting with the Tether and heading back down, while the one that had left headed back up. (It took slightly less than a day for the Tether to complete one rotation, from the perspective of Lys. As the shuttle engaged in this complicated dance with the station, Dorn occupied themself by working out the math on precisely *how* much less, in their head.)

There were so many ways for the Tether-to-Lys shuttle trip to go catastrophically wrong, it was a wonder that nothing *had* gone wrong, for many years. This was what Dorn clung to, after running out of math problems to perform.

Nothing *did* go wrong, and as the shuttle began its final approach Dorn was able to consider things other than dying in space. To that end, their primary fixation became the sheer scope of the space station.

Lys was *massive*. It was impossible to appreciate how very massive it was from the surface, even for someone with a full grasp of the numbers involved. (In short, Lys held a geosynchronous orbit above Dibble, which meant it had to be somewhere in the neighborhood of thirty-thousand kalomaders from the surface. Yet it was not only visible to the naked eye, it was large enough to show advertisements on its underbelly visible to the naked eye at the surface. Dorn never did the math for this, but knew the final number would have to be rather large.)

From the docking station at the back tip of Lys, looking forward, Dorn couldn't even *see* where the station ended.

There were no informational graphics on the shuttle to

explain the history, size, or science undergirding Lys. Dorn was familiar with some of it—as was everyone in Velon—but not all of it. They did not, for instance, actually know the exact distance from sea-level to Lys with any certainty. They could guess, based on what would make the most sense, but it would only be a guess. The station could theoretically be closer to the surface than that, in exchange for expending tremendous amounts of energy to hold the orbit while fighting off the pull of the planet's gravitation. Or, null-gravity could be employed to offset that pull, meaning the station could hypothetically be wherever it wished. This seemed unlikely, because Lys also predated null-grav tech.

Dorn also knew the original Lys station was much smaller, and built by a multi-billionaire. They didn't know how it ended up growing to its current size, but thought the development of null-grav tech was a major factor. (This was counterintuitive, but the same technology that allowed for aero-cars to fly above the surface also enabled the existence of artificial gravity in space.)

The shuttle finally docked. Another alarm sounded, followed by a voice over the intercom declaring that passengers could unhook their safety harnesses and prepare to disembark.

Dorn stepped out of the shuttle and into a receiving area intended for a large number of people. Today, other than them, it had only one person: a short, young, dark-skinned woman with a bright smile and an abundance of energy. She spotted them right away, waved extensively, and jogged over to meet them.

"You made it!" she said, taking their hand, which they hadn't really offered.

"I did," they said evenly. "You must be the person I was told to expect."

"I am! Exty Demara."

"I'm—"

"You're Ichol Daska," Exty said, winking. "Viselle's cousin."

"...Yes, that's right."

"We're all so glad you finally got a chance to visit Lys, after all these years. Come on, let's get your luggage."

She waved over a porter at the other end of the shuttle. He wheeled up a dolly carrying Professor Linus's boxes. Exty took it from him, tipped him with a C-Coin, and led the way from the platform.

"I'm right out front," she said. "And hey, you can relax. You're safe up here. You can take off that hood if you want."

"I'm safe," they said, "and yet I'm Ichol Daska."

"That was the name on the ticket. Don't worry, nobody knows what Ichol looks like. Last anyone knew, he was manning a fishing net off the coast of Botzis. You're fine."

"I would rather leave the hood on, thank you."

"Sure. Here we are."

She stopped at the only vehicle in sight, a curiously designed car that was essentially a half-dome atop four large wheels.

They stared at it without comment. Dorn couldn't remember ever seeing anything quite like it on the surface.

"It was built for up here," Exty said. "They use the same kind of buggy on the moon, but you won't see one down below. Not really practical."

"It accommodates low-atmosphere travel," Dorn said. "I understand."

"Yeah. Heavy too. Eats a ton of power to get around. But it can survive a direct hit from debris up to about the size of your fist. You getting in, or did you want to walk?"

They opened a hatch built into the side of the dome and climbed in, while she loaded the boxes into the rear of the car.

"I was told I'd get an explanation once I arrived," Dorn said, as soon as Exty was in the driver's seat.

"An explanation for what?" she asked.

"What I'm doing here? When I can expect to leave? Where I'm going to go? Why this is happening at all?"

She had her hands up before Dorn got halfway through.

"Whoa, whoa, calm down. You'll get your answers, but not from me. I'm just transportation. Right now I'm taking the most wanted person in Velon around the most exclusive community in the solar system. You're pretty lucky to even be where you are, Dorn Jimbal."

"I thought I was Ichol Daska."

"In the car, you can be Dorn Jimbal."

She got the electric engine started, and they began moving. Ahead of them was an enclosed roadway that threaded between dozens of private estates, all sealed in their own domes.

The conspicuous ostentatiousness of the Lys private estates was legendary. Dorn remembered being enchanted, as a child, by a serial fic vid purportedly based in Lys. They always wondered how true-to-life any of that series actually was.

Frustratingly, the domes were opaque.

"I apologize," Dorn said, "if I came across as being short with you. It's been a trying time."

"That's okay."

"Can you tell me where you're taking me, at least?"

"We're heading for the center. My family's estate."

"*Demara*," Dorn said. "Your last name."

"Archeo was my great grandfather," she said.

"The man who built the city in the sky," Dorn muttered. It was how Archeo Demara was described in the fic vid from their childhood.

"So you've heard of him."

Archeo Demara's mansion was the oldest part of the space station. It was originally built at a time when such things were only barely possible, as a private refuge for members of the Demara clan. In its first iteration, the occupants were in a zero-gravity environment, doing...well, nobody knew what they were doing, but it sounded like fun.

It was said that Archeo's true genius lay not in envisioning a private play area in near-Dibble orbit for himself and others, but in the negotiation for the right to do so. Since Lys was in a geosynchronous orbit, the planet spun beneath it while it remained where it was, on the dark side of Dibble. This meant passing over every country that was situated on the equator. At the time the station went active, none of those countries even considered sub-orbital space to be something they could own, so when a wealthy billionaire showed up offering them *money* for those rights, the countries gladly accepted.

(Eventually, it was legally established that the claim on air rights for any country ended at the troposphere. However, since Demara had already paid for the rights beyond that, his claim was grandfathered. The family continued to own a portion of equatorial space above the planet.)

A hundred years later, with the private vacation palaces on Lys now numbering two hundred and seventeen, and with no limits on continued expansion—the sub-orbital space rights for Lys's orbital plane had been signed away in perpetuity—the only thing keeping Lys from growing was the lack of people wealthy enough to buy their way in.

The drive to the Demara compound was an enormous disappointment, as it continued to be the case that every one of the bubbles they went past was opaque.

"The shells have artificial days going on inside," Exty said, after Dorn sighed a fifth or sixth time. They kept passing signposts indicating which family compound they were driving past. It felt less like the most exclusive vacation spot imaginable and more like a large cemetery. "That's why we can't see in."

"That and privacy, I assume," Dorn said.

"Less important than you might think, up here. If you're on Lys, you *belong* on Lys, whatever that means. That's the assumption."

"What about when they want to look at the stars?"

"Depends. Some will flip the top half of the dome to transparent for a look at the real thing, but a lot of them show a fake night sky when their fake sun goes down."

"That's...obscene."

She shrugged.

"I guess."

They finally reached the center compound, and turned in. The vehicle had to stop twice as it passed through various airlocks.

"There's atmosphere in the tunnel we took to get here," Exty said, "but each estate maintains their own private atmospheres, so we have to go through a decontamination process."

"It's all just air," Dorn said. "What is being decontaminated?"

"There's the station's air, and then there's private air." She laughed. "I know you're making a face under that hood. Maybe you should have waited to use the word *obscene* until after the full tour."

The Demara estate *looked* huge. Dorn couldn't tell how much they were seeing was due to some combination of forced perspective and an artificial sense of depth created by the dome's vid screen. But the mansion looked as large as a Middle Kingdom castle, and the footprint of the land seemed bigger than all of Andel Quarter, so clearly there was *some* manipulation going on.

It was midday in the dome.

"Looks great, doesn't it?" Exty said. "We've had to rebuild four or five times, to keep up. We added the swimming pools, with the river and the lagoon just a few years back. Took forever just to get the water up here."

"How *did* you get the water up here?" Dorn asked. An ongoing question was how Lys managed to survive at all, since the once-daily shuttles were hardly enough to supply two hundred and seventeen estates with all of their collective needs. Just by virtue of their location, none of the properties could self-sustain, long-term.

"Lys gets freight deliveries 20/7," Exty said. "Every estate has a private dock underneath, on the planet-side. *Much* easier with null-grav boosters. They used to use rockets."

She steered the car past the front entrance to the mansion.

"We're not going here?" Dorn asked.

"You can get a tour of the main house later," she said. "Assuming you're sticking around, I mean. We're heading to the guest house."

The *guest house* was a wing of the mansion, rather than a separate building, as the name might imply. Exty brought the car to a stop at a modest (by comparison) set of ivory stairs leading to gold-embossed double doors.

Dorn stepped out, and got their first taste of the Demara family's private atmosphere.

"Lavender," they said.

"What?"

"The air smells of lavender."

"Does it? I guess I don't smell it anymore."

A manservant, or butler, or whatever the Demaras called the help ran down the steps, greeted Exty wordlessly, and proceeded to unload the boxes, ignoring Dorn entirely.

"Jig will take care of the stuff," Exty said. "Let's get you in. We're already late."

Dorn decided it wouldn't be worth it to ask what they were late for, and just followed their guide into the building.

Past the gilded double doors, they went through a velvet-appointed hallway and into a wood-paneled study. There was an enormous bank of computers and vid screens along one wall, looking entirely out-of-place with the rest of the room's décor.

(Overstuffed leather couches and chairs on one side, cold silvery steel and glass on the other.)

A tall, muscular bald man was pacing in front of the computers. He didn't appear to realize he was no longer alone in the room.

Exty held up a finger to let Dorn know this was not the time to speak.

The man stopped at one screen, tapped something on the keyboard, waited five seconds, nodded, and then turned.

"The boxes?" he asked Exty.

"Jig's bringing them."

"Good. Leave us." He looked at Dorn. "Dorn Jimbal. Apologies for all you've been through. My name is Ba-Ugna Kev. We have a lot to talk about. Please, have a seat."

Appendix

TELLING TIME ON THE PLANET DIB

Readers from the planet Earth will likely find the references to time in the Tandemstar series disorienting. Dib has a longer orbital period around its twin suns than the Earth does, is slightly smaller than Earth, and spins slightly faster. The result is a longer year and a shorter day.

Days and Years

The days on Dib are still broken into hours, minutes and seconds. However—and here is where this is bound to further confuse the reader—the hours, minutes and seconds on Dib are *not* the same length of time as Earth's hours, minutes, and seconds.

On Earth, there are 24 hours in a day, sixty minutes in an hour, and sixty seconds in a minute. We will call this E-time, as employed in the following statement: "There are 86,400 E-seconds in one E-day."

We'll call the days, hours, minutes and seconds on Dib, Db-time. One Db day equals 19 E-hours, 27 E-minutes and 8 E-seconds. This means that 1 Db-day = 70,028 E-seconds.

70,028 is 0.81 of 86,400, and so 1 Db-day = 0.81 E-day.

Naturally, Dibblings know nothing about Earth hours and minutes, and don't measure their days by saying they last 19 hours, 27 minutes and eight seconds. That would be silly. Their day is broken into blocks of 20 hours, hence: 1 Db-day = 20 Db-hours. Db-hours continue to be broken into lengths of 60 minutes, and each minute will be 60 seconds.

As we've already established, 1 Db-day = 70,028 E-seconds. If there are 20 Db-hours in 1 Db-day, then 1 Db-hour = 58.36 E-minutes.

One Dib year is the rough equivalent of 21 Earth months and 14 Earth days. (For this exercise, we will be calling an Earth month 30.4375 days. This was arrived at by taking the length of a year—365.25 days—and dividing by 12.)

Twenty-one E-months is therefore equal to 639.1875 E-days. Take the leftover 14 E-days, and:

1 Db-year = 653.1875 E-days.

(The reader is advised to take a break at this point. Have a drink, if one is available. This is getting worse.)

There are sixteen Dib months in a Dib year. This means one Dib month is equal to 40.824 Earth days. Converting upward, 40.824 E-days = 33.08 Db-days, therefore 1 Db-month = 33.08 Db-days.

That leads to one Dib year equaling 529.28 Dibble days.

Finally: 1 Db-year = 1.788 E-years, and the inverse, 1 E-year = 0.559 Db-year.

This means a 20-year old Earthling would be 11.1 years old on Dib. An eighty-year old Earthling—the average lifespan for Earthlings and Dibblings alike—would be 44.7 Db years old.

The Seasons

Notably, Dibblings don't always count their age by years. Their calendar is divided into four month blocks, called seasons. These function much in the same way as Earth seasons, and for the same reason we're using hours, minutes, seconds, days, months and years, these seasons will continue to be (informally) summer, autumn, winter, spring. So, the 80 year-old Earthling might be 44.7 Db-years old, but they might *say* they were 178 seasons old.

There are only four names for their months: Dalexion, Hantober, Sevvitch, and Zenita. Each year contains four Dalexions, four Hantobers, four Sevvitches, and four Zenitas.

This is obviously confusing, but it respects the spirit of the Dibblings' approach to counting the passage of time by quarters of the year rather than by the year. At the same time, saying one's birthday is the 28th of Hantober doesn't entirely acknowledge the concept of the year, and so most Dibblings add the season when referencing the months. Informally, this is expressed with the full season name—a Summer Dalexion, or a Spring Zenita—but formally the seasons appear in the form of a prefix.

The prefixes have a murky linguistic origination. They are: summer = sha, autumn = shi, winter = do, spring = ta.

Ergo, if one's birthday is on the 28th of Hantober, and one was born in autumn, a Dibbling would say they were born on the twenty-eighth day of Shi-Hantober.

The counting of years will be addressed separately, but note that the new year begins on the first day of the summer season.

Finally, there's the matter of the days in the month. Possibly to avoid any conversion headaches for Dib-based science fiction authors, each month has thirty-three days, with two exceptions. First, the final month of the year—Ta-Zenita—has an extra, thirty-fourth day. It's a holiday, and there's much drinking. Second, thanks to that niggling extra .28 of a day in the year, a thirty-fourth day is added, once every four years, to the month of

Do-Sevvitch. (This extra day is not added once every thirty-three years.) The Leap Day of Do-Sevvitch is not celebrated. It's considered cursed, and in more superstitious times, babies born on this day were summarily drowned.

These are more enlightened times.

About the Author

Gene Doucette is a hybrid author, albeit in a somewhat roundabout way. From 2010 through 2014, Gene published four full-length novels (*Immortal*, *Hellenic Immortal*, *Fixer*, and *Immortal at the Edge of the World*) with a small indie publisher. Then, in 2014, Gene started self-publishing novellas that were set in the same universe as the *Immortal* series, at which point he was a hybrid.

When the novellas proved more lucrative than the novels, Gene tried self-publishing a full novel, *The Spaceship Next Door*, in 2015. This went well. So well, that in 2016, Gene reacquired the rights to the earlier four novels from the publisher, and re-released them, at which point he wasn't a hybrid any longer.

Additional self-published novels followed: *Immortal and the Island of Impossible Things* (2016); *Unfiction* (2017); and *The Frequency of Aliens* (2017).

In 2018, John Joseph Adams Books (an imprint of Houghton Mifflin Harcourt) acquired the rights to *The Spaceship Next Door*. The reprint was published in September of that year, at which point Gene was once again a hybrid author.

Since then, a number of things have happened. Gene published three more novels—*Immortal From Hell* (2018), *Fixer Redux* (2019), and *Immortal: Last Call* (2020)—and wrote a new novel called *The Apocalypse Seven* that he did not self-publish; it was acquired by JJA/HMH in September of 2019. Publication date is May 25, 2021.

Gene lives in Cambridge, MA.

For the latest on Gene Doucette, follow him online

genedoucette.me
genedoucette@me.com

Also by Gene Doucette

SCI-FI

The Spaceship Next Door

The world changed on a Tuesday.

When a spaceship landed in an open field in the quiet mill town of Sorrow Falls, Massachusetts, everyone realized humankind was not alone in the universe. With that realization, everyone freaked out for a little while.

Or, almost everyone. The residents of Sorrow Falls took the news pretty well. This could have been due to a certain local quality of unflappability, or it could have been that in three years, the ship did exactly nothing other than sit quietly in that field, and nobody understood the full extent of this nothing the ship was doing better than the people who lived right next door.

Sixteen-year old Annie Collins is one of the ship's closest neighbors. Once upon a time she took every last theory about the ship seriously, whether it was advanced by an adult ,or by a peer. Surely one of the theories would be proven true eventually—if not several of them—the very minute the ship decided to do something. Annie is starting to think this will never happen.

One late August morning, a little over three years since the ship landed, Edgar Somerville arrived in town. Ed's a government operative posing as a journalist, which is obvious to Annie—and pretty much everyone else he meets—almost immediately. He has a lot of questions that need answers, because he thinks everyone is wrong: the ship is doing something, and he needs Annie's help to figure out what that is.

Annie is a good choice for tour guide. She already knows everyone in town and when Ed's theory is proven correct—something is apocalyptically wrong in Sorrow Falls—she's a pretty good person to have around.

As a matter of fact, Annie Collins might be the most important person on the planet. She just doesn't know it.

~

The Frequency of Aliens

Annie Collins is back!

Becoming an overnight celebrity at age sixteen should have been a lot more fun. Yes, there were times when it was extremely cool, but when the newness of it all wore off, Annie Collins was left with a permanent security detail and the kind of constant scrutiny that makes the college experience especially awkward.

Not helping matters: she's the only kid in school with her own pet spaceship.

She would love it if things found some kind of normal, but as long as she has control of the most lethal—and only—interstellar vehicle in existence, that isn't going to happen. Worse, things appear to be going in the other direction. Instead of everyone getting used to the idea of the ship, the complaints are getting louder. Public opinion is turning, and the demands that Annie turn over the ship are becoming more frequent. It doesn't help that everyone seems to think Annie is giving them nightmares.

Nightmares aren't the only weird things going on lately. A government telescope in California has been abandoned, and nobody seems to know why.

The man called on to investigate—Edgar Somerville—has become the go-to guy whenever there's something odd going on, which has been pretty common lately. So far, nothing has panned out: no aliens or zombies or anything else that might be deemed legitimately peculiar... but now may be different, and not just because Ed can't find an easy explanation. This isn't the only telescope where people have gone missing, and the clues left behind lead back to Annie.

It all adds up to a new threat that the world may just need saving from, requiring the help of all the Sorrow Falls survivors. The question is: are they saving the world with Annie Collins, or are they saving it from her?

The Frequency of Aliens is the exciting sequel to *The Spaceship Next Door*.

Unfiction

When Oliver Naughton joins the Tenth Avenue Writers Underground, headed by literary wunderkind Wilson Knight, Oliver figures he'll finally get some of the wild imaginings out of his head and onto paper.

But when Wilson takes an intense interest in Oliver's writing and his genre stories of dragons, aliens, and spies, things get weird. Oliver's stories don't just need to be finished: they insist on it.

With the help of Minerva, Wilson's girlfriend, Oliver has to find the connection between reality, fiction, the mythical Cydonian Kingdom, and the non-mythical nightclub called M Pallas. That is, if he can survive the alien invasion, the ghosts, and the fact that he thinks he might be in love with Minerva.

Unfiction is a wild ride through the collision of science fiction, fantasy, thriller, horror and romance. It's what happens when one writer's fiction interferes with everyone's reality.

Fixer

What would you do if you could see into the future?

As a child, he dreamed of being a superhero. Most people never get to realize their childhood dreams, but Corrigan Bain has come close. He is a fixer. His job is to prevent accidents—to see the future and "fix" things before people get hurt. But the ability to see into the future, however limited, isn't always so simple. Sometimes not everyone can be saved.

"Don't let them know you can see them."

Graduate students from a local university are dying, and former lover and

FBI agent Maggie Trent is the only person who believes their deaths aren't as accidental as they appear. But the truth can only be found in something from Corrigan Bain's past, and he's not interested in sharing that past, not even with Maggie.

To stop the deaths, Corrigan will have to face up to some old horrors, confront the possibility that he may be going mad, and find a way to stop a killer no one can see.

Corrigan Bain is going insane ... or is he?

Because there's something in the future that doesn't want to be seen. It isn't human. It's got a taste for mayhem. And it is very, very angry.

Fixer Redux

Someone's altering the future, and it isn't Corrigan Bain

Corrigan Bain was retired.

It wasn't something he ever thought he'd be able to do. The problem was that the *job* he wanted to retire from wasn't actually a job at all: nobody paid him to do it, and nobody else did it. With very few exceptions, nobody even knew he was doing it.

Corrigan called himself a fixer, because he fixed accidents that were about to happen. It was complicated and unrewarding, and even though doing it right meant saving someone, he didn't enjoy it. He couldn't stop —he thought—because there would always be accidents, and he would never find someone to take over as fixer. Anyone trying would have to be capable of seeing the future, like he did, and that kind of person was hard to find.

Still, he did it. He's never been happier.

His girlfriend, Maggie Trent of the FBI, has not retired. Her task force just shut down the most dangerous domestic terrorist cell in the country, and she's up for an award, and a big promotion.

Everything's going their way now, and the future looks even brighter.

Unfortunately, that future is about to blow up in their faces...literally.

And somehow, Corrigan Bain, fixer, the man who can see the future, is taken completely by surprise.

Fixer Redux is the long-awaited sequel to ***Fixer***. Catch up with Corrigan, as he tries to understand a future that no longer makes sense.

~

FANTASY

The Immortal Novel Series

~

Immortal

"I don't know how old I am. My earliest memory is something along the lines of fire good, ice bad, so I think I predate written history, but I don't know by how much. I like to brag that I've been there from the beginning, and while this may very well be true, I generally just say it to pick up girls."

Surviving sixty thousand years takes cunning and more than a little luck. But in the twenty-first century, Adam confronts new dangers—someone has found out what he is, a demon is after him, and he has run out of places to hide. Worst of all, he has had entirely too much to drink.

Immortal is a first person confessional penned by a man who is immortal, but not invincible. In an artful blending of sci-fi, adventure, fantasy, and humor, IMMORTAL introduces us to a world with vampires, demons and other "magical" creatures, yet a world without actual magic.

At the center of the book is Adam.

Adam is a sixty thousand year old man. (Approximately.) He doesn't age or get sick, but is otherwise entirely capable of being killed. His survival has hinged on an innate ability to adapt, his wits, and a fairly large dollop of luck. He makes for an excellent guide through history ... when he's sober.

Immortal is a contemporary fantasy for non-fantasy readers and fantasy enthusiasts alike.

Hellenic Immortal

"Very occasionally, I will pop up in the historical record. Most of the time I'm not at all easy to spot, because most of the time I'm just a guy who does a thing and then disappears again into the background behind someone-or-other who's busy doing something much more important. But there are a couple of rare occasions when I get a starring role."

An oracle has predicted the sojourner's end, which is a problem for Adam insofar as he has never encountered an oracular prediction that didn't come true ... and he is the sojourner. To survive, he's going to have to figure out what a beautiful ex-government analyst, an eco-terrorist, a rogue FBI agent, and the world's oldest religious cult all want with him, and fast.

And all he wanted when he came to Vegas was to forget about a girl. And maybe have a drink or two.

The second book in the Immortal series, Hellenic Immortal follows the continuing adventures of Adam, a sixty-thousand-year-old man with a wry sense of humor, a flair for storytelling, and a knack for staying alive. Hellenic Immortal is a clever blend of history, mythology, sci-fi, fantasy, adventure, mystery and romance. A little something, in other words, for every reader.

Immortal at the Edge of the World

"What I was currently doing with my time and money ... didn't really deserve anyone else's attention. If I was feeling romantic about it, I'd call it a quest, but all I was really doing was trying to answer a question I'd been ignoring for a thousand years."

In his very long life, Adam had encountered only one person who appeared to share his longevity: the mysterious red-haired woman. She appeared throughout history, usually from a distance, nearly always vanishing before he could speak to her.

In his last encounter, she actually did vanish—into thin air, right in front of him. The question was how did she do it? To answer, Adam will have to complete a quest he gave up on a thousand years earlier, for an object that may no longer exist.

If he can find it, he might be able to do what the red-haired woman did, and if he can do that, maybe he can find her again and ask her who she is ... and why she seems to hate him.

But Adam isn't the only one who wants the red-haired woman. There are other forces at work, and after a warning from one of the few men he trusts, Adam realizes how much danger everyone is in. To save his friends and finish his quest he may be forced to bankrupt himself, call in every favor he can, and ultimately trade the one thing he'd never been able to give up before: his life.

Immortal and the island of Impossible Things

"I thought I'd miss the world."

Adam is on vacation in an island paradise, with nothing to do and plenty of time to do nothing.

It's exactly what he needed: beautiful weather, beautiful girlfriend, plenty of books to read, and alcohol to drink. Most importantly, either nobody on the island knows who he is, or, nobody cares.

"This probably sounds boring, and maybe it is. It's possible I have no compass to help determine boring, or maybe I have a different threshold than most people. From my perspective, though, the vast majority of human history has been boring, by which I mean nothing happened, and sure, that can be dull. On the other hand, nothing happening includes nobody trying to kill anybody, and specifically, nobody trying to kill me. That's the kind of boring a guy can get behind."

Nothing last forever, though, and that includes the opportunity to *do* nothing. One day, unwelcome visitors arrive in secret, with impossible knowledge of impossible events, and then the impossible things arrive: a new species.

It's *all* impossible, especially to the immortal man who thought he'd seen all there was to see in the world. Now, Adam is going to have to figure out what's happening and make things right before he and everyone he loves ends up dead in the hot sun of this island paradise.

Immortal From Hell

Not all of Adam's stories have happy endings

"Paris is romantic and quests are cool. But the threat of a global pandemic kind of sours the whole thing. The good news was, if all life on Earth were felled by a plague, it looked like this one could take me out too. It'd be pretty lonely otherwise."

--Adam the immortal

When Adam decides to leave the safety of the island, it's for a good reason: Eve, the only other immortal on the planet, appears to be dying, and nobody seems to understand why. But when Adam—with his extremely capable girlfriend Mirella—tries to retrace Eve's steps, he discovers a world that's a whole lot deadlier than he remembered.

Adam is supposed to be dead. He went through a lot of trouble to fake that death, but now that he's back it's clear someone remains unconvinced. That wouldn't be so terrible, except that whoever it is, they have a great deal of influence, and an abiding interest in ensuring that his death sticks this time around.

Adam and Mirella will have to figure out how to travel halfway across the world in secret, with almost no resources or friends. The good news is, Adam solved the travel problem a thousand years earlier. The bad news is, one of his oldest assumptions will turn out to be untrue.

Immortal From Hell is the darkest entry in the Immortal series.

Immortal: Last Call

"*I'm something like sixty-thousand years old, and I've probably thought more*

about my own death than any living being has thought about any subject, ever. I used to be unduly preoccupied with what might constitute a "good death", although interestingly, this has always been an after-the-fact analysis. What I mean is, following a near-death experience, I'll generally perform a quiet review of the circumstances and judge whether that death would have been objectively good, by whatever metric one uses for that kind of thing. I'm not nearly that self-reflective while in the midst of said near-death experience. Facing death, the predominant thought is always not like this."

A disease threatening the lives of everyone—human and non-human—has been loosed upon the world, by an arch-enemy Adam didn't even know he had.

That's just the first of his problems. Adam's also in jail, facing multiple counts of murder, at least a few of which are accurate. He may never see the inside of a courtroom, because there remains a bounty on his head—put there by the aforementioned arch-enemy—that someone is bound to try to collect while he's stuck behind bars.

Meanwhile, Adam's sitting on some tantalizing evidence that there might be a cure, but to find it, he's going to have to get out of jail, get out of the country, and track down the man responsible. He can't do any of that alone, but he also can't rely on any of his non-human friends for help, not when they're all getting sick.

What he needs is a particularly gifted human, who can do things no other human is capable of. He knows one such person. He calls himself a fixer, and he's Adam's—and possibly the world's—last hope. That's provided he believes any of it.

Immortal: Last Call is the sixth book in the *Immortal Novel Series*, and also the end of a long journey for one immortal man.

~

Immortal Stories

~

Eve

"...if your next question is, what could that possibly make me, if I'm not an angel or a god? The answer is the same as what I said before: many have considered me a god, and probably a few have thought of me as an angel. I'm neither, if those positions are defined by any kind of supernormal magical power. True magic of that kind doesn't exist, but I can do things that may appear magic to someone slightly more tethered to their mortality. I'm a woman, and that's all. What may make me different from the next woman is that it's possible I'm the very first one..."

For most of humankind, the woman calling herself Eve has been nothing more than a shock of red hair glimpsed out of the corner of the eye, in a crowd, or from a great distance. She's been worshipped, feared, and hunted, but perhaps never understood. Now, she's trying to reconnect with the world, and finding that more challenging than anticipated.

Can the oldest human on Earth rediscover her own humanity? Or will she decide the world isn't worth it?

The Immortal Chronicles

Immortal at Sea (volume 1)

Adam's adventures on the high seas have taken him from the Mediterranean to the Barbary Coast, and if there's one thing he learned, it's that maybe the sea is trying to tell him to stay on dry land.

Hard-Boiled Immortal (volume 2)

The year was 1942, there was a war on, and Adam was having a lot of trouble avoiding the attention of some important people. The kind of people with guns, and ways to make a fella disappear. He was caught somewhere between the mob and the government, and the only way out involved a red-haired dame he was pretty sure he couldn't trust.

~

Immortal and the Madman (volume 3)

On a nice quiet trip to the English countryside to cope with the likelihood that he has gone a little insane, Adam meets a man who definitely has. The madman's name is John Corrigan, and he is convinced he's going to die soon.

He could be right. Because there's trouble coming, and unless Adam can get his own head together in time, they may die together.

~

Yuletide Immortal (volume 4)

When he's in a funk, Adam the immortal man mostly just wants a place to drink and the occasional drinking buddy. When that buddy turns out to be Santa Claus, Adam is forced to face one of the biggest challenges of extremely long life: Christmas cheer. Will Santa break him out of his bad mood? Or will he be responsible for depressing the most positive man on the planet?

~

Regency Immortal (volume 5)

Adam has accidentally stumbled upon an important period in history: Vienna in 1814. Mostly, he'd just like to continue to enjoy the local pubs, but that becomes impossible when he meets Anna, an intriguing woman with an unreasonable number of secrets and sharp objects.

Anna is hunting down a man who isn't exactly a man, and if Adam doesn't help her, all of Europe will suffer. If Adam *does* help, the cost may be his own life. It's not a fantastic set of options. Also, he's probably fallen in love with her, which just complicates everything.

CPSIA information can be obtained
at www.ICGtesting.com
Printed in the USA
LVHW021650130521
687357LV00010B/546